California, Commission in Lunacy, E. T. Wilkins

Insanity and Insane Asylums

California, Commission in Lunacy, E. T. Wilkins

Insanity and Insane Asylums

ISBN/EAN: 9783337381868

Printed in Europe, USA, Canada, Australia, Japan

Cover: Foto ©Andreas Hilbeck / pixelio.de

More available books at **www.hansebooks.com**

INSANITY AND INSANE ASYLUMS.

REPORT OF E. T. WILKINS, M. D.,

COMMISSIONER IN LUNACY

FOR THE STATE OF CALIFORNIA,

MADE TO

HIS EXCELLENCY H. H. HAIGHT, GOVERNOR,

December 2d, 1871.

CONTENTS.

CHAPTER I.

INTRODUCTORY.

CHAPTER II.

INSANITY A DISEASE OF THE BRAIN.

CHAPTER III.

INSANITY AS IT NOW EXISTS.

CHAPTER IV.

CAUSES OF INSANITY—SOME OF THE INFLUENCES OPERATING IN ITS DEVELOPMENT.

CHAPTER V.

INFLUENCE OF SOCIAL DISTINCTIONS.

CHAPTER VI.

APPARENT INCREASE OF INSANITY.

CHAPTER VII.

INSANITY IN FRANCE.

CHAPTER VIII.

INSANITY AMONG THE ANCIENTS.

CHAPTER IX.

INSANE ASYLUMS, LOCATION, SIZE, SITES, ETC.

CHAPTER X.

INSANE ASYLUMS—DOCTOR MANNING'S REPORT.

CHAPTER XI.

CRIMINAL INSANE.

CHAPTER XII.

CHRONIC INSANE.

CHAPTER XIII.

TREATMENT OF INSANITY.

CHAPTER · XIV.

INSANITY IN GENERAL.

CHAPTER XV.

ECONOMY OF PROVIDING AMPLE CURATIVE ACCOMMODATIONS.

CHAPTER XVI.

PLAN BEST ADAPTED TO CARE AND TREATMENT OF THE INSANE.

INDEX.

APPENDICES.

INSANITY

AND

INSANE ASYLUMS.

CHAPTER I.

INTRODUCTORY.

Powers, Duties, and Appointment of Commissioner—Importance of the Commission—Asylums Visited—Number of Patients in Asylums Visited—Other Institutions Visited—Plans of Asylums—Statistical Tables—Meetings of. Superintendents Attended—Importance of such Meetings—Books Obtained for the State Library—Sources of Information—Acknowledgments.

POWERS, DUTIES, AND APPOINTMENT OF COMMISSIONER.

An Act authorizing the appointment of a Commissioner to visit the principal Insane Asylums of the United States and Europe, approved February eighteenth, eighteen hundred and seventy, directs the Commissioner to visit such asylums as soon as possible, and to collect and compile all accessible and reliable information as to their management, the different modes of treatment, and the statistics of insanity, especial attention being called to the asylums of Great Britain, Ireland, France, and Germany. He is further directed to make a written report to the Governor, in which he shall embody at length a history of the management adopted at such asylums, a statement of the different modes of treatment in use, and such statistics as he may deem reliable.

The Governor conferred the honor of this appointment upon me, and being in entire accord with my tastes and desires, having for a long time felt a deep interest in the subject to be investigated and an earnest sympathy for that class of our fellow beings in whose behalf the investigation was ordered to be made, I entered at once upon the duties assigned me.

IMPORTANCE OF THE WORK.

Appreciating the importance of the subject, and feeling that the people, and especially those whose duty it is to make our laws, protect our citizens, and provide for the care and maintenance of our unfortunates, should have all the light that the wisdom and experience of the learned men in other States and countries could shed upon a subject about which so little is known by the great mass even of the reading public, the work was entered upon with some misgivings, but a sincere hope that the laudable object of the mission might be crowned with success.

The law is a comprehensive one, and opens a wide field for interesting investigation and extensive research; one in which many an eminent man has spent a lifetime of labor and of thought, which it has been our object to search for, to find, and to appropriate.

We have not gone forth with the expectation or even the hope of originating anything upon the subject, but rather to collect the accumulated truths gathered by the wisdom and experience of other men in other lands, that we might bring them home to California and strew them broadcast before our people. We did not for a moment suppose that a tithe of this information could be embodied in a report, however elaborate. The diversity of subjects necessarily touched upon would render it impossible to enter fully into the consideration of any; yet it is hoped that the attention of those who desire further light on a matter of so much interest to the State, the citizen, and the philanthropist may be directed to the channel where it exists in abundance, and where it may be found by a little patient and careful research. To all such, therefore, who can find in the accompanying report only a fragment of what they desire to know, let us say, look to the shelves of our State Library, recently replenished with a liberal list of the most valuable works ever contributed by the mind of man to the science of psychology, and you will find *nearly all* that exists on the important subject to which we desire to attract your especial attention.

Having spent a sufficient length of time at Stockton to become thoroughly informed with regard to the condition, construction, and requirements of our asylum, its general management, *good features*, and *glaring defects*, we started out to compare them with what could be found in other States and countries. These comparisons have in some respects been in our favor, and, as might naturally be expected, against us in others—in what particulars we will endeavor to point out in due time, and trust, while we commend our virtues to our brethren for their adoption, we will with equal alacrity and liberality give up our defects and substitute them with some of the excellent features of other institutions.

ASYLUMS VISITED.

During these investigations, one hundred and forty-nine Insane Asylums in complete working order have been visited, making an average of two each week during the whole period. Forty-five of these were in the United States, one in Canada, fifteen in Italy, three in Bavaria, seven in Austria, eleven in the German States, two in Switzerland, thirteen in France, eight in Belgium, three in Holland, twenty-four in England, ten in Scotland, and seven in Ireland, the names, locations, and names of the Superintendents of which will be found in the table following:

Name of Asylum.	Location.	Name of Superintendent.
UNITED STATES:		
Insane Asylum of California	Stockton, California	G. A. Shurtleff.
Alameda Park	Alameda, California	Euston Treanor.
St. Vincent	St. Louis, Missouri	
State Lunatic Asylum	Fulton, Missouri	C. H. Hughes.
St. Louis County Asylum	Near St. Louis, Mo	Charles W. Stephens.
Eastern Asylum	Williamsburg, Va	D. R. Brower.
Western Asylum	Staunton, Va	F. T. Stribbling.
Central Lunatic Asylum	Near Richmond, Va	D. B. Conrad.
Maryland Hospital	Baltimore, Maryland	R. F. Steuart.
Mount Hope Retreat	Near Baltimore	William H. Stokes.
Eastern Lunatic Asylum	Lexington, Kentucky	John W. Whitney.
Western Lunatic Asylum	Hopkinsville, Ky	James Rodman.
Tennessee Hospital	Near Nashville	J. H. Callender.
North Carolina Insane Asylum	Raleigh	Eugene Grissom.
South Carolina Insane Asylum	Columbia	J. F. Ensor.
Government Asylum	Near Washington, D. C	Charles C. Nichols.
State Lunatic Hospital	Harrisburg, Pa	John Curwen.
Pennsylvania Hospital	Philadelphia, Pa	Thomas G. Kirkbride.
Insane Dep't Philadelphia Almshouse	Philadelphia. Pa	D. D. Richardson.
Friends' Asylum	Philadelphia, Pa	J. H. Worthington.
State Lunatic Asylum	Trenton, New Jersey	H. A. Buttolph.
State Lunatic Asylum	Utica, New York	John P. Gray.
Kings County Lunatic Asylum	Flatbush, Long Island	Edw. R. Chapin.
Bloomingdale Asylum	Bloomingdale, N. Y	D. Tilden Brown.
New York City Lunatic Asylum	Blackwell's Island	R. L. Parsons.
Willard Asylum	Ovid, N. Y	J. B. Chapin.
Brigham Hall	Canandaigua, N. Y	George Cook.
State Criminal Asylum	Auburn, N. Y	James W. Wilkie.
General Hospital for the Insane	Middletown, Conn.	A. M. Shew.
Retreat for the Insane	Hartford, Conn	John S. Butler.
Vermont Asylum for the Insane	Brattleboro	William H. Rockwell.
Maine Insane Hospital	Augusta	Henry M. Harlow.
New Hampshire Asylum for the Insane	Concord	James P. Bancroft.
Butler Hospital for the Insane	Providence, R. I	John W. Sawyer.
State Lunatic Hospital	Worcester, Mass	Merrick Bemis.
State Lunatic Hospital	Northampton, Mass	Pliny Earle.
State Lunatic Hospital	Taunton, Mass	William W. Godding.
McLean Asylum for the Insane	Somerville, Mass	George F. Jelly.
Boston Lunatic Asylum	Boston, Mass	Clement A. Walker.
Michigan Asylum	Kalamazoo	E. H. Van Deusen.
Iowa Hospital for the Insane	Mount Pleasant	Mark Ranney.
Illinois State Hospital for the Insane.	Jacksonville	Henry F. Carriel.
Indiana Hospital for the Insane	Indianapolis	Orpheus Everts.
Longview Asylum	Longview, Ohio	O. M. Langdon.
Southern Ohio Lunatic Asylum	Dayton, Ohio	R. Gundry.
CANADA:		
Provincial Lunatic Asylum	Toronto	Joseph Workman.
ITALY:		
Provincial Lunatic Asylum	Genoa	
Capo di Chino Asylum (private)	Naples	Dr. Avesa.
Morotrofio	Aversa	Antonio Raffo.
Santa Maria di Pieta	Rome	Joseph Girolami.
Santa Margherita	Perugia	Cav. Guiseppe Neri.
Bonifazio (provincial Insane Asylum)	Florence	Dr. Cardini. (?)
Provincial Asylum	Bologna	Frances Foucarti. [rio.
San Servalo	Venice	P. Prosdocimo, D. Sale-
St. John and St. Paul	Venice	Antonio Berti.
Senavra	Milan	
Insane Asylum	Mombello	Rinaldo Gectano.
Dufour	Milan	F. Franceso Corbetta.
Colombo	Milan	Achille Colombo.
Rossi Asylum	Milan	Antonio J. Bonfanti.
Presso San Celso	Milan	Serafino Biffi.

Name of Asylum.	Location.	Name of Superintendent.
BAVARIA:		
Royal District Asylum	Munich	Aug. Solbrig.
District Lunatic Asylum	Irsee	J. M. Kiderle.
District Lunatic Asylum	Diggendorf	Dr. Ast.
AUSTRIA:		
Tyrolese Provincial Asylum	Hall	Joseph Stolz.
Institute for Care and Cure of the Insane	Linz	A. Knörlein, Director. Dr. Schasching, Phy'n.
Royal Institute for Care and Cure of Insane	Vienna	Dr. Spurzheim.
Private Insane Asylum	Dobling	Dr. Leidordorf.
Asylum for Chronic Insane	Klosterneuburg	Dr. Mildner.
District Lunatic Asylum	Brunn, Moravia	Dr. Langer.
Royal Bohemian Asylum	Prague, Bohemia	Dr. Fischel.
	Sleep, Bohemia	Dr. Kratochril.
SAXONY AND GERMAN STATES:		
Sonnenstein	Sonnenstein, Saxony	H. Lessing.
Private Asylum	Pirna, Saxony	O. Lehman.
Asylum for Chronic Insane	Hubertusburg, Saxony	George Ehrst.
Charity Hospital	Berlin	Dr. Westphal.
District Lunatic Asylum	Neustadt, Prussia	Dr. Sponholz.
District Lunatic Asylum	Halle	Dr. Köppe.
Thonberg Asylum	Thonberg, near Leipsic.	E. W. Guntz.
District Lunatic Asylum	Gottingen	Ludwig Meyer.
District Lunatic Asylum	Frankfort	H. Hoffman.
District Lunatic Asylum	Heppenheim	Dr. Ludwig.
Illenau Asylum	Achern	C. Roller.
SWITZERLAND:		
Public Asylum	Zurich	D. Gudden.
Public Asylum	Waldau, near Berne	Dr. Fetscherin, Phy'n, Dr. Schaerer, Direct'r
FRANCE:		
Department Asylum	Stephansfeld (Strasb'g).	Dr. Hildebrand, Phy'n, R. du Matey, Director
Antiquaille	Lyons	J. Arthaud, Director and Physician.
St. Jean de Dieu	Lyons	Dr. Carrier, Physician, J. de Matha, Director.
St. George	Bourg	
Chartreuse Asylum	Dijon	Dr. Bruno, Director and Physician.
Asylum for Insane of St. Yonne	Auxerre	Dr. Ceilleux, Director and Physician in Chief
St. Anne	Paris	M. Bayent, Director; M. Dagonet, Phy'n.
La Saltpêtrière	Paris	M. Phélip, Director.
Doctor Blanche's Asylum	Passy, Paris	Dr. Blanche.
National Asylum	Charenton	Dr. Calmeil.
Colony Fitz James	Clermont	Gustave Labitte, Phy'n, M. J. Labitte, Direct'r
Quatre-mares St. Yon	Rouen	Dr. Ed. Dumesnil.
St. Yon	Rouen	Dr. Morel.
BELGIUM:		
Asylum of Ansard Glaine	Liege	Dr. C. Anten.
Liege Hospital	Liege	
Colony at Gheel	Gheel	Dr. Bulckens.
Insane Asylum	Antwerp	T. Targue.
Guislain Asylum	Ghent	B. Ingels.
St. Joseph	Ghent	Dr. Nermenten.
Sts. Julien and Michael	Bruges	Dr. Van den Abeele,
Du Strop (private)	Ghent	Dr. Nermenten.

Name of Asylum.	Location.	Name of Superintendent.
HOLLAND:		
Reinier Van Arkel	Bois le Duc	T. Frybouh. (?)
Meerenberg Asylum	Near Haarlam	B. H. Everts.
City Asylum	Rotterdam	G. Vrolck.
ENGLAND:		
Royal Infirmary	Liverpool	Dr. Stockwell.
County Lunatic Asylum	Rainhill	T. L. Rogers.
St. Luke's Madhouse	London	Dr. Eager.
Bethlem Hospital	London	W. Rhys Williams.
Grove Hall, Bow	Bow, London	Dr. Stocker.
County Lunatic Asylum	Hanwell	W. C. Begley, Male Dep't; J. M. Lindsay, Female Dep't.
County Lunatic Asylum	Colney Hatch	Eagar Sheppard, Male Dep't; W. G. Marshall, Female Dep't.
Surrey County Lunatic Asylum	Brookwood	Thomas N. Brushfield.
Sussex County Lunatic Asylum	Hayward s Heath	S. W. D. Williams.
Essex Lunatic Asylum	Brentwood	D. C. Campbell.
Bristol Borough Asylum	Stapleton	G. Thompson.
Glamorgan County Lunatic Asylum	Bridgend	David Yellowlees.
County Lunatic Asylum	Wotten. n'r Gloucester.	E. Toller.
Barnwood House	Gloucester	A. J. Wood.
Buckingham County Pauper Lunatic Asylum	Stone	John Humphrey.
Borough Lunatic Asylum	Birmingham	T. Green.
County of Warwick Pauper Lunatic Asylum	Hatton, near Warwick.	W. H. Parsey.
Derbyshire County Pauper Lunatic Asylum	Mickleover	John Hitchman.
West Riding Pauper Lunatic Asylum	Wakefield	J. Crichton Browne.
Friends' Retreat	Near York	J. Kitching.
York Lunatic Asylum	York	F. Needham.
Newcastle-upon-Tyne Borough Lunatic Asylum	Newcastle	R. H. B. Wickham.
Cumberland and Westmoreland Lunatic Asylum	Near Carlisle	T. S. Clouston.
Littlemore Asylum	Littlemore, Oxford	R. H. H. Sankey.
SCOTLAND:		
Edinburgh Royal Asylum	Morningside	David Skae.
Saughton Hall (private)	Near Edinburgh	Dr. Low.
Fife and Kinross District Asylum	Near Cupar, Co. Fife	John B. Tuke.
The Colony of Kennoway	Kennoway	
Royal Asylum	Dundee	James Rorie.
Hull Cross Asylum	Musselburgh	
District Asylum	Inverness	Thomas Aitken.
District Asylum	Stirling	F. W. A. Skae.
White House Asylum (private)	Musselburgh	Mrs. Thompson, Sup't; Dr. Thompson, Phy'n
Royal Asylum	Glasgow	Alexander Mackintosh.
Royal Asylum	Perth	Lauder Lindsay.
IRELAND:		
District Asylum	Belfast	Robert Stewart.
Richmond District Asylum	Dublin	Joseph Lalor.
Bloomfield Retreat	County Dublin	H. A. Lodge, Sup't Male Dep't; Mary Pryor, Female Dep't; J. H. Wharton, Physician.
Maryborough District Asylum	Maryborough	J. H. Hatchell.
Cork District Lunatic Asylum	Cork	Thomas Power.
Killarney Asylum	Killarney	W. W. Murphy.
Central Asylum for Criminal Lunatics	Dundrum	

NUMBER OF PATIENTS IN ASYLUMS VISITED.

The number of patients treated in these asylums during the last year was seventy-six thousand six hundred and seven, or an average of five hundred and fourteen for each institution. In addition to the asylums mentioned, a number of asylums in process of erection, lunatic wards of Poor Houses, Idiot and Deaf and Dumb Asylums, ordinary hospitals, penitentiaries, and other governmental, State, county, and city establishments have been visited and examined, and such features noted as appeared might at any time be of interest or importance to the State.

PLANS OF ASYLUMS.

A large number of plans of asylums, rules, regulations, etc., have been procured, a portion of which will be found in the appendix, and all are at the service of the State.

STATISTICAL TABLES.

The statistical tables have cost much time and patient labor, and are believed to be as complete as any ever published on this subject, and the facts set forth in them have been gathered from the latest and most reliable sources known to exist.

MEETINGS OF SUPERINTENDENTS ATTENDED.

It has been our good fortune to have attended the meeting of the Superintendents of American Institutions for the Insane at Hartford last year, and those of a similar character for France, in Paris, and of Great Britain, in London during the present year. It is needless to dilate upon the high character and intellectual capacity that distinguish the men who compose these associations, nor upon the great service they have rendered to humanity by sending forth the results of their individual and collective experiences to enlighten mankind and relieve the distresses of their fellow men. They are the rays of light that dispel the mists and drive away the thick clouds by which the mind of man is enveloped when the brain is diseased. "Their's, indeed, is a mission of mercy, and verily they shall reap their reward."

IMPORTANCE OF SUCH MEETINGS.

So important do these annual meetings appear to our mind we do not hesitate to express the opinion that it should be made the duty of the Superintendent of every asylum, or an assistant, to attend each meeting, feeling assured that the opportunity presented for an interchange of opinions with those engaged in a like calling could not fail to be both agreeable and instructive to himself, but beneficial to those committed to his care and the State in whose service he is engaged. We feel under especial obligations to them, and to all others who have contributed to our pleasure or added to our stock of information.

BOOKS OBTAINED FOR STATE LIBRARY.

A large number of books, reports, and essays on insanity and State medicine have been obtained for the State Library by purchase or donation from various sources and countries, comprising in the list nearly all of the standard works of the most celebrated authors who have written upon the subject of insanity, and the most recent and reliable information on the statistics of lunacy that could be found. Among these are the works of Allen, Anderson, Arlidge, Bingham, Browne, Bucknill and Tuke, Burrows, Conolly, Crowther, Dunn, Ellis, Gall, Hill, Hills, Hoods, Jacobi, Morrison, Prichard, Seymour, Sieveking, Williams, Winslow, including Journal of Psychological Medicine, 1848 to 1863, and the more recent productions of Van Der Kolk, Brown, Sankey, Mandsley, Blanford, Fry, Casper, Griesinger, Davis; translation of Pinel, Cox, Liddell; translation of Esquirol, Mayo, and a set of the Journal of Mental Science from commencement of volume two to the present time. Also, very nearly a complete set of the Reports of the Commissioners in Lunacy, and other valuable documents presented by Mr. Wilkes, one of the Commissioners; a partial set of the Reports of the Scotch Commissioners, and other documents presented by Sir James Cox and Dr. Sibbald, of that Board; the last Report of the Commissioners for Ireland; special reports of all the asylums visited, where these were published and attainable; essays on a variety of subjects; rules and regulations of asylums, general and special; descriptions of asylums by sundry persons; reports of Special Commissioners, and many other documents of more or less interest. Among the French works will be found those of Foville, Dagonet, Calmiel, Falvet, Morel, Mundy, Motet, and others. From Prussia, a volume of general statistics for eighteen hundred and sixty-seven; a valuable treatise on construction and plans of asylums for the insane, containing the opinions of many of the most eminent psychologists of that country, and a brief account of all the asylums of the German Confederation in eighteen hundred and sixty-five, by Dr. H. Laeur, together with a few other documents of minor importance. Besides the reports, more or less complete, of all the asylums visited in the United States, a variety of documents, including statistics of the insane and idiotic for eighteen hundred and seventy, essays, lectures; reports of Commissioners sent into other States and countries, and those of a local character; reports of Boards of Charity of New York, Massachusetts, Ohio, and Pennsylvania, of the Cities of New York and Boston, and a number of other documents of interest and importance, and from most countries plans of asylums, more or less complete, of some of the best institutions known to exist, embracing every variety, from the palatial hospital to the modest cottage.

The professional man will find much that is trite and familiar in this report, but it must not be forgotten that it is not so much for him as for the public that it has been prepared.

SOURCES OF INFORMATION.

The information which it contains has been derived from various sources. The work of other men's brains has been freely appropriated. Their experiences we have endeavored to use to the best advantage; and even the errors committed by some of them have taught us valuable lessons, as it is sometimes as necessary to know what to avoid as what to adopt.

ACKNOWLEDGMENTS.

Much has also been learned from personal intercourse with men of ability in all the countries we have visited, and we can never forget nor ever cease to be grateful for the many acts of courtesy, kindness, and attention that we have received at their hands. To Drs. Shurtleff, Stribbling, Kirkbride, Gray, Buttolph, and Walkar, in each of whose establishments we spent several days in the early part of our investigations, we are especially indebted for the kind manner in which they took us by the hand and started us "right foot foremost" in the path of our duty. Nor have we forgotten the attentions and courtesies of a single Superintendent whose asylum we visited in America or Europe.

CHAPTER II.

INSANITY A DISEASE OF THE BRAIN.

What is insanity? This question has been often asked, but perhaps has never been satisfactorily answered, for the simple reason that insanity assumes so many forms and differs so widely in different persons that no definition can possibly embrace all of its phases. Many persons have given definitions of this subtle malady, but not one has met with that universal concurrence necessary to render it the true and only or even the generally received definition. We do not propose to enter this list, but as much must be said on the subject in the following pages it is best, perhaps, that a selection should be made.

In a lecture delivered before the Royal College of Surgeons, March first, eighteen hundred and sixty-one, by David Skae, M. D., F. R. C. S., Physician to the Royal Edinburgh Asylum, he defined it to be "a disease of the brain affecting the mind." We accept this definition as the best of all, because it is the most simple. It makes but little difference how the brain becomes diseased, whether primarily or by reflex action from the disease of some other organ of the body, so the fact as stated be true that the brain must be diseased ere the mind is affected.

CHAPTER III.

INSANITY AS IT NOW EXISTS.

The Subject Generally—Insanity in England—In Scotland—In Ireland—In France—In Italy—In Prussia—In Austria—In German States—In Bavaria—In Switzerland—In Belgium—In Holland—In Denmark—In Sweden—In Norway—In New South Wales —In the United States—In California.

THE SUBJECT GENERALLY.

In considering the subject of insanity, it is proper first to inquire to what extent it exists in the world and in our midst. To do this we have prepared tables exhibiting the population of various countries, divided into self supporting and pauper classes (where these have been separated), and in all cases the total population, number, and distribution of the insane at the latest dates at which these facts could be obtained; the proportion of the insane to population, the ratio per thousand, the proportion of pauper insane to pauper population, the proportion of insane under treatment to population, the number in hospitals and asylums at latest date; numbers admitted, cured, died, and treated during the year; the number of asylums in each country; the principal assigned causes of the disorder and of death; together with the numbers resident at beginning of the year; numbers admitted, cured, and died during the year, and the percentage of recoveries and of deaths to admissions and to numbers treated in the asylums visited in different countries; to which we have added similar facts for Norway, Sweden, and the Colony of New South Wales.

INSANITY IN ENGLAND.

Population, 1870.

Self supporting classes	21,006,631
Paupers	1,083,532
Total population	22,090,163

Number and Distribution of the Insane, January 1st, 1870.

	Private.	Pauper.	Totals.
County and Borough Asylums	259	27,721	27,980
Registered Hospitals	1,969	400	2,369
Metropolitan Licensed Houses	1,666	1,034	2,700
Provincial Licensed Houses	1,478	726	2,204
Naval and Military Hospitals and Royal India Asylum	198	....	198
Workhouses	....	11,358	11,358
With relatives or others	356	7,086	7,442
Broadmoor Criminal Asylum	354	108	462
Totals	6,280	48,433	54,713

Proportion of insane to population, one in four hundred and three; or, ratio per one thousand, two and forty-seven one hundredths. Proportion of pauper insane to pauper population, one in twenty-two; or, ratio per one thousand, forty-four and sixty-nine one hundredths. Proportion of insane (under treatment) to population, one in six hundred and fifteen; or, ratio per one thousand, one and sixty-two one hundredths.

The number of Insane in Hospitals, Asylums, and Licensed Houses, January 1st, 1870	35,913
Admitted during the year	11,462
Cured	3,955
Died	3,790
Number treated in 1870	47,375

Per cent of recoveries on admissions	34
Per cent of recoveries on number treated	8
Per cent of deaths on admissions	33
Per cent of deaths on number treated	8

Number of Asylums, etc., for the Insane in England and Wales.

County and Borough Asylums	50
Registered Hospitals	16
State Asylums	4
Metropolitan Licensed Houses	41
Provincial Licensed Houses	65
Total number of Institutes for the Insane	176

The average weekly cost per head in County Asylums is nine shillings five and one eighth pence, or two dollars and twenty-eight cents.

The principal assigned causes of insanity are: hereditary, intemperance, domestic trouble, epilepsy, mental anxiety, puerperal condition and critical period, paralysis.

The principal causes of death are: general paralysis, diseases of the lungs, diseases of the brain, epilepsy, debility and old age, apoplexy.

In twenty asylums visited in 1870, the number of patients resident was	12,116
Admitted	3,670
Number treated	15,786
Cured	1,369
Died	1,220

Per cent of cures on admissions	37
Per cent of cures on number treated	8
Per cent of deaths on admissions	33
Per cent of deaths on number treated	7

INSANITY IN SCOTLAND.

Population, January 1st, 1870.

Self supporting classes	3,142,503
Paupers (May 14th, 1869)	80,334
Total population	3,222,837

Number and Distribution of the Insane.

	Private.	Pauper.	Totals.
In Royal and District Asylums	914	3,547	4,461
In Private Asylums	249	54	303
In Parochial Asylums		553	553
In Lunatic Wards of Poorhouses		574	574
In General Prison		49	49
In Training Schools for Imbeciles	83	30	113
In Private Dwellings	49	1,469	1,518
Totals, January 1st, 1870	1,295	6,276	7,571

Besides the number of insane given above, it is estimated that there are about two thousand unreported, making the total number nine thousand five hundred and seventy-one.

Proportion to the population, one in three hundred and thirty-six; or, ratio per one thousand, two and ninety-six one hundredths. Proportion of insane (under treatment) to population, one in six hundred and six; or, ratio per thousand, one and sixty-four one hundredths. Proportion of pauper insane to pauper population, one in thirteen; or, ratio per one thousand, seventy-eight and twelve one hundredths.

Number of insane in asylums, January 1st, 1870	5,317
Admitted during the year	2,015
Cured	832
Died	491
Number treated in 1870	7,332

Per cent of recoveries to admissions	41
Per cent of recoveries to number treated	11
Per cent of deaths to admissions	24
Per cent of deaths to number treated	7

Number of Institutions for the Insane.

District Asylums	10
Royal Asylums	7
Private Asylums	9
Parochial Asylums	5
Total Asylums	31
Lunatic Wards of Poorhouses	15
Total	46

The average weekly cost of maintenance of pauper lunatics in Royal and District Asylums is nine shillings and nine and one fourth pence; in Private Asylums, ten shillings and two and a half pence; in Parochial Asylums, eight shillings and five and a half pence; making a general average cost of nine shillings and five and three fourths pence, or two dollars and twenty-nine cents.

The principal assigned causes of insanity are: climacteric changes, old age, intemperance, child bearing.

The principal causes of death are: consumption, general debility and old age, organic disease of brain, inflammation of lungs, general paralysis.

In six asylums visited in 1870, the number of patients resident was	1,995
Admitted	1,030
Treated	3,025
Cured	365
Died	206

Per cent of cures on admissions	35
Per cent of cures on number treated	12
Per cent of deaths on admissions	20
Per cent of deaths on number treated	6

INSANITY IN IRELAND.

Population, 1870.

Total population 5,195,236

Number and Distribution of the Insane, December 31st, 1870.

	Private.	Pauper.	Totals.
In District Asylums	122	6,533	6,655
In Private Asylums	638	....	638
In Jail	....	1	1
In Workhouses	....	2,754	2,754
In Lucan	....	43	43
In Central	....	167	167
Lunatics at large	6,936	....	6,936
Totals	7,696	9,498	17,194

Proportion of insane to population, one in three hundred and two; or, ratio per one thousand, three and thirty one hundredths. Proportion of insane (under treatment) to population, one in seven hundred and twenty-nine; or, ratio per one thousand, one and thirty-seven one hundredths.

Number of insane in asylums, January 1st, 1870	7,121
Admitted during the year	2,532
Cured	1,088
Died	708
Number treated in 1870	9,653

Per cent of recoveries on admissions	43
Per cent of recoveries on number treated	11
Per cent of deaths on admissions	27
Per cent of deaths on number treated	7

Number of Establishments for the Insane.

District Asylums	23
Private Licensed Houses	20
Asylums for Criminals	1
Total	44

• The average weekly cost per head in District Asylums is eight shillings and eleven and a half pence, or two dollars and seventeen cents.

The principal assigned causes of insanity are: hereditary, grief, fear and anxiety, intemperance and irregularity of living, disease of the brain, bodily injuries and disorders.

The principal causes of death are: thoracic disease, cerebral disease, debility, and old age.

In eleven asylums visited in 1870, the number of patients resident was	2,437
Admitted	1,206
Treated	3,643
Cured	457
Died	256

Per cent of cures on admissions	37
Per cent of cures on number treated	12
Per cent of deaths on admissions	21
Per cent of deaths on number treated	7

INSANITY IN FRANCE.

Population, 1866... 37,988,905

Number and Distribution of the Insane, 1866.

	Insane.	Idiots.	Totals.
In asylums...	31,992	3,980	35,972
At home...	18,734	35,973	54,707
Totals	50,726	39,953	90,679

	Males.	Females.	Totals.
Insane..	24,190	26,537	50,726
Idiots..	22,736	17,217	39,953

Proportion of insane to population, one in seven hundred and forty-seven; or, ratio per one thousand, one and thirty-three one hundredths. Proportion of idiots to population, one in nine hundred and fifty. Proportion of insane and idiots to population, one in four hundred and eighteen; or, ratio per one thousand, two and thirty-eight one hundredths. Proportion of insane and idiots (under treatment) to population, one in one thousand and fifty-seven; or, ratio per one thousand, ninety-four one hundredths.

Population, 1860.. 37,170,942

Number of insane in hospitals and asylums, January 1st, 1860..	28,761
Admitted during the year..	10,786
Cured or improved...	4,337
Died	4,970
Number treated in 1860...	39,546

Per cent of recoveries on admissions..	40
Per cent of recoveries on number treated..................................	11
Per cent of deaths on admissions	46
Per cent of deaths on number treated	12

Number of Asylums for the Insane in eighteen hundred and sixty (public and private establishments), ninety-nine.

In eighteen hundred and fifty-three, the average weekly cost per head was one dollar and twenty-one cents.

The principal assigned causes of insanity, as per reports eighteen hundred and fifty-three, were: hereditary, epilepsy and convulsions, intemperance, destitution and misery, loss of fortune.

The principal causes of death: paralysis, disease of brain, pneumonia, insanity, brain fever.

In thirteen asylums visited in 1870, the number of patients resident was	7,938
Admitted (in eleven of these)	3,324
* Cured (in eleven of these)	873
Died (in eleven of these)	1,292
Number treated (in eleven of these)	11,262

Per cent of recoveries on admissions	26
Per cent of recoveries on number treated	7
Per cent of deaths on admissions	38
Per cent of deaths on number treated	11

INSANITY IN ITALY.

Population, 1864 22,291,181

By the addition of Venice, in 1866, the population was increased to 24,263,320.

Number of insane in asylums, January 1st, 1867 8,191

Proportion of insane (under treatment) to population, one in two thousand nine hundred and sixty-two; or, ratio per one thousand, thirty-three one hundredths.

Number in asylums, January 1st, 1867	8,191
Admitted	4,909
Discharged	3,210
Died	1,504
Number treated during the year	13,100
Number remaining January 1st, 1868	8,386

Per cent of discharges on admissions	65
Per cent of discharges on number treated	24
Per cent of deaths on admissions	30
Per cent of deaths on number treated	11

* Leaving out the Asylum La Salpêtrière (for chronic cases only), the per cent of cures on admissions would be twenty-seven.

Fifteen asylums were visited in eighteen hundred and seventy.

In fourteen of these the number resident was	4,259
In thirteen of these the admissions were	1,967
In twelve of these the number treated was	5,316
In thirteen of these the number cured was	764
In thirteen of these the number died was	621

Per cent of recoveries on admissions	38
Per cent of recoveries on number treated	13
Per cent of deaths on admissions	31
Per cent of deaths on number treated	10

The average weekly cost of maintenance of indigents in eight public asylums is one dollar and seventy-seven cents.

Principal causes of death: disease of the lungs, paralysis, marasmus.

Principal assigned causes of insanity: pillagra, hereditary, intemperance.

INSANITY IN PRUSSIA.

Population, 1864..19,252,363

Number of Insane Under Treatment.

In Public Asylums	4,796
In Private Asylums	944
Total	5,740

Proportion of insane (under treatment) to population, one in three thousand three hundred and fifty-four; or, ratio per one thousand, twenty-nine one hundredths.

Number of Asylums.

Public Asylums	32
Private Asylums	27
Total	59

Expenses of Public Asylums, six hundred and fourteen thousand six hundred and sixty-four thalers, or four hundred and forty-eight thousand seven hundred and four dollars and seventy-two cents, which gives a weekly cost per head of one dollar and eighty cents.

In two asylums visited in 1870, the number of patients resident was	1,065
Admitted	297
Cured	105
Died	110
Number treated	1,362

Per cent of cures on admissions	35
Per cent of cures on number treated	7
Per cent of deaths on admissions	37
Per cent of deaths on number treated	8

The average weekly cost of maintenance of indigents in these two asylums is one dollar and ninety-five cents.

Principal assigned causes of insanity: The Director at Halle says that eighty per cent of cases of insanity are from hereditary causes.

Principal causes of death: general paralysis, epilepsy.

Population, December, 1867 23,971,337

The total number of insane	16,929
The total number of idiots	21,031
Total number of unsound mind	37,960

Proportion of insane and idiots to population, one in six hundred and thirty-one, or ratio per one thousand	1.58
Proportion of insane to population, one in fourteen hundred and sixteen, or ratio per one thousand	.70

INSANITY IN AUSTRIA.

German Austria, exclusive of Hungary.

Population, 1864 13,000,000

Number of Insane in Asylums.

In Public Asylums	3,065
In Private Asylums	150
Total	3,215

| Proportion of insane (under treatment) to population, one in four thousand and forty-three, or ratio per one thousand............... | .24 |

Number of Asylums.

Public Asylums..	14
Private Asylums...	4
Total...	18

Expenses of Public Asylums, eight hundred and seventy-three thousand seven hundred and fifty-six florins, or four hundred and twenty-two thousand eight hundred and ninety-seven dollars and ninety cents, which gives an average weekly cost per head of two dollars and sixty-five cents.

In six asylums visited in 1870, the number of patients resident was..	2,302
Admitted...	1,741
Cured..	377
Died...	543
Number treated..	4,043

Per cent of cures on admissions	21
Per cent of cures on number treated.................................	9
Per cent of deaths on admissions	31
Per cent of deaths on number treated................................	13

The new asylum, Klosterneuberg, was also visited. It was opened in eighteen hundred and seventy, so there was no report for the year. The number resident was one hundred and twenty-three.

The average weekly cost of maintenance of indigents in the Public Asylums visited was two dollars and thirty-nine cents.

The Statistical Bureau gives three hundred and ninety-seven thousand and ninety dollars as the cost of supporting four thousand four hundred and ninety-nine pauper patients in eighteen hundred and sixty-nine—

| An annual cost per head of.. | $88 26 |
| A weekly cost per head of... | 1 70 |

The principal assigned causes of insanity: inherited or congenital tendency, affliction, poverty, remorse, intemperance.

The principal causes of death: disease of the lungs, paralysis of the brain, marasmus.

INSANITY IN THE GERMAN STATES.

Population, 1864.. 13,747,637

Number of Insane in Asylums and Hospitals.

In Public Asylums...	9,962
In Private Asylums	633
Total	10,595

Proportion of insane (under treatment) to population, one in twelve hundred and ninety-seven, or ratio per one thousand	.77

Number of Asylums.

Public Asylums	46
Private Asylums	18
Total	64

In ten asylums visited in 1870, the number of patients resident was	2,495
Admitted	1,046
Cured	276
Died	290
Number treated	3,541

Per cent of cures on admissions	26
Per cent of cures on number treated	7
Per cent of deaths on admissions	27
Per cent of deaths on number treated	8

At Illenau the numbers for ten years were obtained. They were as follows:

Admissions	4,086
Cures	1,570
Deaths	597
Number treated	4,512

Per cent of cures on admissions...	38
Per cent of cures on number treated	34
Per cent of deaths on admissions...	14
Per cent of deaths on number treated.....................................	13

The average weekly cost of maintenance for indigents in the Public Asylums visited was one dollar and sixty cents.

INSANITY IN BAVARIA.

Population, 1864.. 4,807,440

Number of Insane Under Treatment.

In Public Asylums..	1,831
In Private Asylums...	19
Total	1,850

Proportion of insane (under treatment) to population, one in two thousand five hundred and ninety-eight, or ratio per one thousand	.38

Number of Asylums.

Public Asylums...	9
Private Asylums..	2
Total...	11

In 1861 the population was	4,689,837
The total number of insane...	4,899
Proportion to population, one in nine hundred and fifty-seven, or ratio per one thousand	1.04

In the six District Lunatic Asylums the number of patients October 1st, 1865, was...	1,651
Admitted during the year..	529
Cured...	171
Died	150
Number treated in 1865–6..	2,180

Per cent of recoveries on admissions	32
Per cent of recoveries on number treated	7
Per cent of deaths on admissions	28
Per cent of deaths on number treated	6

The average weekly cost of maintenance per head in the above District Asylums was, in 1865–6, two dollars and fifty-three cents.

Causes of insanity not specified; but in about twenty-nine per cent of the whole number of cases the insanity was hereditary.

The principal causes of death: consumption, general paralysis, pleurisy and pneumonia, marasmus.

In three asylums visited in 1870, the number of patients resident was	658
Admitted	324
Cured	112
Died	57
Number treated	982

Per cent of recoveries on admissions	34
Per cent of recoveries on number treated	11
Per cent of deaths on admissions	17
Per cent of deaths on number treated	5

INSANITY IN SWITZERLAND.

Population, 1860	2,510,494

In two asylums visited in 1870, the number of patients resident was	462

The report for the asylum at Waldau is as follows:

Number resident	295
Admitted	83
Cured	32
Died	19
Number treated	378

Per cent of cures on admissions...	38
Per cent of cures on number treated.......................................	8
Per cent of deaths on admissions	22
Per cent of deaths on number treated........:.................................	5

Average weekly cost of maintenance of indigents is one dollar and sixteen cents.

INSANITY IN BELGIUM.

Population, 1865... 4,984,451

Number and Distribution of the Insane, December 31st, 1865.

	Private.	Pauper.	Totals.
In hospitals and asylums..............................	1,579	3,852	5,431
Estimated number at large who are supported by their families..	2,000	....	....
Totals..	3,579	3,852	7,431

Proportion of insane to population, one in six hundred and seventy one, or ratio per one thousand...	1.49
Proportion of insane (under treatment) to population, one in nine hundred and seventeen, or ratio per one thousand..................	1.09

Number of insane under treatment in hospitals, January 1st, 1865.	5,441
Admitted during the year...	1,851
Cured	642
Died	595
Number treated in 1865..	7,292

Per cent of recoveries on admissions...	34
Per cent of recoveries on number treated...........................	8
Per cent of deaths on admissions .....:.......................................	32
Per cent of deaths on number treated..	8

Number of Asylums for the Insane, 1865.

For male patients only	17
For female patients only	17
For both sexes	17
Total	51

Twenty-seven of these asylums are for private patients and paupers; sixteen are for private patients only, and eight for paupers only.

The average weekly cost of pauper patients varies from five francs and four centimes to ten francs and fifty centimes, or from ninety-five cents to two dollars.

The fifty-one asylums of Belgium have a total capacity of five thousand three hundred and eighty-seven patients.

The principal assigned causes of insanity are: poverty, losses, etc., intemperance, domestic trouble, disappointment.

The principal causes of death are: cerebral marasmus, general paralysis, consumption, chronic bronchitis.

In eight asylums visited in 1870, the number of patients resident was	3,029
Admitted into five of these asylums	769
Treated in five of these asylums	3,567
Cured in five of these asylums	232
Died in five of these asylums	311

Per cent of recoveries on admissions	30
Per cent of recoveries on number treated	8
Per cent of deaths on admissions	40
Per cent of deaths on number treated	8

INSANITY IN HOLLAND.

Population, 1868.. 3,592,415

Number of patients in Lunatic Hospitals, January 1st, 1868	3,179
Admitted	994
Cured	380
Died	358
Number treated in 1868	4,173

Per cent of cures on admissions	38
Per cent of cures on number treated	9
Per cent of deaths on admissions	36
Per cent of deaths on number treated	8

Proportion of insane (in asylums) to population, one in eleven hundred and thirty, or ratio per one thousand	.88

Number of Lunatic Asylums...... 12

Cost of Maintenance.

At Reinier Van Arkel:

First class, seven hundred florins, and twenty-five florins as entrance fee.

Second class, four hundred florins, and twelve florins as entrance fee.

Third class, two hundred and twenty-five florins, and are clothed by the Institute.

At Meerenberg:

First class, one thousand florins.

Second class, seven hundred and fifty florins.

Third class, five hundred florins.

Fourth class, three hundred florins.

Fifth class, two hundred and seventy florins.

At Rotterdam (for indigents):

Two hundred and forty florins. Twelve other patients pay one florin per day extra for better accommodations.

Average weekly cost for indigents, one dollar and eighty-eight cents.

The principal assigned causes of insanity (mentioned in reports) are: hereditary, intemperance.

The principal causes of death are: marasmus, consumption, apoplexy, general paralysis.

In three asylums visited in 1870, the number of patients resident was	1,245
Admitted	321
Treated	1,566
Cured	123
Died	145

Per cent of recoveries on admissions	38
Per cent of recoveries on number treated	7
Per cent of deaths on admissions	45
Per cent of deaths on number treated	9

INSANITY IN DENMARK.

Population, 1860...	2,605,024
Total number of insane...	5,135

Proportion to population, one in five hundred and seven, or ratio per one thousand...	1.97

Proportion of insane (under treatment) in public institutions to population, one in sixteen hundred and thirteen.*

INSANITY IN SWEDEN.

Population, 1860...	3,859,728
Total number of insane...	7,512

Proportion of insane to population, one in five hundred and thirteen, or ratio per one thousand..	1.94

Patients in Asylums.

	Private.	Pauper.	Totals.
1861 †...	469	530	1,026
1864 ‡...	553	598	1,151
1867 ‖...	630	641	1,271

Calculated population, 1864..	4,091,594

Proportion of insane under treatment, 1867, to population, one in three thousand two hundred and nineteen, or ratio per one thousand...	.31

* See Knörlcin's Report of Asylum at Linz, published in 1866, p. 78.
† Helso och Sjukvärden, 1861, pp. 30, 31.
‡ Helso och Sjukvärden, 1864, pp. 26, 27.
‖ Helso och Sjukvärden, 1867, pp. 14, 15.

4

Number of insane in asylums and Houses for the Insane, January 1st, 1864	1,095
Admitted during the year	332
Cured and improved	163
Died	91
Number treated	1,427
Number January 1st, 1865	1,151

Per cent of cured and improved on admissions	49
Per cent of cured and improved on number treated	11
Per cent of deaths on admissions	27
Per cent of deaths on number treated	6

Proportion of insane (under treatment) to population, one in three thousand five hundred and fifty-four, or ratio per one thousand	.28

Annual cost per head, three hundred and twenty-eight rix dollars and seventy-nine öre (three hundred and forty-seven dollars and sixty-eight cents, nearly), averaging six dollars and sixty-eight cents per week.

According to the census of 1855 the population was	3,641,011
Number of insane	3,893
Proportion to population, one in nine hundred and thirty-five, or ratio per one thousand	1.06

INSANITY IN NORWAY.

Population, 1864.. 1,668,254

Number of patients in asylums January 1st, 1864	557
Admitted	394
Cured	124
Died	35
Number treated in 1864	951
Number in asylums January 1st, 1865	583

Per cent of recoveries on admissions	31
Per cent of recoveries on number treated	13
Per cent of deaths on admissions	8
Per cent of deaths on number treated	3

Proportion of insane (in asylums) to population, one in two thousand eight hundred and sixty-one, or ratio per one thousand .... | .34

Number of asylums.. | 8

According to census of 1855 the population was.................... | 1,490,047
Total number of insane.. | 1,329
Proportion to population, one in eleven hundred and twenty-one, or ratio per one thousand.................................... | .89

Doctor Bucknill, in eighteen hundred and fifty-seven, reckons the proportion of insane to the population as one in five hundred and fifty-one.

Number of asylums in 1867 .... | 9

Number of patients in asylums January 1st, 1867.................. | 667
Admitted... | 423
Cured.. | 140
Died... | 41
Number treated... | 1,090
Number in asylums January 1st, 1868............................... | 727

Per cent of recoveries on admissions............................... | 33
Per cent of recoveries on number treated.......................... | 12
Per cent of deaths on admissions.................................. | 9
Per cent of deaths on number treated.............................. | 3

INSANITY IN NEW SOUTH WALES.

Population, 1867... 447,620

Number of insane, including idiots................................ | 1,156
Proportion of insane to population, one in three hundred and eighty-seven, or ratio per one thousand .... | 2.58

The number of lunatics under treatment, exclusive of invalids, in eighteen hundred and sixty-eight, was:

	Pauper.	Private.	Totals.
At Tarban..	397	223	620
At Parramatta..	347	189	536
Totals.....................	744	412	1,156

In eighteen hundred and fifty-five the number of lunatics in the Government Asylums was:

At Tarban...	197
At Parramatta..	279
Total..	476

In eighteen hundred and sixty-eight the number was eleven hundred and fifty-six, an increase of six hundred and eighty in thirteen years, or an annual increase of fifty-two and four one hundredths.

The cost of maintenance is: at Tarban, seven shillings and eight pence; at Parramatta, eight shillings and five pence.

INSANITY IN THE UNITED STATES.

Population, 1870... 38,555,983

Number of Insane.

White...	35,560
Black	1,605
Mulatto	169
Chinese	35
Indian	13
Total..	37,382

Number of Idiots.

White	21,324
Black..	2,743
Mulatto	445
Chinese	5
Indian...	10
Total..	24,527

Number of insane and idiots................................. 61,909

Proportion of insane to population, one in ten hundred and thirty-one, or ratio per one thousand...	.97
Proportion of idiots to population, one in fifteen hundred and seventy-two, or ratio per one thousand..................................	.63
Proportion of insane and idiots to population, one in six hundred and twenty-three, or ratio per one thousand........................	1.06

Number of insane under treatment.*....................................	17,735
Proportion of insane under treatment to population, one in two thousand one hundred and seventy-three, or ratio per one thousand..	.46

Number of patients in asylums, 1870 †................................	15,792
Admitted during the year †..	10,229
Cured †...	3,357
Died †	1,851
Number treated †..	26,021

Per cent of cures on admissions.......................................	33
Per cent of cures on number treated.................................	13
Per cent of deaths on admissions.....................................	18
Per cent of deaths on number treated...............................	7

Number of Asylums.

Public Asylums..	50
Private Asylums	16
Total..	66

The principal assigned causes of insanity: ill health, spermatorrhœa, intemperance, domestic trouble, physical disease, religious excitement, epilepsy.

Principal causes of death: exhaustion (from various causes), epilepsy, general paralysis, and consumption.

* As nearly as can be ascertained from returns.

† Report for forty-nine asylums. Returns could not be obtained from the others.

In thirty-nine asylums visited in 1870, the number resident was...	12,907
Admitted	8,639
Cured..	3,240
Died	1,519
Number treated...	21,504

Per cent of cures on admissions..	37
Per cent of cures on number treated...	15
Per cent of deaths on admissions	17
Per cent of deaths on number treated..	7

Years.	Population.	Insane.	Idiots.	Total.	No. Insane Hospitals.	No. Insane in Hospitals.	Per ct. sup'd with hospital accommod's.
1850.......	23,191,876	15,610	15,787	31,397	28	4,730	30.30
1860.......	31,443,322	23,999	18,865	42,864	46	*8,500	35.42
1870	38,555,983	37,382	24,527	61,909	66	17,735	47.44

INSANITY IN CALIFORNIA.

Population, 1870...	560,247

Native population	350,416
Foreign population..	209,831
Total...	560,247

Number of Insane.

	Males.	Fem'les	Totals.
White	789	304	1,093
Black..	15	2	17
Mulatto	....	....	....
Chinese..	29	4	33
Indian	2	1	3
Totals	835	311	1,146

* See Journal of Insanity, Vol. XVIII, p. 2.

Number of Idiots.

	Males.	Fem'les	Totals.
White	48	29	77
Black	2	....	2
Mulatto	1	1	2
Chinese	4	1	5
Indian	1	....	1
Totals	56	31	87

Insane and Idiots classified as Native and Foreign.

	Insane.	Idiots.	Totals.
Native	408	70	478
Foreign	738	17	755
Totals	1,146	87	1,233

Proportion of insane to population, one in four hundred and eighty-nine, or ratio per one thousand	2.04
Proportion of idiots to population, one in six thousand four hundred and thirty-nine, or ratio per one thousand	.15
Proportion of insane and idiots to population, one in four hundred and fifty-four, or ratio per one thousand	2.20

Number of insane under treatment	1,047
Proportion under treatment to population, one in five hundred and thirty-five, or ratio per one thousand	1.86

Proportion of native to total insane	35.60
Proportion of foreign to total insane	64.40
Total	100.00

Number of patients in Asylum January 1st, 1870......................	920
Admitted during the year..	562
Cured..	221
Died	156
Number treated...	1,483

Of the whole number of insane, ninety-one and three tenths per cent are under treatment.

CHAPTER IV.

CAUSES OF INSANITY, AND SOME OF THE INFLUENCES OPERATING IN ITS DEVELOPMENT.

General Observations—Assigned Causes—Physical Causes—Moral Causes—Observations upon Assigned Causes—Principal Assigned Causes—Insanity Found in all Countries—Enumeration of the Insane—Tables Relating to Enumeration—Enumerations Imperfect—Difficulties in the way of a Perfect Enumeration—Influence of Age—Influence of Age in the Different Races—Influence of Sex—Influence of Marriage.

GENERAL OBSERVATIONS.

From the formidable array made by such an army of insane men and women, as it is seen with its banners flying in every civilized country, it behooves us to pause and give it thought; to ascertain as nearly as may be what causes are most prolific in its production; what conditions of society most readily lead to its development, and how best to meet its attacks and arrest its onward march, "more terrible than an army of banners." Let us first inquire into the causes producing this malady. In ancient times insanity was attributed to supernatural causes, but as science advanced and shed its light upon the human race this superstition passed away, until at the present time the causes which lead to it are known to be as varied as those which affect the physical system, as will be seen from the following table, taken from a paper on the supposed increase of insanity, read before the Association of Medical Superintendents of American Institutions for the Insane, by Dr. Jarvis, of Massachusetts, at their annual meeting at Philadelphia, May, eighteen hundred and fifty-one:

ASSIGNED CAUSES OF INSANITY.

Physical Causes.	*Moral Causes.*
Congestion of the brain.	Mental labor and excitement.
Disease of the brain.	Mental fatigue.
Phrœnitis.	Mental shock.
Epilepsy.	Mental perplexity.
Arachnoiditis.	Excessive study.
Apoplexy.	Study of metaphysics.
Convulsions.	Study of phrenology.
Hydrocephalus.	Excitement of lawsuit.
Nervous irritation.	Politics.

Physical Causes.	*Moral Causes.*
Excessive pain.	Political commotions.
Neuralgia.	Excitement of Mexican war.
Typhus fever.	Excitement of visiting.
Nervous fever.	Sea voyage.
Bilious fever.	License question.
Scarlet fever.	Anti-rent.
Intermittent fever.	Fourierism.
Yellow fever.	Preaching sixteen days and nights.
Gastritis.	Blowing fife all night.
Measles.	Application to business.
Gout.	Reading vile books.
Dyspepsia.	Seclusion.
Dysentery.	Sudden joy.
Erysipelas.	Hope.
Phthisis.	Faulty education.
Rheumatism.	Day dreaming.
Bilious rheumatism.	Extatic admiration of works of art.
Suppression of hemorrhoids.	Seduction.
Suppression of perspiration.	Domestic affliction.
Suppression of secretions.	Domestic trouble.
Suppression of eruption.	Family affairs.
Suppression of tumor.	Bad conduct of children.
Suppression of fistula.	Ill treatment.
Smallpox.	Ill treatment from husband.
Varioloid.	Ill treatment from parents.
Irritation of the spine.	Abuse from husband.
Disease of the spine.	Infidelity of husband.
Ill health.	Infidelity of wife.
Ill health and solitude.	False accusation.
Ill health and perplexity in busi-	Imprisonment for crime.
ness.	Difficulty in neighborhood.
Ill health and family trouble.	Avarice.
Ill health and pecuniary difficulties.	Anticipation of wealth.
Ill health and lawsuit.	Speculation in stocks.
Old age.	Speculation in morus multicaulis.
Irregular decay of powers in old	Speculation in lottery tickets.
age.	Perplexity in business.
Congenital.	Pecuniary difficulties.
Hereditary.	Disappointment in business.
Injuries.	Loss of money.
Concussion of brain.	Loss of property.
Lesion of brain.	Reverse of fortune.
Blow on the head.	Fear of poverty.
Fracture of the head.	Death of relations.
Burn on the head.	Death of husband.
Malformed head.	Death of father.
Fall.	Death of son.
Kick on the stomach.	Sickness and death of a friend.
Surgical operation.	Sickness and death of friends.
Mesmerism.	Sickness and death of kindred.
Insolation.	Murder of a son.
Want of exercise.	Anxiety.

Physical Causes.	*Moral Causes.*
Sedentary habits.	Anxiety and loss of sleep.
Idleness.	Anxiety for absent friends.
Insolation and drinking cold water.	Home sickness.
Exposure to excessive heat.	Fright.
Exposure to cold.	Disappointment.
Bathing in cold water.	Disappointment in love.
Sleeping in a barn filled with new hay.	Disappointment in ambition.
Tight lacing.	Unrequited love.
Excess of quinine.	Want of employment.
Metallic vapor.	Want of occupation.
Prussic acid vapor.	Destitution.
Charcoal vapor.	Mortified pride.
Pregnancy.	Ungoverned passion.
Parturition.	Virulent temper.
Abortion.	Misanthropy.
Puerperal.	Jealousy.
Cold in childbed.	Envy.
Lactation.	Duel.
Sexual derangement.	Religious anxiety.
Disease of uterus.	Religious excitement.
Irregular menstruation.	Remorse.
Profuse menstruation.	Millerism.
Suspended menstruation at change of life.	Mormonism.
Suppressed menstruation.	Struggle between the religious principle and power of passion.
Hysteria.	Epidemic influences.
Carbonic acid gas.	
Working in white lead.	
Acetate of lead.	
Excessive labor.	
Bodily exertion.	
Loss of sleep.	
Intemperate use of snuff.	
Intemperate smoking.	
Intemperate opium eating.	
Syphilis.	
Vice.	
Immorality.	

And winds up by saying: "These are not all the diseases, accidents, events, etc., that can disturb the regular action of the brain."

OBSERVATIONS UPON ASSIGNED CAUSES.

From this formidable list of assigned causes of mental disturbance we see there is scarcely a disease of the body, an emotion of the mind, or a feeling of the heart that may not act as an exciting, if not an actual cause in the dethronement of man's reason. "Dr. Ludwig, of the Heppenheim Asylum, expressed the opinion that the cause of insanity is extremely obscure and not easily defined, and thinks that most of the assigned causes are made at the writing desk of the Committing Boards;

that predisposition must exist, and that the form is only the effect, not the cause." We very well know that mistakes are often made by Committing Boards, even when composed of physicians, and that symptoms are too often mistaken for disease; nevertheless we cannot agree with Dr. Ludwig and other German Superintendents who assign nearly all cases of lunacy to hereditary taint. Intemperance was admitted by a few of those with whom we conversed to be a cause of mental disturbance, but all others were set aside as unworthy of being assigned a place. Dr. Koëppé, the intelligent Director and Physician in Chief of the celebrated Asylum at Halle, in Prussian Saxony, informed us that eighty per cent of those committed to his Asylum were from hereditary causes, and that this was in accord with the experience of the Superintendents of other institutions in Germany. To say the least, this does not agree with the opinions of the learned and practical men who have charge of Asylums in most other countries, and especially in Great Britain and the United States.

The preceding list was inserted as a matter of general interest. The following table comprises the principal assigned causes of insanity:

COMPARATIVE VIEW OF THE PRINCIPAL ASSIGNED CAUSES OF INSANITY IN SEVERAL COUNTRIES.

Unit'd States.	England.	Scotland.	Ireland.	France.	Germany.	Prussia.	Austria.	Italy.	Belgium.	Holland.
Ill health. Spermatorrhea. Intemperance. Domestic trouble. Epilepsy. Physical disability. Religious excitement. Epilepsy.	Hereditary. Intemperance. Domestic trouble, Epilepsy. Mental anxiety. Puerperal condition and critical period, Paralysis.	Climacteric changes, Old age. Intemperance. Child bearing.	Hereditary. Grief, fear, and anxiety Intemperance and irregula'ty of living; Disease of brain. Bodily injuries and disorders.	Hereditary. Epilepsy and convuls'ns. Intemperance. Destitution and misery Loss of fortune.	Hereditary. Intemporance.	Hereditary. Intemperance.	Inherited or congenital tendency. Affliction, poverty, remorse. Intemperance.	Pellagra. Hereditary. Intemperance.	Poverty. losses, etc. Intemperance. Domestic trouble. Disappointment.	Hereditary. Intemperance.

INSANITY FOUND IN ALL COUNTRIES.

As the causes enumerated in this Chapter operate with more or less power and energy in producing insanity, we learn that it is found in all countries and among all nations, but is more prevalent among civilized than among savage people. It is true that we have no statistical data upon which to predicate this assertion, as no census of the insane has ever been taken in savage or semi-barbarous nations. From those who have resided in these countries, and from travellers who have gone among them, we learn that but little insanity is known among them. Caleb Cushing, former United States Minister, states that after a somewhat protracted residence in China he had concluded there were but few lunatics to be seen or heard of. Mr. Williams, an American missionary, after a residence of twelve years, says that he only saw two who were "upside down," as the Chinese call it, during the whole time.

All travellers agree that it scarcely exists in Nubia, and that it is extremely rare in Egypt. In eighteen hundred and forty-four, according to a statement in the London Medical Gazette, there were only fourteen in Cairo, being one to twenty-three thousand five hundred and seventy-two of the population. A few isolated cases have been reported by Doctors Moreau and Furnari, among the tribes bordering on the African shores of the Mediterranean, but agree in the general conclusion as to its scarcity. Doctor Furnari thinks it is in consequence of their "total abstinence."

Doctor De Forest, of the Syrian Mission, in a letter to Doctor Butler, of America, says: "It is impossible to obtain accurate statistics of the insane here, but I think the disease far less frequent than in our own land." He gives a fearful picture of the treatment of those who are unfortunate enough to be insane. Doctor Paulding, in the Boston Medical and Surgical Journal (1852), bears testimony to the same facts.

Doctor Wise, Superintendent of an asylum in Bengal, states as the result of his experience, "that insanity is less frequent and assumes a less acute form among the East Indians than among the civilized nations of Europe." Captain Wilkes, of the United States Exploring Expedition, in a letter to Doctor Brigham, says: "During the whole of my intercourse with the natives of the South Sea I met no deranged person. I am confident that had any instance of mental derangement among the natives occurred, it would have been observed by us."

We all know in this country that for a long time it was supposed that no Indian had been known to become insane; and so we might show of all other countries where savages are found in similar conditions, if deemed important. That it exists in much larger proportions in Europe and America scarce needs be stated, as it is a fact well known to all who have paid the least attention to the subject, and will be abundantly proved in this report. That it is not due to any peculiarity of race will also be shown, at least with regard to some of these peoples, when brought in contact with more civilized nations and subjected to the influences by which it is developed.

It is believed to be due to causes inherent in man, or connected with his condition, habits, and exposures.

Some of these causes belong to the body, as physical diseases—apoplexy, epilepsy, palsy, scrofula, injuries to the head, general ill health, consumption—and some are called moral causes, such as anxiety, excessive study, grief, remorse, distress, struggles for gain, ambition. Some of these causes apply to the savage as well as civilized nations, while others are applicable exclusively, or nearly so, to a condition of civilization. They vary in their frequency, intensity, and power, and consequently the mental diseases also differ in frequency and durability; to what extent we will endeavor to show, in a measure at least, hereafter. For the present we desire to exhibit their combined effect upon those subjected to their influence.

ENUMERATION OF THE INSANE.

Most nations in their enumerations take account of the insane; thus we find their numbers as seen in the following tables:

TABLE.

COUNTRY.	Census of......	Population.	Numbers of Insane and Idiots.			Proportion of—		
			Insane	Idiots.	Total.	Insane to Population.	Idiots to Population.	Total to Population.
United States	1870	38,555,983	37,382	24,527	61,909	1 in 1,031	1 in 1,572	1 in 623
England.......	1870	22,090,163	....	....	54,713	....	....	1 in 403
Scotland.......	1870	3,222,837	....	....	9,571	....	....	1 in 336
Ireland	1870	* 5,195,236	11,122	6,072	17,194	1 in 467	1 in 855	1 in 302
France	1866	37,988,905	50,726	39,953	90,679	1 in 747	1 in 950	1 in 418
Prussia	1867	23,971,337	16,929	21,031	37,960	1 in 1,416	1 in 1,139	1 in (31
Belgium........	1865	4,984,451	....	....	7,431	....	....	1 in 6/1
Total........	....	136,008,912	....	....	279,457	....	....	1 in 486

TABLE.†

COUNTRIES.	Census taken once in :	Census of	Populat'n.	Number of Insane.			Proport'n to Populat'n
				Males.	Feml's	Totals.	
Ireland	10 years	1861	5,798,967	3,500	3,565	7,065	1 in 821
England and Wales........	10 years	1861	20,066,224	11,249	13,096	24,345	1 in 824
Newfoundland	10 years	1857	122,638	50	38	88	1 in 1,394
Nova Scotia..................	10 years	1861	330,857	166	174	340	1 in 973
Prince Edward's Island..	7 years	1861	80,857	....	....	148	1 in 546
United States	10 years	1860	31,445,080	....	....	23,999	1 in 1,310
France	5 years	1856	36,012,669	....	....	35,031	1 in 1,028
Savoy..........................	·4 years	1861	542,535	143	167	310	1 in 1,750
Belgium	10 years	1856	4,529,560	2,019	1,998	4,017	1 in 1,128
Holland	10 years	1859	3,308,969	1,038	1,101	2,189	1 in 1,547
Hanover	3 years	1861	1,888,048	1,591	1,493	3,084	1 in 612
Prussia	3 years	1858	17,739,913	....	....	1,559	1 in 1,427
Saxony	3 years	1861	2,225,240	....	....	4,899	1 in 957
Bavaria.......................	3 years	1861	4,689,837	2,576	2,323	1,338	1 in 1,286
Wurtemburg.................	3 years	1861	1,720,708	690	648	954	1 in 301
Hesse Darmstadt	3 years	1861	856,907	446	508	5,135	1 in 507
Oldenburg	....	1855	287,163	2,543	2,592	3,893	1 in 935
Denmark......................	5 years	1860	2,605,024	1,898	1,995	1,329	1 in 1,121
Sweden	5 years	1855	3,641,011	619	710	1,750	1 in 2,881
Norway	10 years	1855	1,490,047				
Piedmont	10 years	1858	5,041,853				

* Calculated population.

† From Vital Statistics of Ireland.

TABLE.

COUNTRIES.	1844.*			1850.†	1857.‡	1860.§	1867.‖
	Population	Insane.	Ratio.	Ratio.	Ratio.	Ratio.	Ratio.
Spain............	4,058,000	569	1 in 7,180	1 in 7,181	....	1 in 1,667	....
Italy	16,789,000	3,441	1 in 4,876	1 in 3,785	....	1 in 3,690	....
Belgium	3,816,000	3,763	1 in 1,014	....	....	1 in 816	....
Holland	2,302,000	2,300	1 in 1,001	....	....	1 in 1,223	....
France	32,000,000	32,000	1 in 1,000	1 in 1,000	1 in 795	1 in 1,773	1 in 444
United States.	17,069,453	17,457	1 in 977	....	....	....	....
Malta & Gozzo	120,000	130	1 in 932	....	....	....	....
Westphalia ...	1,283,142	1,535	1 in 846	....	....	....	....
England	13,089,358	16,222	1 in 807	1 in 666	1 in 577	1 in 700	1 in 432
Ireland	7,784,586	10,059	1 in 774	....	....	1 in 2,125	1 in 325
Scotland	2,365,807	3,652	1 in 648	1 in 400	....	1 in 513	1 in 368
Norway	1,051,300	1,909	1 in 551	1 in 531	1 in 551	1 in 550	....
Brunswick.....	262,948	488	1 in 539	....	....	....	....
CITIES.							
London..........	1,400,000	7,000	1 in 200	....	....	....	....
Paris............	890,000	4,000	1 in 222	....	....	....	....
Petersburg ...	377,000	120	1 in 3,142	....	....	....	....
Naples	370,000	479	1 in 772	....	....	....	....
Cairo	330,000	14	1 : 23,572	....	....	....	....
Madrid	204,000	60	1 in 3,400	....	....	....	....
Rome	154,000	320	1 in 480	....	....	....	....
Milan	151,000	618	1 in 244	....	....	....	....
Turin	114,000	331	1 in 341	....	....	....	....
Florence.......	80,000	236	1 in 339	....	....	....	....
Dresden	70,000	150	1 in 446	....	....	....	....
Brunswick.....	37,583	104	1 in 361⅓	....	....	....	....

ENUMERATIONS IMPERFECT.

These statements of the insane are doubtless imperfect in all countries, and certainly very imperfect in some of them. It is impossible to obtain full accounts of the insane through public offices as at present organized, and any other and more perfect system would probably be deemed too expensive by most Governments. We have reason to believe that many are concealed from public view, and that families refuse to report them to ordinary officers.

DIFFICULTIES IN THE WAY OF PERFECT ENUMERATION.

Massachusetts seems to have understood and appreciated these difficulties at an early date, and in eighteen hundred and fifty-four appointed a Commission, consisting of Levi Lincoln, Doctor Edward Jarvis, and Increase Sumner, to ascertain the number and condition of

* See London Medical Gazette, April, 1844.
† American Journal of Insanity, Vol. VII, p. 286.
‡ Bucknill & Tuke on Insanity, p. 47.
§ Journal of Insanity, Vol. XVII, p. 348.
‖ Manning's Reports, p. 109.

the insane in the State; distinguishing as accurately as may be between the insane, properly so considered, and the idiotic or *non compos;* between the furious and harmless; curable and incurable; and between the natives and foreigners, and the number of each who are State paupers. (See Insane and Idiots, Mass. 1854).

This Commission addressed circulars to every physician in the State, setting forth the facts that they desired to obtain, and asking their assistance and coöperation. There were at that time fifteen hundred and fifty-six physicians in the State, of whom all but four responded, giving every case within their knowledge.

Besides these, many of the clergy, Overseers of the Poor, and other persons known or supposed to be interested in or informed upon the subject were consulted and their assistance asked.

After twelve months of constant, persistent, and untiring labor the most complete, able, and satisfactory report ever made of the insane and idiots in any State or country was the result. It was not only important to Massachusetts, but to all other States and countries. The subject of inquiry was of a general character, and the facts found and inferences deduced as applicable to all the world as to Massachusetts.

Without going into the details of the modus operandi by which the information was obtained, it is sufficient to state the result in a few particulars. Of the lunatics found, fifteen hundred and twenty-two were paupers, and eleven hundred and ten were supported by their own property or by their friends, making a total of two thousand six hundred and thirty-two, or one to every four hundred and twenty-seven of the population; whereas an enumeration made by another Commission, in a different way, a few years previously (eighteen hundred and forty-eight), showed only one to five hundred and ninety-two of the population. The United States census of eighteen hundred and sixty showed one to five hundred and eighty-five, and in eighteen hundred and seventy, one to five hundred and forty-seven. These figures demonstrate the imperfections of general enumerations, and the difference exhibited by a census perfectly taken. This difference, we think, may safely be added to the enumerations made in other countries.

INFLUENCE OF AGE.

Among the causes of insanity, age is supposed to have its influence; at all events, it is a fact established by the observations of most men who have written upon the subject that a larger proportion become insane between the ages of thirty and forty than at any other period of life. The general enumerations of the insane do not show their ages, but this is stated in all those who are, committed to hospitals, and thus the deficiency is in a measure supplied, and we are thereby enabled to arrive at approximate conclusions.

There are, however, some notable exceptions to this general rule. The experience of Esquirol at Charenton showed the largest number of admissions between twenty and thirty. The experience of Doctor Erle at Bloomingdale, and that of Doctor Hood during ten years at Bethlem, is in accord with that of Esquirol at Charenton, though the whole experience of Esquirol was in accordance with the general rule, while that of Doctor Tuke was in favor of the earlier period, between twenty and thirty. It will be seen by the following table that in France, Italy, and

Holland the greatest number become insane between the ages of thirty and forty, while in Ireland and at the York Retreat the greater number was between twenty and thirty. The table also shows that the numbers decrease as we ascend or descend the scale. This result may be attributed to the fact that at that period of life both males and females are more exposed to the various exciting causes than at any other. It is contended by some authors, however, that the age between thirty-five and forty exercises a special influence over the production of insanity; but of this we have no other evidence than that already cited. The following table will show the influence of age, illustrated by statistics of different countries:

TABLE.

Influence of Age, illustrated by Statistics of Different Countries.

AGE.	FRANCE. 1853. Number	FRANCE. 1853. Proportion at each to total known ages.	IRELAND. District Asylums, 1870. Number	IRELAND. District Asylums, 1870. Proportion at each to total known ages.	ITALY. Florence Asylum, 1868. Number	ITALY. Florence Asylum, 1868. Proportion at each age to total.	HOLLAND. 1844 to 1864. Number	HOLLAND. 1844 to 1864. Proportion at each age to total.	TOTAL. Number	TOTAL. Proportion at each to total of known ages.
Under 10 years	1,809	5.90	2	.08	3	.96	66	.56	2,738	6.08
10 to 20 years...			187	8.14	18	5.73	653	5.57		
20 to 30 years......	5,912	19.27	713	31.05	68	21.66	2,681	22.87	9,374	20.83
30 to 40 years......	8,470	27.61	593	25.83	77	24.52	3,045	25.98	12,185	27.08
40 to 50 years......	7,011	22.86	374	16.29	66	21.02	2,370	20.22	9,821	21.82
50 to 60 years......	4,610	15.03	229	10.00	41	13.06	1,672	14.27	6,552	14.56
60 to 70 years......	2,022	6.59	145	6.31	24	7.64	867	7.40	3,058	6.79
Over 70 years......	839	2.74	53	2.30	17	5.41	367	3.13	1,276	2.84
Unknown	2,203	....	37	....	....	....	....	....	2,240	....
Totals............	32,876	....	2,333	....	314	....	11,721	....	47,244	....

Doctor Tuke says: "During the forty four years between seventeen hundred and ninety-six and eighteen hundred and forty, of those admitted at the Retreat the greater number (one third of the whole) were *attacked* between twenty and thirty years of age. Each subsequent decennial period is marked by a gradually decreasing proportion. Thus, of every hundred cases at the origin of the disorder there were, at successive periods of life, as follows:

0–10	10–20	20–30	30–40	40–50	50–60	60–70	70–80	80–90
.96	12.77	32.53	20.00	15.9	10.6	6.3	.97	.24

" Now it is obvious that to render these statistics of any value they must be compared with the numbers living in the same community at the same periods of life. This means of comparison we afford in the following table.

" Of every hundred individuals there were living, at successive decennial periods of life, as follows:

0–10	10–20	20–30	30–40	40–50	50–60	60–70	70–80	80–90
16.7	18.9	15.4	12.4	11.9	10.8	7.8	4.9	1.2

" From which it is evident that the large proportion of persons who become insane, of those admitted at the Retreat, between twenty and thirty years of age, cannot be explained by the greater proportion of the number living at that period. On the contrary, there were more living under ten years of age and between ten and twenty. These facts, therefore, exhibit an increased liability to insanity connected with the age between twenty and thirty; or man during that period is brought into contact with an increased number of the causes of insanity. It is probable that it is the combination of these two circumstances which induces this result."[*]

In eighteen hundred and fifty the greatest number of inhabitants of a given age in the United States was under ten, the next greatest between ten and twenty, and so on, gradually decreasing to the end. We presume that these proportions have been maintained to the present time; and as we have not by us any census of a later date setting forth this particular fact, we have made use of it in preparing the following table, taking, however, the number of insane for eighteen hundred and seventy instead of eighteen hundred and fifty, and leaving idiots out of the computation. From this it will be seen that though there are many more persons living under ten, between ten and twenty, and between twenty and thirty, than between thirty and forty, still the number of insane of the latter age are greatly in excess of those of any other age.

---

[*] See Bucknill & Tuke on Insanity, p. 245.

Table.

Influence of Age illustrated by Statistics of the United States.

AGE.	Population	No. Insane, 1870.	Proportion at each age to total of known ages.	
			Popula'n	No. Ins'e
Under ten years	6,739,041	324	29.08	.87
From ten to twenty years	5,420,421	1,992	23.38	5.36
From twenty to thirty years	4,277,318	7,096	18.46	19.09
From thirty to forty years	2,825,819	9,109	12.19	24.51
From forty to fifty years	1,846,660	7,976	7.97	21.46
From fifty to sixty years	1,109,540	5,264	4.79	14.16
From sixty to seventy years	609,926	3,307	2.63	8.90
From seventy to eighty years	257,234	1,569	1.11	4.22
From eighty to ninety years	77,382	455	.33	1.22
From ninety to one hundred years.	11,695	62	.05	.17
One hundred years and upwards..	2,555	15	.01	.04
Unknown	14,285	213	....	....
Totals	23,191,876	37,382	100.00	100.00

INFLUENCE OF AGE IN THE DIFFERENT RACES.

The following table has been made for the purpose of showing the susceptibility to insanity of the different races inhabiting our continent, and the ages at which they are most liable to the seizure of this terrible malady.

TABLE.

Influence of Age in different Races.

AGE.	White. Male.	White. Female.	White. Total.	Black. Male.	Black. Female.	Black. Total.	Mulatto. Male.	Mulatto. Female.	Mulatto. Total.	Chinese. Male.	Chinese. Female.	Chinese. Total.	Indian. Male.	Indian. Female.	Indian. Total.	Total. Male.	Total. Female.	Total. Total.
Under 1 year	26	30	56	4	4	8										30	34	64
From 1 to 5	130	108	238	11	8	19										143	117	260
From 5 to 10	289	297	586	23	32	55	2	1	3							315	333	648
From 10 to 15	661	549	1,210	58	59	117	3	4	7							727	617	1,344
From 15 to 20	3,448	3,195	6,643	186	216	402	8	9	17	8	1	9	2	1	3	3,765	3,431	7,096
From 20 to 30	4,376	4,356	8,732	137	188	325	21	18	39	14	1	15	3	2	3	4,547	4,562	9,109
From 30 to 40	3,581	4,019	7,650	116	165	281	17	17	34	2	1	3	2	1	4	3,715	4,261	7,976
From 40 to 50	2,385	2,706	5,091	54	102	156	14	24	38				1		1	2,447	2,817	5,264
From 50 to 60	1,473	1,709	3,182	43	71	114	7	9	16							1,521	1,798	3,307
From 60 to 70	664	824	1,488	26	51	77	5	5	10							692	877	1,569
From 70 to 80	191	251	422	10	21	31	2	2	4				1		1	203	253	455
From 80 to 90	18	33	51	6	5	11		1	1							24	38	62
From 90 to 100	4	4	8	1	6	7										15	10	15
100 and upwards				1	1	2												
Unknown	133	70	203							7	1	8				141	72	213
Totals	17,379	18,181	35,560	676	929	1,605	79	90	169	31	4	35	9	4	13	18,174	19,208	37,382

The preceding table shows a most interesting fact, that may or may not be overthrown by further investigation and longer experience. It will be observed that while the general rule under discussion holds good with the Chinaman and the Indian, that both the black and mulatto are most liable to become insane between twenty and thirty, and that this is true with regard to both males and females. This may be the result of accident; but from our knowledge of the race, derived from a long residence among them in the Southern States, we are of the opinion it is the result of a natural law. Their development, both intellectual and physical, is of much earlier growth and maturity than that of the Caucasian, and as insanity seems to attack the human race most frequently at that age when all the faculties are in fullest maturity, and most powerful, energetic action, there would seem to be no reason why the negro should be an exception to the general law. These reflections, however, are made more to direct the attention of future investigation to the subject than with a view to the promulgation of a new theory or the enunciation of a new idea.

INFLUENCE OF SEX.

The susceptibility of the sexes to insanity has been a debateable question from the days of Cælius Aurelianus to the present time, most of those participating in the discussion seeming to be guided by their individual experience or their immediate surroundings. Aurelianus, Pinel, Haslam, and their followers taking sides with the women, while Esquirol, Copeland, Browne, and others took the other side of the question. In our country, Doctor Rush was of the opinion that more women were insane from the fact that they are exposed to several exciting causes from which men are exempt, apparently overlooking another fact, that men are liable to many causes from the influence of which females are partially or entirely removed. Doctor Jarvis, one of the closest observers and most thorough investigators whose writings have come under our observation, came to the conclusion some twenty years ago, after exhausting all the information that existed on the subject at that time, that a few more men than women become insane. (Jarvis on the Comparative Liability of Males and Females to Insanity; see American Journal of Insanity, Vol. VII, p. 142.) And from the following table of first admissions into the Asylums of England, Ireland, France, Belgium, Holland, and Bavaria, during the period specified, it would seem that the conclusion at which he then arrived still holds good; though according to the United States census for eighteen hundred and seventy the reverse of this would seem to be true in our country, as the number of males was eighteen thousand one hundred and seventy-four; the number of females, nineteen thousand two hundred and eight, or an excess of one thousand and thirty-four females.

TABLE,

Showing the Influence of Sex.

COUNTRIES.	Period.	Number of First Admissions.		
		Males.	Females.	Totals.
England...........................	1870	5,124	4,966	10,090
Ireland............................	1870	1,141	971	2,112
France.............................	1853	3,959	3,487	7,447
Belgium...........................	1865	865	690	1,555
Holland............................	1844 to 1864	4,747	4,526	9,273
Bavaria (Asylum at Irsee)....	1858 to 1868	388	324	712
Totals......................	....	16,224	14,964	31,188

The various arguments made and facts adduced to prove the one theory or the other, are conclusive evidence to our mind that there is but little difference in the gross number of the sexes. As classes they seem about equally subject to this malady, yet different causes operate in various proportions on the sexes. Men are more intemperate, which is well known to be one of the most prolific causes of insanity, its victims being in proportion of about four men to one woman. More men are engaged in hazardous enterprises and doubtful business speculations, in gambling and other dissipation, more subject to disappointment and failure in business operations, more use their brains excessively in study, in scientific investigations and ambitious projects, and more are liable to ordinary accidents and the casualties and exposures of war.

On the contrary, domestic trials, ill health, loss of relatives, and disappointments in love act more powerfully on women, while a few other causes belonging to peculiarities of organism affect them only. We must conclude, therefore, that the liability of the excess to insanity is very nearly equal, and that any difference in numbers in different countries and localities depends more on the exposure to the various causes that produce it than to difference of liability in the sexes; and these must vary with different nations, different periods of the world, and different habits of the people. The fact that the percentage of recoveries is slightly greatest among females, and *a fortiori*, the percentage of deaths among males, is too well established to require an argument. The reason of this is obvious; we have already seen that the causes operating on the sexes are different in some important particulars; general ill health and the puerperal condition adding largely to the list among females, give to insanity its most curable cases; while epilepsy, palsy, and masturbation are more frequent causes among men, and are among the most incurable cases.

INFLUENCE OF MARRIAGE.

The experience of all writers upon the subject, as far as our observation has extended, shows conclusively that a greater number of single than married persons become insane, notwithstanding there are more of the latter class of the ages most subject to insanity.

TABLE,

Showing the Influence of Marriage.

CIVIL CONDITION.	Ireland. 1870.			Bavaria. (District Asylums, 1865.)			France. 1853.			Italy. (Florence, 1867 and 1868.)			United States. (Pennsylv'a Hospital for Insane, 1841 to 1870).			Totals.		
	Male.....	Female.	Totals...	Male.....	Female.	Totals...	Male.....	Female.	Totals...	Male.....	Female.	Totals...	Male.....	Female.	Totals...	Male.....	Female.	Totals...
Single............	3,006	2,251	5,257	815	629	1,444	9,278	8,800	18,078	468	367	835	1,472	1,084	2,556	15,039	13,131	28,170
Married..........	701	747	1,448	283	291	574	4,047	4,446	8,493	156	274	430	1,332	1,183	2,515	6,519	6,941	13,460
Widowed	113	310	423	45	117	162	791	1,888	2,679	34	109	143	133	331	464	1,116	2,755	3,871
Unknown	170	162	332	......	......	......	2,297	1,329	3,626	......	......	......	......	......	......	2,467	1,491	3,958
Totals	3,990	3,470	7,460	1,143	1,037	2,180	16,413	16,463	32,876	658	750	1,408	2,937	2,598	5,535	25,141	24,318	49,459

From the foregoing table we find that out of every one h
patients whose civil condition was known, sixty-one and ninety-c
hundredths were single, twenty-nine and fifty-eight one hundredth;
married, and eight and fifty-one one hundredths were widowed.
It appears from the census of eighteen hundred and fifty-one ;
the condition of the entire population of Great Britain (aged twe
and upwards) was in respect of marriage as follows: *

Unmarried.	Married.	Widowed.	Totals.
3,456,310	6,852,695	1,178,559	11,487,664
30.2	57.6	10.2	100

The greater liability of single than of married persons to insanity is
explained in part by the fact that a much larger proportion of the
unbalanced, odd, idle, worthless, restless, dissipated, and improvident
do not marry. The causes of their celibacy and insanity are radically
the same. We know that marriage often leads to insanity; domestic
troubles and afflictions, and all cases of puerperal insanity being the
most prominent. Yet, on the other hand, it seems to prevent a much
larger number of cases than it produces. The kindly and calming
influences of the domestic circle, the greater regularity of habits, the
freedom from inordinate passions and dissipated tendencies, all have
their due effects in keeping the mind in a proper state of equilibrium,
which is sanity.
It further appears from the foregoing table that while the greatest
numbers and largest proportions of the insane are among the single and
the smallest among the married population, that the widowed occupy an
intermediate proportion, thus proving conclusively that marriage is one
of the most powerful agencies in preventing the increase of this dread-
ful malady.

CHAPTER V.

INFLUENCE OF SOCIAL DISTINCTIONS.

Diseases of the brain are peculiar to no class in society. They are
found in all ranks of men—the high and the low, the refined and the
vulgar, the educated and the ignorant, the rich and the poor—but not in
the same proportion in all classes. The brain is not the mind, but the
organ through which it operates and through which it manifests itself.
There are manifold causes and various conditions by which it is disturbed. Many and various events and external circumstances; many
conditions of the body and nervous system affect this organ morbidly.
These pervert its functions, and produce mental disorder. These disturbing causes are distributed in various proportions among the different
classes of society; none are entirely free. Some causes are common to

* See Bucknill & Tuke on Insanity, p. 255.

ıen, and others are the especial dangers that hover over
several classes.   The distinctions in society are manifest
le, but not more certain than the variety of dangers that
ıental health.
condition of man, that has been fixed upon him from the
is the necessity of protection and sustenance, and his first
ıction is his desire to obtain them.   To some the means of
.e easily.   Their sagacity, industry, and faithfulness procure
ıot only what they need, but enable them to create a surplus
for future emergencies and for more expensive and luxurious
All of these have a competence, and some have great wealth,
fear of want.   These constitute the higher, but by no means the
class of society.   Another and larger class, with less mental and
power or opportunity, obtain what they need from day to day,
ıave thrift enough to secure the means of meeting the ordinary
es of life and the necessities of sickness and age when they cease to
or.   A third and very large class in every country, called the labor-
.g class, not because they work more than the others, but because, hav-
ıng no capital, they obtain their subsistence by the labor of their hands
exclusively.   They earn from day to day what they consume, and lie
down at night no richer than they were in the morning.   They sustain
themselves as long as strength lasts, but when sickness overtakes them
or old age falls upon them, having accumulated no capital to fall back
upon they become dependent upon the charity of friends or public
bounty for support.

Below these in the social scale are the entirely dependent or pauper
class, who are housed, fed, and clothed by the general treasury.   These
are found most numerous in old and least so in new countries.   All of
these classes are subject, though in different degrees, to insanity.   Beside
the courses of mental disorder that are common to all, some appear more
frequently and act with more destructive power on some classes, while
they are rarely known in others.   As a general law the most favored
class have the best natural endowments of body and mind, the best
physical health, the best mental and moral training and discipline.
These give them their position and enable them to sustain themselves
therein.   Their wisdom and sagacity, their power of consideration and
of adapting means to the desired ends, their faithfulness to the law of
their being, and discreet self management, insure this prosperity and
the world's confidence.

Fortune is not the blind goddess as commonly represented, scattering
her favors without regard to conditions and circumstances, making some
rich who never sought for her blessings, and others poor in spite of their
well laid plans and earnest endeavors.   As a rule, accident and chance
have but little to do with this matter.   Success is almost always the
result of fitting plans and faithful execution.   "Herein is wisdom justified of her children, and folly may make a similar boast, the child is
after the similitude of the parent."   The wisdom may be merely of this
world, and applied to a narrow field wherein riches are gathered, or one
wherein the flowers of fashion bloom.   It may be a better wisdom that
leads to self culture, to learning, to the generous and peaceful graces of
character.   Whatever it may be, it is sufficient for its purpose.   Without
this wisdom of the appropriate kind no man attains to his desired ends.
A man may be a fool in everything else, but he is neither foolish nor
weak in that in which he succeeds.   Success in any line of life is then

evidence of wisdom appropriate to that purpose, and of strength sufficient for its accomplishment.

The simple fact that men are in the higher social ranks of culture, character, or wealth, must be accepted as prima facie evidence that they have good minds, well developed, trained, and balanced; that they have strength and discipline of character by which they reached their present position and retained themselves in it. Being generally persons of good health and sound mind they have in themselves better defences against insanity than the lower classes that are less liberally endowed and less favored by education and self discipline. Nevertheless, the more favored and prosperous classes have their peculiar dangers that threaten their soundness of mind. Here, temptations to excessive mental labor in business, study, in the pursuit of riches and knowledge, ambitious projects and political strife, all have their influence. In this country, where no child is bound to follow the paths of his father, where all the avenues to wealth and distinction are open to any who desire to enter, and the race of life is free to every competitor, whatever may be his history and preparation, there are some in every rank who are struggling with all their energy to grasp what is almost within or even beyond their reach. Some of these who succeed find themselves in a false position, which they are not prepared to fill, and are compelled still to fight the battle to sustain themselves in form and appearance, for which they were not educated. In this class are the dangers of great reverses in business, of graceful and fashionable dissipation, and sometimes of gross sensuality; of disregard to the natural laws of health, in late and unusual hours, unreasonable eating, inadequate costume, etc. All these tend to over work or disturb the brain, and sometimes the mind is disordered and insanity follows.

The class next below the highest, just described, is composed of persons of comparatively limited fortune. They have less strain upon their mental powers. Generally they have a more even course of life, and are more contented with their position; their moderate gains meet all their necessities and secure them against suffering in days of sickness and age; yet there are those among them who are earnestly striving to rise to the higher place, and whose ambition lays too heavy a tax on their physical and mental energies. Some break down under this unnatural strain upon their powers. In this class there is less waste of health and force, in graceful dissipation than in the class above them, and in coarse and vulgar dissipation than in the classes below. These have fewer causes of insanity peculiar to themselves than either of the other classes; and though they furnish the smallest number of victims to this disorder, yet they have their dangers, under which some of their members lose their mental health.

The poor have not been wanting among mankind from the earliest records; nor until the human constitution, with the natural passions and appetites, shall be changed, and men and women conform their habits to the laws of health and restrain their self-indulgence, will the *poor* fail to appear in every successive generation.

In the world's careless estimation, poverty is simply an absence of the outward means of life, food, clothing, shelter, and the real and apparently sufficient way of relief is to supply these wants or give their value in money. This is but a superficial view of this matter. Poverty is deeper and earlier than present ascertained destitution. It is in a great measure an original element in the man; in his constitution; in his development and education, and in his character.

This class is filled from causes opposite to those that fill the highest class. The primary grounds of prosperity, sagacity, coördinating power, physical strength, industry, perseverance, self-discipline, are deficient in the poor. As a class, they have less health and intellectual force; less perfect development and education. More of them are of unbalanced mind, of unreliable judgment; they are more changeable in purpose; their plans are less in harmony with their circumstances and the means at their control, or their power of execution. Here are found more of the victims of low and gross dissipation—the intemperate, the debauched; more of those who suffer from hereditary diseases.

The members of this class are generally laborers for wages, and a large proportion are unskilled, doing the work that simply requires muscular force with the least mental exertion. They earn a bare subsistence while in health, with little or no surplus to depend upon in sickness and old age. They exemplify the old law, that "from him that hath not shall be taken, even that which he hath." One element of poverty begets another, and this creates a third, and still others follow, until the low condition of the man, without and within, is complete. As his earnings are small his nutrition is meagre, clothing inadequate, dwelling narrow and unhealthy. He must live with his family in small and unventilated rooms, and breathe impure air; his frame, therefore, is not strengthened; his brain is inactive, his mind cloudy; he must consequently accept the coarsest work for the lowest wages, that afford no means of strengthening his body or elevating his mind to the power of more profitable labor. Depressed, languid, torpid, he often seeks relief in artificial stimulants, and adds another fountain from which poverty flows. His hard and exhausting toils destroy his buoyancy of spirit, take away his hope, and neutralize his ambition to rise to a better scale of life.

From the original and constitutional character of the poor, and from their habits and exposure, there is much insanity among them. Poverty and insanity often spring from the same source. Persons who are weak in intellect, undisciplined, unbalanced, fickle, or excitable, are wanting in the elements of success, and are poor for this reason. Their mental and moral condition are the sources of much insanity. Their imperfections or perversities grow into mental disorder. These are not insane because of their destitution, nor yet poor because of their insanity; but they are both because they have in their brains the elements of poverty and mental disorder. So, also, intemperance and other sensual indulgences creates the double destruction of estate and mental health. Drunkenness is one of the most fruitful causes both of insanity and pauperism.

The paupers, the lowest in the social scale, have still more the elements of weakness. There are among them more than among others defective and disordered constitutions; more diseases both of body and mind. In some, their disability, original or acquired, was manifest; others have been weighed in the world's balance of business or labor of some kind and found wanting. The deficiencies and perversities of the previous class (the poor but independent laborers) are intensified in this. At least the paupers live nearer the borders of insanity than others, and a much larger portion pass that bound into lunacy. Beside these causes inherent in and acting on the dependant class to produce insanity, they receive a large supply of recruits from the other and more favored classes on account of mental disorder. Some men, sufficiently secure in their self sustaining power, by their skill and exertions supply all their wants until they lose their reason, when labor, and production, and income cease together. If the mental disorder be not relieved, and life-long insanity be established, the accumulated capital will soon be exhausted, and the patient and his family fall upon the public treasury for support.

In some cases the family may yet have power to support themselves, especially if the lunatic be not the head and principal producer, but cannot add to this the board and care of the patient. Then they throw him upon the town or State, and join him to the pauper class, while the rest of the family remain in the ranks of the independent. These last described are not made insane by their poverty, but their insanity made them paupers. In this way insanity hangs about the necks of its victims in all the social ranks, depriving them of the power of production, and consuming an undue proportion of the family substance. Under this burden they gravitate downward, and may ultimately reach the lowest depths of pauperism. Another and important fact is discovered; that a very large portion of the lunatics in the pauper class are chronic cases, who have been a long time disordered, and whose day of healing is past, and whose malady will end only in death.

From all these and manifold other causes the proportion of insanity among the paupers is very great as compared with that of the higher ranks, and indeed with all the independent classes of society.

The annual reports of the Commissioners in Lunacy for England show the number of lunatics in the independent classes and among the paupers. From these and other British reports on population and on the poor the following facts as to numbers are derived, and the proportion of lunatics in the classes are calculated from these facts:

During the ten years, eighteen hundred and sixty-two to eighteen hundred and seventy-one, the average annual independent population was twenty million three hundred and thirty-eight thousand seven hundred and ninety-two. The average annual number of independent lunatics was five thousand nine hundred and seventy-three. The ratio of lunatics in this class was one in three thousand four hundred and five. The average annual number of paupers was one million twenty-one thousand eight hundred and seventy-two. The average annual number of pauper lunatics was forty-two thousand seven hundred and sixty-four. The ratio of lunatics in this class was one in twenty-four. The proportionate ratios of lunatics to their respective classes were three thousand four hundred and five to twenty-four, or one hundred and forty-two times as great in the pauper as in the independent classes of English society.

The pauper lunatics are in the asylums and workhouses, or are otherwise subject to official supervision—their numbers therefore are known and accurately stated. The independent lunatics are in the public and private asylums and hospitals, and under the guardianship of the State, through the Lord Chancellor and his agents, and under the observations of the Commissioners in Lunacy; but there may be others not known to these authorities who are kept at their homes or privately boarded elsewhere. These are not included in this statement of the independent insane. But the number of these who have escaped the vigilant inquiries of the Government officials cannot be very great; admitting, however, that there were as many as were revealed and reported or even three or four times as many, still the differences of the burden of lunacy resting on the pauper class is enormous in comparison with that which the more favored classes are doomed to suffer.

There was a similar disproportion of insanity in the pauper and independent classes of Massachusetts, as shown by the report of the Commissioners in eighteen hundred and fifty-four, and it is probable that the same exists in every civilized country.

Unfortunately, we have no means of showing this in the United States and most other countries, though the accompanying table shows that they constitute a majority of the insane in Scotland, Ireland, and Belgium, as well as in England, notwithstanding the proportion of the pauper population would not exceed a twentieth of the whole in any of these countries:

COUNTRY.	Population.	Total Insane and Idiots.	Pauper Insane and Idiots.	Proportion of—	
				Pauper Insane and Idiots to Total Insane and Idiots.	Pauper Insane and Idiots to Population.
England	22,090,163	54,713	48,433	88 per cent	1 in 456
Scotland	3,222,837	9,571	6,276	65 per cent	1 in 513
Ireland	5,195,236	17,194	9,498	55 per cent	1 in 546
Belgium	4,984,451	7,431	3,852	52 per cent	1 in 1294
Total	35,492,687	88,909	68,059	76 per cent	1 in 521

It has been explained elsewhere and must not be overlooked, however, that a large majority of these pauper lunatics are no more furnished by the pauper element in society in these countries than are the non-paying patients in our own institutions; most of them were self-sustaining and independent citizens till misfortune assailed them and deprived them of their reason and the power to labor. Yet all must admit that pauperism is one of the most prolific sources from which insanity is supplied. Here is a grave question for the consideration of those in authority, whether they may not, by providing means sufficient to accommodate and care for every one who becomes insane, thereby affording proper treatment in the early stages of the disease, restore most of these unfortunate victims of this direful malady to health, the power to serve themselves, their families, and the State, and whether this is not a duty which every commonwealth owes to itself and to its members?

CHAPTER VI.

APPARENT INCREASE OF INSANITY.

For many years it has been apprehended that this fearful malady was increasing, not only in our own country, but in all other civilized nations; and as early as eighteen hundred and fifty-one Doctor Ja. read a paper on the subject before the Association of Medical Superintendents of American Institutions for the Insane, in which he said: "It is a recent thing that any nation has enumerated its insane, and I cannot discover that any nation has ascertained and reported this twice, and thus offered us data for the comparison."

Since that time other nations have taken an account of their insane, and some of them several times, but only to prove that insanity has increased, at least apparently, and in some countries very rapidly, within comparatively a short time. Thus the following table, from official reports, will show the result in the countries named:

UNITED STATES—TWENTY YEARS.

Year.	Population.	Number of Insane and Idiots.	Ratio per 1,000 to Population.	Proportion to Population.
1850	23,191,876	31,397	1.35	1 in 738
1860	31,443,322	42,864	1.36	1 in 733
1870	38,555,983	61,909	1.60	1 in 623

ENGLAND—TEN YEARS.

1862	20,336,467	41,129	2.02	1 in 494
1865	20,990,946	45,950	2.18	1 in 456
1868	21,649,377	51,000	2.35	1 in 424
1871	22,704,108	56,755	2.49	1 in 400

SCOTLAND—TEN YEARS.

1862	3,083,989	6,341	2.05	1 in 486
1865	3,136,057	6,468	2.06	1 in 484
1868	3,188,125	6,931	2.17	1 in 459
1871	3,358,613	7,808	2.32	1 in 430

IRELAND—NINETEEN YEARS.

1851	6,552,385	15,098	2.03	1 in 434
1856	6,164,171	14,141	2.29	1 in 435
1861	5,798,967	16,749	2.88	1 in 346
1870	5,195,236	17,194	3.39	1 in 303

FRANCE—FIFTEEN YEARS.

| 1851 | 35,783,170 | 44,970 | 1.25 | 1 in 795 |
| 1866 | 37,988,905 | 90,679 | 2.38 | 1 in 418 |

This shows that the ratio of insane and idiots per one thousand in the United States in eighteen hundred and fifty was one and thirty-five one hundredths, or one in seven hundred and eight, and in eighteen hundred and seventy, one and sixty one hundredths, or one in six hundred and twenty-three.

In England, in eighteen hundred and sixty-two, it was two and two one hundredths, or one in four hundred and ninety-four, and in eighteen hundred and seventy-one, two and forty-nine one hundredths, or one in four hundred. In Scotland, in eighteen hundred and sixty-two, it was two and five one hundredths, or one in four hundred and eighty-six, and in eighteen hundred and seventy-one, two and thirty-two one hundredths, or one in four hundred and thirty. In Ireland, in eighteen hundred and fifty-one, it was two and thirty one hundredths, or one in four hundred and thirty-four, and in eighteen hundred and seventy-one, three and thirty-nine one hundredths, or one in three hundred and two. In France, in eighteen hundred and fifty-one, it was one and twenty-five one hundredths, or one in seven hundred and ninety-five, and in eighteen hundred and sixty-six, two and thirty-eight one hundredths, or one in four hundred and eighteen.

But even these statements must not be taken as altogether correct. In the paper of Doctor Jarvis, already referred to, he shows how very carelessly the returns from France had been made, and so it may have been with those from which our figures were taken: Statistique de la France, 1866, second series, Vol. XVII. In the United States we have also shown that all of the insane and idiots have probably not been found. In England, Scotland, and Ireland, the reports are mainly official, showing the number in institutions for custody and cure, in pauper establishments where they are kept merely for support, and those under the guardianship of the Lord Chancellor's Commissioners.

It is probable there are many others who belong to neither of these categories. Nor must these facts induce the conclusion that insanity, if it has increased at all, has done so in anything like the proportion here indicated. The existence of a fact and our knowledge of it are two very different things. Electricity has existed for all time, but our knowledge of its properties and the purposes to which it may be usefully applied is of very recent date. So it may be in many respects with our knowledge of the insane. We have already shown that many had existence in Massachusetts who could not or had not been found by one set of Commissioners who were found by another Commission whose method of search was different and whose work was more thorough. Nor must it be overlooked that since greater attention has been paid to the insane than formerly many more are brought to light and seek the benefit of asylum accommodation. Add to this the important fact that the duration of life among the chronic insane has been much increased by the greater amount of care and the more humane treatment which they receive, and we can readily account for at least a portion of the apparent increase.

It is exceedingly interesting to trace this apparent increase of insanity in the various countries of the world, and easy to show how much more rapidly the increase has been brought to light in those countries where the most humane and liberal provisions have been made for their accommodation. We will show, however, that it is not confined to the present epoch, nor to any particular country; but that it has always and everywhere come forth from its recesses and hiding places whenever suitable hospitals for the reception of its victims were provided. Thus Bucknill & Tuke state that "in the short space of nineteen years the estimated proportion of the insane in England rose from one in seven thousand two hundred to one in seven hundred and sixty-nine;" while on the first of January, eighteen hundred and seventy-one, there was one to four hundred. This is simply insanity revealed by increased attention. The following extracts from the paper of Dr. Jarvis on this subject will show the results in several States and countries at a former period:

"Thus we find that whenever the seeds of this interest are once sown and allowed to germinate and grow, it spreads continually thereafter. Whenever the attention of the people of any country is called to this subject, and a hospital is built, there follows a remarkable increase of the cases of insanity revealed to the public eye and asking for admission.

"In the year eighteen hundred and thirty-two, when the McLean Asylum at Somerville, Massachusetts, contained sixty-four patients, the State Lunatic Hospital was established at Worcester for one hundred and twenty patients. This was as large a number as was then supposed would need its accommodation. In eighteen hundred and thirty-six one new wing, and in eighteen hundred and thirty-seven another new wing, and rooms for one hundred more patients were added to the Worcester Hospital, and at the same time the McLean Asylum contained ninety-three lunatic inmates. In eighteen hundred and forty-two the Worcester Hospital was again enlarged by the addition of two new wings, and now these are all filled to overflowing, having four hundred and fifty patients in May, eighteen hundred and fifty-one, while at the same time there were two hundred at the McLean Asylum, two hundred and four at the City Lunatic Hospital at Boston, and one hundred and fifteen in the county receptacles for the insane at Cambridge and Ipswich, beside thirty-six in the jails; making one thousand and fifteen lunatics in the public establishments of Massachusetts in eighteen hundred and fifty-one, instead of the one hundred and eighty-two which were there in eighteen hundred and thirty-two"—an increase of eight hundred and thirty-three in nineteen years.

"Besides these there is now a great demand for the admission of patients who cannot be accommodated in these establishments already built, and there is so much interest elicited in their behalf, and the friends of the lunatics are so alive to the necessity of providing means of relief for all of these sufferers, that the Legislature has just now authorized the erection of a new hospital sufficiently large to receive two hundred and fifty patients.

"The State Hospital at Augusta, Maine, was opened in December, eighteen hundred and forty, with only thirty patients. In eighteen hundred and forty-five it was so crowded that the Trustees asked for more rooms. In eighteen hundred and forty-seven the building was enlarged, and one hundred and twenty-eight patients were admitted.

8

In eighteen hundred and forty-eight the house was all filled, and more were offered than could be accommodated, and the Superintendent asked the Legislature to build still another wing, to enable him to meet the increased demand.

"The New Hampshire Hospital was opened in eighteen hundred and forty-two, and received twenty-two patients; these were all that were offered. In eighteen hundred and forty-three these were increased to forty-one; in another year, eighteen hundred and forty-four, there were seventy; in eighteen hundred and forty-five there were seventy-six; in eighteen hundred and forty-six there were ninety-eight; and in eighteen hundred and fifty they reached the number of one hundred and twenty. In the meantime additions have been made to meet this growing demand for more and more accommodations.

"The number of patients in the Eastern Virginia Asylum at Williamsburgh has increased more than two hundred per cent in fifteen years—from sixty in eighteen hundred and thirty-six, to one hundred and ninety-three in eighteen hundred and fifty.

"Those in the Western Virginia Asylum at Staunton, have increased more than eight hundred per cent in twenty-three years—from thirty-eight in eighteen hundred and twenty-eight, to three hundred and forty-eight in eighteen hundred and fifty.

"The average number of patients in the Ohio State Lunatic Asylum at Columbus, was sixty-four in eighteen hundred and thirty-nine, and three hundred and twenty-eight in eighteen hundred and fifty—being an increase of more than four hundred per cent in eleven years.

"Now, no one would imagine that the population of these several States has increased in these ratios of the increase of the lunatics in their asylums within these respective periods. But it will readily be supposed that the opening of these establishments for the cure or the protection of lunatics, the spread of their reports, the extension of the knowledge of their character, power, and usefulness by the means of the patients that they protect and cure, have created and continue to create more and more interest in the subject of insanity and more confidence in its curability. Consequently, more and more persons and families who, or such as who formerly kept their insane friends and relations at home, or allowed them to stroll abroad about the streets or country, now believe that they can be restored or improved, or at least made more comfortable in these public institutions, and therefore they send their patients to these asylums and thus swell the lists of their inmates.

"For the same reason the people in the vicinity of lunatic hospitals send more patients to them than those at a greater distance. Thus the County of Worcester, Massachusetts, has sent one lunatic out of every one hundred and sixteen of its population, while the most remote counties of the State have sent only one in three hundred and sixty-one of their people to the State Hospital since its first establishment.

"In New York, the County of Oneida has sent one in three hundred and sixty-one, and the remotest counties sent only one in fifteen hundred and twenty-three of their people to the State Lunatic Asylum at Utica.

"In Kentucky, the people of Fayette County sent one in eighty-nine of their people to the Lunatic Hospital at Lexington, while the farthest counties sent only one in sixteen hundred and thirty-five of their population to that institution.

"Similar differences in the use of the public hospital are found in

Maine, New Hampshire, Connecticut, Ohio, Maryland, Tennessee; and doubtless in other States the same will be found on investigation.

"To infer the number of lunatics in the community from the number in the hospitals is about as unsafe as to infer the number of births from the number of children in the schools. The first element here is wanting: that is, the proportion of all the children that are sent to school. Now, as this is very different in Massachusetts and England, and Spain and Egypt, no reasonable man would venture to compare the number of births in these several countries by the population of their school houses. The provision for the cure and custody of the insane in these countries differs as widely as their provision for the education of children; and yet writers have given us the comparative numbers on this ground, as in London one in two hundred, because there were seven thousand in the metropolitan hospitals, and in Cairo one in thirty thousand seven hundred and fourteen, because there were fourteen in the hospitals of that city.

"It must be further considered that many of these statements that were put forth as positive facts are given in such round numbers as to afford good reason for supposing that they or their elements are estimates rather than actual enumerations.

"Thus, in some works on this subject, there are stated to be thirty-two thousand lunatics in France; sixteen thousand in the United States; seven thousand in London; four thousand in Paris; two thousand in Pennsylvania, and one thousand in Massachusetts. Millingen says the proportion of lunatics to the people is one in one thousand in England, and in France one in one thousand.

"One department in France, Ariege, gives three hundred vagabond lunatics for four successive years, without change, but these suddenly, in the fifth year, diminish to two hundred and fifty, and in the seventh year disappear entirely. Another department, Seine Inferieure, reports two hundred lunatics for seven successive years, and another three hundred for three successive years in private families. Saone Haute reports none, either in private families or as vagabonds, for two years, when suddenly in one year there appears to be one hundred and ninety-three. Sarthe reports two hundred and seventy-three lunatics in families in eighteen hundred and thirty-seven, and then they all disappear and are reported no more. Mayence reports eight in families and as vagabonds in eighteen hundred and thirty-five. These are increased to two hundred and nine in eighteen hundred and thirty-seven, and diminished to twenty-one in eighteen hundred and thirty-eight, and to eight, the original reported number, in eighteen hundred and forty-one. There are so many of these apparent inaccuracies, such full and round numbers, and such unvarying totals where there must be some change, and such sudden and violent changes, out of all relation to the ordinary circumstances of society, that we are compelled to look with distrust upon the whole, and consider it as but little better than mere guess work, with more or less foundation in fact."

As more attention has been paid to the insane within the last twenty-five years than ever before, we may fairly conclude that their numbers have been more accurately ascertained and reported, at least in some countries. The foregoing extracts prove how rapidly this malady appeared to increase prior to eighteen hundred and fifty-two in all the States and countries where liberal provision had been made for its proper treatment. We have shown its increase in England and the

United States since that time, and the Chapter on insanity in France affords a comprehensive view of the disorder in that country. But let us see what has been the result in the several States and Territories of the United States, respectively, within the last twenty years. The following table shows the population, the number of the insane, the number of idiots, and the ratio of each to the total population, in eighteen hundred and fifty, eighteen hundred and sixty, and eighteen hundred and seventy. It will be observed that the ratio of the insane has increased from one in fourteen hundred and eighty-five to one in thirteen hundred and ten during the first period of ten years, and to one in ten hundred and thirty-one in eighteen hundred and seventy; while during the whole period of twenty years the idiots are not so numerous in proportion as they were in eighteen hundred and fifty, being at that time in ratio of one in fourteen hundred and seventy-six, and in eighteen hundred and seventy, one to fifteen hundred and seventy-one. We have neither time nor space to analyze each State separately, but the curious can do so for themselves, as the facts appear in the tables.

TABLES.

TABLE,

Showing Insane, Idiotic, and total Population of the United States for 1850 and 1860, with the ratio of Insane and of Idiotic to total Population at those dates.

STATES AND TERRITORIES.	1850. Population	1850. Insane	1850. Idiotic	1850. Ratio of Insane to Population	1850. Ratio of Idiotic to Population	1860. Population	1860. Insane	1860. Idiotic	1860. Ratio of Insane to Population	1860. Ratio of Idiotic to Population
Total United States	23,191,876	15,610	15,706	1 to 1,485	1 to 1,476	31,429,891	23,999	18,865	1 to 1,310	1 to 1,666
Alabama	771,623	233	476	1 to 3,311	1 to 1,621	964,296	257	537	1 to 3,572	1 to 1,795
Arkansas	200,897	63	115	1 to 3,332	1 to 1,825	435,427	87	176	1 to 5,005	1 to 2,474
California	92,597	2	7	1 to 46,299	1 to 13,228	380,015	456	42	1 to 833	1 to 9,047
Connecticut	370,792	470	287	1 to 789	1 to 1,291	460,151	281	226	1 to 1,637	1 to 2,036
Delaware	91,532	68	92	1 to 1,346	1 to 994	112,218	60	67	1 to 1,870	1 to 1,674
Florida	87,445	11	36	1 to 7,949	1 to 2,429	140,439	25	68	1 to 5,618	1 to 2,065
Georgia	906,185	324	664	1 to 2,797	1 to 1,344	1,057,237	491	724	1 to 2,153	1 to 1,460
Illinois	851,470	238	363	1 to 3,578	1 to 2,345	1,711,753	683	588	1 to 2,506	1 to 2,911
Indiana	988,416	563	938	1 to 1,755	1 to 1,053	1,350,479	1,035	907	1 to 1,304	1 to 1,488
Iowa	192,214	42	94	1 to 4,577	1 to 2,044	674,948	201	289	1 to 3,357	1 to 2,335
Kansas						107,110	10	17	1 to 10,711	1 to 6,300
Kentucky	982,405	527	907	1 to 1,864	1 to 1,083	1,155,713	623	1,058	1 to 1,855	1 to 1,092
Louisiana	517,762	200	174	1 to 2,588	1 to 2,975	709,433	169	247	1 to 4,198	1 to 2,872
Maine	583,169	561	577	1 to 1,040	1 to 1,010	628,276	704	658	1 to 892	1 to 954
Maryland	583,034	546	391	1 to 1,068	1 to 1,491	687,034	560	305	1 to 1,227	1 to 2,252

	A	B	C	D	E	F	G	H	I	J
Massachusetts	1 to 1,729	1 to 585	712	2,105	1,231,065	1 to 1,257	1 to 592	791	1,680	994,514
Michigan	1 to 2,249	1 to 2,984	333	251	749,112	1 to 2,103	1 to 2,990	189	133	397,654
Minnesota	1 to 5,226	1 to 6,481	31	25	162,022	1 to 6,077	1 to 6,077	1	1	6,077
Mississippi	1 to 2,941	1 to 2,910	269	272	791,305	1 to 2,732	1 to 4,701	222	129	606,526
Missouri	1 to 2,300	1 to 1,523	510	770	1,173,317	1 to 1,910	1 to 2,603	357	202	682,044
Nebraska	1 to 9,614	1 to 5,768	3	5	6,857					
Nevada	1 to 970	1 to 644	336	506	326,072	1 to 905	1 to 841	351	378	317,976
New Hampshire	1 to 1,841	1 to 1,141	365	589	672,031	1 to 1,168	1 to 1,292	419	379	489,555
New Jersey	1 to 1,679	1 to 901	2,314	4,317	3,887,542	1 to 1,840	1 to 1,229	1,665	2,321	3,097,394
New York	1 to 1,012	1 to 1,504	980	660	992,667	1 to 1,094	1 to 1,704	794	510	869,039
North Carolina	1 to 1,308	1 to 1,020	1,788	2,293	2,339,599	1 to 1,455	1 to 1,504	1,361	1,317	1,980,329
Ohio	1 to 3,497	1 to 2,281	15	23	52,464	1 to 3,323	1 to 2,659	4	5	13,294
Oregon	1 to 1,577	1 to 1,051	1,842	2,766	2,908,370	1 to 1,575	1 to 1,208	1,467	1,914	2,311,786
Pennsylvania	1 to 1,788	1 to 606	101	288	174,621	1 to 1,294	1 to 680	114	217	147,545
Rhode Island	1 to 1,746	1 to 2,220	403	317	703,812	1 to 1,920	1 to 2,085	348	249	698,507
South Carolina	1 to 1,259	1 to 1,734	881	640	1,109,847	1 to 1,185	1 to 2,464	846	407	1,002,717
Tennessee	1 to 2,990	1 to 4,808	201	125	601,039	1 to 2,044	1 to 5,746	104	37	212,592
Texas	1 to 1,198	1 to 455	263	693	315,116	1 to 1,050	1 to 561	299	560	314,120
Vermont	1 to 1,247	1 to 1,354	1,279	1,179	1,596,083	1 to 1,202	1 to 1,466	1,182	970	1,421,661
Virginia	1 to 3,018	1 to 2,741	257	283	775,873	1 to 3,248	1 to 5,655	94	54	305,391
West Virginia										
Wisconsin										
Arizona										
Colorado	1 to 4,839		1	204	34,197					
Dacota	1 to 2,780	1 to 368	27		4,839	1 to 3,975	1 to 2,217	13	23	51,687
District of Columbia					75,076					
Idaho										
Montana	1 to 2,338	1 to 3,341	40	28	93,541	1 to 1,308	1 to 5,595	44	11	61,547
New Mexico	1 to 8,059	1 to 2,686	5	15	40,295	1 to 11,380	1 to 2,276	1	5	11,380
Utah		1 to 3,859		3	11,578					
Washington										

TABLE,

Showing Insane, Idiotic, and total Population of the United States for 1870, with the ratio of Insane and of Idiotic to total Population.

STATES AND TERRITORIES.	Population	Insane	Idiotic	Ratio of Insane to Population.	Ratio of Idiotic to Population.	Total Insane and Idiotic	Ratio of Insane and Idiotic to Population
Totals in the United States and Territories	38,555,963	37,382	24,527	1 to 1,031	1 to 1,571	61,909	1 to 622
Totals in the States	38,113,253	36,786	24,395	1 to 1,036	1 to 1,562	61,181	1 to 622
Alabama	996,992	555	721	1 to 1,796	1 to 1,382	1,276	1 to 781
Arkansas	484,471	161	289	1 to 3,009	1 to 1,676	450	1 to 1,076
California	260,247	1,146	87	1 to 489	1 to 6,439	1,233	1 to 454
Connecticut	537,454	772	341	1 to 696	1 to 1,576	1,133	1 to 482
Delaware	125,015	65	69	1 to 1,923	1 to 1,811	134	1 to 932
Florida	187,748	29	100	1 to 6,474	1 to 1,877	129	1 to 1,455
Georgia	1,184,109	634	871	1 to 1,868	1 to 1,359	1,505	1 to 786
Illinois	2,539,891	1,625	1,244	1 to 1,563	1 to 2,041	2,869	1 to 885
Indiana	1,680,637	1,504	1,360	1 to 1,117	1 to 1,235	2,864	1 to 586
Iowa	1,191,792	742	533	1 to 1,606	1 to 2,236	1,275	1 to 934
Kansas	364,399	131	109	1 to 2,781	1 to 3,343	240	1 to 1,518
Kentucky	1,321,011	1,245	1,141	1 to 1,061	1 to 1,157	2,386	1 to 553
Louisiana	726,915	451	286	1 to 1,612	1 to 2,541	737	1 to 986
Maine	626,915	792	628	1 to 792	1 to 998	1,420	1 to 441
Maryland	780,894	733	362	1 to 1,065	1 to 2,157	1,095	1 to 713
Massachusetts	1,457,351	2,662	778	1 to 547	1 to 1,873	3,440	1 to 423
Michigan	1,184,059	814	613	1 to 1,455	1 to 1,931	1,427	1 to 829

Minnesota	439,706	302	134	1 to 1,456	1 to 3,281	436	1 to 1,008
Mississippi	827,922	245	485	1 to 3,379	1 to 1,707	730	1 to 1,134
Missouri	1,721,295	1,263	779	1 to 1,362	1 to 2,309	2,042	1 to 842
Nebraska	122,993	28	25	1 to 4,392	1 to 4,919	53	1 to 2,320
Nevada	42,491	2	2	1 to 21,246	1 to 21,246	4	1 to 10,622
New Hampshire	318,300	498	325	1 to 639	1 to 979	823	1 to 386
New Jersey	906,096	918	436	1 to 987	1 to 2,078	1,354	1 to 669
New York	4,382,759	6,353	2,486	1 to 690	1 to 1,762	8,839	1 to 495
North Carolina	1,071,361	779	976	1 to 1,375	1 to 1,097	1,755	1 to 610
Ohio	2,665,260	3,414	2,338	1 to 781	1 to 1,139	5,752	1 to 463
Oregon	90,923	122	55	1 to 745	1 to 1,653	177	1 to 513
Pennsylvania	3,521,791	3,895	2,250	1 to 904	1 to 1,565	6,145	1 to 573
Rhode Island	217,353	312	123	1 to 697	1 to 1,767	435	1 to 499
South Carolina	705,006	333	465	1 to 2,119	1 to 1,517	798	1 to 884
Tennessee	1,258,520	925	1,091	1 to 1,361	1 to 1,153	2,016	1 to 624
Texas	818,579	270	451	1 to 3,031	1 to 1,815	721	1 to 1,135
Vermont	330,551	721	325	1 to 458	1 to 1,017	1,046	1 to 315
Virginia	1,225,163	1,125	1,130	1 to 1,089	1 to 1,084	2,255	1 to 543
West Virginia	442,014	374	427	1 to 1,181	1 to 1,035	801	1 to 551
Wisconsin	1,054,670	846	560	1 to 1,247	1 to 1,882	1,406	1 to 750

TERRITORIES.

Totals in the Territories	442,730	596	132	1 to 743	1 to 3,354	728	1 to 608
Arizona	9,658	1		1 to 9,658		1	1 to 9,658
Colorado	39,864	12	3	1 to 3,322	1 to 13,288	15	1 to 2,657
Dacota	14,181	3	3	1 to 4,727	1 to 4,727	6	1 to 2,363
District of Columbia	131,700	479	50	1 to 275	1 to 2,634	529	1 to 248
Idaho	14,099		1	1 to 14,999	1 to 14,999	2	1 to 7,499
Montana	20,595	2	1	1 to 10,298	1 to 20,595	3	1 to 6,865
New Mexico	91,874	50	46	1 to 1,837	1 to 1,997	96	1 to 957
Utah	86,786	25	23	1 to 3,471	1 to 3,773	48	1 to 1,808
Washington	23,955	23	5	1 to 1,041	1 to 4,791	28	1 to 855

9

TABLE,

Showing the Population, with numbers and proportions of Insane and Idiots, Classified according to Race, in the United States in 1870.

RACE.	Population.	Insane.	Idiotic.	Ratio of Insane to Population.	Ratio of Idiotic to Population.	Total of Insane and Idiotic....	Ratio of Insane and Idiotic to Population...
Whites..........	33,586,989	35,560	21,324	1 to 944	1 to 1,579	56,884	1 to 590
Colored	4,880,009	1,774	3,188	1 to 2,750	1 to 1,530	4,962	1 to 983
Chinese	62,254	35	5	1 to 1,807	1 to 12,450	40	1 to 1,556
Indians	25,731	13	10	1 to 1,979	1 to 2,573	23	1 to 1,118

Nevada will of course come out with flying colors, since all of the insane of that State, with two exceptions, have been credited to us. As the table shows a larger proportion of the insane to population in the District of Columbia than in almost any other community in the world—being one to two hundred and forty-eight—we deem it not only just, but proper, to show why this is so. The Government Asylum, located in the District, is not only intended for those who reside within its limits, but also for the soldiers and sailors of the army and navy of the United States; and as these are brought from all parts of the Union, of course the list is swelled far beyond the ordinary proportion in other communities. The causes leading to the rapid development of insanity in this State will be considered in relation to other matters pertaining to California.

CHAPTER VII.

INSANITY IN FRANCE—GENERAL STATISTICS OF THE INSANE FROM 1854 TO 1866—DR. MOTET'S ANALYSIS OF LEGOYT'S WORK.

Having alluded in the preceding Chapter to the imperfect manner in which the insane in France had been enumerated, even at so late a date as eighteen hundred and fifty, we take pleasure in laying before our readers the following able and interesting analysis of M. Legoyt's great work on the Statistics of the Insane, by Dr. Motet, Secretary of the Medico-Psychological Society of France, who kindly presented us with a copy.

This able review of one of the most important public documents ever published in France cannot fail to interest and instruct all who read it. We believe it gives a better idea and affords a more comprehensive view of the number and condition of the insane in France than any work that has hitherto been offered in the English language; and though it treats of some topics upon which we have already touched it is given entire:

DR. MOTET'S ANALYSIS OF LEGOYT'S WORK.*

The subject of insanity has for some time actively interested the French mind. People are now no longer satisfied with barren sympathy; they question, they are anxious. Each one imagines it his right and his duty to probe this deep wound of society, and doubtless with a laudable, but sometimes inopportune zeal, reforms are proposed on all sides; an almost radical modification of the legislation which here regulates the condition of the insane is desired. A word which in our country is never uttered without exciting a tumult—liberty—is the watchword at which rally a great number of writers who lack only one thing, a little experience. To these publicists who are animated by the best intentions, we will not reply by cold disdain. We have remarked elsewhere † and we gladly repeat it here, generous illusions are deserving respect; everything which relates to insanity acquires a dignity, a magnitude just in proportion to this measureless misfortune, and those who, excited by a deep sympathy, demand of us by what right we violently separate from society a being whose reason is affected, deserve to be answered not merely by denying their competence, but by arguments and facts of a nature to justify our conduct.

Moreover, the time has passed when knowledge was an exclusive monopoly in the hands of a few. Social problems are debated in open day. We cannot stay the movement of thought, which, after all, tends toward progress; and to be silent will be to expose ourselves to deserve the reproach which, from habit, is still easily enough addressed to us, of seeing nothing beyond a narrow specialty. It would be a singular inconsistency for us to refuse to examine the elements of an investigation which every one may possess. The *Moniteur* of April 16, 1866, published a report of the Minister of Commerce, the impression of which cannot yet have been effaced. These figures, which seem to increase each year, and which statistics present from time to time to the impatient but legitimate curiosity of economists and philanthropists, need to be commented on and discussed; what is of especial importance is to give them a correct interpretation, and, accepting them as the stern expression of facts unfortunately too true, not to force results from them—not to deduce too hasty, and therefore, very probably, erroneous conclusions from them. Many minds, even the best, accepting them without question, and seduced by their eloquence (the expression is restricted to a particular signification), imagine it their duty to take up arms against us. Although silence sometimes serves a just cause better than too much discussion, it seems to us that we ought not to be silent to-day. We have at our command the elements which are always wanting to those who can only make abstracts of accounts. Is it that we consider fruitless those patient investigations which present to us, at stated periods, the balance of our intellectual and moral condition? Such is not our idea. We well know (for we have been aided by it) what labor and research have been necessary to present at once the imposing array of figures which constitutes the statistics of the insane in France from 1854 to 1860. M. Legoyt possesses a thorough experience in these matters, and we are merely just in tendering to him here the tribute of praise which he deserves:

---

* Translated by Miss Martha W. Sawyer, Harrison Square, Massachusetts.

† Of the possibility and propriety of allowing certain classes of insane to leave special asylums and of placing them either at agricultural improvement or with their own families. (Medical Congress at Lyons, 1864); (The Insane before the Law). Paris, 1866.

he has well completed a thankless task, the scattered materials for which would have remained in confusion if he had not collected them, substituting in place of chaos a fruitful harmony. It is not, then, a criticism which we are about to make; it is a complement of instruction which we would present. To harsh figures we would oppose facts; what seems to us important is to explain how results, apparently deplorable, are due to the influence of causes very readily appreciable; in short, to solve a question which has been put to us, and which, in our opinion, will place us in a most humiliating situation if we leave it unanswered.

The sequestration of the insane in public or private asylums is, at the same time, a measure of public order and of personal safety. The lunatic is a sick person who has the right, by very reason of the special disease with which he is affected, to special care; he is also a being dangerous to those around him; in presence of this terrible scourge, the most prepossessed minds cannot refuse to admit it, family devotion is, for the most part, fruitless; they are exhausted by vain efforts; the most generous sacrifices result only in cruel deception; they are obliged, sooner or later, to adopt the serious measure of placing in an asylum the patient whom they can neither protect nor take care of at home. We understand too well how serious are the questions which sequestration involves, even when it is most justifiable, to seek always to hasten it. Although cure is a performance too often compromised by unwise delay, we are but feebly disposed to blame the family affection which resists our advice and waits until the last moment to take leave; but we do not hesitate to blame those who entertain unjust suspicions and represent the asylum as the sepulchre of intelligence. It is too lightly flinging the shroud over the head of the dying; it is too seriously undervalueing the wisdom and the honor of the physicians who devote themselves to a task always sad. The lunatic is not fatally condemned to leave the little reason which still remains in those establishments which the vivid imaginations of some philanthropists transform into a kind of extinguisher. There is something better to be done than to address petitions to the Senate; it is necessary to give an account of things, not to seize, with unreflecting haste, the malicious lucubrations of unfortunate minds still affected, although they may present the fairest appearance. But to restrain impulse in France would be to reform our national character, and although these excesses may not be to our taste, they have, as a point of departure, a sentiment so elevated as to merit being reduced to their just value without passion on our part; we have, moreover, good reasons enough to produce to maintain, without fear, an attitude of defense, and never to attempt to assume an aggressive attitude towards those who try to save, by a bold *coup de main*, their compromised cause. We shall proceed in this matter in a calmer way, consulting rather the experience of our predecessors than our own; but, nevertheless, we do not wish to be hastily accused, or to have it thought that we have gained nothing during thirty years. We do not think, whatever may be said, that we are behind neighboring nations; our legislation, if it is not perfect, does not deserve the reproach which it receives, of being, the greater part of the time, insufficient or arbitrary. One cannot deny, without systematically closing his eyes to evidence, that nowhere is the solicitude of the State, of the Government, more active than in our country. We find a proof in these statements which we now possess, and which we wish to explain to all. We have been preceded in this design by our learned colleague, Dr. Brierre de Boismont, who published in this collection an excellent analysis of the statistical works of M. Legoyt.* We cannot do better than to follow his steps; finding ourselves, moreover, in perfect conformity with his views, we shall be obliged to refer to points already noticed by him.

The number of establishments, public and private, devoted to the insane was one hundred and eleven in eighteen hundred and fifty-three. At the close of eighteen hundred and sixty there were only ninety-nine, as several of them may have been suppressed on account of their trifling importance or of their incomplete or irregular organization. On the first of January, eighteen hundred and fifty-four, their population was twenty-four thousand five hundred and twenty-four lunatics of both sexes. This number increased in the succeeding years, but the progression has been much less rapid than in the period between eighteen hundred and thirty-five and eighteen hundred and fifty-three. The following table will show this:

January 1st, 1854	24,524
January 1st, 1855	24,896
January 1st, 1856	25,485
January 1st, 1857	26,305
January 1st, 1858	27,028
January 1st, 1859	27,878
January 1st, 1860	28,761
January 1st, 1861	30,239

The increase was enormous from eighteen hundred and thirty-six to eighteen hundred and forty-six, each quinquennial period presenting an increase of five and a half per cent; but since eighteen hundred and forty-six the progression has been greatly diminished. It appears:

From 1846 to 1851	3.71 per cent.
From 1851 to 1856	3 87 per cent.
From 1856 to 1861	3.14 per cent.

These results should not astonish. The increase in the population of asylums corresponds to the relief which they bring to the lot of the insane—a new organization, in which much more attention is given to the conditions of material life of the patients than formerly. On the other hand, the foundation of new establishments; the confidence inspired by officers and physicians; and, it must be allowed also, the greater facility of communication. The changes brought about within thirty years in our customs, in our needs, all favored this movement of entry. It was the necessary result, foreseen in advance, of a new order of things. Now the equilibrium tends to become reëstablished, and we doubt not that from this time for some years a sensible diminution will be proved in the still continuous increase of which statistics accuse us. Everything has contributed to increase these numbers; and it is from settled convictions that we assert that there has not actually been the

*Annals of Public Hygiene and Legal Medicine, Second Series, vol. xi, p. 197. Motet.

enormous increase which is indicated. The investigations have been more carefully made during these last ten years than they had ever been. Those of whom information was sought understood the importance of such work, and the French Statistical Bureau has been able to collect materials much more complete than those heretofore placed at its disposal. This result, the extent of which will be better appreciated in the future, is due to the active and persevering energy with which M. Legoyt has inspired every department of his administration.

If the population of the asylums increases, the proportion of the insane in relation to the population of France ought also to increase; but it is important constantly to bear in mind, in presence of these figures, the increased extent each year of public assistance; more patients relieved and treated; that is all which can be deduced from them. Thus it is estimated in

Year.	Population of France.	Insane Under Treatment.	Proportion to Population.
1851	35,783,170	21,353	1 to 1,676 inhabitants.
1856	36,139,364	25,485	1 to 1,418 inhabitants.
1861	36,717,254	30,239	1 to 1,214 inhabitants.

This is not the exact proportion of the insane to the total population of the Empire; we must add the insane remaining in families, of which the number was in eighteen hundred and fifty four nearly twenty-four thousand four hundred and thirty-three individuals; in eighteen hundred and fifty-six, thirty-four thousand and four; in eighteen hundred and sixty-one, fifty-three thousand one hundred and sixty—which makes for this last year, including the insane treated in asylums, about two insane to one thousand inhabitants. To what, then, is this increase due? To the idiots and cretins being included in the statistical tables, and it is impossible on seeing their number increase from twenty-five thousand two hundred and fifty-nine in eighteen hundred and fifty-six to forty-one thousand five hundred and twenty-five in eighteen hundred and sixty-one, not to conclude, as M. Legoyt has judiciously done, that there was a serious error, the more easily committed since the greater part of the idiots and cretins remain at home; since previous to eighteen hundred and sixty-one they were confounded with the general population, and since, if in accordance with the more complete instructions given to the Census Marshals, they have been classed apart, it is not surprising that results so different in appearance have been obtained. This reason (a more rigid, more exact appreciation of mental condition) should be the true one.

It is scarcely probable that the number of idiots increased everywhere at once. But one thing is certain, that in eighteen hundred and fifty-six there were only two thousand eight hundred and forty idiots in the asylums, and in eighteen hundred and sixty-one three thousand seven hundred and forty-six of them were counted. The influence of Ferrus had made itself felt; he had, in a remarkable report, described the inconvenience which might arise by withdrawing imbeciles and idiots from the action of the law, and the administrative power had adopted his views. The number would have increased much more if they had not made so great a restriction in the admission of idiots. It would doubtless be desirable that all who belong to indigent families should be effectually relieved. There is, in this way, a progress to be effected, and some efforts have already been made; but it is difficult to think of placing indefinitely in an asylum inoffensive beings who live a wholly vegetative life. It is at the same time imposing too heavy a tax upon the department, and, on the other hand, increasing a burden which is already too real in a large number of our asylums. Moreover, under the general name of idiots is included a class of beings who are not entirely useless. There are imbeciles, feeble minded, as they are called in some localities, who are good workers and who regularly accomplish a slightly complicated task. Until now they have been unnoticed in statistical statements; they appear there now, and augment by so much the total number. The situation is not then so deplorable as might have been supposed, and we believe that the deviation will be much less for several years from now.

What we have remarked concerning the influence of the reorganization of asylums upon the increasing number of insane under treatment is especially noticeable in the statements of the admissions. One is convinced, by consulting them, that the greatest increase corresponds to the period nearest to the promulgation of the law of eighteen hundred and thirty-eight. M. Legoyt divides the period from eighteen hundred and thirty-five to eighteen hundred and sixty into five sub-periods, and he finds that the proportional increase has been, annually:

YEARS.	Per ct.
From 1840 to 1844	7.94
From 1845 to 1849	3.38
From 1850 to 1854	3.83
From 1855 to 1860	2.00

Here is also the exact number of admissions from 1854 to 1860:

1855	9,303	1858	10,314
1856	9,246	1859	10,086
1857	10,024	1860	10,785

Which gives, as the annual mean of admissions, about nine thousand three hundred and fifty-three insane, seven hundred and twenty-seven idiots, and eleven cretins; hence, of one hundred patients admitted, there were ninety-two insane, seven idiots, and one cretin.

The admissions are voluntary, that is to say, requested by the families, or officially ordered by the authorities. The tables which we have here do not make a distinction which is, nevertheless, of some importance. Nearly two thirds of the admissions into the departmental asylums are made officially; in the departments for pensionnaires, in the private institutions, including Charenton, there is nothing like it. This occurs, doubtless, from the negligence of the families of the indigent insane,

from the slighter disturbance of private interests which the presence of
an insane person creates, and also from prejudices which have not yet
entirely disappeared among the poorer classes, and which are no longer
shared by the better educated classes. The voluntary entries were:

In 1856 in the proportion of..	30.20 per cent.
In 1857 in the proportion of..	31.19 per cent.
In 1858 in the proportion of..	32.02 per cent.
In 1859 in the proportion of..	30.61 per cent.
In 1860 in the proportion of..	32.02 per cent.

The official entries were:

In 1856 in the proportion of	69.80 per cent.
In 1857 in the proportion of..	68.81 per cent.
In 1858 in the proportion of..	67.98 per cent.
In 1859 in the proportion of..	69.39 per cent.
In 1860 in the proportion of..	67.98 per cent.

In wealthier families, where the physician is called, if not at the commencement of the insanity, at least as soon as it becomes serious, the
situation is different. Judicious advice is given and often promptly followed. They do not wait for the interference of the authorities to effect
an entry; they hope, on the contrary, that by combating the disease in
season they will have better opportunities of eradicating it, and the
official entry, which is so common to asylums, becomes almost the exception in private establishments. This may be seen by the following figures, which are a statement of the admissions into the hospital (*maison
de santé*) directed by Dr. Mesnet and myself:

1856—54 admissions, of which 9 were official.............	16.65 per cent.
1857—68 admissions, of which 8 were official.............	11.76 per cent.
1858—74 admissions, of which 9 were official.............	12.15 per cent.
1859—74 admissions, of which 7 were official.............	9.45 per cent.
1860—54 admissions, of which 4 were official.............	7.40 per cent.
1861—59 admissions, of which 4 were official.............	7.14 per cent.

No other conclusion of interest can be drawn from it; in the asylums
the entries, which are, after all, a kind of public assistance, should be
under the supervision of the administrative power, and the right of control which it reserves is not excessive. It is known, moreover, that it
never refuses to open the doors of its special establishments when a
request really justifiable is made; the entry, which, for paupers, is always
made by means of the authorities, takes the name of official entry for
that reason; but, if we except insane vagabonds, incendiaries, and homi-
cides, the Mayors and Prefects never make the decision before having
been sought by the family. One need not, then, infer from these figures
(which might at first surprise) too frequent or too great an intermeddling

of the administration in the sequestration of the insane. For the large towns, which, like Paris, have private hospitals, the official entries have taken place only in desperate cases; and when·an insane person has been arrested upon the highway his family is immediately notified, if possible, and invited to designate the establishment in which they wish the patient to be entered. At Paris, it is the Prefect of Police who makes the arrest. He uses the right which the law gives him to protect public order and personal safety, and one cannot complain when authority takes the place of an absent or negligent family. We insist upon this point, for this right of authority is now contested with more passion than propriety; if all the difficulties, all the embarrassments which are constantly created by the insane in society were well understood; if the consequences of their acts were examined without prejudice, and intervention always useful, never arbitrary, would perhaps be less promptly censured. And allow us to say, there are insane and idiots for whom sequestration in an asylum would be a blessing; they would escape ill treatment, detestable calculations dictated by base cupidity; recent facts which have been developed by tribunals have shown but too well how far cruelty and ill usage of poor, defenceless beings may be carried. We believe, therefore, that it is well to leave to the Mayors and Prefects the liberty of the initiative, and that to withdraw it would be to promote the development of abuses already but too common.

The number of women in the asylums is always a little larger than of the men, and nevertheless the admissions are in an inverse proportion. The reason of this fact is that the discharges and deaths, and the mean length of residence, differ much for the two sexes. The mortality and the discharges attain a higher figure among males than females. We shall refer again to this subject. The following are the figures corresponding to the period eighteen hundred and fifty-four to eighteen hundred and sixty, for the patients present at the end of each year:

YEAR.	Males.	Females.
1854	12,036	12,860
1855	12,221	13,264
1856	12,632	13,673
1857	12,930	14,098
1858	13,392	14,486
1859	13,876	14,885
1860	14,582	15,657

This difference had been already noted from eighteen hundred and forty-two to eighteen hundred and fifty-four. The proportion was, per hundred, forty-seven and seventy-seven one hundredths males, and fifty-two and twenty-three one hundredths females. From eighteen hundred and fifty-four to eighteen hundred and sixty it is nearly the same, for we find among one hundred patients forty-eight and ten one hundredths males, and fifty-one and ninety one hundredths females. This is not the case among idiots and cretins. Subtracting these from the total number of insane under treatment, we find among one hundred idiots and cretins fifty-one and twenty-two one hundredths males, and forty-eight and seventy-eight one hundredths females.

One of the most interesting subjects of study is that of the curability or incurability of the insane under treatment. But who does not comprehend at the same time how researches of this nature must lack correctness? Let us, therefore, attach but an indifferent importance to the figures furnished us by statistics. They are approximate results, which could only acquire a real value in case it were possible to estimate singly the statistics of each asylum after having deducted from its lists the epileptic, the paralytic imbeciles (les déments paralytiques), the idiots and the cretins, for whom incurability is no longer a presumption, but a certainty. We shall not insist upon this point; when the discharges by recovery are presented to us we shall find more exact means of estimation, and such as will better merit our consideration.

At what age is insanity most common? Statistics previous to eighteen hundred and fifty-four agree with those which have just been published; it is from thirty-five to forty years that we find the most insane of both sexes. It is likewise the period of life at which males and females expend the most physical and intellectual activity. It is the age of complete development; it is also that at which trials are most numerous. Thus of seven thousand two hundred and ninety-two insane persons admitted (mean year) for the first time, from eighteen hundred and fifty-six to eighteen hundred and sixty, we find:

YEARS.	Males.	Females.	Total.
From 20 to 30 years	762	688	1,450
From 30 to 40 years	1,107	888	1,995
From 40 to 50 years	857	676	1,533

Beyond this period of life the proportion of females increases; at a single period there is almost an equality; it is from fifty to fifty-five years—we find four hundred and ninety-five males and four hundred and fifty-eight females.

YEARS.	Males.	Females.	Total.
From 60 to 70 years	243	324	567
Above 70 years	101	182	283

Among idiots and cretins it is from twenty to thirty years that the greatest number of admissions takes place. That is readily understood; it is the time at which these unfortunates become most troublesome to the family and to society, especially those whose physical development is not too incomplete, and who manifest all sorts of impulses—blind passions which it is often difficult to control. What is the result in the families of these poor creatures for whom constant watchfulness is necessary, and who become a deeper and deeper source of anxiety? They embarrass labor and they oppress by too heavy a tax an account already limited; it becomes necessary to part with them, and to ask their admission into the asylum. Above fifty years the number of admissions is reduced a little; it might descend to zero without our being astonished, for idiots rarely live to that age; it seems probable to us that they must have inserted in the table individuals who are only imbeciles; for the latter, indeed, the duration of life is more extended than for idiots.

The civil condition of the insane admitted for the first time, from eighteen hundred and fifty-six to eighteen hundred and sixty, has been stated most carefully, and offers us the following results:

	Males.	Females.	Total.
Single	9,545	7,624	17,169
Married..	7,731	6,671	14,402
Widowers and widows........................	1,327	2,718	4,045
Civil condition unknown......................	545	298	843
Totals...	19,148	17,311	36,459

The number of unmarried insane is of itself as considerable as that of the married and widowed insane. All statistics agree upon this point. Is it because celibacy predisposes one to insanity? This problem has long been agitated, and the solutions are various. An unmarried person retains a greater freedom to temptation, and he yields more readily to those allurements which family relations diminish, if they do not entirely efface; life is less regular, less calm; in trial it is less encouraged, less supported, and having, generally, no one near to care for him if attacked by insanity, the doors of the asylum or of the hospital will open far more readily to him than to any other. The causes of the numerical superiority of unmarried persons in the admission are therefore complex. They have not escaped the sagacity of M. Legoyt, who has judiciously described them. As to widowhood* it seems to exercise a more unfavorable influence upon females than upon males; but to make a correct estimate it is necessary to find out whether women do not oftener remain in the condition of widowhood than men, and whether, also, the moral causes do not play the most important part in these new conditions.

As for the preceding statistics, the examination of the professions furnishes a sad lesson. It is from among the laborers of thought that insanity receives most victims.† For the period included between eighteen hundred and fifty-four and eighteen hundred and sixty these statements give the enormous number of forty-six hundred and twenty persons engaged in the liberal professions. Compared with the total number of admissions this result presents a proportion of ten per cent. See the following table:

---

* I have no English word more nearly corresponding to "veuvage" than widowhood, which I use for both sexes.

† Our investigations lead us to believe the reverse of this to be true in all other countries than France.

YEARS.	Number engaged in the Liberal Professions
1854 to 1855	1,839
1856..	511
1857..	544
1858..	497
1859..	658
1860..	571
Total	4,620

During the same time there were sixty-eight thousand nine hundred and ninety-two admissions. If in round numbers we deduct twenty thousand idiots and cretins, there remain forty-eight thousand nine hundred and ninety-two admissions, of which four thousand six hundred and twenty represent individuals having received a liberal education. Clergymen and members of religious orders amount to twelve hundred and forty-eight; physicians, apothecaries, and midwives, to six hundred and thirty-three; professors, learned men, and men of letters, one thousand and ninety-three; artists, sculptors, painters, musicians, eight hundred and sixty. The rest of the catalogue are notaries, advocates, bailiffs, and public officers or employés. The other professions are far from furnishing so large a quota. This is, as M. Brierre de Boismont has remarked, another argument in favor of the opinion of those who think that the progress of civilization affects the development of insanity. It is just to add, nevertheless, that it is among this class of persons that the excitements of life are most incessant, that ambition is most feverish, and that the sensibility to display constantly kept in exercise is liable to the greatest extremes. Military and seafaring men are not spared; then come, finally, stockholders and proprietors, the manual or industrial professions, domestics or hired laborers, and farmers. The inhabitants of towns constitute more than one half the annual admissions, and yet the proportion of the people of the rural districts to those of the towns is as three to one. There are many causes which effect this result. The insane person is more easily guarded in the rural districts than in towns; his presence in the family does not so necessarily become the occasion of difficulties and embarrassments of all kinds; there is more room for him, and fewer causes of annoyance; if he is sometimes noisy, the neighbors are not disturbed by his cries, so he may remain at home a long time if he is inoffensive. The citizen, even if he were just as docile and easily governed, becomes, from the fact of his insanity, a source of consant anxiety. The asylum or private establishment which will open its doors to him will give him a material benefit which he cannot obtain at home, where, for various reasons, he would be habitually confined to his chamber. On the other hand, in a family whose means are quite limited the incapacity of one of its members becomes a source of expense which the entry into an asylum at the present very moderate charge immediately reduces. These are constant facts, and if we add thereto the excitements constantly renewed, the need of luxury and more active enjoyment, the more frequent deception, the watching, the excess, etc., we shall understand the enormous disproportion which is presented to us in the following figures:

1856 to 1860.	Insane......	Idiots and Cretins...
Inhabitants of towns.....	18,228	950
Inhabitants of the country.....	16,914	1,481
Residence unknown.....	1,317	98
Totals.....	36,459	2,529

M. Brierre de Boismont ascertained the same facts in preceding statistics, and the reasons by which he supports them remain true in our day. There is a perfect accordance, just as in the researches made to ascertain which are the departments which furnish the most insane. They are still the Seine, Seine Inférieure, Seine and Marne, the Rhône, Seine et Oise, the Eure, the Loiret, the Bouches du Rhône, the Côte d'Or, and the Yonne.

To conclude that which relates to admissions, we still find, as in the past, that the Summer months are the months of the most numerous admissions—that the Winter months are less fruitful.

The study of causes presents difficulties of more than one kind. We must not rely upon the very rigid estimates of statistics essentially official. There is not a physician having lived among the insane who does not remember the extreme embarrassment in which he has often found himself when he has tried to analyze the diverse influences which have produced the development of insanity. It is very rare to find only one of the number to which we can with certainty ascribe the actual derangement. Be that as it may, there is a portion of truth in the tables which M. Legoyt has prepared; and as it was not possible for him to obtain more accurate statements, we will accept them. Among these causes hereditary takes the lead. Modern works, those of Baillarger in particular, have represented its full importance. Of twenty-eight thousand six hundred and twenty-one insane of both sexes, of whom the friends have given the necessary information, there are reckoned four thousand and fifty-six whose father or mother had been attacked by insanity; and pursuing the analysis still further, of the insane admitted in eighteen hundred and fifty-nine and eighteen hundred and sixty it has been found that hereditary transmission is in some degree obedient to the law of propagation from sex to sex. The insane mother transmits the insanity to her daughters, the father to his sons. We reproduce the following table, which relates to fifteen thousand two hundred and thirteen insane:

CAUSES.	Males.	Females.	Total.
Issue of an insane father..........................	412	294	706
Issue of an insane mother..........................	356	403	759
Issue of an insane father and mother*..........	83	110	199
Issue of a father and mother not insane........	2,367	2,132	4,499
Unknown...	4,862	4,194	9,056
Totals*...	8,080	7,133	15,213

This gives, out of one thousand insane males, two hundred and sixty-four bearing the hereditary taint, one hundred and twenty-eight from the father's side, one hundred and ten from the mother's, twenty-six from both sides at the same time; of one thousand insane females, one hundred from the father's side, one hundred and thirty from the mother's, and thirty-six from both sides.

What is the share of the causes called physical and of the moral causes in the development of insanity? For a great number, as we have already said, it is very difficult to succeed in separating them fully. Sometimes they succeed each other as consequences the one of the other; sometimes they are so closely linked that any distinction becomes impossible; but what is beyond doubt is that drunkenness presents itself in a great number of cases. M. Brierre de Boismont tried vainly to diminish its influence when he wrote: "The man who drinks to divert his thoughts from disappointment, and becomes insane, has at first acted under the influence of a moral cause." This reasoning, which justly exhibits the complications which may exist among physical and moral causes, is only applicable to a small minority. Now that attention is aroused in this direction, it is beyond doubt that insanity receives the greater number of its victims from among persons addicted to the use of alcoholic drinks. The nature of intoxication may be curious to determine, for if it is true that, under one form or another, it is always the alcohol absorbed which acts upon the cerebral functions, it is no less true that certain preparations into which it enters in a highly concentrated degree give a more rapid progress to the disease, and a peculiarly serious character. A remarkable fact, and one which our personal researches have presented in all statistical tables, is that it is not in wine countries that delirium tremens is most frequent. It is in the large towns, in cities where industry is most developed and most active, where there is the greatest agglomeration of population, that delirium tremens is most common. It is, moreover, more frequently found at the north than at the south; and we do not consider ourselves guilty of exaggeration in attributing to the improvements made in the distillation of beet root, potatoes, and grains a large share of the increase in the number of the insane. One is justifiably startled at finding that more than one fourth of the persons whose insanity is attributed to physical causes suffer the penalty of alcoholic excess. Of eight thousand seven hundred and ninety-seven persons, three thousand and fourteen were drunkards. Even women pay their

* This is a correct copy of the figures presented in the original, but there is evidently an error, which I conclude is in either the males or females of the third item—eighty-three for eighty-nine, or one hundred and ten for one hundred and sixteen.

tribute to this degrading cause. They are, however, in much smaller number—four hundred and forty-one out of seven thousand and sixty-nine. After this comes, in order of frequency, advanced age (l'âge avancé), diseases of various organs, epilepsy, various diseases of the nervous system, Onanism and venereal excesses, destitution and misery, accidents and wounds. Among females, disorders of the genital organs, appearing either at the time when the uterine functions are most active or when they cease, are one of the most frequent physical causes of insanity. The proportion is one thousand five hundred and ninety-two out of seven thousand and sixty-nine.

Among moral causes, domestic disappointment plays the most important part. Of four thousand nine hundred and nineteen men, nine hundred and eighty became insane from this cause; of five thousand four hundred and thirty-eight women, one thousand five hundred and sixty-nine under the same influence. This is a little more than one fourth, especially if we add thereto the disappointments resulting from loss of friends, and which may, in a great majority of cases, appear among domestic disappointments (chagrins.) Afterwards come disappointments resulting from loss of fortune (851), from disappointed ambition (520), excitement of religious feelings (1095), excess of intellectual labor (358), love (767), jealousy (456), pride (368), anger (123), remorse (102), isolation and solitude (115), simple imprisonment (113), imprisonment in cell (26), nostalgia (78), from a total of ten thousand three hundred and fifty-seven of both sexes.

Under this title ("Aggravating Circumstances") is found one of the most instructive paragraphs of all M. Legoyt's publication. General paralysis is there considered as the complication of insanity, and its relation to the total population of the asylums is precisely stated. A comparison between preceding and present statistics presents an increase of one half; and for ourselves, who live in special circle, in a private hospital where only the insane of the wealthier classes are received, we do not find this number so great. For ten years we have seen general paralysis becoming more frequent; it appears sooner in the life of man, and if one considers that this terrible malady attacks without mercy the most gifted, one cannot help feeling profound pity for the poor creatures who, in the midst of their insanity, retain the most delusive ambition—who, with simple credulity, delight in the most deceptive chimeras. The dementia (démence) which attacks them almost unawares, the diminution of their strength together with that of their intellect, the progressive deterioration, which may be traced, step by step, is one of the saddest and most heart-rending pictures which can be imagined. Nothing stays its victorious march; with scarcely, from time to time, a few periods of abatement, abruptly broken by the return of cerebral congestion, with epileptic (épileptiformes) convulsions, and death, after eighteen years or two months of a purely vegetative existence, coming to end the sad trial —this is what we have daily before our eyes. Paralytic imbeciles (les déments paralytiques) now present, in the admissions, a number relatively large. From eighteen hundred and forty-two to eighteen hundred and fifty-three the proportion was: for males, six per cent; for females, three per cent. From eighteen hundred and fifty-six to eighteen hundred and sixty the number increases to twelve per cent for males, and remains three per cent for females. " Cèst que la paralysie générale semble reconnaître pour cause tout ce que sur excite l'appareil encéphalo-rachidieu;" in its etiology is found excess of all kinds, as well of pleasure as of labor, and the ambitious delirium which is one of its commonest characteristics is very often only the incessant preoccupation of those whom it attacks in the midst of their need of relaxation, of their insatiable desires. It is only too certain that, in these later years, general paralysis has had many more victims; what we have ourselves observed is confirmed by general statistics. Among epileptics the proportion seems to have diminished; we do not well explain to ourselves from what influences; we state this result. From eighteen hundred and forty-two to eighteen hundred and fifty-three it was, for males, eight and eight tenths per cent; among females, six and four tenths. From eighteen hundred and fifty-six to eighteen hundred and sixty it is only four and thirty-one hundredths among males, and three and seventeen one hundredths among females. Something here has escaped us, and we are inclined to think that in preceding statistics the number of epileptics under treatment were given; in the present, that of the epileptics admitted during the period, which is very different. In both cases the males are represented by a higher figure than the females.

Hitherto we have considered only a single side of the question. It remains for us to see what becomes of the insane admitted and treated in the asylums—that is to say, to study the discharges before or after recovery, and the deaths.

The proportional number of the insane discharged before or after recovery was fourteen and forty-six one hundredths per cent from eighteen hundred and fifty-four to eighteen hundred and sixty. This number is a little less than that of the period eighteen hundred and forty-two to eighteen hundred and fifty-three, during which it was sixteen and thirty-six one hundredths per cent. But that which was proved at that epoch is also found to-day—more males are discharged than females. Insanity of alcoholic origin, which is generally cured quickly, being more common among males than among females, will in part explain this difference, if we do not also find, to the disadvantage of females, all chronic diseases of the uterus, difficulties succeeding delivery, irregular menstruation, etc. Depression has not so deep or so lasting an influence among males. These are all so many favorable causes which lead to a more certain and speedy recovery. Be this as it may, the proportion of discharges after recovery seems to have diminished— that of discharges before recovery to have increased a little. We do not think, for our part, that the difference can be very great. Many patients leave our establishments, public or private, reclaimed by their friends before their recovery can be completed. The heads of the office report them as improved, but not cured. It is necessary, in order that the estimate may be correct, to know what has become of these convalescents, who for the most part, attain perfect health. These documents are wanting; all correction is impossible, and the numbers have only an entirely relative value. Thus the mean of discharges after recovery, from eighteen hundred and fifty-four to eighteen hundred and sixty, was only seven and seventy-seven one hundredths per cent of patients treated; of discharges before recovery, six and sixty-eight one hundredths per cent. Brierre de Boismont had good reason to say, in eighteen hundred and fifty-nine, that it should not be estimated thus. Too many elements are found in these statistics, and cannot be officially separated to make the estimate correct. · Who does not see at once that the general paralytics included in the total number of insane (for example) fatally condemned to incurability, the epileptics, nearly all in the same condition, make of themselves alone the proportion of the chronic insane considerable; the proportion per cent of cures is reduced at once before them, and to attain a really scientific, really correct data, we should take the acute forms presumed to be curable, and then see the results obtained. If we should adopt this course, which after all will not lead to very great complications in the formation of tables, we shall not be discouraged by the disheartening figure of seven or eight per cent of cures. This is the weapon of which the opponents of the law of eighteen hundred and thirty-eight most readily make use.

Indeed, to one who has not the power to explain it there is something very sad in these official statements. We are not reduced to a situation as discouraging as might at first be believed; and M. Legoyt himself comes to our aid by saying that among the insane treated who are most certainly cured are military and seafaring men. Why? Because they are men in the strength of youth, who are generally attacked by acute, curable forms of mental alienation; because they are submitted to a careful examination at the commencement, and because the disease is treated almost as soon as it appears. General paralysis, which we justly accuse of increasing the number of our failures, does not yet appear among them. It is from thirty-five to forty-five years that it commits the greatest ravages. Let one deduct from the total number of insane treated the epileptics, the paralytics, the idiots, and the cretins; let him retain the acute forms, in indicating each year the probable prognostics of those remaining under treatment, and he will see that the recoveries are not so rare as he thinks. As to the discharges before recovery, we do not attach any more importance to them than they deserve. What are they generally? Fruitless trials which, after short duration, result in return to the asylum. They are escapes followed sooner or later by reëntry; they are also transfers from one establishment to another, of which care had been taken to keep an account. A more correct data, and conformable, moreover, to the observations collected by the *chefs de service*, is that of length of treatment among the insane cured. Of thirteen thousand six hundred and eighty-seven insane discharged after recovery, sixteen hundred and sixty-three were discharged after a residence in the public or private establishments of one month or less. The greater number, eighteen hundred and eighty-seven, were discharged after five or six months of treatment; fifteen hundred and nineteen after seven or eight months; seventeen hundred and forty-eight in the second month. It is, then, in the first months which follow the attack of insanity that the cures are most numerous; let us add, also, that they are most certain; yet it might have been important to describe the forms which are most quickly relieved. All insanity of alcoholic origin, especially if the habit of drinking is not inveterate (if there has not been a previous attack), is decided in a period of from one month to six weeks. An attack of mania or of true melancholy (*mélancolie franche*) runs its course in five or six months; a few, nevertheless, have lasted a shorter time. Here the influence of cause makes itself felt, and the influence of constitution; and if one could determine the date of the appearance of the derangement, in view of these speedy cures, he would see that the insane who are soonest improved are those who have been most promptly treated. Moreover, we join without reserve in the idea which M. Legoyt has thus expressed: "It is evident that it is the interest of families, and consequently of society, that the insane should be placed under treatment as promptly as possible." As to the season of the year at which the recoveries take place, the following has been observed of one thousand recoveries:

11

Months.	Males.	Females.
December, January, February....................................	206	195
March, April, May...	255	248
June, July, August...	280	283
September, October, November..............................	259	274
Totals..	1,000	1,000

We deem it proper, also, to show the effects of the seasons on mortality, and for this purpose insert the following from the Thirteenth Scotch Report:

"Cold increases the mortality among all classes of the population, and accordingly the deaths in asylums are most numerous in the colder months. But it is worthy of notice that while the mortality of both sexes is higher in Winter than in Summer, there is a difference in the tendency to death in the two sexes in the two seasons.

"Of every one hundred deaths which took place in asylums in the six years from eighteen hundred and sixty-five to eighteen hundred and seventy, fifty-three and fifty-four one hundredths took place in Winter, and forty-six and forty-five one hundredths in Summer. The number of deaths of both sexes is greatest in Winter, but the tendency to death is in Summer greater among females than males. This is shown by the following table:

Table,

Showing the Mortality in Summer and Winter in the Asylums of Scotland for six years, 1865–1870.

Summer. May to October.		Winter. November to April.	
Male Mortality.	Female Mortality.	Male Mortality.	Female Mortality.
620	690	789	721

As to age, it is from twenty-five to thirty-five years that the greatest success is obtained; beyond this age the number of recoveries gradually decreases, as the activity of the mental faculties also diminishes. The following are approximately the causes among about one half of the patients recovered of whom, alone, any positive information could be obtained. Drunkenness, seventeen hundred and thirty-eight; domestic disappointments, eleven hundred and seventy-one; various diseases, seven hundred and sixty-one; diseases peculiar to females, seven hundred and twenty-three; religious excitement, four hundred and sixty. Hereditary tendency has been noted among fifteen hundred and twenty-two cured—about fifteen per cent.

The mortality appears to have increased slightly in the asylums in the period included between eighteen hundred and fifty-four and eighteen hundred and sixty. In the preceding years it was thirteen and seventy-five one hundredths per cent; in these last seven years it has been fourteen and three one hundredths per cent. It is unnecessary to seek for reason other than the cholera epidemic of eighteen hundred and fifty-four. It decreased in eighteen hundred and fifty-nine to thirteen and eighteen one hundredths per cent, and in eighteen hundred and sixty to twelve and fifty-seven one hundredths. Of an equal number, one hundred and thirty-one males die to one hundred females. More than twelve per cent of the mortality among the insane took place within the first month of residence in the asylum, and this number, relatively very large, has given rise to explanations which are not in accordance with facts. It is said that "the cause of these speedy deaths must be the arrest, the violent agitation, the deep disappointment which patients must experience on being abruptly separated from their families—confined, without knowing the reason, in this violent way." This is not the truth. The insane who die so quickly bring to the asylum the diseases under which they sink. We have means to prove that there is only a very small number who have a semi-consciousness of change of place.

Not to extend the limits of this resumé, we shall present the figures for three years only. We have gathered them ourselves, we know all the particulars of the disease, and we can prove that moral disturbances have counted for nothing in the rapidity of the fatal termination. What we have noticed many officers have also observed, and Brierre de Boismont has devoted himself to refute an opinion which has not failed to produce a sad impression. Figures seem to err. It is evident that more than one fourth of the total number of deaths are to be attributed to the first three months. But why? It is because frequently there are brought to the asylum poor patients attacked sometimes with cerebral tumors; sometimes with organic diseases of the respiratory, digestive, or circulatory organs; sometimes with pneumonia and fevers; sometimes with alcoholic intoxication with complication. They have been cared for as far as could be at home. They have only been sent away when frightful hallucination, continued shrieks, and ungovernable impulses have made it dangerous or impossible. A few days more and they would have died at home. They are brought; the journey is very fatiguing to them; they arrive exhausted; they sink in the midst of a delirium which has not even allowed them time to perceive that they have been confided to the hands of strangers. The asylum, then, should not be accused; it is the first disease, of which insanity is then only an accidental manifestation.

One may better judge from the following table, which sums up our professional observations.

In eighteen hundred and sixty-four, of fifteen deaths (eleven males, four females), six died in less than a year after their admission:

AGE.	Nature of the Disease.	Length of Residence.
1. 70 years	Delirium tremens, third attack; epileptic (épileptiformes) convulsions	Left May 7th, 1863; relapse; reëntered January 9th, 1864; died the 13th; four days.
2, 33 years	Acute delirium, agitation, and constant shrieks (cris); nervous exhaustion	Three weeks.
3. 48 years	Consumptive; cavernes aux deux sommets; délire de persécutions	Eight days.
4. 80 years	Sordid avarice; privations of all kinds; allowing himself to starve in a garret. Interference of the Commissioner of Police. Inanition	Two days.
5. 31 years	Typhoid fever, with hallucination and délire de persécutions; pneumonie hypostatique	Twenty-nine days.
6. 17 years	Young woman married fifteen days previous. Acute delirium; proved hereditary	Fifteen days.

In eighteen hundred and sixty-five, of eleven deaths (nine males, two females), five died in less than six weeks after admission:

AGE.	Nature of the Disease.	Length of Res.
1. 45 years	Complete dementia (démence) with general paralysis; cerebral congestion; epileptic convulsions.................	One month.
2. 28 years......	General paralysis à marche galopante; méningo encéphalite suraigué................................... ...	Six weeks.
3. 34 years	Méningo encéphalite; maniacal delirium; official entry: nervous exhaustion produced by constant agitation....	Eight days.
4. 36 years	Dementia, with general paralysis progressing rapidly; appearance of disease six months before; venereal excess; increasing debility (affaiblissement)...............	Fourteen days.
5. 54 years	Consumptive; hallucination and délire de persécutions; agitation; death rather sudden............................	One month.

In eighteen hundred and sixty-six the mortality reached a very high figure. From January first to September first we had twelve deaths— ten males, two females. Five males and one female died in the first month. We have rarely had a year more unfortunate in this respect. It will be seen in consequence of some sad circumstances, all accidental, moreover, that the length of residence has been so short.

AGE.	Nature of the Disease.	Length Residence.
1. 87 years	Appearance ten days previous; carried to the City Hospital, where his stay was impossible from his excitement and shrieks; acute delirium; pulse filiforme	Twenty-four hours
2. 44 years	General paralysis; complete dementia; convulsed condition	Six weeks.
3. 28 years	Young priest; sick for a month at the seminary; excitement and shrieks which terrified his colleagues and prevented their keeping him longer; six hours travel by rail; extreme exhaustion; pulse at one hundred and twelve; typhoid condition..................	Three days.
4. 43 years	General paralysis, dating three years back; cared for until now at home, but for some time creating all sorts of difficulties; intestinal obstructions; ballonnement énorme du ventre; asphyxie par compression	A half hour.
5. 26 years	Alcoholic excess having caused two previous attacks of delirium tremens; sick for fifteen days in a hotel, where he continued to drink; frightful hallucination, shrieks, and violence; on entering, coldness of the extremities; pas de pouls	Fifteen hours.
6. 39 years	Woman. Dread; sleeplessness; délire lypémaniaque; refused food; then acute delirium; maniacal excitement..	Fifteen days.

It may be thought that we have dwelt too long upon this point; but it seemed to us important to present these facts with some details; it is not possible to imagine them when one has only figures before his eyes; but to every impartial mind it will be very apparent that the mental condition of those persons who died so quickly after their admission scarcely allowed them to appreciate the new situation provided for them by entry into the asylum. Not the arrest, then; not excited feelings— nothing but serious physical conditions, which of themselves were sufficient to produce death. Thus that sort of accusation which charges the asylum with a mortality whose very natural explanation need not be so far-fetched, falls of itself.

There still remain a few subjects of comment. M. Legoyt completed his work by researches which, properly speaking, only the administration promotes. We do not stop there; we think we have said enough to set forth the qualities which characterize his work, at the same time conscientious, impartial, and moderate in its estimates. If we do not always agree with him, it is because we look from a different point of view, placed as we are in conditions of special observation which allow us to go to the root of things. But we are pleased to acknowledge that it was impossible to have done better; and such as it is, the statistics from eighteen hundred and fifty-four to eighteen hundred and sixty constitute one of the most interesting documents of the annals of mental alienation.

Does this important work which we wish to show accuse us of a situation as fearful as has been represented? We do not think so. It is impossible to deny an increase in the number of admissions; but it is just also to acknowledge that if the special causes which we have enumerated have favored this increase, there is now a tendency towards an equilibrium, which we hope soon to see definitely established. Our regretted colleague, Parchappe, has noticed, with all the authority of a long experience, a few of these questions, in a discourse delivered last year before the Medical Psychological Society at Paris.* We will not attempt, after him, to rehabilitate our asylums; whoever desires to be enlightened will ascertain very quickly the general movement, which, on all sides, tends towards progress, towards perfection, and, consequently, towards the amelioration of the lot of the insane. The statistics themselves prove to what extent everything is regularly conducted, seriously observed. The documents of which it is constituted were not obtained by an idle or ill-directed administration. There is in the superior as in the inferior ranks of administrative hierarchy a unity of aims and tendencies which should suffice to reassure those who are disturbed because they do not well understand the subjects upon which they comment; for ourselves, who are witness of these efforts, who heartily unite in them, we cannot, without regret, see our intentions undervalued; we regret that we are judged with a frivolity which we should not have suspected among men whose habits of serious investigation should have given them an immunity from such deviations. We think that, in view of this formidable scourge, insanity, it were more generous to assist us, to sustain us in our sad task, than to create obstacles and to discourage us sometimes by unjust suspicions. Happily, duty accomplished brings its recompense with it; and if, in later times, we have been the object of attacks little deserved, this justice will at least be done us, that we have never refused to reply, not upon the ground of delusive theories, but upon that of facts. It has seemed expedient for our cause to review the work of a man as enlightened as capable, placed by his official situation in that quiet region penetrated neither by the spirit of party nor adventurous ideas. We have made numerous drafts upon M. Legoyt, and when, in some matters of detail, we disagree with him, it is because we have had in our hands documents which he always lacked. The statistics which he has published, more complete than those which preceded, are, in our idea, a work of rare value. They are one of the best arguments which can be presented to those who try to believe that we allow ourselves to be soothed by that easy quiet which accepts the past for fear of disturbing the future.

CHAPTER VIII.

INSANITY AMONG THE ANCIENTS.

COMPARATIVE VIEW OF THE CONDITION AND TREATMENT OF THE INSANE AT DIFFERENT
PERIODS AND IN DIFFERENT COUNTRIES.

In the time of the Ancients—In the Middle Ages—In the Eighteenth and Nineteenth
Centuries—In England—In France—In Rome—In the Germanic Confederation—
Observations upon Foregoing Subjects—Cruel Treatment the Result of Ignorance—
New York Poor Houses—Amelioration in the Treatment of the Insane as compared
with Former Periods—Proof of the Advantage of Moral Treatment.

The ancients regarded insanity as the result of some supernatural power; a visitation from some God, at whose shrine the person affected had refused to worship, or as a punishment for irreverence or crime; but the psychologists of modern times have endeavored to explain its mysterious effects on scientific principles. Some contend that the mind

------

*Annals Médico-Psychologiques, 1865, p. 66.

alone is diseased; others that it is a disease of both body and mind; while the great majority regard it as " a disease of the brain affecting the mind;" and while the latter theory accords with our views, and is most readily understood, we propose to enter into no argument with those who have advanced and still maintain a different view, nor is it a part of the purpose of this report to enter into any metaphysical discussion on the various theories that have been advanced in this or any former period of time.

That it is a disease in some shape, all will admit. That it is extremely curable when properly treated in its earliest stage, none will deny. That it is equally intractable and unmanageable after it has fixed itself upon its hapless victim, is a fact that those best acquainted with its subtle nature most deplore. It seems to be an inevitable if not a natural attendant upon the human race. It has been present among men from the beginning, or from the earliest records to the present day.

The feigned madness of Ulysses,* immediately prior to the Trojan war, is perhaps the earliest reference in antiquity to the existence of mental disease—otherwise the madness of Saul claims priority. Ajax was seized with madness after the arms of Achilles had been awarded to his rival Ulysses. Orestes is also described as a madman by his sister Electra.

The "heaven inspired Cassandra" was regarded by the Trojans as insane. Plato alludes to the connection of divination and insanity, the prophetess at Delphi and the priestess at Dodona both being considered as insane. The Sybil and others being classed in the same category, they were said to possess the mad art.

Several other allusions are made to madness by Plato and other writers of antiquity. Euripides makes many allusions to madness, and the power of Bacchus to produce it. Lycurgus, King of the Edones in Thrace, refused to worship Bacchus, in consequence of which the God visited him with madness. The three daughters of Praetus, Lysippe, Iphinoe, and Iphianassa, are fabled to have become insane in consequence of neglecting the worship of Bacchus. They ran about the fields, believing themselves to be cows. Praetus is represented to have applied to Melampus to cure his daughters of insanity, but refused to employ him when he demanded a third part of his kingdom as a reward, reminding us of the enormous sums received by Willis for his attendance on George III and the Queen of Portugal. This neglect of Praetus was punished, and madness became contagious among the Argive women. The persons affected, however, as also the daughters of Praetus, were restored on Melampus being feed in a more liberal manner. Athamas, King of Thebes, and Ino, his second wife, were both said to be insane. Medea, the niece of Circe, Cambyses, Clomenes, King of Sparta, and many others might be mentioned. Hippocrates makes many allusions in his writings to mania, melancholia, and epilepsy. He says that men ought to know that from nothing else but thence (the brain) come joys, despondency, and lamentations. By the same organ we become mad and delirious; and fears and terrors assail us, some by night and some by day.

Diocles (B. C. 300) and Asclepiades also discuss this subject in their writings, and the Roman poets frequently allude to it. Persius and Juvenal both speak of hellebore as a remedy for madness.

From the foregoing extracts we learn that the causes of insanity were

---

* See Bucknill & Tuke on Insanity.

supposed to be very different in the olden time and at the present day. We might therefore very naturally expect a different mode of treatment corresponding with the pathological opinions of the two periods. This, to a certain extent, is true, yet it will be interesting to the non-professional reader to learn how this fearful malady was treated by the doctors of that day. It is a remarkable fact, as we learn from Bucknill & Tuke, that some of them at least were as earnestly opposed to the use of mechanical restraint as were Pinel, Charlesworth, Hill, or Conolly, who immortalized their names in the seventeenth century by advocating in theory and carrying out in practice the non-restraint system that has done so much to ameliorate the condition of the insane in the asylums of the present day in most of the enlightened countries of the world. Bleeding, so much in vogue at a later day, was also condemned by one at least of these celebrated men, as we will see by the following:

OPINIONS OF ANCIENT MEDICAL WRITERS ON THE TREATMENT OF THE INSANE. *

Music is the first recorded remedy employed, so far as we are aware, for the relief of madness. That ancient musician of whom it has been said that he struck tones that were an echo of the sphere harmonies, "took an harp and played with his hand; so Saul was refreshed and was well, and the evil spirit departed from him." Music appears to have been strongly recommended by Asclepiades.

Asclepiades was certainly one of the most definite in his directions in regard to the treatment of the insane. As we have already said, he prescribed music. He especially recommended that the patient should abstain from food, drink, and sleep, in the early part of the day; that in the evening he should drink water, that then gentle friction should be applied, while later still, liquid food should be given, with a repetition of the frictions. By these means sleep was supposed to be induced. He regarded as worse than useless the application of narcotic fomentations, referring specially to hyoscyamus, mandragora, and poppies. Such reference to these remedies is interesting, as showing their use prior to the time in which he flourished. He directed that the patient should be placed in the light. To employ bleeding, was, he thought, little short of madness. According to Cælius Aurelianus, Asclepiades ordered his patients to be chained. Feuchtersleben in his Medical Psychology, states that Asclepiades recommends "that bodily restraint should be avoided as much as possible, and that none but the most dangerous should be confined by bonds;" referring to Celsus and Cælius Aurelianus as his authorities for the opinions of Asclepiades, whose works are lost; but neither of these writers appears to assert so much. Themison, another disciple of Asclepiades, and who is often regarded as the real founder of the School of the Methodici, styled "phlebotomotos" by Cælius, followed, to a considerable extent, in the steps of his predecessor as regards treatment; but prescribed the bath and more liberal regimen, and ordered astringent fomentations (constrictira fomenta).

The treatment recommended by the celebrated Celsus, in his chapter entitled, *De tribus insaniæ generibus*, may next be considered. On the whole, the directions of this physician are harsh, and scarcely merit the praise which some authors have bestowed upon them. It is true, that he admits, in regard to those who ramble in their discourses or attempt

---

* Bucknill & Tuke on Insanity.

some trifling injury with their hands, that it is unnecessary to employ any rough, coercive measures. He deemed it proper, however, to subdue those who were more violent by a very compulsory treatment, "lest they should injure themselves or others." Their audacity must be coerced, and they must be brought to submission by blows, as in the case of any one else who requires restraint. Excessive mirth must be checked ·by scolding. If conciliatory measures fail, patients must be cured by some kind of torment; thus, should they be detected in false-hood or deceit, they must be hungered, or bound in chains, or flogged. By these means, he assures us, they will before long, through the influ-ence of fear, be thoroughly disposed to come to terms, to eat anything; and even their memory, he says, will thus be refreshed. For to startle them suddenly, and greatly to terrify them, is profitable in this disease; anything, in short, by which the mind is violently disturbed. To close up all the avenues of pity this humane physician also says that you are not to believe anyone who thus subdued, while he is desirous of being released from his bonds, pretends that he is sane, however prudently and piteously he may converse, since this very deceit is the result of madness. On which enlightened principle it is difficult to understand how Celsus himself would have escaped had he once been so unfortunate as to be suspected of insanity. Celsus by no means, however, over-looked all medical treatment. He approved of venesection, and of cup-ping applied to the head, which, he observes, will have the effect of inducing sleep. Should any symptom render bleeding unsuitable, the next best remedy is abstinence, followed by an emetic and a purgative of white hellebore, and if possible the employment of friction twice in the ‚day. He is here speaking of those cases in which sadness appears to be the result of black bile. No longer under the influence of apprehension from the violence of the patient, Celsus directs that fear should be removed from his mind, and cheerful hopes excited; pleasure being sought in fables and sports, and whatever else may be conducive to health. Patients are to be judiciously encouraged in their several occu-pations, and their groundless fears are to be lightly reproved. Cold water is also to be poured upon the head of the patient, and his body immersed in water and oil. In maniacal cases, warm fomentations might be applied to the shaven head; when, in consequence, the febrile symp-toms abate, we are to have recourse to friction; but we must use it more sparingly in those cases in which the patients are exhilerated than in those in which they are depressed. In the maniacal paroxysm itself, however, Celsus had not much faith in medical applications; indeed, he was afraid that by such means the fever would be increased. There-fore in such cases, says he, do nothing with the patient but confine him.

Severe as was Celsus upon the insane.who were guilty of deception. he had no hesitation in employing similar means towards the patient, We need not quarrel with the direction, that should the patient refuse to swallow the doctor's favorite hellebore mixture he is to be deceived by having it mixed in his food; but we may well dissent from the pro-priety of another direction, namely: that should it be necessary to inspire fear, and should the patient be a rich man, you are to announce to him the false intelligence of a lost estate.

The good effect of a full diet in some cases of insomnia was very properly pointed out. Other somniferous remedies prescribed by Celsus were friction, exercise after food, and by night the sound of a waterfall,

but chiefly the rocking motion of a suspended bed. Nor were the soothing influences of music in melancholy overlooked. The mind was also
to be called forth in some cases by reading aloud, and occasionally errors
might be made in order to elicit the critical powers of the patient.
Cælius regarded it as essentially necessary to place the maniacal in a
room moderately light and warm, and to avoid everything of an'exciting character. Pictures were not to be allowed, nor was the window to
be too high, nor was the room to be in the upper story, the reason being
added that many when seized with madness have thrown themselves
out. The bed was to be firm, and so placed that the patient could not
be disturbed by the sight of persons entering the room; it was to be of
straw, soft, and well beaten, but not broken. If the patient was in danger of injuring himself, soft wool moistened was applied to the head,
neck, and chest; thus instead of having a padded room Cælius padded
his patient. The duty of attendants, in regard to deception, is clearly
laid down. They were to beware on the one hand of seeming to confirm the patient's delusions, and thus increase his disorder, and on the
other they were to be careful not to exasperate him by too much opposition, but at one time by indulgent condescension, at another by insinu-
ation, endeavor to correct his delusion. Should the patient attempt to
escape and be with difficulty restrained or exasperated with seclusion,
then, says Cælius, with admirable perception, you must employ more
attendants. Let these, he adds, without the patient perceiving the real
object in view, engage themselves in applying friction to his limbs.
Further: should this treatment fail, and the violence be great, a ligature
may be resorted to, being quietly applied, and the limbs protected by
wool. Should the patient have been accustomed to submission and reverence, this, he observes, will not require frequent repetition—for such
repetition would induce contempt, and when patients do not yield to
such a course of treatment, then it becomes necessary to subdue them
by inducing fear or awe. Should the patient's eyes be affected by the
light, they must, according to our author, be shaded; but, he adds, with
great discrimination, in such a way that other parts of the body may
not be deprived of light. Cælius directed that abstinence from food
might be carried so far as to induce slight hunger, adding that the
strength may be reduced by bleeding, if the malady require it, even
during such abstinence should there be nothing present to contra indicate it. The food was to be light and digestible, as bread softened in
warm water, or a preparation of wheat lightly boiled with honey, etc.
Alternate days of fasting and feeding were likewise recommended.
Benefit also might be derived from clysters, and the application of an
emollient cataplasm to the region of the heart.

Should the disorder become stationary, Cælius advises the head to be
shaved, and cupping to be applied, first over the chest, then between the
shoulders ("for these parts sympathize with the head"), and next to
the head. A restless and sleepless condition was to be relieved by
carrying the patient about on a litter or in a chair. To this was to be
added the monotonous sound of running water. Fomentations, by
means of warm sponges, were to be applied over the eyelids, with the
idea of relaxing them, and in the hope of exerting a curative influence
over the meninges of the brain. As reason returned, moderate exercise
was strongly recommended—riding, walking, and exertion of the voice.
The patient was to read compositions containing inaccuracies, in order
the better to exercise the understanding; but Cælius adds a caution that
this must not be too difficult, lest the patient be overdone with laborious

mental exercise, which were as detrimental to the mind as immoderate exertion to the body. Theatrical entertainments were to follow for those laboring under melancholy, and scenes of a solemn or tragic character were to counteract excessive hilarity and excitement.

Subjects of disputation might be added as the patient recovered, conducted in a low tone of voice, the preference being given to narrative and demonstrative subjects. Further, individuals known to the patients were to be employed to converse with them, in a manner calculated to encourage and amuse them. These various mental exercises were to be followed by rubbing with oil, and a gentle walk. Here, our author suddenly remembers that much of the preceding treatment could not be carried out with the illiterate; for such, he prescribes questions having reference to their particular callings; as, on farming, for the agriculturist; navigation, for the sailor; and for those ignorant even of these, questions of a general nature must be propounded. Shampooing, as well as inunction, was an important remedy with Cælius, including frictions of the head. The diet was to be improved as the patient's health returned, wine being forbidden in the first instance, gradually allowed after the use of fruit, but then only of light quality.

As the mind recovered its tone, the patient was allowed to go and hear the disputations of the philosophers, from the persuasion that the passions of grief, fear, and anger were thus dissipated. If, on the contrary, the patient relapsed, the former treatment was to be resumed, adding exposure of the body to the heat of the sun, the head being covered. The administration of an emetic made from the root of white hellebore, was to be added, to which, if the patient objected, vomiting was to be promoted by tickling the fauces. The ears were to be injected with water containing a little nitre, honey, nettle seed, or mustard; the rationale given being, that even through the channels of the senses, a restorative virtue may be conveyed to the membranes of the brain, especially as patients are often affected with tinnitus aurium. Finally, the cure of the patient was to be established by travelling and sea voyages.

After thus stating the mode of treatment which recommended itself to his judgment, Cælius proceeds to condemn the practice of some who had preceded him. Some of the Methodici, he observes, have recommended close confinement in a dark room, forgetting that the patient's dislike to it may aggravate his disorder, and that too much seclusion from the air causes dense bodies to perspire, and that the omission of ordinary occupations will aggravate cerebral congestion. He then denounces the extreme abstinence which was recommended, in forgetfulness of the fact that such a course disorders the bodily powers and is one which the patient will be unable to bear. The supporters of such regimen referred to the taming of wild beasts as analogous and as a proof that madness may be thus repressed; but Cælius, anticipating the practice of the present day, states that they should have known better from a consideration of the effect of hunger upon the sane in inducing rage. He does not hesitate to assert that the starving system will induce madness rather than cure it. He then refers to a subject of especial interest to us in our time, and his observations are calculated to humiliate us, exhibiting, as they do, a far seeing philanthrophy which those who have treated the insane have, until very lately, failed to imitate. Cælius observes that they also order the patients to be bound with chains, without any consideration that the bound parts must necessarily be chafed, and how much more properly the patients might be restrained by the care of attendants than by senseless chains. He is alike indignant against those who would coerce by flagellation, especially about the face and head, which, so far from relieving the disease, only induces swellings and sores; in addition to which, the returning consciousness of the patient could not but be hurt by the sense of his wounds.

In regard to the relative advantages of cold and warm applications, Cælius speaks of those who endeavor to induce sleep by warm fomentations of poppy, thyme, roses, etc., and observes, in accordance with the view attributed by Cælius to Asclepiades, that the result is heaviness of the head, but not sleep—constriction being induced, when relaxation is required. He then refers to an opposite school who made use of cold applications, believing the disorder to be caused by heat; ignorant, he observes, that internal heat is an undoubted sign of congestion, and not, as they think, the cause of the disease. He condemns the hydropathic treatment as being calculated to increase congestion, and therefore to aggravate the patient's disorder. In regard to the important question of venesection in mania, Cælius comments upon the practice of those who employed excessive bleeding from both arms to the extent of syncope and even death, and observes that the abstraction of blood from both arms is not to be practiced in consequence of the fearful prostration of strength which may follow. Clysters he regarded as worse than useless, often inducing dysentery in consequence of the active ingredients which they contained. Among the many strange and opposite modes of treatment to which the insane have been subjected, intoxication was not overlooked. Some, our author observes, recommend intoxication, since madness is often caused by it; but without sufficient discrimination, since injudiciously used it may prove injurious. The pleasures of love, which were prescribed by Titus and Themison, were strongly condemned by Cælius, who regards as impious and absurd the attempt to indulge propensities which required restraint.

In the chapter which treats of melancholy, Cælius observes that the treatment is the same as has been already prescribed for the maniacal. He would not bleed, nor depress the patient by purging him with hellebore and aloes, but at once soothe and invigorate him by emollient and astringent applications. The celebrated Galen, of Pergamos, flourished at a period but little subsequent to Cælius Aurelianus. He is said to have died at the age of ninety, A. D. one hundred and ninety-three. His treatment was based upon the humoral pathology, which was in such high repute among the ancients, and which exercised an almost universal influence on their practice. He lays it down that, if moisture produces fatuity and dryness sagacity, just in proportion to the excess of moisture over dryness the sagacity will be diminished. Hence, he advises the practitioner to aim above all things at preserving a just medium between these opposite qualities. He recommends that "should you be of opinion that the whole of the patient's body may contain melancholy blood" you are to employ venesection, especially from the median cephalic vein. He adds, that should the blood flowing from it not appear to be of a melancholy quality, the vein must immediately be closed; and that should the contrary be the case, you are to abstract as much blood as the state of the patient and his habit of body shall permit. If, however, madness arise from idiopathic disease of the brain, bleeding is by all means to be avoided. In forming an opinion on this subject, regard was to be had to the patient's constitution and temperament. The fat, the fair, and the flabby were not to be supposed to possess any melancholy humor; but the lean, dark, and hairy, and those in whom the veins are large, are the most subject to its accumulation. He gives a long enumeration of the kinds of food which induce melancholy, as the flesh of oxen, goats, but especially asses and camels, and also wolves, dogs, hares, and snails. Among herbs, the cabbage only is mentioned. Thick and black wine was to be particularly avoided, "as from it the melancholy humor is made." This melancholy humor is spoken of by Galen as a condition of blood "thickened, and more like black bile which, indeed, exhaling to the brain, causes melancholy symptoms to affect the mind." We frequently also notice, he observes, that when yellow bile is contained in the stomach, the head is painfully affected; but it immediately recovers when the stomach is relieved from bile by vomiting. In mild cases of insanity Galen prescribed the bath and nourishing food.

IN THE MIDDLE AGES.

We have thus taken a hurried glance at the opinions of the ancients with regard to the pathology of this mysterious disease, and of the treatment employed by them for its cure or amelioration, and it is strange, indeed, that we hear but little more of it until about the period of the reformation. It is true that an asylum is said to have existed at Jerusalem about the fifth century, but little seems to be known of its character, history, or the modes of treatment employed. Again, at a period assigned by tradition, about eleven centuries ago, the tragic death of the Irish girl, the Princess Dymphna, who was slain by the hand of her own father, led to the establishment of a church and altar at Gheel, in Belgium, where those afflicted with "minds diseased" were carried to intercede with the spirit of the patron saint for relief; and a number of these unfortunate victims, more or less numerous, are supposed to have been kept there ever since; till now it has grown into one of the most remarkable institutions for the insane that anywhere exists.

The next asylum established, so far as we are able to ascertain, was that of "Reinier Van Arkel," at Bois le Duc, in Holland. It bears the name of its philanthropic founder, who established it in fourteen hundred and forty-two, for the care and custody of six unfortunate persons who had been deprived of their reason. From this small beginning, it has continued to increase, till it now has capacity for six hundred patients; but on the first of December, eighteen hundred and seventy, three hundred of its inmates were removed to a new asylum, just finished, a short distance from the city. At the time of our visit— seventh of July, eighteen hundred and seventy-one—there were one hundred and seventy men and one hundred and fifty-six women within its walls. The old asylum is immediately on one of the business streets of the city, and has been so often added to and enlarged that it can be said to possess no particular plan. It still retains many evidences of the age in which it was built, and shows more clearly than anything we have elsewhere seen, the wonderful and beneficent improvements that have been made in the character of the buildings for the treatment of the insane. Small dark cells, with high small windows, and cribs in which to *cage* the excited patients, may still be seen, and we regret to say have not yet been entirely abolished in this and one or two other asylums visited on the continent. The douche, solitary confinement, and confinement to the chair, are also used in some cases, not as a part of the treatment, but for punishment—showing how difficult it is even yet, in some countries, to shake off old habits and adopt new ideas in the treatment of the insane. The inquiring mind of the young and intelligent physician, Dr. Frijbank, will doubtless soon lead him to discard all of these old appliances, and to adopt the more humane and enlightened practice of the age in which he lives. Indeed, it is but just to say that he has already done so in most respects.

As another link in the history and treatment of this malady, the following extracts will show the condition of the insane in asylums in the eighteenth and nineteenth centuries:

IN ENGLAND.

"The reader of Cœlius Aurelianus cannot but feel astonished when he finds that nearly eighteen hundred years after that humane physician flourished it could be said in the House of Commons, by the Earl of Shaftesbury (then Lord Ashley), that the whole history of the world, until the era of the Reformation, does not afford an instance of a single receptacle assigned to the protection and care of these unhappy sufferers, whose malady was looked upon as hardly within the reach or hope of medical aid. If dangerous, they were incarcerated in the common prisons; if of a certain rank in society, they were shut up in their houses, under the care of appropriate guardians. Chains, whips, darkness, and solitude were the approved and only remedies.

"It is, indeed, to be feared that the directions of Celsus have exercised a most prejudicial influence, even till within a very recent period; and it is not difficult to recognize them in the writings of the classical Cullen, who did not omit to recommend the employment of 'stripes' in the treatment of the maniacal.

"The kind of treatment pursued by the highest medical men four hundred years ago is pretty clearly indicated by what has been handed down to us relative to the psychological history of King Henry VI, in whom mental disease was hereditary. Thus we are informed that five physicians and surgeons were appointed to attend the royal patient, and were empowered to administer 'electuaries, potions, and syrups, confections and laxative medicines, in any form that might be thought best; baths, fomentations, embrocations, unctions, plasters, shavings of the head, and scarifications.'

"It is not a little singular that Bethlem Hospital, which has become on various occasions so notorious for its ill treatment of the insane, should in the first instance have provided for their care with benevolent intentions, and under some favorable auspices. It was in the year fifteen hundred and forty-seven that Henry VIII took possession of the monastery or hospital of St. Mary of Bethlem, and presented it to the City of London, with an order that it should be converted into a house for the reception of lunatics. It was situated in Bishopsgate Ward, without the city wall, between Bishopsgate street and Moorfields. Stow describes it in his time as standing in an obscure and close place in the neighborhood of many common sewers, and as also too small to receive and entertain the great number of distracted persons, both men and women, who stood in need of it."

In consequence of the want of further provision for lunatics in London, a large building was erected in sixteen hundred and seventy-five in Moorfields, where the hospital stood until eighteen hundred and fourteen. There was, in a short time, accommodation for one hundred and fifty patients; whereas, in the old building, there were usually but fifty or sixty. In the rules made March thirtieth, sixteen hundred and seventy-seven, to which it is interesting to refer, it is ordered *inter alia*, that such of the lunatics as are fit should be permitted to walk in the yard until dinner time, and then be locked up in their cells; and that no lunatic that lies naked, or is in a course of physic, should be seen by anybody without an order of the physician. It is further humanely ordered that no officer or servant shall beat or abuse any lunatic, or employ any force to them, but upon absolute necessity for the better governing of them. Dr. Tyson, who was physician to Bethlem from sixteen hundred and eighty-four to seventeen hundred and three, informs us that, as to the care and cure of the patients, here is undoubtedly the greatest provision made for them of any public charity in the world; each having a convenient room and apartment to themselves, where they are locked up at night, and in it a place for a bed, or if they are so senseless as not to be fit to make use of one, they are every day provided with fresh, clean straw. Those that are fit for it, at convenient hours have liberty to walk in the long galleries, which are large and noble. For the Summer time, to air themselves, there are two large grass plats—one for the men, the other for the women; in the Winter, a stove for each apart, where a good fire is kept to warm them. In the hot weather, a very convenient bath place to cool and wash them; which is of great service in airing their lunacy, and is easily made a hot bath for restoring their limbs when numb, or cleaning and preserving them from scurvy, etc. Their diet is extraordinary good and proper for them, which every week is viewed by a committee of the Governors. * * * There is nothing of violence suffered to be offered to any patient, but they are treated with all the care and tenderness imaginable. If raving or furious, they are confined from doing themselves or others mischief; and it is to the credit of the hospital that in so great a number of lunatics that are constantly kept there, it is very rare, in many years, any one patient makes away with himself. * * * The time of cure is uncertain; some have been cured in a month, others in two or three, and some continue distracted many years." This was written early in the eighteenth century.*

In seventeen hundred and thirty-four, considerable additions were made to Bethlem, and, in consequence of its still proving inadequate to meet the demand, Saint Luke's Hospital was established in seventeen hundred and fifty-one, by voluntary subscription. It was situate on the north side of Upper Moorfields, in a locality called Windmill Hill.

From this period to the latter part of the eighteenth century but little progress was made in the treatment of the insane, and in the condition of the houses where they were received; indeed, as respects Bethlem it is probable that its state had retrogaded rather than advanced. In the middle of the century (seventeen hundred and fifty-five) a work was published the title of which appears significant, this was "Folly Predominant; with a Dissertation on the Impossibility of Curing Lunatics in Bedlam." From time to time during this period a work made its appearance on the subject of insanity. Thus, in seventeen hundred, Herwig published his "Art of Curing Sympathetically or Magnetically; with a Discourse on the Cure of Madness;" and, five years later Fallowes enlightened the world with his "Method of Curing Lunatics."

---

*In the General Regulation of Bethlem Hospital for 1792 we find the following orders: "No lunatic shall be put in chains without the instructions or approval of the apothecary. "The feet of the lunatics who are chained shall be carefully examined, well rubbed and covered with flannels every morning and evening through the Winter; and if any morbid symptoms require the presence of the surgeon, he shall at once be informed."—Sections 9 and 10.

Blakeway wrote in seventeen hundred and seventeen ("Essay toward the Cure of Religious Melancholy,") and Frings in seventeen hundred and forty-six (Treatise on Phrensy.) Batty wrote his treatise on madness in seventeen hundred and fifty-seven. But none of these works deserved or gained much reputation. Perfect, whose first work on the subject was written in seventeen hundred and seventy-eight, made some valuable contributions to the knowledge then possessed regarding insanity. His treatment appears to have consisted chiefly in venesection, emetics, setons, digitalis, antimony, and electricity. Dr. T. Arnold published the first edition of his excellent "Observations on the nature, kinds, etc., of Insanity," in seventeen hundred and eighty-two. This work, however, contains little or nothing in regard to treatment. A few years afterwards (seventeen hundred and eighty-nine), "A Treatise on the real cause and cure of Insanity," was published by Harper, which, although it possesses no merit, has, however, the honor of having been criticised by Pinel. In seventeen hundred and ninety appeared "Observations on the general and improper treatment of Insanity," by Faulkner; and the "Observations on Maniacal Disorders," by Pargeter, in seventeen hundred and ninety-two. But none of these writings appear to have exercised any material effect in ameliorating the condition of the insane in England. This, unfortunately, is but too correctly described in the following graphic sketch from the pen of Dr. W. A. F. Browne ("What Asylums were, are, and ought to be:") "Let us pass a few minutes," he says, "in an asylum as formerly regulated, and from the impression made by so brief a visit let us judge of the effects which years or a lifetime spent amid such gloomy scenes were calculated to produce. The building is gloomy, placed in some low confined situation, without windows to the front, every chink barred and grated—a perfect gaol. As you enter a creak of bolts and the clank of chains are scarcely distinguishable amid the wild chorus of shrieks and sobs which issue from every apartment. The passages are narrow, dark, damp, exhale a noxious effluvia, and are provided with a door at every two or three yards. Your conductor has the head and visage of a Carib; carries (fit accompaniment) a whip and a bunch of keys, and speaks in harsh monosyllables. The first common room you examine—measuring twelve feet long by seven wide, with a window which does not open—is perhaps for females. Ten of them, with no other covering than a rag round the waist, are chained to the wall, loathsome and hideous; but, when addressed, evidently retaining some of the intelligence and much of the feeling which in other days ennobled their nature. In shame or sorrow, one of them perhaps utters a cry; a blow, which brings the blood from the temple, the tear from the eye—an additional chain, a gag, and indecent or contemptuous expression—produce silence. And if you ask where these creatures sleep, you are led to a kennel eight feet square, with an unglazed airhole eight inches in diameter. In this, you are told, five women sleep. The floor is covered, the walls bedaubed with filth and excrement; no bedding but wet decayed straw is allowed, and the stench is so insupportable that you turn away and hasten from the scene."

"From the evidence given before the memorable committee of the House of Commons, in eighteen hundred and fifteen, notwithstanding the equivocation and evasion which marked many of the replies, it is not difficult to form an estimate of the condition of the English asylums generally, more especially the York Asylum and Bethlem Hospital. Nor was the condition in which they were found at that period alone revealed; their past condition was at the same time rendered manifest.

"A miserable and empirical routine marked the treatment. To the question: 'Has there not been a rule in the hospital for a certain number of years that, in certain months of the year, particular classes of the patients should be physicked, bled, bathed, and vomited at given periods?' the reply from Bethlem was in the affirmative. Twice in the year the patients, with few exceptions, were bled. 'After they have been bled,' said the physician, in evidence, 'they take vomits once a week, for a certain number of weeks; after that, we purge the patients. That has been the practice, invariably, for years—long before my time.'

"In regard to the means of coercion employed, it was stated that the patients 'are generally chained to the wall with manacles.' When inquiry was made regarding the use of strait waistcoats, it was replied, 'I do not believe there are any strait waistcoats in Bethlem now, or very few indeed; they generally use irons.' The objection to strait waistcoats was that the patients 'could not help themselves in strait waistcoats; they are so exceedingly long in the hospital without being seen by anybody, in a dark place; in Winter, from four o'clock to six or seven in the morning. If they were in a strait waistcoat they could not assist themselves the least in the world.' When, in the following year, the head keeper of Bethlem Hospital was asked : 'Was it not the practice in old Bethlem—not in the late gallery, but in the gallery pulled down—for eight, ten, or more patients to be fastened to the tables, almost in a state of perfect nakedness?' he replied: 'Yes; they used to think they tore their clothes all to pieces; some of them would do that.' 'In point of fact, were they not fastened to the tables, sitting in a state of perfect nudity?' Answer—'They used to be so at the table; they were chained all around.'"

With these records of the barbarity and cruelty practiced in the asylums of England, and so forcibly described in the able work of Bucknill & Tuke, from which they have been quoted, we need not be surprised at their having been made the basis of a sensational novel by Charles Read, even after they had ceased to exist, nor that the prejudices against these institutions should still hold a place in the minds of the people everywhere.

THEIR CONDITION IN FRANCE.

Esquirol says of the insane in France: "I have seen them naked or covered with rags; with nothing but a layer of straw to protect them from the cold dampness of the ground upon which they lay. They were kept upon food of the coarsest kind; they were deprived of fresh air to breathe, and of water to quench their thirst, and even of the most necessary things of life. I have seen them given up to the brutal supervision of jailors. I have seen them in their narrow cells, filthy and unwholesome, without air or light, chained in such dens as one might fear to confine ferocious beasts." "Similar to these were the abodes of the insane throughout Europe."

IN ROME AND LIMERICK.

"In Rome iron rings, armed with chains, and fixed in the wall, serve to confine the furious and turbulent maniacs, who are fastened by their necks and feet." "In one room were two rings fixed to the wall; one ring was to embrace the neck, the other the ankle, and the poor maniac was doomed to stand or suspend himself by the neck." "The accommodations in the asylum at Limerick appear to be such as we should not appropriate for our dog kennels." "One victim was confined in one of the oblong troughs, chained down. He had evidently not been in open air for a considerable time, for when I made them bring him out he could not endure the light. Upon asking him how often he had been allowed to get out of the trough, he said: 'Perhaps once a week, and sometimes not for a fortnight.' He was not in the least violent; he was perfectly calm."[*]

IN THE GERMANIC CONFEDERATION.

In eighteen hundred and forty-five the Journal Psychiatrie and Psychological Medicine was established, with Doctor Damerow, of the institution in Halle, as its principal editor, and Doctors Flemming and Roller—the latter of the Illenaw Asylum—as associates. Although printed at Halle, as a matter of convenience to Doctor Damerow, it is published at Berlin. If an opinion may be formed from the vigor with which it has been conducted, as well as the long list of collaborators—men distinguished as physicians of the insane or for their knowledge of psychical medicine and the jurisprudence of insanity, not in Germany alone, but in Denmark, Holland, and Switzerland—it will not lack for material, and is established upon a permanent basis. Its editor in chief is one of the most prominent advocates of the doctrines of the Psycho-Somatic school, but both his associates are Somatics. Among its collaborators are found all the gradations of theory from the somatic to the psychic.

Since the death of Heinroth, Dr. Ideler, of Berlin, is the acknowledged leader of the psychic school. But as time has progressed the conflict of opinion has measureably subsided. The attention of physicians has been diverted from the comparatively barren field of hypothetical controversy to the more useful domain of practical science, the improvement of hospitals, and the treatment of their inmates.

From the foregoing historical sketch, chiefly of the literature of insanity, it may be justly inferred that little, if anything, was done during the last century for the improvement of the receptacles for the insane in Germany. The initiative, however, was taken even in the few writings which were published, as these were the preliminary steps which led to more important practical action. The asylum at Vienna, but of late years not very favorably known as the Narrenthurm, was completed and opened in seventeen hundred and eighty-four, and was at that period the best establishment of the kind, as it was the only one exclusively devoted to the insane, throughout the German nations. As the eighteenth century was departing, Heinroth, having finished his studies at Paris, carried the principles of his illustrious preceptor within the German borders, and thus added a new and important element to the cause of improvement. An idea of the condition of the German asylums at the commencement of the present century may be derived from the language of one of their native authors, Reil, who, in his "Rhapsodies upon the application of the Psychical Curative Treatment in Mental Disorders," published in eighteen hundred and three, wrote as follows: "They are mad-houses, not merely by reason of their inmates, but more especially because they are the very opposite of what they were intended to be. They are neither curative institutions nor such asylums for the

---

[*] Browne's Lectures, Edinburgh, 1837.

incurable as humanity can tolerate; they are for the most veritable dens. Has man so little respect for the jewel which makes him man, or so little love for his neighbor who has lost that treasure, that he cannot extend to him the hand of assistance and aid him in regaining it? Some of these receptacle are attached to hospitals, others to prisons and houses of correction; but all are deficient in ventilation, in the facilities for recreation; in short, they are wanting in all the physical and moral means necessary to the cure of their patients."*

OBSERVATIONS UPON FOREGOING SUBJECTS.

The foregoing extracts from various well known authorities have been made not only to show the condition of the insane, the character of the establishments in which they were kept, and the methods of treatment adopted and pursued in such cases by the most learned and eminent men in the several countries under consideration, but also to direct attention to the fact that though sundry efforts had been made by men of learning and ability to establish journals of mental science in Germany during the latter part of the eighteenth and early part of the nineteenth centuries, they all signally failed, not from lack of ability on the part of those who edited and conducted them, but for want of support by the public. The first of these magazines was commenced in seventeen hundred and eighty-three, but lived only a short time. The next periodical devoted exclusively to the subject of insanity was established by Doctor Reil, and published at Halle, in Prussian Saxony, in the year eighteen hundred and five, the philosopher Kayssler having contributed largely to its pages. It, too, soon shared the fate of its predecessor, and died for the want of appreciation and support, too little interest as yet being felt in a class of persons supposed to be possessed by devils. In eighteen hundred and eighteen Nasse made another effort, and commenced his Journal of Psychological Medicine, and being conducted with great ability and unusual zeal, awakened a more lively interest in the subject and its unfortunate victims. But the time for success had not yet arrived, and after a desperate struggle for eight years it, too, went down to join the list of the departed. Still another journal was started in eighteen hundred and twenty-nine; and yet another, by Doctors Jacobie and Flemming, in eighteen hundred and thirty-eight, but all with similar results. Many valuable essays and books have in the mean time been given to the world by various German writers; but it was not till eighteen hundred and forty-five, as already stated, that a journal was established, with Damerow of Halle as its head, and Flemming and Roller—the latter still at Illenaw—as assistants, that a psychological journal has been able to stem the current and stand the test of time.

Since that time many able writers have appeared upon the field of psychological medicine and made valuable contributions to science. Among these, none stood higher either at home or abroad than the lamented Griesinger, who has left behind him in his works a monument more grand, beautiful and enduring than any that could be erected of marble or bronze.

It is also worthy of notice that there was but one public asylum in all

---

*Institutions for the Insane in Germany, by Pliny Earle, M. D.

Germany in seventeen hundred and eighty-four*—the "Norrenthurm" at Vienna—while at the present time, as will be seen in the list of asylums. in the German Confederation,† there are ninety-two public and forty-nine private institutions devoted to the care and maintenance of this hitherto neglected class of human beings. And although most of these do not come up to our ideas of first class asylums, as viewed from an American or English standpoint; nevertheless, some of them are well built, conveniently arranged and ably conducted, and would be a credit to any country. Indeed, it may be said that very nearly all of those established within the last twenty years are of this class.

CRUEL TREATMENT THE RESULT OF IGNORANCE.

It would appear strange indeed, and, if we did not know to the contrary, absolutely incredible, that such cruelties, such barbarous practices as have been noticed in the foregoing pages could have been tolerated for so long a time among the refined, intelligent, and highly civilized people of Europe without a single effort—previous to the French revolution—on the part of humanity to relieve the distresses of this class of their fellow creatures. Ignorance, in law, is no excuse, and yet ignorance is the only excuse that mankind can offer for the neglect of these wretched creatures. They were regarded during these long centuries as being possessed of devils, as enemies of society, and as doomed forever, so soon as they were known to be madmen. Even yet this idea has not been eradicated from the minds of some people, while many still believe the disease to be incurable from the beginning, and its accession a disgrace to the unfortunate victim and his family. It is high time for the people to lay aside these false notions, and accept the fact that insanity is simply the effect of a diseased brain, and that all persons are liable to its invasion.

NEW YORK POORHOUSES.

But let us look into this matter at home, and see if we cannot find that these abuses and cruel practices, unfortunately, have not been confined to English and continental institutions. The following extracts will show their condition in the poorhouses of New York at a comparatively recent period. In eighteen hundred and fifty-seven a committee, consisting of Mark Spencer, George Bradford, and M. Lindley Lee, reported the results of inquiries and examinations made the Summer before. The following sentence is from that report:

"The poorhouses throughout the State may be generally described as badly constructed, ill arranged, ill warmed, and ill ventilated. The rooms are crowded with inmates, and the air, particularly in the sleeping apartments, is very noxious, and to casual visitors, almost insufferable."

In eighteen hundred and sixty-five a Committee of which Dr. Sylvester D. Willard was Chairman made a report, from which we extract the following:

---

*Note.—The Alexianer Convent at Aix-la-Chappelle has been a receptacle for the insane for five hundred years; and the "Bloekdick" (private asylum), near Bremen, was established in 1750, and rebuilt in 1839.

†See Appendix B.

"It is not without a confession of pain and humiliation that the Commissioners announce the deplorable condition of the insane poor; the 'notorious and sickening abuses' which they found in many of the public establishments known as County Poorhouses. With unquestionable truth they affirm that 'the State has shifted off from itself upon the counties a duty which it ought ever to have recognized as imperative and sacred.' Nearly every county house was visited. As the record of particular instances is more convincing and more affecting than general statements and summary conclusions, a few facts are condensed from the report, the selection being made from counties in the Hudson River hospital district. Let us look first at Albany. Here, under the shadow of the State Capitol, were seventy-six insane persons shut up in thirty-one rooms, each of which was intended and is only large enough for one. A number of these rooms had three occupants in each; the ventilation in some of them was very imperfect. Notwithstanding the deficient accommodations, rendering all classification impossible, recent cases are frequently received and held for treatment, with what probability of improvement under such conditions can easily be seen. The insane poor of Duchess County are bestowed in eighteen cells constructed in prison style, with heavily grated doors and barred windows; board partitions separate these cells, and wooden bunks serve for bedsteads; for want of proper appliances the cells cannot be made comfortable in cold weather; two of the men were loaded with chains. For her insane Richmond County has provided four dark cells. One poor creature has spent fourteen years in a small outhouse—a cripple, bent nearly double—and without a rag of clothing! The poorhouse in Saratoga County is nearly fifty years old; the floors and walls of this venerable structure are much broken, and the roof leaks. Though not far from the Ballston Springs, the water is scarce there. The cells of the insane measure seven and a quarter by six and a quarter feet, and each contains a wooden bunk, and nothing else; these cells get all their light and air through gratings in the doors; in these dungeons individuals have been confined for ten and even for eighteen successive years, never going outside, except during the short annual visits of the Board of Supervisors. In one case there had been an illegitimate birth, under circumstances most distressing and revolting. Warren County is thus described: 'Insane filthy in their persons, and stench from the place intolerable. Four cells in the building, all unfit for use. Rats the only scavengers. No medical attendance. Building entirely unsuited to the purpose.'"

Very little is said in praise of Franklin, Essex, Washington, Greene, Putnam, Sullivan, Westchester, and Queens Counties. At the time of the inspection the number of insane persons who were shut up in cells or secured by chains was two hundred and thirteen. In view of the whole picture the Commissioners might well exclaim: "Will the people of New York, when they comprehend the inhuman treatment which the insane poor sometimes receive, leave a system in unchecked operation which admits of such enormities?"

We are rejoiced to say that the people of New York have comprehended this subject, and have nobly responded to this question in a manner not to be mistaken, and with a generosity worthy of that great State. Her legislators, advised and encouraged by her wise executive officers, have made appropriations, provided lands, selected sites, and ordered the erection of asylums for the proper care and treatment of *every insane person within her borders.*

AMELIORATION IN THE TREATMENT OF THE INSANE AS COMPARED WITH
FORMER PERIODS.

Let us call attention for a moment to some of the causes that led to
an amelioration of the condition of the insane, both in England and on
the continent, and to some of the men who were conspicuous in directing
public opinion in so important a matter, and instrumental in carrying out
the humane doctrines they proclaimed. A brief review of the life and
writings of Dr. Conolly appeared in the American Journal of Insanity
for April, eighteen hundred and seventy; a few extracts from which will
subserve the purposes we have in view:

Former Coercive Treatment.

Few of us in America know, except from history or from travel on
the continent, the extent to which mechanical restraints were used in
Great Britain previous to eighteen hundred and forty, and are now in
the other European countries.

Dr. Conolly found on taking charge of the Asylum at Hanwells—
eighteen hundred and thirty-nine—each ward provided with a closet full
of restraining apparatus, and every attendant used them at will. Many
patients were always in restraint. Six new restraining chairs had been
recently added to the stock, making forty-nine in all (pp. 53, 54). The
instruments of mechanical restraint were so abundant as to amount,
when collected together, to about six hundred; half of them handcuffs
and leg locks (pp. 18, 20).

This may be assumed as a specimen of the provision in the asylums of
Great Britain and Europe at that time, and these means nearly represented the ideas of the people at large, the governors or magistrates
who had the outer superintendence of these establishments, and the
physicians who had them under their immediate charge.

Pinel.

Although Pinel had wrought what was deemed almost miracles in setting the manacled maniacs free without evil consequences to those who
were in contact with them, yet few had dared to follow him, and the
lunatic remained in great measure as he was before. The world still
clung to the faith of olden time—that the insane were the devil's possessions, and those thus possessed should be, if not punished, at least
restrained, to prevent injury to the fearful community.

Treatment in Middle Ages.

Nevertheless, there had been a wonderful improvement upon the cruel
customs of the barbarous ages. In those dark periods the religious
houses were in some sort used as hospitals, and some of them took care
of the insane. At one of these establishments of the Franciscans, who
believed in and practiced on themselves the severest mortifications and
self-chastening, the same rule was applied to their patients, and they
gave each lunatic ten lashes a day. In another each patient was bled
every June. Stripes, however, were but one form of cruelty, and the
slightest of the kind. In the old asylums all the most terrible engines
of torture, to carry out the theory of punishment, were resorted to.
The inventions to give pain were marvelous. There were chairs of

restraint in which the patient could not move limb or body, and whirling chairs, in which the unfortunate lunatic was whirled at the rate of one hundred gyrations a minute (p. 47).

These and other practices equally cruel were continued in Germany as late as seventeen hundred and ninety. In some asylums the patients were kept in a state of partial famine, chained, covered with dirt and filth, but half clothed, and their insufficient clothing seldom changed; cages of iron were in use, in which some of the lunatics were kept for years. These miseries were inflicted, not from carelessness, but from what was believed to be real humanity (p. 48).

In an earlier age, some iron cages were made sufficiently large to hold one or more patients. These were movable and suspended by chains over water, in tanks or pools, with the patients standing in them; they were let down into the water, until it reached their chins or mouths, leaving them only a breathing place. There they were kept as long as they could endure the position and the bath. This was an established part of the treatment or punishment. The worst of these practices had passed away before the time of Pinel and his followers.

York Asylum.

Among the bad, the York Asylum was the worst. A female member of the Society of Friends being placed as a patient in this institution in seventeen hundred and ninety-one, died under suspicious circumstances. They immediately determined to establish an asylum under their own control, in which there should be no secrecy. William Tuke was the great founder of this new hospital, and from the first he and his associates pursued those principles in its management that Pinel was then proposing, and which have now become the established rule of practice in Great Britain and the United States. They did not abolish all restraints, yet they began this work, retaining only those of the milder kind.

Lincoln Asylum.

Dr. Charlesworth, in the Lincolnshire Asylum, in eighteen hundred and twenty-one, began his experiments of substituting the milder for the severe restraints. He persevered in this great work year after year, regardless of opposition and undaunted by difficulties, and at length arrived at the total abolition, which he found both a practicable and a more comfortable and successful method of controlling the patient. Mr. Gardner Hill was also engaged in the same work, with the same result.

Dr. Conolly at Hanwell.

Still chains, handcuffs, and leg blocks were in general use in the asylums of Great Britain and the continental nations when Doctor Conolly entered the Hanwell Asylum, as Resident Physician, on the first of June, eighteen hundred and thirty-nine. He was familiar with the writings and practices of Pinel, Charlesworth, and Hill. He had confidence in the success of these measures and in their applicability to any other hospital. At once he determined to try the experiment on the patients at Hanwell.

He began his work June first. There were then over forty under mechanical restraint. Immediately he commenced removing the shackles, fetters, etc., from those who were the most promising, or who suffered most, and proceeded gradually until the whole were removed in less than four months. In his work on the treatment of the insane he quotes from the asylum records:

"After the first of July, when I required a daily return to be made to me of the number of patients restrained, there were never more than eighteen so treated in one day. After the thirty-first of July the number never exceeded eight; after the twelfth of August it never exceeded one, and after the twentieth of September no restraints at all were employed."

On the thirty-first of October, in his first report to the Quarter Sessions, he said: "Since the twenty-first of September not one patient has been under restraint. No form of straight waistcoat, no handcuffs, no leg locks, nor any contrivance confining the trunk or limbs, or any of the muscles, is now in use. The coercion chairs, about forty in number, have been altogether removed from the wards" (p. 20).

In his eleventh and last report he says: "For ten years no hand or foot has been fastened in this large asylum, by day or night, for the control of the violent or the despairing; no instrument of mechanical restraint has been employed, or even admitted into the wards, for any reason whatever; no patient has been placed in a coercive chair by day or fastened to a bedstead by night. Every patient, however excited or apparently unmanageable, arriving at the asylum in restraints has been immediately set free, and remained so from that time. The results, more and more seen in every successive year, have been increased tranquility, diminished danger, and so salutary an influence over the recent and newly admitted and most recent cases, as to make the spectacle of the more terrible forms of mania and melancholia a rare exception to the general order and cheerfulness of the establishment" (p. 33).

Effect of Removal of Restraints.

The effect of this removal of restraints was at once noticed in the general tone of the whole hospital. The excited were sooner calmed, the irritable less easily disturbed, and a general quiescence prevailed more than before. The wards were managed with less difficulty. The new system tended to remove, as far as possible, all causes of excitement from the irritable, to soothe, encourage, and comfort the depressed, to repress the violent by methods that leave no ill effect on the temper, no painful recollections in the memory, and in all cases seize every opportunity of promoting a restoration of the healthy exercise of the understanding and the affections (p. 27.) Mania not exasperated by severity, and melancholia not deepened by want of ordinary consolations, lose the exaggerated character in which they were formerly beheld. Hope takes the place of fear, serenity is substituted for discontent, and the mind is left in a condition favorable to every impression likely to call forth salutary efforts (p. 28.)

Effect of Dr. Conolly's Method on other Physicians.

Many physicians, managers of other institutions in Britain, visited Dr. Conolly, and a few from the continent. These became converts to his views and strong friends of his plans. One asylum after another followed him, until, before many years, non-restraint seemed to be the universally accepted doctrine of the whole psychological profession in England and Scotland.

Proof of the Advantage of Moral Treatment.

As proof of the advantage of moral over mechanical means of treatment, Dr. Broadhurst points to "the general quietness and decorum of his establishment, the cheerful aspect of the patients, the comparative freedom from acts of destructive violence, the large proportion constantly engaged in useful occupation, a decreased mortality, and an increased percentage of cures." (p. 78.)

Mr. Wilkes, formerly Superintendent of the Stratford Asylum, now Commissioner of Lunacy, writes: "The effect of the change upon the old inmates was in marked degree beneficial."

The excitement of the patients generally diminished. They were less noisy and restless at night; destructive propensities and objectionable habits were, in many instances, overcome. With greater opportunities of doing mischief, less occurred. And now, without a window in any way protected, and a much larger number of patients, there is probably less breakage of glass than there ever was. (p. 79.)

Reputation of Dr. Conolly.

He was very much consulted in the cases of the greatest importance, and was considered the chief authority in all matters of doubt. Ever affable and courteous, he drew many to his house from his own country and from abroad, and alienists from the continent and from America found and enjoyed the most cordial hospitality. Several of the psychological physicians of the greatest power on the continent were among his visitors and became the strongest friends of his doctrine of non-restraint. Among these were Doctor Griesinger, of Berlin; Baron Mundy and Meyer, of Germany; Morel, of France; and Guislain, of Belgium.

They used their utmost exertion to introduce the practice into their several countries, but, except in the institutions within their immediate influence, they made but few converts; and Continental Europe was yet to accept the new method and to unchain its lunatics.

Doctor Conolly's opinions in regard to the Management of the Insane.

In the management of the insane he considered the provision of large establishments, however desirable as a matter of economy, was at the cost of some of the remedial powers of the institution and of the chances of restoration of the patients, and that the proper conduct of lunatic asylums requires the whole power of mind and heart that belong to the superintending physician; and that whenever the governors or directors of each institution require their medical officers to leave their high vocation and sacred responsibility of watching mental disorders and guiding mental weakness, and give their time and thought to the subordinate matter of finance and stewardship, to collect bills, and watch the market, they take from the suffering patients a part of that influence upon which their best hope of recovery is founded.

Such were the life and character of Doctor Conolly, and such were his works, as described by his friend Sir James Clark, and as known, in part, to most of us. Few men have fulfilled a nobler destiny; few will be remembered with more affection and gratitude.

Restraint and Seclusion.

The use of mechanical means of restraint and the protracted seclusion of patients in their rooms—although the former of them may be, and as I believe is, occasionally desirable but not absolutely necessary in the management of our hospitals for the insane—ought both always to be regarded as evils of no trifling magnitude, and to abate which, as far as possible, no effort should be left untried. They both tend to produce a relaxation of vigilance, and it cannot be too often repeated that whatever tends to make vigilance unnecessary is undesirable about a hospital for the insane. Besides leading patients into bad habits, the frequent use of the means referred to in a ward induces attendants and others to look upon them as a common recourse in cases of difficulty or danger, to regard them as their grand reliance in every emergency, and to forget the great power of other measures that are entirely unobjectionable—the value of tact and kindness and sympathy in controlling the violence and dangerous propensities of the insane. And yet, without a proper force of attendants and an efficient classification the use of mechanical means of restraint and the protracted seclusion of certain classes of patients is almost unavoidable.

Objectionable as I deem the use of restraining apparatus in a hospital for the insane, it cannot be too earnestly insisted on that it is no advance to give up mechanical means of restraint and to substitute the frequent and long continued seclusion of the patients. Occasionally an individual may really be more comfortable and much better off in the open air, with some mild kind of restraining apparatus on his person, than he would be confined to his room without it; for this kind of long continued seclusion is pretty sure, sooner or later, to lead to habits revolting in themselves and most unfortunate for the future prospects of the patient.

The subject is introduced here as a reason why no false notions of economy should be permitted to influence any Board of Trustees to ask the Superintendent of an institution to attempt its management with a force so inadequate as to compel him, against his better judgment, to resort to means so objectionable, and which are so destructive to the comfort and proper treatment of his patients.

Labor, Outdoor Exercise, and Amusements.

Having referred to the unfavorable results of an habitual use of restraint and seclusion in a hospital for the insane, it is proper to indicate in more detail some of the means by which those unfortunate effects may be obviated.

A properly constructed building, admitting of a liberal classification of the patients, and the employment of an adequate number of intelligent and kind assistants, is indispensable for such an object. The design in establishing every such institution being the restoration and comfort of the afflicted, the relief of their families, and the protection of the community, there can be no question but that it is sound economy to provide everything that will effect these objects promptly and in the most thorough manner.

Without adequate provision for outdoor exercise and occupation for the patients, and a liberal supply of means of amusement, the excitement of the wards and the violent and mischievous propensities of their inmates will be apt to be such as to require modes of management that might otherwise be easily dispensed with. The first cost of some of these arrangements will necessarily be considerable, but the ultimate results can hardly fail to be so gratifying as to satisfy the most rigid stickler for economy that the only wise course is to provide liberally of everything likely to be beneficial to the patients.

The farm and garden offer admirable means of useful occupation to the insane at certain periods of the disease; for, useful as they are to a large number, no greater indiscretion could be committed than attempting to set all insane men at work in every stage of their malady.

To those accustomed to such pursuits, as well as to many who have been differently occupied, regular, moderate labor in the open fields or in the garden contributes most essentially to their comfort and tends to promote their recovery. Labor, then, is one of our best remedies; it is as useful in improving the health of the insane as in maintaining that of the sane. It is one of the best anodynes for the nervous; it composes the restless and excited; promotes a good appetite and a comfortable digestion, and gives sound and refreshing sleep to many who would without it pass wakeful nights.

The provision of adequate and comfortable workshops, in a convenient position and under the care of competent superintendents, may be made a source of profit to an institution, and furnish another means of labor of an interesting kind to a large number of the insane.

The usual means of amusement, which demand active muscular exercise, should not be neglected. A gymnasium, suitable in its fitting up for insane men, and a calistheneum for insane women, will be found useful. The various games of ball; the exercise of using a car on a circular railroad; the care of domestic animals, as well as regular walks on the grounds or in the neighborhood, are also among the kinds of exercise that will be enjoyed by many patients; while means of carriage riding seem almost indispensable for many, who from physical and other causes cannot resort to the more active forms which have already been referred to.

Within doors the means of keeping a comfortable house are, in addition to the medical treatment, the constant presence among the patients of intelligent attendants, active supervisors, and judicious teachers or companions, always ready to check the commencement of excitement, to separate quarrelsome individuals, and to change the train of thought of those who seem disposed to be troublesome. The means to effect the objects in view are very numerous, and the tact of an individual is shown in selecting those that are most applicable to a case.

The introduction of regular courses of lectures, interesting exhibitions of various kinds, and musical entertainments in the lecture rooms of our hospitals for the insane, has done much to break up the monotony of hospital life, which is so common a source of complaint among the insane.

Regular courses of instruction in well furnished school rooms, reading aloud by the teachers to the patients of the more excited wards, the use of well selected libraries, the inspection of collections of curiosities, the use of musical instruments and various games, are all among the many means which an ingenious Superintendent will suggest for the benefit and amusement of his patients, and which ought to be provided for in every institution for the insane.

In most of the asylums in the United States the dance is either added to this list or substituted instead of some of its items. It is a favorite amusement among the patients wherever it is allowed; and we have been informed by some of the Superintendents that patients will often control themselves for a whole week with a promise that they may be allowed the privilege of going to the next dance.

CHAPTER IX.

INSANE ASYLUMS, LOCATION, SIZE, SITES, ETC.

Location—Influence that Distance ought to have on Location—Effect of Multiplying Hospitals—Effects of Railroads and other Facilities of Travel—Hospitals Better Known to Neighboring People—Observations on Foregoing Topics—New York State Lunatic Asylums—General Suggestions—Propositions relative to the Structure and Arrangements for American Institutions for the Insane—English Lunacy Commissioners on Sites, Construction, Size, etc.—Suggestions of the Scotch Board—Size of Hospitals—Quantity of Land Necessary—Comments upon Kirkbride's Views.

LOCATION.

The location of an asylum has, perhaps, as great an influence over its usefulness as any other matter connected with its establishment, and those to whom this important trust may be delegated, here or elsewhere, cannot be too careful with the selection they may make. There are certain general rules that should *never* be overlooked nor disregarded by them, as on their action may depend, in a great degree, the success of the asylum to be established at the present time, as well as those that must, in the progress of events, come after it.

The admissions in our Asylum during the last ten years was an average of three hundred and fifty-eight each year, and the average annual increase has been sixty-seven. If we take a shorter period, these numbers will be augmented. We see by the report of Dr. Shurtleff, that "for the past five years the annual admissions have averaged about four hundred and fifty, and the net increase has been about eighty." With the increasing population, we may estimate with certainty that no decrease in these numbers will take place, if indeed, in the providence of God, and the better habits of the people, it be permitted to remain at these figures. This proportion of increase would give us eight hundred additional insane persons in the next ten years. But let us suppose that insanity will continue in its present ratio to the population, or one to four hundred and eighty-nine inhabitants, and that the population increases no more in the next decade than during the last, and it will be seen that more than eight hundred will be added to the regiment of insane men and women already in our Asylum at Stockton. It therefore behooves us, in any present provision we may make to meet the pressing necessities of immediate demands, to look wisely to the future, and so shape our action that it may have its proper bearing on similar provision to be made at some subsequent and not distant time to come.

INFLUENCE THAT DISTANCE OUGHT TO HAVE ON LOCATION.

That the importance of locating an asylum in convenient proximity to the greatest number who will be likely to require its use may be thoroughly understood and appreciated, we have made the following extracts from a Treatise on the Influence of Distance from and Nearness to an Insane Hospital on its Use by the People, prepared for the State of New York, by Edward Jarvis, M. D.:

"An insane hospital is, and must be to a certain extent, a local institution. People will avail themselves of its privileges in some proportion to their nearness to it. No liberality of admission, no excellence of its management, no power of reputation can entirely overcome the obstacle of distance, expense, and of the difficulties of transporting lunatics, or the objection of friends to sending their insane patients far from home, and out of the reach of ready communication.

"The operation of this principle, in some degree, seems probable to any one who gives a thought to the matter; but the facts, the particular history of those institutions in which the records of the homes of their patients are kept, show that the objection of distance prevails with all of them, and that those hospitals have been and are used by those who live near by much more than by those who live farther off; and consequently they are practically much more local in their usefulness than they are intended or are supposed to be.

"The State Hospital at Utica was opened in eighteen hundred and forty-three, and offered to the people of every county, both near and remote, on the same conditions. The people of Oneida, Schoharie, Orange, Washington, and Chautauqua, were alike invited to send their insane on the same terms. Between them there was and could be no difference of advantage after their patients should be placed in the hospital; the only difference was in the distance between their homes and the institution, in the labor, cost, and burden of traveling to a hospital with a lunatic. To make this matter more certain and to show the difference of enjoyment to the eye, the whole State has been divided into four districts, according to their distance from the hospital.

"The First District is Oneida County, in which the hospital is situated.

"The Second District consists of eleven counties: Chenango, Cortland, Fulton, Herkimer, Lewis, Madison, Montgomery, Onondagua, Oswego, Otago, Schoharie. These are mostly within sixty miles of Utica.

"The Third District includes seventeen counties, which are from sixty to one hundred and twenty miles distant: Albany, Broome, Cayuga, Columbia, Delaware, Greene, Hamilton, Jefferson, Rensselaer, Saratoga, Schenectady, Seneca, Tioga, Tompkins, Warren, Washington, Wayne.

"The Fourth District includes the most distant counties, which are from one hundred and twenty to three hundred and fifty miles from Utica : Allegheny, Cattaraugus, Chautauqua, Chemung, Clinton, Dutchess, Erie, Essex, Franklin, Genesee, Livingston, Monroe, Niagara, Ontario, Orange, Orleans, Putnam, Queen, Richmond, Rockland, Schuyler, Steuben, St. Lawrence, Suffolk, Sullivan, Ulster, Westchester, Wyoming, Yates.

"These four districts include all the counties of the State, except New York and Kings, which have each hospitals of their own, and therefore little or no occasion or inducement to send patients to Utica.

"The population of each of these districts has been ascertained and calculated for each of the twenty-three years, eighteen hundred and forty-three to eighteen hundred and sixty-five inclusive, since the hospital was opened. The number of patients sent to the hospital from each district within that period has also been ascertained.

"Taking, then, the sum of the annual populations for twenty-three years, and dividing it by the number of patients sent in that time, shows the proportion of patients which each district has sent out of its whole number of people. These numbers and facts are presented in the following statement:

"For these twenty-three years—eighteen hundred and forty-three to eighteen hundred and sixty-five—Oneida County sent one in two thousand seven hundred and seventy-two of their number to the hospital. The Second District sent one in five thousand eight hundred and twenty of their number to the hospital; the Third District sent one in seven thousand three hundred and fifty-one of their number to the hospital; the Fourth District sent one in eleven thousand five hundred and thirty-five of their number to the hsopital.

POPULATION AND PATIENTS OF DISTRICTS.

SUMMARY.	Districts.			
	I.	II.	III.	IV.
Sum of the annual population for twenty-three years	2,292,643	10,528,406	16,337,520	28,146,477
Patients sent to the hospital in twenty-three years	827	1,809	2,222	2,440
Average annual population	99,680	457,756	710,327	1,223,760
Average patients sent to the hospital	36	78	96	106
Population to one patient sent to the hospital in each year	2,772	5,820	7,351	11,535

"This shows a great disproportion in the uses made of the hospital by the people of the near and of the remote counties.

"Taking a basis of one thousand for the extent of the enjoyment of the hospital by the remotest districts, the proportionate enjoyment of the districts will be: Fourth, one thousand; Third, one thousand five hundred and sixty-eight; Second, one thousand nine hundred and eighty-one; First, four thousand one hundred and ninety-six.

"The advantages of the hospital enjoyed by Oneida County have been more than double those enjoyed by the counties next beyond, but within sixty miles; they are nearly threefold those enjoyed by the counties which are from sixty to one hundred and twenty miles distant; and more than four times as great as those enjoyed by the people of the counties which are more than one hundred and twenty miles distant.

"It will not be supposed that the insane persons who needed the hospital care or treatment in these districts were in these proportions. It cannot be supposed that the number of lunatics in Oneida County is twice as great as that in Oswego; Fulton, Schoharie, Herkimer, and the counties beyond Oneida, but within sixty miles; or four times as great as that in counties one hundred and twenty and more miles from this district.

"The State censuses of eighteen hundred and fifty-five and eighteen hundred and sixty-five show the number of the insane in the several counties of New York. Arranging these in the districts herein described, according to their distance from Utica, they were in proportion to the population:

POPULATION TO ONE LUNATIC IN NEW YORK.

DISTRICT.	1855.	1865.
First	1,224	1,300
Second	1,525	1,611
Third	1,457	1,396
Fourth	1,788	1,904

"This diversity of advantage of an insane hospital enjoyed by the people of near and remote districts is not an accident, nor a peculiarity of New York alone. It is a general and probably universal principle—a natural and necessary law of nature or humanity; for in all other States whose hospital records of patients' residence have been obtained, the same law is found to be in operation, and the people send their patients to these institutions in proportion to their nearness.

"In twenty-six States, for various periods of years, insane hospitals have been in operation, whose doors are and have been open alike to all of their people. The reports of most of these institutions state the number which have been sent to them from each county. From the others, copies of the records of facts have been obtained, showing the number which the various parts of the States have contributed to fill the wards of these institutions. In order to determine the extent and application of the law of distance in the use of hospitals, these other States and two of the British Provinces have been examined and analyzed in the same way as New York.

"They have been divided into concentric districts, making the county in which the hospital is situated the first, and the contiguous counties the second district, and the others more distant. The populations of these several districts have been calculated and determined for each of the years in which the hospital has been in operation, or in which the records of the residence of the patients were kept and have been obtained, and the comparison made of the proportion of patients to population of the several districts.

"It should be here stated that, in making these concentric circular divisions, it has been impossible to make them perfectly regular, with an exactly equal radius from the common centre, or equal distance of the inner and outer boundary from the hospital, for the counties are very diversely and irregularly shaped, some of them, as in Maine, being nearly one hundred and fifty miles long. While, then, a district may be stated to be within certain specified distances from the hospital, circles drawn upon the radii would, on both sides, exclude some part of the territory that belongs to it, and include some that belongs to its neighbor. Nevertheless, these irregularities of border or exceptions to the rule will not militate with the general plan nor vitiate any calculations made upon or deductions made from this analysis of the States and hospital receptions.

"Twenty-two States and two British Provinces furnish the conditions requisite for the purpose of this report, and are included in the calculations and statements.

POPULATION TO ONE PATIENT ANNUALLY SENT TO LUNATIC HOSPITALS.

STATES.	Number of Years.	Districts.				
		I.	II.	III.	IV.	V.
Maine	1840–65	2,835	5,171	5,630	7,890	
New Hampshire	1842–65	2,440	3,470	6,280		
Massachusetts	1833–53	2,229	3,872	4,953		
Rhode Island	1849–65	3,094	5,279			
New York	1843–65	2,772	5,820	7,351	11,535	
New Jersey	1848–66	2,253	3,714	5,905		
Pennsylvania	1850–57	6,061	10,793	17,686	23,748	
East Pennsylvania	1857–66	5,884	10,497	17,414	53,629	
West Pennsylvania	1857–66	3,650	10,585	22,382		
Maryland	1850–64	7,034	10,122	23,009		
Virginia	1828–59	5,472	10,314	21,570	24,433	25,105
North Carolina	1856–60	4,875	6,433	9,707	10,982	45,779
Mississippi	1858.....	*15,018	7,026	13,290	16,151	21,276
Louisiana	1848–58	6,653	15,235	16,645	21,399	25,822
Tennessee	1852–59	3,923	8,318	13,164	20,440	*15,826
Kentucky	†1824–55	3,198	10,670	12,964	24,132	27,801
Ohio	1838–66	5,060	7,304	11,712	28,873	
Illinois	1847–64	3,306	7,865	9,317	11,753	15,585
Michigan	1859–65	3,162	9,229	11,089	14,208	58,039
Missouri	†1851–64	5,910	12,553	13,989	15,983	26,933
Canada	1853–66	3,184	7,227	7,744	12,608	14,582
Nova Scotia	1858–64	467	1,023	1,768	3,057	

" In all these States the privileges of the hospitals are offered equally to the people of the counties. The patients of Oneida and Allegany Counties in New York, of Mercer and Warren Counties in New Jersey, of Dauphin and Venango Counties in Pennsylvania, can enter on the same terms, enjoy the same advantages, and for the same price. The only difference is the burden of cost, care, and labor of travel from their homes to the place of healing. And yet the actual use of the hospital by and the practical value of these institutions to the people of the remote districts have been only one fourth as great in New York, about one third as great in New Jersey, and less than one third as great in Pennsylvania as they have been in the districts near to them.

" Similar discrepancies in favor of the central counties and against the district counties are seen to have existed in all the other States whose record has been obtained.

EFFECT OF MULTIPLYING HOSPITALS.

" This principle has been remarkably manifested whenever and wherever a second hospital has been opened in any State and placed in a district remote from the one previously in operation. The people who

---

* There is apparently something unexplained in the record of one county in each of those districts.

† Excluding 1844, 1845, 1846, and 1847.

‡ Excluding 1861, 1862, and 1863.

sent a few patients to the distant institution now sent many to the hospital which was brought to their neighborhood. The number of lunatics that found a place of healing was suddenly and permanently increased.

"In Massachusetts, the hospital at Worcester was the only State institution for the insane in the Commonwealth from eighteen hundred and thirty-three to eighteen hundred and fifty-four, when the second hospital was opened in Taunton, Bristol County, for the southeastern part of the State. The Worcester establishment continued to receive all the patients from the northern, central, and western counties until eighteen hundred and fifty-eight, when the third hospital was opened at Northampton, Hampshire County, for the western district. In both of these districts there was a sudden and large increase of the insane whose friends sought and used these new places of healing for them. During the eight years—eighteen hundred and forty-five to eighteen hundred and fifty-three—previous to the opening of the Taunton Hospital the people of Bristol County had sent one hundred and fifty-one patients to Worcester, which was an annual average of one patient in four thousand four hundred and thirty-four inhabitants. During the eight years after the hospital was opened within their borders they sent three hundred and twenty-four patients to it, which was an annual average of one patient in two thousand one hundred and ninety-four people.

"In the former period the people of Plymouth County sent one in three thousand seven hundred and nineteen of their number, and in the latter period one in two thousand seven hundred and seventy-four.

"Barnstable, Dukes, and Nantucket Counties sent in the former period one in four thousand one hundred and eighteen, and in the latter one in three thousand five hundred and seventy-three to the hospitals.

POPULATION FOR ONE PATIENT SENT ANNUALLY TO THE STATE HOSPITALS.

COUNTIES.	1845 to 1853.			1854 to 1862.			Rate of increase......
	Patients......	Sum of populations......	People to one patient......	Patients......	Sum of populations......	People to one patient......	
Bristol................	151	669,581	4,434	324	810,903	2,194	102.1
Plymouth............	132	493,215	3,719	204	565,981	2,774	34.
Barnstable ⎫ Nantucket ⎬ .... Dukes ...... ⎭	104	429,319	4,118	118	421,662	3,573	15.2
Totals............	387	1,592,115	4,111	646	1,798,546	2,784	42.9

"During the four years—eighteen hundred and fifty-four to eighteen hundred and fifty-eight—the people of Hampshire County sent thirty-seven patients to the Worcester Hospital, which was an annual average of one in four thousand and eight inhabitants. In the four years after the opening of the third hospital in their midst, the same people sent eighty-five persons, or one in one thousand seven hundred and eighty-seven of their number to its care.

"Franklin County sent in the former period nineteen patients, or one in six thousand five hundred and seventy-four people, to Worcester; and in the latter period fifty-two, or one in two thousand four hundred and nineteen people, to Northampton. Berkshire County is geographically fifty miles nearer to Northampton than to Worcester. But a range of mountains lies between, and the roads are difficult for travelers, who can use only private conveyances, except the Western Railroad to Springfield, and the Connecticut River Railroad from Springfield to Northampton. This practically reduces the difference of distance between the two hospitals to thirty miles. And many when once in the cars on the Western Road find it easier to continue fifty-four miles further to Worcester, than to change cars and go twenty miles to Northampton, with their patients. Therefore the increase is less in Berkshire County than in the others. Nevertheless, there was an increase.

"Before eighteen hundred and fifty-eight the Berkshire people sent thirty-three patients, or one in six thousand nine hundred and thirty-seven people, yearly to Worcester, and after that they sent to Worcester and Northampton forty-seven patients, or an average in each year of one in four thousand seven hundred and fifteen people.

"To the towns in the eastern part of Hampden County, Worcester is nearer and more accessible than Northampton. Most of the people must necessarily use the Western Railroad, whether going to Worcester or Northampton, and all must change cars at Springfield if they go to Northampton, but not if they go to Worcester.

"The people of Hampden County sent in the former period one in two thousand one hundred and eighty-five of the living to Worcester, and in the latter, one in one thousand nine hundred and eighty-eight in each year.

POPULATION TO ONE PATIENT SENT TO HOSPITAL BEFORE AND AFTER NORTHAMPTON HOSPITAL WAS OPENED.

Western District.

COUNTIES.	1855 to 1858, four years.				1859 to 1862, four years.			Increase.
	Patients sent.	Sum of annual population.	People to 1 patient.		Patients sent.	Sum of annual population.	People to 1 patient.	Per cent patients sent.
Berkshire...............	33	212,437	6,437		47	221,640	4,715	38.6
Franklin................	19	124,916	6,574		52	125,830	2,419	171.2
Hampshire.............	37	148,294	4,008		85	151,897	1,787	124.3
Hampden...............	101	220,680	2,185		116	230,784	1,988	9.9
Total Counties.....	190	706,327	3,717		300	730,151	2,433	52.7

"The people of Hampshire County nearly trebled the number and proportion of their patients in the hospital. The people of Franklin and Bristol more than doubled them, and the other counties also increased them very greatly, and thus so many more of their lunatics found places of healing and protection when the hospital was brought to their neighborhood and within their reach.

EFFECT OF RAILROADS AND OTHER FACILITIES OF TRAVEL.

" Facilities of travel, navigable rivers, canals, railroads, public highways, public conveyances, which render communication easy and cheap, and intercourse familiar, and virtually diminish distance from the hospital, increase the ratio of patients that are sent to it. We therefore find that three counties which are situated along the course of rivers, canals, roads, etc., leading directly to the situation of the hospitals, have sent more patients to these institutions than other counties of equal population and at equal distances, but not favored with these facilities of communication. Ten counties in New York along the line of the railroad, canal, etc., east and west of Utica, with easy means of travel, sent two thousand one hundred and fifty-one patients to Utica, or one in seven thousand two hundred and sixty-six. While during the same period ten other counties, northeast and southwest from Utica, with no easy means of communication, sent six hundred and forty-seven patients, or one in eleven thousand nine hundred and thirty-four of their number to the State Hospital. Taking all these facts into view, we have here indisputable proof of the effect of distance in diminishing the practical benefits of lunatic hospitals to the people of any district. In all these States these hospitals are as open and their advantages as freely granted to the patients from the most remote towns as to those in their very neighborhood. It is not hinted, or even suspected, that the lunatics whose friends reside afar off are not as kindly, as faithfully, and as successfully treated, and at as small a cost, as those whose friends are so near as to keep a watchful vigilance over their welfare.

HOSPITALS ARE BETTER KNOWN TO THE NEIGHBORING PEOPLE.

" The idea of the hospital purposes and its management is familiar to those who live in its vicinity. They know its means, its objects, and its administration; they know the character of its officers and its attendants. They are frequently witnessing its operations and results in the many who are going to and returning from it in improved or restored mental-health. Whenever they think of the possibility of their becoming insane, the idea of the hospital presents itself to their minds in the same connection almost as readily as the idea of their own chambers, their own physician, and the tender nursing of their own family is associated with the thought of having a fever or dysentery; and when any one of their family or friends become deranged the hospital occurs to them as a means of relief, and they look upon it as a resting place from their troubles.

" But this ready association of the hospital with lunacy and this generous confidence in its management diminishes as we recede from it. The people in the remoter places know the general facts; but distance lends an obscurity to the notion, and thus the character of the hospital and its administration do not stand before them as the thought of home and domestic arrangements, of which they can cheerfully and trustfully avail themselves in any emergency. To them the hospital seems a strange place; perhaps a place of unkind restraint, or even of needless confinement, rather than a home of tenderness. Its officers are to them strangers rather than friends; and its attendants, though good and honest persons, are not as household comforters and nurses, or even as neighbors, whose ready and affectionate sympathy is sure, and on whom they are accustomed to call in time of trouble, and to whom they unhesitatingly commit the care of their disordered and distressed relatives or children.

"Then the unwillingness to be far separated from their suffering or weakened friends operates with many. This is, indeed, a mere feeling or sentiment; but it is converted into practical facts, and retains some at home who would otherwise be sent to and cured in a hospital if it were nearer to them. The State Lunatic Hospital, when it is used, is no better to the people of Oneida than to those of Cattaraugus and Clinton; but so long as a portion of the people of the remote counties do not feel so their insane friends are not sent there.

"The difficulties and expense of sending lunatics over long distances, or unfrequented and indirect roads, or by private conveyances, are perhaps the most effectual obstacle in the way, and more than any other diminish the number of patients with the increase of miles that separate them from the hospital.

"For these reasons the towns in the neighborhood of the public hospital in this State have enjoyed more than four times as much of its benefits as the remote towns; and all the other hospitals mentioned in this article have been compelled to confer their blessings in a similar and some of them in a much greater disproportion upon the people of the neighboring than upon those of the distant districts of the State to which they respectively belong.

"We think we have here presented facts enough to establish it as a general principle that the advantages of any public lunatic hospital, however freely and equally they may be offered to all the people of any State, are yet to a certain degree local in their operation, and are enjoyed by people and communities to an extent in proportion to their nearness to or distance from it.

"Whenever and wherever the same causes exist the same effects must be produced, and any hospital that may be hereafter established must be subject to the same law. This law of nearness, inviting and increasing the patients, and of distance, preventing and diminishing the number in hospital, is our very nature, and must operate in the future as well as the past. The people will be influenced by the same motives in time to come, as they have been in the years that have gone by."

OBSERVATIONS ON FOREGOING TOPICS.

Thus we are shown, by the interesting paper prepared with the greatest care by this able and accurate observer, that insane asylums dispense their blessings almost in proportion to their convenience to the people. We also learn from other sources that the proportion of cures from the nearer counties is much greater than those in the second radius of distance, and so on with corresponding ratio to the third and fourth. This is what we might naturally expect, as those who live near the hospital would be sent to it for treatment at the earliest period after the attack, while those living at the greatest distance would defer the separation from the afflicted member of the family to the latest moment, and too often till all hope of relief has passed away.

It is interesting to notice in this connection that since the publication of Doctor Jarvis' paper the State of New York has inaugurated an entirely new policy, and we are informed by Doctor Charles S. Hoyt, Secretary of the Board of State Commissioners of Public Charities, in a letter recently received from that gentleman, that it has been determined to bring every insane person within its borders under the supervision of its officers; and that bills have already been passed authorizing the establishment of first class asylums for the accommodation, care, and treatment of all the insane in the State.

The following brief description of these asylums, with amount of appropriation for each, as well as their location, will best convey an idea of the noble work that has been undertaken, and may serve to guide us in the judicious location of our new asylum:

THE NEW YORK STATE LUNATIC ASYLUM, AT UTICA.

This asylum, the only State institution for the insane fully completed, was organized by the Legislature in eighteen hundred and forty-two, and opened for patients in eighteen hundred and forty-three.

The buildings consist of a central edifice, two front and two rear wings, a cross wing, additional wings, and outbuildings. The front and centre are constructed of stone, and the other portions mainly of brick. The central building is four stories in height above the basement, and one hundred and twenty by seventy-six feet on the ground. The front wings are three stories high, and each has an area of two hundred and fifteen by thirty-five feet. The rear wings are of the same height, two hundred and fifty feet each in length, and thirty feet in width. The cross wing is two stories high, twenty-five feet wide, and three hundred and fifty feet long. One of the additional wings is two, and the others are one story in height. The former has an area of eighty-five by twenty-five feet, and the latter one hundred and sixty-three by thirty-four feet. The entire edifice presents a front of five hundred and fifty, and the flanks a depth of two hundred and fifty feet. It is heated by steam, lighted by gas, and ventilated in the most approved manner. The outbuildings are a mortuary, bakery, coal house, work shops, boiler and engine house, containing also the fans for ventilation, and drying and ironing rooms, wash house, farm buildings, carriage house, barns, ice house, etc.

The asylum, as first erected, and until eighteen hundred and fifty-two, had room for only four hundred and fifty (450) patients. Since that date, the original buildings have been remodeled, the additional wings erected, and the cross wing adapted to the insane, by which the institution has been made to accommodate six hundred (600) patients. It also furnishes apartments for the resident officers and necessary attendants and employés. Cost—six hundred and sixty-one thousand and sixty-five dollars and fifty-eight cents.

THE WILLARD ASYLUM FOR THE INSANE, AT OVID.

This institution, designed for the chronic pauper insane, heretofore provided for in the county poorhouses, and for those who may be hereafter discharged from the State Asylum at Utica as incurable, was established by an Act of the Legislature, passed April fifth, eighteen hundred and sixty-five. The site, known as the "State Agricultural Farm," contains four hundred and seventy-five (475) acres, near the Village of Ovid, on the east shore of Seneca Lake. The erection of the building was commenced in the Spring of eighteen hundred and sixty-six, and it was so far advanced as to be opened for patients in October, eighteen hundred and sixty-nine.

The main asylum building is situated near the lake. The plan of this edifice comprises a central building for the Superintendant's residence and offices, and a north and a south wing, with extensions from the extremities of these to the rear, for patients. It is a plain, substantial, three story brick structure, well planned and arranged, and furnished with the appliances and conveniences requisite for its purposes.

In addition to the main asylum, there is the "Agricultural College Building," on the premises when acquired by the State, and now known as the "Branch." This building, situated about one mile from the main edifice, was remodeled and fitted up the past year, and occupied by female patients in November last. It is a plain, substantial brick structure, in good preservation, and appears to be well adapted for the purposes to which it is applied. The Trustees estimate it to have cost one hundred and fifty thousand dollars.

The cost of the buildings now in use for the insane, and the Trustees' estimated cost for the completion of those in process of erection and proposed, is shown by the following statement:

Cost of the main asylum and branch in use, including furniture, out buildings, etc. (as stated above)	$446,998 44
For the completion of the south wing, including the amount already expended (estimated)	81,728 67
For the extension to the north wing, erecting a single group of detached buildings, furniture, fences, further water supply, etc. (estimated)	200,000 00
Total	$728,727 11

The completion of the buildings as proposed will give accommodations for the insane as follows: in the main asylum, five hundred (500); the "branch," two hundred (200); single group of cottages, two hundred (200); total, nine hundred (900) patients.

The Trustees of this asylum express the opinion that its capacity may be very properly extended by the erection of additional groups of detached buildings similar to the one proposed at different points on the farm, so as to include nearly if not all the chronic pauper insane of the State not suitably provided for otherwise. In the judgment of these officers this would prove economical, by lessening the cost of the buildings per capita, and utilizing the labor of the insane, and at the same time secure to them under a single responsible direction and control, better treatment and care. This subject is one of such great public importance, not only as affecting the insane, but as to the cost of providing for their maintenance, that the Board deems it proper to present it to the attention of the Legislature.

THE HUDSON RIVER STATE HOSPITAL FOR THE INSANE

Was established by the Legislature March sixteenth, eighteen hundred and sixty-seven. The site, previously selected by Commissioners appointed by the Governor, contains three hundred (300) acres. Its location is on the east bank of the Hudson River, two miles north of the City of Poughkeepsie.

The plan of this hospital comprises a central edifice for administrative purposes, and a north and a south wing, composed of four sections each, for patients. It also includes a chapel, general kitchen, boiler and engine house, workshops, gas house, etc., to be situated at the rear of the central structure.

The erection of the building was commenced in September, eighteen hundred and sixty-seven. The three extreme sections of the south wing are nearly finished and partly furnished, and it is stated, if funds were provided, could be soon ready for patients. The boiler and engine house are built and two boilers set; the foundations for the four remaining boilers required for the entire building are laid; the great chimney, containing flues for the boilers, kitchen range, bake shop, gas retorts, and central ventilating shaft, is also built; the underground air duct is made, and the main sewer laid from the chimney to the river. The reservoir for the full capacity of the hospital is two thirds completed, and the arrangements for water are said to be adequate for its present purposes.

The hospital is being constructed of North River brick, with a better quality for face work. The window heads are of Ohio stone, with blue stone introduced to increase the artistic effect. The centre building and a part of two sections of each wing will be three, and the residue two stories in height.

The portions of the building erected will accommodate one hundred and twenty (120) patients, and when the hospital is completed according to the plans adopted it will furnish room for four hundred (400).

The Medical Superintendent reports that the estimated cost of the building when the plans were adopted was six hundred and sixty-six thousand dollars; but in the event of the continuance of the inflated prices for materials and labor heretofore paid it will cost, when completed according to these plans, twelve hundred thousand dollars. It is stated, however, by this officer, that this estimate may be modified by the gradual decrease in prices now taking place, and the advantages to be derived from the increase of power from the boilers, in the use of the machinery, etc., but that no great reduction can be anticipated. The institution is designed for the treatment of cases of acute insanity, and the building is being constructed with the adaptations and appointments necessary to carry out its objects.

THE BUFFALO STATE ASYLUM FOR THE INSANE

Was organized under chapter three hundred and seventy-eight, laws of eighteen hundred and seventy. The site, previously selected by designated Commissioners, consists of two hundred (200) acres, situated near Buffalo, and was presented by that city to the State.

The Managers report that the ground plan of the building has been adopted, and that the plan of the elevation will probably be soon approved, and the work of erection commenced.

The Board had expected information as to the estimated cost of the building from the Managers, but it has not been received. We learn that it is to be constructed of brick, with arrangements for the treatment of cases of acute insanity, and with capacity for the accommodation of five hundred (500) patients. The general estimate of superintendents of insane asylums for the erection of plain, substantial buildings of such character, and appropriately furnishing the same, at the present prices for material and labor, is one thousand six hundred dollars per inmate. On this estimate it will cost, when completed, eight hundred thousand dollars.

· The following statement shows the capacity and cost of the State Asylums for the insane in use, and the estimated capacity and cost of those in process of erection, or for which appropriations have been made, when completed according to the several plans adopted, as hereinbefore referred to:

NAMES OF ASYLUMS.	Capacity.	Cost of the buildings.
The New York State Lunatic Asylum at Utica.	600	$661,065 58
The Willard Asylum for the Insane at Ovid....	900	728,727 11
The Hudson River State Hospital for the Insane at Poughkeepsie..........................	400	1,200,000 00
The Buffalo State Asylum for the Insane at Buffalo..	500	800,000 00
The New York State Homœopathic Asylum for the Insane at Middleton..........................	200	360,000 00
Total..	2,600	$3,749,792 69

In conclusion, the Board deems it proper to submit a general view of the present number of the insane in custody, of their condition in respect to recovery, of the present provision made for them, and the requirements for the future.

It will be observed that there were at the close of the first year, four thousand four hundred and eighty-four (4,484) insane persons in public institutions. Of these, nine hundred and twenty-five (925) were in the State Asylums, and one hundred and forty-eight (148) in incorporated institutions receiving State aid. The Counties of New York and Kings contained one thousand nine hundred and sixty-seven (1,967); and there were in the County Poorhouses and City and County Asylums one thousand four hundred and forty-four (1,444). Thus we see that the State of New York has not only determined to provide asylums for the reception of all of her insane population, but has wisely chosen locations in different portions of the State, that they may be easily accessible to all of her citizens who may be so unfortunate as to require their healing influences; though while we commend the generous liberality and munificent appropriations that distinguish this noble act of humanity, we cannot advise our legislators to follow her example in all respects. In the enlightened policy of providing suitable hospitals for all who require their use, we most heartily and unequivocally concur; but we cannot see the necessity of such lavish expenditure in building palacial residences for a class of persons who can neither appreciate the magnificence of the edifice, nor pay for the luxury. The Poughkeepsie Asylum, it appears, will cost three thousand dollars for each patient to be accommodated; which, according to our view, is at least twice as much as any State institution should cost under any circumstances; and for buildings alone, we are satisfied that one thousand dollars ($1,000) per patient is enough. It is true that all asylums of this class should present an attractive and cheerful appearance, its architectural proportions should be in good taste, plain, neat, and substantial; but all expenditures simply for ornamentation should be scrupulously avoided, otherwise charity may be crippled at the expense of pride and vanity.

But this is a digression from the subject under discussion. We have desired to show, and trust we have succeeded, that asylums are intended for the use of the people, and to be most useful they must be accessible. This being admitted, it will be easy to conclude that our next hospital for the insane should be located somewhere on or near the Bay of San Francisco, and within easy reach of that city. At what particular locality, must necessarily depend on many important circumstances and indispensable conditions; and that the commission to which this responsible duty should be confided may not, from inadvertence, overlook or neglect any of them, we append the following suggestions from the Association of Medical Superintendents of American Institutions for the Insane, and of the English and Scotch Boards of Commissioners in Lunacy, who, from their great ability and long experience, would not be likely to make unnecessary recommendations on the one hand nor overlook important matters on the other.

PROPOSITIONS RELATIVE TO THE STRUCTURE AND ARRANGEMENT OF AMERICAN INSTITUTIONS FOR THE INSANE, 1853.

I. Every hospital for the insane should be in the country, not within less than two miles of a large town, and easily accessible at all seasons.

II. No hospital for the insane, however limited its capacity, should have less than fifty acres of land devoted to gardens and pleasure grounds for its patients. At least one hundred acres should be possessed by every State hospital or other institution for two hundred patients—to which number these propositions apply, unless otherwise mentioned.

III. Means should be provided to raise ten thousand gallons of water, daily, to reservoirs that will supply the highest parts of the building.

IV. No hospital for the insane should be built without the plan having been first submitted to some physician or physicians who have had the charge of a similar establishment, or are practically acquainted with all the details of their arrangements, and received his or their full approbation.

V. The highest number that can with propriety be treated in one building is two hundred and fifty, while two hundred is a preferable maximum.

VI. All such buildings should be constructed of stone or brick, have slate or metallic roofs, and, as far as possible, be made secure from accidents by fire.

VII. Every hospital having provision for two hundred or more patients should have in it at least eight distinct wards for each sex—making sixteen classes in the entire establishment.

VIII. Each ward should have in it a parlor, a corridor, single lodging rooms for patients, an associated dormitory, communicating with a chamber for two attendants, a clothes room, a bath room, a water closet, a dining room, a dumb waiter, and a speaking tube leading to the kitchen or other central part of the building.

IX. No apartments should be provided for the confinement of patients, or as their lodging rooms, that are not entirely above ground.

X. No class of rooms should ever be constructed without some kind of window in each, communicating directly with the external atmosphere.

XI. No chamber for the use of a single patient should ever be less than eight by ten feet, nor should the ceiling of any story occupied by patients be less than twelve feet in height.

XII. The floors of patients' apartments should always be of wood.

XIII. The stairways should always be of iron, stone, or other indestructible material, ample in size and number, and easy of ascent, to afford convenient egress in case of accident from fire.

XIV. A large hospital should consist of a main central building with wings.

XV. The main central building should contain the offices, receiving rooms for company, and apartments entirely private for the Superintending Physician and his family, in case that officer resides in the hospital building.

XVI. The wings should be so arranged that if rooms are placed at both sides of a corridor the corridors should be furnished at both ends with movable glazed sashes for the free admission of both light and air.

XVII. The lighting should be by gas, on account of its convenience, cleanliness, safety, and economy.

XVIII. The apartments for washing clothing, etc., should be detached from the hospital building.

XIX. The drainage should be underground, and all the inlets to the sewers should be properly secured to prevent offensive emanations.

XX. All hospitals should be warmed by passing an abundance of pure fresh air from the external atmosphere over pipes or plates, containing steam under low pressure, or hot water, the temperature of which at the boiler does not exceed two hundred and twelve degrees Fahrenheit, and placed in the basement or cellar of the building to be heated.

XXI. A complete system of forced ventilation in connection with the heating is indispensable to give purity to the air of a hospital for the insane, and no expense that is required to effect this object thoroughly can be deemed either misplaced or injudicious.

XXII. The boilers for generating steam for warming the building should be in a detached structure, connected with which may be the engine for pumping water, driving the washing apparatus, and other machinery.

XXIII. All water closets should, as far as possible, be made of indestructible materials, be simple in their arrangement, and have a strong downward ventilation connected with them.

XXIV. The floors of bath rooms, water closets, and basement stories should, as far as possible, be made of materials that will not absorb moisture.

XXV. The wards for the most excited class should be constructed with rooms on but one side of a corridor, not less than ten feet wide, the external windows of which should be large, and have pleasant views from them.

XXVI. Whenever practicable, the pleasure grounds of a hospital for the insane should be surrounded by a substantial wall, so placed as not to be unpleasantly visible from the building.

Additional Declarations, 1866.

The following comprehensive resolutions were proposed by Dr. Nichols, of the Government Hospital for the Insane at Washington, and adopted by the Convention of Medical Superintendents of American Institutions for the Insane, in eighteen hundred and sixty-six, and emphatically reaffirmed in eighteen hundred and sixty-seven. They comprise a full and clear declaration of sound principles, tested by experience:

1. The large States should be divided into geographical districts of such size that a hospital, situated at or near the centre of each district, will be practically accessible to all the people living within its boundaries, and available for their benefit in case of mental disorder.

2. All State, county, and city hospitals for the insane should receive all persons belonging to the vicinage designed to be accommodated by each hospital, who are affected with insanity proper, whatever may be the form or nature of the bodily disease accompanying the mental disorder.

3. All hospitals for the insane should be constructed, organized, and managed substantially in accordance with the propositions adopted by the association in eighteen hundred and fifty-one and eighteen hundred and fifty-two, and still in force.

4. The facilities of classification or ward separation possessed by each institution should equal the requirements of the different conditions of the several classes received by such institution, whether these different conditions are mental or physical in their character.

5. The enlargement of a city, county, or State institution for the insane, which, in the extent and character of the district in which it is situated, is conveniently accessible to all the people of such district, may properly be carried, as required, to the extent of accommodating six hundred patients, embracing the usual proportions of curable and incurable insane in a particular community.

Resolutions offered in the same Association in 1870.

Resolved, That this Association reaffirm in the most emphatic manner its former declarations in regard to the construction and organization of hospitals for the insane; and it would take the present occasion to add that at no time since these declarations were originally made has anything been said or done to change in any respect its frequently expressed and unequivocal convictions on the following points, derived as they have been, from the patient, varied, and long continued observations of most of its members:

First—That a very large majority of those suffering from mental disease can nowhere else be as well or as successfully cared for for the cure of their maladies, or be made so comfortable, if not curable, with equal protection to the patients and the community, as in well arranged hospitals specially provided for the treatment of the insane.

Second—That neither humanity, economy, or expediency can make it desirable that the care of the recent and chronic insane should be in separate institutions.

Third—That these institutions, especially if provided at the public cost, should always be of a plain but substantial character; and, while characterized by good taste and furnished with everything essential to comfort, health, and successful treatment of the patients, should avoid all extravagant embellishments and every unnecessary expenditure.

Fourth—That no expense that is required to provide just as many of these hospitals as may be necessary to give the most enlightened care to their insane can properly be regarded as either unwise, inexpedient, or beyond the means of any one of the United States.

These resolutions came before the Association in eighteen hundred and seventy-one, and were unanimously adopted, the following Superintendents voting upon the question:

Yeas—Doctors Ray, Butler, Kirkbride, McDill, Shew, Walker, Hughes, Parsons, Landor, Reidle, Compton, Gundry, Clopton, Grissom, Lewis, Bancroft, Curwen, Evarts, Dickson, Roy, Gray, and Read.
Nays—None.

In the discussion upon their adoption, Doctor Ray used this language:

"Mr. President: I feel very much as Mr. Webster did on one occasion when called upon, as he said, to reaffirm an ordinance of nature. The opinions of the Association on certain points have been so well fixed for many years that I supposed they would never be altered; that they were correct from the very nature of things. I am not clear now about the necessity of bringing up again the subject matter of these resolutions. It does seem to me like reaffirming the laws of nature. The questions implied in these resolutions you are aware have come up at various times before the Association, and have been very thoroughly discussed. It seems to me we have discussed them until they are threadbare. For this reason I do not feel like speaking upon them at present."

In reply to a question asked by Doctor Cook, Doctor Kirkbride made these remarks:

"Speaking for myself, I should say, without any hesitation whatever, that I do mean, as the fourth resolution declares, that every State should provide enough institutions to accommodate all the insane within its borders. It is my firm conviction that the poorest State in this country is perfectly able to provide just as many hospitals as are necessary. I do not believe any Government has the right to say to one family, 'We will take care of your afflicted one,' and say to another, 'We will not take care of yours,' simply because one is a more recent case than the other. If we undertake to provide for a part of the insane, we are bound to provide for all. One family has just as good a right to claim the bounty of the State as another."

Doctor Cook—"You would not exclude chronic cases?"
Doctor Kirkbride—"I certainly would not."

ENGLISH LUNACY COMMISSIONERS ON SITES, CONSTRUCTION, ETC.

[Suggestions and Instructions in Reference to (1) Sites, (2) Construction and Arrangement of Buildings, (3) Plans of Lunatic Asylums, by the Commissioners in Lunacy for England and Wales.]

No. 1—Sites.—General.

1. The site of an asylum should be of a perfectly healthy character, and offer facilities for obtaining a complete system of drainage. A chalky, gravelly, or rocky subsoil is most desirable; but if a clayey subsoil only can be obtained, an elevated position is indispensable.

It should not be near to any nuisances, such as steam engines, shafts of mines, noisy trades, or offensive manufactures; neither should it be surrounded, or overlooked, or intersected, by public roads or footpaths.

Proportion of Land.

2. The land belonging to the asylum should, when practicable, be in proportion of not less than one acre to four patients, so as to afford ample means for agricultural employment, exercise, and recreation; and should be so situated as to offer facilities for any extension which may become necessary at a future period.

Form of Ground.

3. The site of the building should be elevated, as respects the surrounding country, and (if to be obtained) undulating in its surface, and cheerful in its position, and having a fall to the south.

Position and Aspect of Building.

4. The building should be placed near the northern boundary of the land; and it is important that the site should afford a plateau of sufficient extent for the structure, and for ready access from the north; the whole of the southern portion of the land being available for the undisturbed use of the patients.

Locality.

5. The asylum should be as central as possible to the mass of population in the country or district for which it is to be erected, and should be convenient with respect to its easy access by public conveyance in order to facilitate the visits of friends and the supply of stores.

Supply and Quality of Water.

6. It is of the utmost importance that there should be a constant and ample supply of good water, of which a careful analysis should be made with a view of determining the proper materials for pipes and reservoirs, and also to ascertain its fitness for the purposes of drinking and washing. The quantity, exclusive of rain water, should at the dryest season be not less than twenty-five gallons per patient per diem, and the amount should be accurately gauged.

No. 2.—Construction and Arrangement of Buildings.—General Form.

1. The general form of an asylum should be such as to afford an uninterrupted view of the surrounding country, and the free access of sun and air, and be so arranged as to give the principal day rooms on the lowest and middle stories a southern or southeastern aspect.

Entrance and Offices to the North.

2. There should be no road of approach or public entrance on the south side of the asylum. The general entrance, the porter's room, the reception and visitors' rooms, the clerk and steward's office, and storerooms, and the other offices, should be placed on the north side of the building.

Character of Building.

3. As the building is intended for the accommodation of pauper patients, all superfluous external decoration should be avoided; at the same time it should be rendered as cheerful and attractive as due consideration of economy will permit.

Separation of Sexes, and Classification.

4. The accommodation for the male and female patients should be kept distinct on either side of the centre, and the building should be so constructed as to admit of the separation of the male and female patients, respectively, into three classes. As a general rule the numbers in each class should be such as to require the services of not less than two attendants.

Stories.

5. The building may consist of three stories, provided the uppermost story be devoted to sleeping accommodation.

Buildings for Working Patients.

6. Buildings of a cheap and simple character, consisting merely of associated day-rooms and dormitories, without long corridors or other expensive arrangements, should be provided for the use of working patients. These buildings should be placed in connection with the washhouse and laundry on the female side, and be conveniently situate in reference to the workshops and farm buildings on the male side.

For Idiotic and Epileptic Patients.

Provision of an equally simple and inexpensive description should also be made for a portion of the idiotic and epileptic patients, and also for chronic cases.

Size of Chapel and Offices.

7. The chapel and all offices and parts of the building common to the establishment—such as the kitchen and scullery, the washhouse and laundry, the workshops and storerooms, should be sufficiently spacious to meet the prospective wants of the asylum in case of an increase in the number of patients.

Position of Chapel.

8. The chapel should not be placed over the kitchen. It should be capable of comfortably accommodating at least three fourths of the patients. It should have the usual character and arrangement of a church, and contain no special or peculiar provision for the separation of the sexes.

General Dining Hall.

9. A general dining hall, conveniently situate with reference to the kitchen, and capable of being made available for the purposes of recreation, should be provided for the patients of both sexes.

Officers' Residences.

10. A good residence should be provided for the Medical Superintendent, with kitchen and other necessary domestic offices. Suitable apartments of moderate extent should also be provided for the Assistant Medical Officer, the Steward, and the Matron, but for these officers a separate kitchen is not required.

Domestic Servants.

There should also be sleeping accommodation for the domestic servants of the institution, with whom might conveniently be associated those patients who habitually work in the kitchen.

Proportion of Single Rooms.

11. The proportion of single rooms throughout the Asylum need not exceed one third. The single rooms should be chiefly in the wards appropriated to the excited and the sick. A few should be available for special cases in the other wards.

Arrangement of Upper Stories—Passages and Corridors.

12. In the upper stories passages of communication of moderate width should be adopted in lieu of wide corridors, and the dormitories should be placed to the south. Generally, long, wide, and expensive corridors should not be constructed, but only so much passage or corridor provided as may be absolutely necessary to connect the several parts of the building.

Stairs.

13. The stairs should be built of stone, without windows or long, straight flights. The well should be built up, and hand rails should be provided.

Staircases.

14. The staircases should be so arranged that the medical officer, attendants, and others may pass through from one part to another without necessarily retracing their steps.

Material for Floors—Provision Against Fire.

15. All the corridors and day and sleeping rooms should have boarded floors, and it is desirable that the boards should be tongued. It is indispensable that they should be of the best wood, and thoroughly well seasoned. The floors of the sculleries, lavatories, and water closets need not be of wood. There should be a disconnection of the floor and joists at all the internal doorways, by means of a stone sill; and in all cases where a fireproof construction is not adopted similar separations, at not greater distances apart than fifty feet, should be made in the floors and joists of the galleries or corridors. Provision should also be made for a complete fireproof separation of the timbers of the roof at the same distance, and the parapet should be carried through the roof one foot above the slating. Oak floors, capable of being cleaned by dry rubbing, are preferable for the corridors and day rooms.

Plastering.

The walls of the galleries and rooms generally should be plastered.

Number of Beds in Dormitories.

16. No associated bedrooms should be designed to contain less than three beds.

Height of Each Story, and Dimensions of Rooms.

17. The general height of each story should not be less than eleven feet. The associated dormitories should not contain less than fifty feet superficial to each bed or patient.

Dormitories.

The separate sleeping rooms generally should be of not less than the following dimensions, viz: nine feet by seven superficial, and eleven feet high. Those appropriated to sick or bedridden patients should be of somewhat larger dimensions, and some of these should be provided with a fireplace.

Size of Day Rooms.

18. The day rooms, of which there should be at least one in each ward, should contain not less than twenty feet superficial for each patient, and should be calculated for the whole of the patients in each ward, exclusive of corridors or galleries.

Position of Day Rooms.

19. The day rooms should be so arranged as to afford ready communication with the grounds, and those appropriated to the aged and infirm should be on the lowermost stories.

Attendants' Rooms.

20. Rooms should be provided for two or more attendants to each ward, and single attendants' rooms should not be of less dimensions than one hundred and twenty feet, and whenever practicable, these should be placed between two dormitories, with glazed doors of communication.

Windows.

21. The windows of the day rooms and corridors should be large and of a cheerful character, and every one be made to open easily, and so as to allow a free circulation of air, but not so far as to expose patients to danger. The wall below should not be sloped or splayed, but recessed, to admit, if requisite, of a seat. In the dormitories and single rooms the windows should, as a general rule, not be placed more than four feet from the floor.

Shutters.

Sliding shutters should be provided for a majority of the single sleeping rooms.

Doors.

22. The doors of the single rooms should open outward, and be so hung that when open they will fold back close to the wall.

Lavatories, Baths, and Water Closets.

23. In each ward there should be conveniences for washing the person, a slop room containing a sink, a store room or closet, water closets, and a bath. (In many instances the bath room may be so arranged as to be available for two or more wards.) It is very desirable that all water closets, lavatories, etc., should be placed in projections.

Infirmaries.

24. Suitable infirmaries, in the proportion of at least one tenth of the whole, should be provided in which the cubical contents of the sleeping rooms should be greater than in other parts of the building; and every room, including the single rooms, should have an open fireplace. A small day room in each infirmary is also desirable.

Warming.

25. All the day rooms and galleries should be warmed by means of open fireplaces, or open fire stoves, and in large rooms two fires should be provided. Fireplaces should also be built in all associated dormitories. In large rooms, such as the chapel or general dining hall, and in the corridor, further provision for warming may be necessary by means of some simple system of hot water pipes in connection with the open fire stoves or fires.

Ventilation.

26. The ventilation generally should be provided for by means of flues taken from the various rooms and corridors into horizontal channels connecting with a perpendicular shaft, in which a fire box should be placed for the purpose of extracting the foul air.

Smoke Flues.

27. In all cases where descending or horizontal smoke flues are used, they should be entirely constructed of brickwork, rendered or pargetted inside and out; and flues from any of the heating or other furnaces, which are carried up through any of the main walls, should be constructed with a hollow space round them to prevent the inconvenient transmission of heat into the building during the warm periods of the year, and to allow of a moderation of the temperature of the building at other periods, when, owing to a change in the atmosphere, it may become inconveniently hot.

Ventilating Flues.

28. Whenever ventilating flues are constructed of inflamable material, such a quartering, lathed and plastered a distance of at least twenty

17

feet from their point of connection with any shaft, furnace, rarifiying chamber, or smoke flue, must be constructed entirely of brick, stone, or other fireproof material. The rarifying chamber for ventilation, together with the adjoining roof, must be entirely fireproof; and a communication should be made with it by means of a slate or iron door frame.

Drainage.

29. The best and most approved system of pipe or tubular drainage should be adopted, with a sufficient fall, so as effectually to carry off to a sufficient distance from the asylum the soil and all other impurities; and the sewerage should be collected in closed tanks, and so placed and constructed as to render the contents available for agricultural purposes. Means of flushing should be provided.

Airing Courts.

30. The inclosed airing courts need not be more than two in number on each side, and should be of ample extent, so as to afford proper means for healthful exercise. They should all be planted and cultivated, and any trees already existing within them should be preserved for shade. The walls should be sunk in a haha.

Rainwater.

31. The whole of the rainwater from the building should be collected in tanks suitably placed, for the purposes of the washhouse, and if possible, at such levels as will dispense with the labor of pumping. Lead is an objectionable material for pipes and reservoirs, as adulterating the water.

Lightning Conductors.

32. Lightning conductors should be placed on the most elevated parts of the building, and they may be connected with the stacks of iron rain water pipes, which in that case should be fixed so as to answer the double purpose of rain water pipes and lightning conductors.

Farm Buildings.

33. Farm buildings, with suitable stables, etc., for visitors' horses, should be provided.

No. 3—Plans Required.

1. One or more sheets of the ordnance map containing the county, borough, or district, in respect to which the asylum is to be erected, or some other large map, in which the situation of the proposed asylum and all the public roads and footpaths in the vicinity thereof are fully defined.

Scale of 100 feet to an Inch.

2. A general plan of the land (with the block of the buildings and offices) and of the exercise grounds, garden, and road of approach, with the levels of the surface of the ground at the quoins of the building, offices, and fence walls figured thereon.

Scale of 20 feet to an Inch.

3. Plans of the basement, ground, and each other floor of the building and offices, also of the roofs and gutters and of the principal elevation.

Scale of 10 feet to an Inch.

4. Elevation of portions of the principal front, and also of any other parts in which any variation therefrom takes place.

Scale of 5 feet to an Inch.

5. Transverse and longitudinal sections or sufficient portions thereof to show the construction of every portion of the building.

Scale of 1 foot to one half an Inch.

6. Plan and section of one separate sleeping room, dormitory, and eating or day room respectively, or of part of the same, showing the method of warming and ventilating each; also, of the baths and washing rooms and water closets, and the construction of the apparatus for each.

7. An abstract of the draft, contract, and specifications, giving a concise statement of the whole of the intended work, and also a detailed estimate of the building, and the prices at which the different materials and workmanship have been calculated in making the estimate.

8. The thicknesses of the walls, and the scantlings of the timbers of the floors and roofs to be figured.

9. The general system of heating and ventilation proposed to be adopted throughout the asylum, to be fully described in the drawings and specifications.

10. Each plan to show the several classes and number of patients to be accommodated in the wards, day rooms, dormitories, cells, galleries, and airing courts, respectively, to which each plan relates.

SUGGESTIONS OF THE SCOTCH BOARD.

The following suggestions and instructions by the Scotch Board of Commissioners are the only ones differing from those by the English Commissioners:

Suggestions and Instructions in Reference to (1) Sites; (2) Construction and Arrangement of Buildings; (3) Plans of Lunatic Asylums; by the Commissioners in Lunacy for Scotland.

Locality.

(First part of description same as for England and Wales.) The asylum should be within such distance of a town as to command the introduction of gas, water, etc., and of one of sufficient size to afford the means of amusement and recreation for the medical staff, the attendants, and such of the patients as might derive benefit from a change in the asylum routine.

Supply and Quality of Water.

(First part, same as for England and Wales.) The quantity, exclusive of rain water, which should be collected in cisterns on the roof, should, at the dryest season, be not less than forty gallons per patient per diem, and the amount should be accurately gauged.

No. 2—Construction and Arrangements of Buildings—Entrance and Offices to the North.

2. There should be no road of approach or public entrance traversing the grounds.

The general entrance, the porter's room, the reception rooms, the committee room, the store rooms, and the other offices should be so placed as not to interfere with the amenity of the buildings occupied by the patients.

Buildings for Working Patients—For Idiotic and Epileptic Patients— Cottages.

6. (First part, same as for England and Wales.) Provision of an equally simple and inexpensive description might also be made for a portion of the idiotic, imbecile, and fatuous patients, and also for chronic cases; or cottages might be erected for the accommodation of a large proportion of the working and inoffensive patients, who might be placed either under the care of the families of the attendants, or of cottage tenants of the asylum.

Position of Chapel.

8. The chapel should be of easy access, and it should be capable of comfortably accommodating at least three fourths of the patients. (Remainder of description same as for England and Wales.)

General Dining Hall, Library, and Reading Room.

9. A general dining hall, conveniently situated with reference to the kitchen, should be provided for the patients of both sexes; and also a library and reading room, capable of serving for the general purposes of instruction and recreation.

Arrangement of Day Rooms and Dormitories.

12. Passages of communication of moderate width should be adopted in lieu of wide corridors, and the day rooms and dormitories should be placed on one side, and to the south. Under certain circumstances the day rooms and dormitories may occupy the whole breadth of the building.

Cottages.

32. The cottages, if adopted, should be of different sizes, each calculated to accommodate from three to five patients, in addition to the family of the occupier. The male patients should be placed either in single rooms or in dormitories for three or four, and each cottage should contain a water closet.

Farm Buildings.

33. Farm buildings, with suitable stables, etc., should be provided, and

also workshops, suitable for the employment of the patients according to the prevalent occupations of the district.

English Commissioners on Size of Hospitals.

The English Commissioners of Lunacy are of opinion that an asylum to contain four hundred to five hundred patients is the best size, but that on an emergency they may be enlarged to contain six hundred to seven hundred patients without sacrificing the special characters which all modern asylums should possess. When there are more than seven hundred patients, the expenses increase, and all individual treatment vanishes. The Superintendent can only know the patients *en masse*, and not individually, and the establishment grows out of effective supervision, although the number of attendants may be increased. This opinion may be found in the reports of the Commissioners again and again stated during the last ten years. Thus, in eighteen hundred and fifty-seven they state:

"It has always been the opinion of this Board that asylums beyond a certain size are objectionable. They forfeit the advantage—which nothing can replace, whether in general management or the treatment of disease—of individual and responsible supervision. To the cure and alleviation of insanity few aids are so important as those which may be derived from vigilant observation of individual peculiarities; but where the patients are so numerous that no medical officer can bring them within the range of his personal examination and judgment, such opportunities are altogether lost, and amid the workings of a great machine the physician, as well as the patient, loses his individuality. When to this also is added, what experience has of late years shown, that the absence of a single and undivided responsibility is equally injurious to the general management, and the rate of maintenance for the patients in the large buildings has a tendency to run higher than in buildings of a smaller size, it would seem as if the only tenable plea for erecting them ought to be abandoned. To the patients, undoubtedly, they bring no corresponding benefit. The more extended they are, the more abridged become their means of care; and this, which should be the first object of an asylum, and by which alone any check can be given to the present gradual and steady increase in the number of pauper lunatics requiring accommodation, is unhappily no longer the leading characteristic of Colney Hatch or Hanwell."

The Scottish Commissioners are equally opposed to large asylums. They consider that no asylum should contain more than three hundred and fifty patients; that the individual treatment of a larger number is impossible; and that cost increases with anything above that number. These opinions they repeatedly expressed in their various reports.

M. Parchappe, lately Inspector of Asylums in France, says:

"After taking every consideration into account, I think the minimum of patients ought to be fixed at two hundred, and the maximum at four hundred. Below two hundred the economical advantages rapidly decline without compensatory benefit; above four hundred, although the economical advantages augment, it is at the detriment of the utility of the institution in its medical character."

M. Guislain, the eminent Belgian authority, in his large work on insanity, which is quoted by Doctor Arlidge, says:

"It would be absurd to bring together, in the same place, a very large population. It would tend to foster an injurious degree of excitement, would render the management difficult or impossible, would destroy the unity of plan, and neutralize all scientific effort. The maximum number ought not to exceed three hundred or three hundred and fifty insane persons."

Doctor Arlidge, in his work on "The State of Lunacy," mentions the opinions of Roller and Damerow—two of the most eminent of German alienist physicians—on this subject, both of whom consider that asylums for acute cases should be limited to two hundred and fifty, but that those for both acute and chronic cases may admit from four hundred and fifty to five hundred inmates, but no more; and at page one hundred and eighteen states his own opinion that six hundred "represent the maximum which can economically and with just regard to efficient government and supervision, and to the interests of the patients, be brought together in one establishment."

OBSERVATIONS ON FOREGOING PROPOSITIONS.

We have preferred the suggestions of associations and the recommendations of bodies of men high in authority to anything we might have' said on these subjects, for the reason that they will be justly regarded as the results of wisdom and experience, worthy of attention and thoughtful consideration; whereas the same suggestions from us might be considered as the expression of individual opinion, carrying with it no weight of authority. The good of the cause is what we desire to promote, and for this reason have not hesitated in any instance to make free use of the ideas or words that the wisdom of others have given to the world. With no experience of our own, we have endeavored to carry out the instructions of our mission—to collect, compile, and report the result of other men's experience. We have, of course, exercised our own judgment in drawing conclusions, after listening to the arguments and observing the particular operations of theories; and all of our deductions have been made upon this basis. When we say, therefore, that the next asylum should be established for the accommodation of the City of San Francisco and the counties around the Bay, and on this account should be located in that vicinity, we are only carrying out the ideas of others, and obeying a law of common sense and universal experience; and when we suggest that another asylum will be necessary in the northern and still another in the southern portion of the State, ere many years shall have elapsed, it is in obedience to the dictates of the same ideas and natural laws. It will be seen from the foregoing suggestions that the English Board of Commissioners in Lunacy regard hospitals that will accommodate from four to six hundred as the best size for the pauper class of patients; while in Scotland, owing possibly to the fact that both private and pauper patients are more generally received in the same asylums than in England, the Board expressed the opinion that three hundred and fifty should constitute the largest number that could be properly accommodated in one institution. The best authorities at this time in France, Germany, Switzerland, Italy, and Belgium have placed the limits at four hundred, and in the United

States, until very recently, the Superintendents, in their collective capacity, declared that two hundred and fifty should never be exceeded. But in eighteen hundred and sixty-six they so far modified this expression as to say that under certain peculiar. circumstances the number might be carried to the extent of accommodating six hundred patients.

This concession was made, as we have been informed by most of those giving their consent to its utterance, more to what seemed to be a necessity, than from convictions of propriety, most of them still adhering to the correctness of the original declaration—such too, as will be seen from the Massachusetts Report on Insanity and Idiocy, page one hundred and thirty-four, a copy of which will be found in our State Library, was the opinion of most of the Medical Superintendents in Europe and America at the time that report was written.

PRESENT CUSTOM IN ALL COUNTRIES.

Notwithstanding the modifications that have been made in this respect, and notwithstanding the further fact that most of the asylums being erected at the present time are intended for the accommodation of from four hundred to six hundred, both in the Old World and the New, our observations of the practical workings of asylums of all sizes, compels the conviction that *all things* taken into consideration the smaller number—two hundred and fifty—is the best; and that under no circumstances should this number be exceeded under one roof. If this should be deemed too small, it might with propriety be supplemented by additional separate buildings for the accommodation of one hundred and fifty more; one with a capacity for fifty patients of the convalescent class, for both sexes, and two others of equal size—one for the inoffensive and quiet males, who may or may not labor on the farm, in the garden, or shops, and the other for females of the same class, who may work in the laundry or sewing room. Such buildings may be seen at many of the asylums in England and Scotland, as well as on the Continent, and are not only pleasant features, but are considered of so much value in the treatment of the patients, and the general management of the asylums, that we were assured by the Superintendents that they would not dispense with them on any account. They are by no means uniform in the proportions which they accommodate, nor as to the classes we have specified above. They are usually more cheaply constructed than the main buildings, and free from the grated or barred windows and other necessary arrangements made use of in the main building as precautions against escape or injury. They are warmed by open fireplaces, and are surrounded by their own little gardens, redolent with flowers and beautified with shrubs cultivated by the patients. Of course they are never left to themselves, as it is a universal law that no ward of a hospital should, under any circumstances, be left without an attendant, even for a short time; otherwise serious accidents might be the result.

DINING HALLS IN EUROPEAN ASYLUMS.

In Great Britain and Ireland, as well as on the the continent, the patients take their meals in a common dining hall, the males occupying seats on one side the hall and the females on the other. When the numbers are too great for this arrangement to be practicable, two dining halls are provided, one for either sex, and are situated on either side of the kitchen. At Newcastle-upon-Tyne they not only dine in the same hall, but. sit where they please; and it was interesting to observe that while the first tables on the female side of the room were occupied exclusively by them, and so with the males on their side, that the next set of tables had a sprinkling of the opposite sex, and so on till the centre tables were reached, which were occupied by about an equal number of either sex. Doctor Wickham informed us that this was always the case, and that he had never experienced the least excitement or trouble on this account. For these reasons the patients occupying the detached buildings of which we have spoken resorted to the common dining halls for their meals, with the exception of the convalescent patients, who were in some instances provided with meals in their own establishment.

ASYLUM SHOULD NOT BE ENLARGED.

When an asylum of this size has received its intended complement, instead of building still further additions, another should be established in another district of the State, where the population most strongly indicates its need, whether at some other point upon the Bay—should San Francisco still continue to pour its hordes into the new asylum as it has done into the old—or in some more distant part of the State, in the great north or the mild and genial south, must be determined by the condition of things as they may exist at the time. Of one thing we are positively certain, that so long as the habits of our people remain as they have been; so long as the proportion of the foreign population remains the same; so long as the causes of insanity remain unchanged, just so long will insanity continue to be produced and hold its present ratio to the inhabitants of the State.

ONE INSANE TO FOUR HUNDRED AND FIFTY OR FIVE HUNDRED PERSONS.

We may as well make up our minds now as at any future time that every community of four hundred and fifty or five hundred persons will have to support or provide for the treatment and care of one insane person. When this becomes to be a recognized fact among the people, the whole subject will have been stripped of more than half its difficulties and embarrassments, the system for which we have labored will have been established, and the just and regular provision for the insane will be made for their support, as it is now for the common schools or the ordinary and inevitable expenses of the State Government. Until this has been accomplished the constantly recurring and ever renewing question of provisions for the insane will be brought before our Legislature, to occupy its time and perplex its members.

ASYLUM AT STOCKTON OVERCROWDED.

But there is another question that must not be overlooked, in our solicitude for the establishment of a new asylum, and which is a matter of equal concern. It is the present crowded condition of the asylum at Stockton. With accommodations for not more than six or seven hundred patients, there are packed in its wards about eleven hundred—or four hundred more than it can properly accommodate. Doctor Shurtleff tells us in his report, "that beside two patients in the rooms intended for but one, in eight out of the eleven wards, two hundred and twenty-seven patients are sleeping on beds nightly prepared for them in the halls."

Two of these wards, the second and tenth, intended for thirty patients each, now have about eighty each. These wards are poorly ventilated, low, and uncomfortable in the extreme, and should be erased from the face of the earth and the memory of man. They never were fit receptacles for any human being, and have been tolerated altogether too long.

<h3 style="text-align:center">INCREASED MORTALITY.</h3>

To the crowded condition of these wards and the hospital generally must be attributed the increased mortality of the last four years; and should it be our misfortune, which God forbid, to be visited with cholera or other epidemic, there is no place to which these patients could possibly be removed, and they would consequently be swept away like sheep with the rot. Let any member of the Legislature visit these wards at bedtime, and if he does not conclude that it is *a sin and a shame not to do something for their immediate relief*, we will be willing to acknowledge that we ourselves have lost our reason and our heart, and a fit subject for the very wards that we have described, or that he himself is in such condition; for no two sane men could ever agree to the policy of "doing nothing," after having visited them.

How Dr. Shurtleff and his assistants have managed to get along so well, under the disadvantages with which they have been constantly beset, is a matter of wonder and surprise, and the untiring energy and constant watchfulness that has been displayed by them are worthy of the highest commendation, as well as the gratitude of the community at large.

<h3 style="text-align:center">NEW BUILDINGS SHOULD BE FINISHED.</h3>

The new building at Stockton is of the most creditable character, and when completed would be considered a first class asylum anywhere in the world; indeed, with a few modifications, we know of none that would be better suited to the climate in which it is located. The pressing demands for further and immediate room, make it of the greatest importance, nay, an absolute necessity, that it should be completed by the immediate construction of the north wing, and thus finish the work that has been too long delayed. It is not necessary to stop to discuss the question as to whether Stockton is or is not the proper place for the location of an insane asylum. One has been located there, and has been in successful operation for the last twenty years. It could not be removed, even if such an event were desirable. We therefore heartily indorse all that Dr. Shurtleff has said with regard to the necessities of the institution over which he has so long presided, with such marked ability and success.

<h3 style="text-align:center">OTHER PROVISIONS NEEDED.</h3>

The strongest reasons and the plainest motives of sound policy would indicate the propriety of providing for the improvements at Stockton, and for a new asylum in the same bill. The past experience of Doctor Shurtleff, aided by his Board of Trustees, would insure the completion of the work there in the shortest time and best manner; when it would only remain for the Governor or the Legislature to make a judicious selection of the men who are to choose the site, decide upon the plan, superintend the erection of the new building, and control its subsequent management.

COMMISSIONERS.

As great power is commonly placed in the hands of these individuals, it will readily be understood how important it is that they should be men of high character, strict integrity, active benevolence and business habits. They should be willing to inform themselves of the character and responsibility of the high trust confided to them, and should heartily avoid taking any step that might mar to a greater or less extent the usefulness of the institution as long as it may exist.

SITE.

Great caution should be observed in the selection of a site, as the best style of building and most liberal organization can never compensate for the loss sustained by a location that deprives the patients of valuable privileges, or subjects them to annoyances; nearness to manufacturing establishments, houses of correction, penitentiaries, or other public institutions calculated to disturb the quiet or unpleasantly affect the mind of the patients should be especially avoided. Great stress is laid upon all of these matters both by the Commissioners of England and the Superintendents of our own country. As has been observed by Doctor Kirkbride, than whom no better authority can be found: "It is now well established that this class of hospitals should always be located in the country not within less than two miles of a town of considerable size, and they should be easily accessible at all seasons. They should, if possible, be near turnpikes or other good roads, or on the line of a railroad. While two or three miles from a town might be named as a good distance on the former, the facilities afforded by a railroad might make ten or twelve miles unobjectionable; for it is the time spent in passing and ease of access that is most important. Proximity to a town of considerable size has many advantages, as in procuring supplies, obtaining domestic help, or mechanical workmen, and on account of the various matters of interest not elsewhere accessible to the patients. In selecting a site, facility of access from the districts of country from which the patients will be principally derived should never be overlooked."

SHOULD BE IN A HEALTHY LOCALITY.

The building should be in a healthful, pleasant, and fertile district of country; the land chosen should be of good quality and easily tilled; the surrounding scenery should be of a varied and attractive kind, and the neighborhood should possess numerous objects of an agreeable and interesting character. While the hospital itself should be retired, and its privacy fully secured, it is desirable that the view from it should exhibit life in its active forms, and on this account stirring objects at a little distance are desirable. Reference should also be made to the amount of wood and tillable land that may be obtained, to the supply of water, and to the facilities for drainage, and for inclosing the pleasure grounds.

QUANTITY OF LAND NECESSARY.

While it is the duty of the State to provide for and take care of every citizen who may be afflicted with insanity, on the other hand it is no more than right that they should make the burden as light as possible; and although we do not believe in making patients work for the profits of their labor, yet when they have been accustomed to labor on the farm, in the garden, or in shops at home, and when they are well enough to perform this labor at the asylum, not only without detriment but with advantage to their health and improvement in their mental condition, it should be exacted from them; the Superintendent in all cases being the judge as to the results. In most of the asylums in our country too little employment is given to the body, and too little occupation to the mind, to prevent a state of *ennui* that naturally follows the occupation "of doing nothing."

Many cannot labor for medical reasons; others, on account of previous occupations and professions, have not been taught to labor, and require other forms and methods of employment; yet *all* in whom there exists no special reason contraindicating it should be employed in some way during a portion of every day.

Hence every State Asylum should have at least half an acre of land for each patient intended to be accommodated, not only for farming and gardening purposes, but for pleasure and exercise grounds as well, as the latter are the most beautiful and attractive features of every asylum where they exist, and in which the English Asylums especially, so far excel those of all other countries as a rule, and those in our country more particularly, where this feature has been too much neglected.

Supply of Water.

An abundant supply of good water is one of the necessaries of every hospital, and should be secured whatever may be the cost or trouble required to effect it. A very extensive use of baths is among the most important means of treatment, and the large number of water closets that are indispensable in the wards, the great amount of washing that is to be done, as well as various other arrangements requiring a free use of water, and above all, abundant means for extinguishing fire, in case such an accident should occur, make it of the utmost importance that the supply should be permanent and of the most liberal kind.

The daily consumption for all purposes in an institution for two hundred and fifty patients will not be much, if any, less than ten thousand gallons, and tanks to contain more than this amount should be placed in the dome, or highest part of the building.

Drainage.

All the drainage should be under ground; and in selecting a site, facilities for making this very important arrangement should never be overlooked. All the waste water from the kitchen, sculleries, baths, water closets, etc., should be carried off beneath the surface, and to such a distance as will prevent the possibility of its proving an annoyance to the hospital.

All the entrances to the culverts should be trapped, and the culverts should be made so large and with such a descent as will obviate all risks of obstructions. If the rain water from the roof and the surface drainage are taken in another direction, that from the hospital may be made to add greatly to the fertility of the farm; but it is much better to carry all off through the same culvert and lose this advantage, than incur the slightest risk of having the air in the vicinity of the hospital contaminated by these fertilizing arrangements.

Inclosures.

It is desirable that the pleasure grounds and gardens should be securely inclosed, to protect the patients from the gaze and impertinent curiosity of visitors, and from the excitement occasioned by their presence in the grounds.

This inclosure should be of a permanent character, about ten feet high, and so located that it will not be conspicuous, even if it is at all visible from the building. The site, as well as the position of the building on it, should have some reference to this arrangement. If sufficient inequalities of surface exist, the wall or fence, as it may be, should be placed in the low ground, so as not to obstruct the view; but if the country is too level to admit of this, the same end may be attained by placing the wall in the center of a line of excavation of sufficient depth to prevent its having an unpleasant appearance, and yet be entirely effective. Although the first cost of a wall will be about double that of a fence of the proper kind, still, its durability and greater efficiency in every respect will make it cheaper in the end. The amount of land thus inclosed should never be less than thirty acres, while forty or even fifty acres will be a more desirable amount, so that the pleasure grounds of the male and female patients, which, as before observed, should be entirely distinct, may be sufficiently extensive. Important as I regard the permanent inclosure of extensive pleasure grounds and gardens, in the manner suggested, as protecting the patients from improper observation, keeping out intruders, enlarging the liberty of the insane generally, securing various improvements from injury, and permitting labor to be used as a remedy for more patients than could otherwise be done, still it is proper to add, that high walls around small inclosures, and in full view from the buildings, are even less desirable than a simple neat railing, which would neither keep determined visitors out nor active patients in. The first of these objects—keeping the public out—it must not be forgotten, is the prominent one thought of in recommending a wall to be placed around the pleasure grounds of a hospital. The presence and watchfulness of intelligent attendants must still be the grand reliance to prevent the escape of patients, and I regard any arrangement that does away with the necessity of constant vigilance undesirable about a hospital for the insane.

Patients' Airing Courts.

Although it does not seem to me desirable to have a large number of private yards in immediate connection with a hospital for the insane, it will still be found convenient to have two for each sex, of a large size, well provided with brick walks, shade trees, and such other modes of protection from the sun and weather as may be deemed useful. These yards enable many patients, who at certain periods wish to avoid the greater publicity of the grounds, to have the benefit of the open air, and to take exercise at hours when the attendants cannot conveniently leave the wards; but most of the patients should have a more active and longer continued kind of exercise than these yards afford. They should look to the walks in the open fields and about the grounds, which can readily be made a mile long for each sex for their principal exercise.

Four fifths of all the patients will, under proper regulations, be able to take walks of this kind for at least a couple of hours, morning and afternoon, at all seasons; and in warm weather, when proper summer houses and seats are provided, they may thus profitably spend one half the entire day in the open air. It is always much better for patients to be comfortably seated in a pleasant parlor or hall at any season of the year than to be lying on the ground, or otherwise soiling their clothes, and exposing themselves to the risk of taking cold, as is very apt to be the case when certain classes are allowed to consult their own pleasure as to the mode of passing their time while in the small yards adjoining the building.

Size of the Building.

A suitable site having been selected, it will next become necessary to decide upon the size of the institution. Whatever difference of opinion may have formerly existed on this point, I believe there are none at present. All the best authorities agree that the number of insane confined in one hospital should not exceed two hundred and fifty, and it is very important that at no time should a larger number be admitted than the building is calculated to accommodate comfortably, as a crowded institution cannot fail to exercise an unfavorable influence on the welfare of its patients. The precise number that may be properly taken care of in a single institution will vary somewhat, according to the ratio of acute cases received, and of course to the amount of personal attention required from the chief medical officer. In State institutions, when full, at least one half of all the cases will commonly be of a chronic character, and require little medical treatment. Even when thus proportioned, two hundred and fifty will be found to be as many as the Medical Superintendent can visit properly every day, in addition to the performance of his other duties. Whenever an existing State institution built for two hundred and fifty patients contains that number and does not meet the wants of the community, instead of crowding it, and thereby rendering all its inmates uncomfortable, or materially enlarging its capacity by putting up additional buildings, it will be found much better at once to erect an entirely new institution in another section of the State, for under any circumstances the transfer of acute cases from a great distance is an evil of serious magnitude, and constantly deplored by those who have the care of the insane.

Position, Form, and General Arrangements.

The size of the building having been determined, its form and general arrangements will next require attention; and no plan, however beautiful its exterior may appear, nor how apparently ingenious its interior may seem, should be adopted without having been *first submitted to the inspection and received the approval of some one or more physicians who have had a large practical acquaintance with the insane*, and who are thoroughly familiar with the details of their treatment, as well as with the advantages and defects of existing hospitals for their accommodation. So different from ordinary buildings or other public structures are hospitals for the insane, that it is hardly possible for an architect, however skillful, or a Board of Commissioners, however intelligent and well disposed, unaided to furnish such an institution with all the conveniences and arrangements indispensable for the proper care and treatment of its patients. No desire to make a beautiful and picturesque exterior should ever be allowed to interfere with the internal arrangements. The interior should be first planned, and the exterior so managed as not to spoil it in any of its details.

A hospital for the insane should have a cheerful and comfortable appearance; everything repulsive and prison-like should be carefully avoided, and even the means of effecting the proper degree of security should be masked, as far as possible, by arrangements of a pleasant and attractive character. For the same reason the grounds about the building should be highly improved and tastefully ornamented; a variety of objects of interest should be collected around it, and trees and shrubs, flowering plants, summer houses, and other pleasing arrangements should add to its attractiveness. No one can tell how important all these may prove in the treatment of patients, nor what good effects may result from first impressions thus made upon an invalid on reaching a hospital—one who, perhaps, had left home for the first time, and was looking forward to a gloomy, cheerless mansion, surrounded by barren, uncultivated grounds, for his future residence, but on his arrival finds everything neat, tasteful, and comfortable.

Nor is the influence of these things on the friends of patients unimportant. They cannot fail to see that neither labor nor expense is spared to promote the happiness of the patients, and they are thus led to have a generous confidence in those to whose care their friends have been intrusted, and a readiness to give a steady support to a liberal course of treatment.

Great care should be observed in locating the building, that every possible advantage may be derived from the views and scenery adjacent, and especially from the parlors and other rooms occupied during the day. The prevailing winds of Summer may be also made to minister to the comfort of the inmates, and the grounds immediately adjacent to the hospital should have a gradual descent in all directions, to secure a good surface drainage.

PROPOSITIONS RELATIVE TO THE ORGANIZATION OF HOSPITALS FOR THE INSANE.

I. The general controlling powers should be invested in a Board of Trustees or Managers; if of a State institution, selected in such manner as will be likely most effectually to protect it from all influences connected with political measures or political changes; if of a private corporation, by those properly authorized to vote.

II. The Board of Trustees should not exceed twelve in number, and be composed of individuals possessing the public confidence, distinguished for liberality, intelligence, and active benevolence, above all political influence, and able and willing faithfully to attend to the duties of their station. Their tenure of office should be so arranged that when changes are deemed desirable the terms of not more than one third of the whole number should expire in any one year.

III. The Board of Trustees should appoint the Physician, and, on his nomination, and not otherwise, the Assistant Physician, Steward, and Matron. They should, as a Board, or by committee, visit or examine every part of the institution at frequent stated intervals, not less than semi-monthly, and at such other times as they may deem expedient, and exercise so careful a supervision of the expenditures and general operations of the Hospital as to give to the community a proper degree of confidence in the correctness of its management.

IV. The Physician should be the Superintendent and chief executive officer of the establishment. Besides being a well educated physician, he should possess the mental, physical, and social qualities to fit him for the post. He should serve during good behavior, reside on or very near the premises, and his compensation should be so liberal as to enable him to devote his whole time and energies to the welfare of the Hospital. He should nominate to the Board suitable persons to act as Assistant Physician, Steward, and Matron. He should have entire control of the medical, moral, and dietetic treatment of the patients, the unrestricted power of appointment and discharge of all persons engaged in their care, and should exercise a general supervision and direction of every department of the institution. .

V. The Assistant Physician, or Assistant Physicians where more than one are required, should be graduates of medicine, of such character and qualifications as to be able to represent and to perform the ordinary duties of the Physician during his absence.

VI. The Steward, under the direction of the Superintending Physician, and by his order, should make all purchases for the institution, keep the accounts, make engagements with, pay, and discharge those employed about the establishment, have a supervision of the farm, garden, and grounds, and perform such other duties as may be assigned him.

VII. The Matron, under the direction of the Superintendent, should have a general supervision of the domestic arrangements of the house, and, under the same direction, do what she can to promote the comfort and restoration of the patients.

VIII. In institutions containing more than two hundred patients, a Second Assistant Physician and an Apothecary should be employed; to the latter of whom other duties, in the male wards, may be conveniently assigned.

IX. If a chaplain is deemed desirable as a permanent officer, he should be selected by the Superintendent; and, like all others engaged in the care of the patients, should be entirely under his control.

X. In every asylum for the insane there should be one supervisor for each set, exercising a general oversight of all the attendants and patients, and forming a medium of communication between them and the officers.

XI. In no institution should the number of persons in immediate attendance on the patients be in a lower ratio than one attendant for every ten patients; and a much larger proportion of attendants will commonly be desirable.

XII. The fullest authority should be given to the Superintendent to take every precaution that can guard against fire or accident within an institution, and to secure this an efficient night watch should always be provided.

XIII. The situation and circumstances of different institutions may require a considerable number of persons to be employed in various other positions; but in every hospital, at least all those that have been referred to, are deemed not only desirable, but absolutely necessary to give all the advantages that may be hoped for from a liberal and enlightened treatment of the insane.

XIV. All persons employed in the care of the insane should be active, vigilant, cheerful, and in good health. They should be of a kind and benevolent disposition; be educated, and in all respects trustworthy;

and their compensation should be sufficiently liberal to secure the services of individuals of this description.

COMMENTS ON KIRKBRIDE'S VIEWS.*

The foregoing views of Doctor Kirkbride on some of the most important of the many subjects connected with hospitals for the insane, their location, site, and organization, should be carefully considered. No man in America is better or more favorably known, and but few have had so successful a career or so large an experience. His opinions have been accepted by all as the best authority, and if not always concurred in, certainly always command attention. If we have imbibed some of his ideas it may not be regarded as strange or unexpected, since they are supported by reason and confirmed by experience. Others more experienced and able than we are have done likewise. If we differ with him on some points of importance, it is because other men of ability have impressed us with their views, and our observations have led us to different conclusions. We think, for instance, that no Board of Trustees for the management of an asylum should consist of more than seven members—five being still better than seven. Small Boards seem to be more efficient than large ones. They do not leave matters so much to each other, and thus neglect their duties. We believe that detached buildings for the purposes that we have suggested are desirable features in an asylum; he does not. But in most of his views we heartily concur, and only regret they are not as well known by the people as by the profession. Let us hope, at least, that they may be carefully weighed and duly considered by our legislative committees and Boards of Commissioners. The subjects of ventilation, warming, lights, water closets, comparisons between the asylums of different countries, and many other matters of more or less interest, have been so completely and minutely noticed and discussed by Doctor Manning, and his conclusions ordinarily so just as to challenge our approval on most subjects, that we are induced to incorporate the following sketch of his able and interesting report into our own.

CHAPTER X.

INSANE ASYLUMS—DOCTOR MANNING'S REPORT.

Synopsis of Doctor Manning's Report—Comments upon the same.

SYNOPSIS OF DOCTOR MANNING'S REPORT.

Doctor Manning commences his report, made in eighteen hundred and sixty-seven, to the Government of New South Wales, by considering briefly the various existing methods of providing for the insane, which he divides into five classes:

1st. Indigent—supported mainly or wholly by local or General Government.

---

* NOTE.—See Kirkbride on Hospitals for the Insane.

2d. Non-pauper—supported by friends or from their own estates.
3d. Criminal.
4th. Idiots.
5th. Inebriates.

He speaks first of the provision made for them in *private dwellings*, especially in England, Scotland, France, and Belgium; thinks that even in Scotland, where there are peculiar advantages (from the character and sparseness of population) for this method of treatment, the fact that the number of insane thus accommodated has steadily diminished since the visitations of the Board commenced, is worthy of note; and alludes to the evils of this method (see p. 9). *In a new country such a plan is altogether impracticable.* Describes Gheel (pp. 9 to 14).

Next treats upon *farm asylums*, and describes Clermont (p. 15), and in conclusion says: "A full examination of the system of farm asylums shows that it is economical, and calculated to promote the comfort and happiness, and be beneficial to the mental health of the inmates."

Next, *close asylums;* speaks of the poorhouse wards, and quotes from Doctor Willard, of their miserable condition in the United States; then contrasts them with the State asylums; considers it "remarkable that proprietary asylums for pauper patients are unknown in America."

Page 22—Describes general construction and organization of asylums for paupers.
1. *Elevation of position;*
2. *Aspect;*
3. *Distance from town.*
Table of amount of land owned and cultivated by several asylums, p. 25.
Before treating of asylum construction, considers the two questions:
1. *Separation of the acute and chronic cases;*
2. *The size of asylums.*

Arguments for and against separation are presented on pages twenty-eight to twenty-nine. Dr. Manning says : "Upon the whole, it must be considered that the balance of argument is strongly in favor of one asylum, to contain both classes in such proportion as they occur in each district."

In regard to size, he says: "For the new institutions on the continent, wherever placed, the maximum number is fixed at six hundred; and in many cases a much smaller size is preferred;" then presents two tables (p. 30) of asylums in England and of a few in Scotland, France, Germany, and United States, showing number of patients and rate of maintenance.

Treats of Construction under four heads:
Form of building;
Number of stories;
Material;
Architecture.
Form—1. *Corridor, or ward form;*
2. *House form;*
3. *Block, or pavilion form;*
4. *Cottage form.*

His objections to the *corridor form* are "that the asylum is spread over an immense area, is costly in construction from the immense length of corridor and roofing required, and from the absence of all those social and domestic arrangements which characterize an English home."

. The advantages of the *house form* are "that the condition of the patient is assimilated to that of ordinary life by the separation of the sleeping accommodation from that required for the duties and employments of the day, the supervision of the patients by the attendants is more complete, ventilation is more easy, since the windows and doors of the sleeping rooms from which the patients are removed can be kept fully open all day, and those of the day rooms, all night; whilst the cleaning, always a matter of difficulty in the ward plan, is rendered easy from the fact that the floors are in use at different times."

The *block or pavilion plan* is "a still further development of the house plan."

"As supplementing an ordinary asylum, the *cottage system* has worked admirably, but when fully employed the system has not, on the whole, been found to answer. The inconveniences which have been felt in this arrangement have been chiefly from difficulties of supervision owing to the large space over which the asylum extends. The best form of cottages, whether for a complete asylum or as adjunct to an existing institution, are the 'conjoined cottages' designed by Mr. Stack and Doctor Campbell, at the Essex Asylum," (see p. 33 for description, and App. G, Nos. 10 and 11 for plans.)

Page 34—Water supply. This inquiry includes:
1. *The source and mode of supply;*
2. *Quantity;*
3. *Storage;*
4. *Precaution against fire.*

As supplementary to this question are considered arrangements for the cleanliness of patients:
1. *Baths;*
2. *Lavatories;*
3. *Sinks;*

Their situation, material and fittings, and their number. The proportion of baths in English and American Institutes, about one to twenty patients; on the Continent, less.

Page 38—Drainage.

Page 45—Warming, by:
1. *Open fires;*
2. *Hot air;*
3. *Hot water;*
4. *Steam.*

Page 47—Lighting:
1. *Windows;*
2. *Lamps.*

Examining windows is noted:
1. *Position and proportion to wall space:*
2. *Material and method of opening;*
3. *Size of panes;*
4. *Guards and accessories, as shutters, etc.*

Page 52—Ventilation, either artificial—by propulsion or extraction; or natural—by doors, windows, and fireplaces *only*, or by openings in addition to these.

Doctor Manning says; "it is noteworthy also that those with windows, doors, and fireplaces only, and those with the more simple accessories in addition to these, seem as well ventilated as those in which there is an elaborate arrangement of ventilating shafts."

Page 54—Cubic space.—In the new asylum at Madras fifteen hundred cubic feet is the space fixed for European patients.

Day and night accommodation:

1. *Day or sitting rooms.*
2. *Dining rooms.*
3. *Dormitories.*
4. *Airing grounds.*

Considers the question of single rooms or common dormitories quite an important one. It is universally agreed that violent, noisy, dirty patients should be accommodated in single rooms, but it by no means is decided what proportion of patients it is necessary to isolate thus.

Page 59—*Floorings, fittings, and furniture of rooms.*

Page 64—*Staircases and stairs, bells.*

Page 65—Treats of the different provisions made in asylums for *convalescents and quiet patients*, for the *sick and infirm*, and for the *violent and excited*. "The proportion of violent patients for which provision is generally made would appear to be about one tenth."

Kitchens, laundry, chapel, dead-house and cemetery, amusement room, library, are each considered separately in turn, followed by a brief notice of the provision made for employés of all classes.

Page 75—*Organization and government*, which Dr. Manning considers "even of greater importance than asylum construction;" reviews briefly the method in use in different countries, and concludes:

"On examining closely the general condition of asylums, those are almost always found to be best managed in which the physician is the Superintendent, one and supreme; in which the committee of visitors act only through him and with his advice, and in which the appointment and dismissal of all attendants are delegated to him; and those are found to be least satisfactory in which the responsibility is divided; in which the committee of visitors or controlling Board meddle in the internal management of the institution, and direct, themselves or through other officers, any part of it, appoint or dismiss attendants, or clip in any way the authority of the Medical Superintendent."

Page 80—Gives a table of the salaries of Superintendents in some English asylums and the number of assistants.

Then follows a consideration of each of the classes of subordinate employés.

Page 84—Table of proportionate number of attendants to patients in the principal asylums of England, France, Germany, Holland, and the United States. Ages of attendants (in English asylums), from eighteen to thirty-five; generally deemed advisable that they should not be under twenty-one. Discusses the desirability of placing attendants in uniform, but expresses no decided opinion. Diet of attendants and the privileges allowed them follows.

Page 88—Artisans and servants.

Page 91—Hospital dietary, followed by considerations as to clothing of patients; next, labor—several tables relative thereto being given; then follows amusement and school; classification of patients; animals kept at asylums; system of supply (commissariat); provision for relief of patients on discharge; asylum reports.

Page 108—Statistics.

Page 116—Restraint and seclusion.—Doctor Manning quotes from Doctors Bucknill, Wilkes, Ewerts, Meyer, Kirkbride, and Gray, and shows the practice in many asylums. He says: "During the last few years there has been a certain reaction in the feelings of Superintendents of asylums on this subject. In quite half of the asylums visited, although restraint was not practiced, its advantage in certain cases was distinctly admitted, and it does not now meet with the all but wholesale condemnation which was accorded to it some few years ago." After speaking of the use of the shower bath, he concludes as follows:

"It is not a little curious that owing more or less to popular clamor, and to a fear of the abuses to which they are liable, mechanical restraint has been virtually abandoned in Great Britain, and the shower bath has ceased to be used in America, and so a mode of treatment useful in a certain number of cases is lost to the physician in each country."

Page 122—*Accommodation for patients paying for their maintenance.*
Page 125—*Criminal lunatics;* which are divided into two classes:
1. Those who whilst insane commit criminal acts.
2. Those who become insane while undergoing punishment.
He treats of the distinction made between these classes and the manner in which they are provided for; thinks that Scotland is broader in principle and has been more successful in her treatment of this class; then describes at considerable length the Broadmoor Criminal Asylum and the Criminal Lunatic Asylum at Perth, Scotland.
Page 139—*Asylum for idiots.*
Page 148—*Asylum for inebriates.*
Page 154—*Suggestions,* from which are quoted the following paragraphs:

"The moral and material advantages which follow the system of provision for the insane in private dwellings are undoubted."
"It is necessary that population should so increase as not only to form aggregate bodies, towns, and villages, but to form a united, related, fixed, and settled people; and that the masses shall have received a certain education on lunatic matters, by public papers and by the existence of well conducted asylums, before the separate system is adopted. An attempt to place any large number of the insane in private dwellings must necessarily fail in a new country, colony, or State. Neither the Belgian system nor the Scotch is possible in New South Wales at present, but the advantages of these should be ever kept in view, and the whole asylum organization should tend towards the development of such systems in the maturer age of the colony."
"The close asylum, however, has been in long years past, and must be in the years yet to come, the chief method in which the insane of all countries, in the acute stages of their maladies, are provided for."

Page 157—Doctor Manning quotes from Doctor Wilson, the Catholic Bishop of Hobart Town, in reference to locating a hospital near a large city, as follows:

"The advantages of having a hospital near a large city are incalculable. Here are a few:
"1. The securing judicious visitation of a properly selected Board of Commissioners for the general management of so important an institution, a measure absolutely necessary for its permanent well working.

"2. The means of procuring the best medical and surgical assistance when required.

"3. The opportunity afforded almost daily to convalescent, quiet, and orderly patients of visiting the city for amusement, going through the markets, sometimes strolling through the public pleasure grounds, and obtaining that change so beneficial to them, both mentally and physically.

"4. Affording facility to humane and well qualified persons of gratifying in the asylum, not unfrequently of an evening, patients whose minds are in a state to profit by such kind offices, with music, instrumental and vocal, recitations of short and cheerful pieces, or appropriate readings, and such like friendly acts.

"5. Of affording patients likely to profit by such visits the means of attending such public exhibitions in the city as offer from time to time suitable for them. Many other advantages might be mentioned."

On page one hundred and sixty-six Doctor Manning says:

"The site to be chosen for an asylum is a matter of primary importance. On it must depend in no small degree the comfort, happiness, and health, both mental and bodily, of the inmates, as well as the cost of the institution and the whole working of its internal economy.

"An elevated position is desirable, because more healthy—commanding, as a rule, more extended views, both from the rooms and airing grounds, and affording greater facilities for drainage and ventilation.

"In the suggestions and instructions to architects, issued by the Commissioners for England and Scotland, it is suggested that 'it should not be near to any nuisances, such as steam engines, shafts of mines, noisy trades, and offensive manufactories; neither should it be surrounded, or overlooked, or intersected by public roads or footpaths;' 'that the site of the building should be elevated as respects the surrounding country, and, if to be obtained, undulating in its surface and having a fall to the south.'"

Doctor Manning continues:

"The subsoil should, if possible, be calcareous, gravelly, or rocky; but if the position is elevated and the drainage good, a clayey subsoil, such as is occupied by more than one of the best English asylums, is not objectionable."

The advantages to be derived from proximity to a large town are:

1. *Facility of access for patients and their friends, Commissioners, Inspectors, and other Government officials, medical officers, etc.*
2. *Diminished cost of conveyance of coal, stores, and provisions.*
3. *Facility for amusement of patients.*
4. *Supply of gas and water.*
5. *Increased facilities for procuring good attendants and for inducing them to remain for a longer time.*

The special need of the attendants (who are always with the insane) for change and amusement away from the institution is spoken of at considerable length.

In reference to *land*, Doctor Manning recommends "the proportion of one acre to every two patients," "instead of the minimum of one acre to every four patients, suggested by the British Commissioners." "The full amount which will be required for the institution, according to its estimated eventual extent, should, if possible, be acquired at once. It might either be cultivated by the patients in the institution, if sufficiently numerous for the purpose, partly cultivated by hired labor, or let on short lease till the number of patients was sufficient to work it; but as much as possible of it should be brought under cultivation—fruits, root or cereal crops, grown according to the nature of the soil, the wants of the institution, and the capabilities of the inmates. The more an asylum is self supporting in this respect the greater will be the economy of expenditure.

"It has been calculated that the labor of the insane is only equal to one fifth of that of the sane, so that one hundred patients are equivalent only to twenty healthy field laborers. In most asylums there will be found one inmate in every five suitable for field labor, so that in an asylum of five hundred patients, there will be about one hundred inmates capable of such employment. But if it is supposed that only half this number can be so employed, it will be equivalent to the constant labor of ten healthy men; and what these are capable of effecting in agriculture and horticulture can be estimated by all those conversant with the matter."

In regard to the question of the separation of acute and chronic cases, Doctor Manning says: "The solution of this, like many other practical questions regarding asylums, depends very much upon the population of the district, upon the nature of the existing buildings, and upon the special aims which it is intended to combine with their erection (e. g., clinical instruction). Wherever a large population is crowded within a small space, and two asylums can be made fairly accessible to the whole population of the district, the greatest argument against the separation of acute and chronic cases ceases to exist."

In regard to the size of asylums, Doctor Manning quotes the opinions expressed by many eminent authorities, and concludes as follows:

"Weighing well all the opinions of eminent men on this subject, and the arguments with which they are backed, and judging from personal inspection of existing asylums, the opinion may be expressed that from four to five hundred is the preferable size for an asylum, and that six hundred should never be exceeded. The asylums which are working smoothly and well, with every care for the treatment of patients, and effective supervision, are, as a rule, below this number; and " "for economical reasons, from four to five or six hundred is the preferable number. The maintenance rate generally increases where the population is below or above it."

TABLE,

Giving a List of certain American and European Asylums, with the Amount of Land about them and the Amount used for Pleasure Grounds (Airing Courts included).

[Manning's Report.]

ASYLUM.	Acres of Land.	Pleasure Ground.
Worcester County	100	20
Sussex County	200	30
Essex County	96	10
Three Counties	252	20
New Surrey	150	...
Middlesex County (Colney Hatch)	150	80
Gloucester County	80	10
Derby County	100	50
Lancashire County	96	25
Leicester County	80	15
Stafford County (New)	100	...
Stafford County (Old)	77	17
Lincoln County	40	10
Bristol Borough	32	14
Cotton Hill Lunatic Hospital	80	10
Northampton Hospital	75	15
Retreat, York	30	28
Elgin District Hospital	92	12
Perth Hospital	60	...
Haddington Hospital	12	2
Fife Hospital	57	7
Montrose Royal	110	30
Government Asylum, Washington	230	105
Pennsylvania State	130	18
Northampton (Mass.) State	200	...
New Jersey State	120	45
New York	200	60
Evreux, Département Eure	150	60
Quatre Mares, Département	100	...
Seine Inferieure	.....	...
Sainte Anne, Département Seine	14	...
Ville Evrard, Département Seine	750	...
Vancluse, Département Seine	700	...
Colony of Fitz James, at Clermont	1000	...
Meerenberg, Holland	70	20
Guislain's Asylum, Ghent	35	15
Hamburg	65	20
Illenau	42	12
Frankfort	40	10
Gottingen	20	...

Table,

Showing Number of Patients and Assistants in certain Asylums, with the Salaries of the Superintendents in certain of the English and Scotch Asylums.

[From Manning's Report.]

ASYLUM.	No. of Patients.	No. of Assistants.	Salary of Superintendents	ASYLUM.	No. of Patients.	No. of Assistants.
Bristol	206			Quatre Mares	715	1
Derby	342	1		St. Yon	950	2
Leicester	391	1	£500	St. Anne	600	...
Stafford	469	1		Ville Evrard	600	1
Lincoln	502	1	650	Evreux	500	1
Sussex	510	1	550	Guislain's Asy., Ghent	450	1
Three Counties	534	1	550	Meerenberg	600	4
Worcester	540	1	600	Hamburg	350	2
Essex	554	1	800	Frankfort	200	1
Gloucester	590	2	500	Göttingen	300	2
New Surrey	650	1	600	Illenau	450	6
Lancashire, Lancaster	836	2	600	Washington	380	3
Lancashire, Prestwich	962	2	750	New Jersey State	500	2
York, West Riding	1,124	2		Pennsylvania State	380	2
Colney Hatch	2,026	2	600	Northampton	420	1
Perth District	220	1	350	New York State	608	3
Cupar	213	1	300			
Montrose	380	1	400			

CONSTRUCTION.

To make the lunatic as much "at home" as possible, to make the household arrangements of an asylum resemble those of a large private dwelling house so far as is consistent with salubrity of structure, economy of expenditure, and facility of supervision and management, should be the leading principle in the construction and internal arrangements of asylums.

Asylum construction must depend somewhat on the classification of the patients which is considered necessary.

The classification recommended is:

1. *Recent cases.*
2. *Sick and infirm.*
3. *Violent and noisy.*
4. *Ordinary patients.*

In an asylum for five hundred patients, at least six divisions for each sex are necessary; and in this case the "ordinary" patients may be placed in two divisions; but with a smaller number, three or four will suffice; the "recent" and "ordinary" cases being amalgamated or not. Thirty to forty patients are a sufficient average number for each division.

For a small asylum the maximum population of which is never to exceed two hundred, the modified cottage plan is the one to be most recommended.

For an asylum built originally for one hundred and fifty or two hundred patients, but intended for enlargement, so as eventually to contain four hundred, the "house" plan or the pavilion plan are most fitted for the original structure.

For an asylum built originally to contain five hundred patients in six divisions, the pavilion or block plan may be mainly adopted and supplemented by cottages; or plans may be so modified as to embrace the house, pavilion, and cottage plan, blended into one harmonious whole, as in the New Surrey Asylum.*

If the three plans are combined to form one asylum the two classes who require most constant care and attention (the sick and the acute cases recently admitted) should be placed in the part built on the "house" plan, which will be under one roof with the administrative department, and so within easy access of the Resident Physician.

The ordinary patients and the violent class may be placed in detached blocks, two or three in number for each sex; and the small asylum town thus built be supplemented by cottages for idiotic and convalescent patients.

The cottage plan is particularly fitted for patients of good education. It adds vastly to their comfort to separate them from the other inmates. For convalescent patients also, the association with sane people is very beneficial, and they by this means are allowed greater liberty, and are able to resume gradually their accustomed life, instead of passing at once from the asylum ward and its artificial existence to the realities of actual life abroad.

The special block for violent and noisy patients, which should be the smallest division of the house, should have connected with it and opening from it, a one-storied building, capable of containing four or five patients. It should consist of corridor and single rooms, and should have one or more small airing courts, opening either from the corridor or the rooms.

The question as regards the number of stories in an asylum must depend chiefly on the uses to which the rooms on the ground floor are applied. If the ground floor is to be divided into day room and dining rooms, and so the patients occupy only half of it at once, the number for which it will serve will not be greater than can be contained in one dormitory floor; but if the dining room accommodation is provided elsewhere, the space for sitting or day room accommodation will be doubled, and made sufficient for the number of patients who can be accommodated in two stories built over it. The space required for sitting and day room in asylums is reckoned to be about half that required for the night.

The material to be selected for asylum construction may fairly be that which is most readily procurable, so long as it is durable and not porous. So long as the windows are of large size, the particular style may fairly be left to the architect entrusted with the planning of the building.

A full supply of pure water is an important requisite in an asylum,

* See Appendix F, plates 5, 6, 7.

and no site should be chosen where this cannot be obtained. If the asylum be near the town, the town supply will be found cheaper and altogether more convenient than any other arrangement; but when at a distance, the supply from a well or spring, especially if this is close to the buildings, is the best method, since the steam engine which will always be necessary to pump and fill tanks, may be made to serve other purposes also, as turning machinery, either at the laundry or farm buildings, whilst the boilers which supply it may be used also for heating hot water for baths and lavatories, the kitchen and laundry. No supply from a running stream should be used without careful filtration, and if water is procurable in any other way, surface drainage should not be resorted to, since, with this method in use, high farming is almost impossible, without running risk of dire illness to the inmates from animal poison contained in the water. The quantity required for the use of an asylum, even when earth closets are used, is not less than fifteen to twenty-five gallons per head per diem.

For safety in case of fire, Dr. Manning says: "Reliance should be placed mainly on hydrants, for which proper hose should be kept always at hand, placed both outside in the grounds and inside on the staircases. These should be connected both with the ordinary water supply and with the tank; and where a steam engine exists, the pipes should be so arranged that the water may be played by steam power. Fire drill, at which attendants and patients should assist, should be practised at fixed intervals, and the hose and other appliances kept always in order. In asylums in which force of water sufficient to play the hose cannot be obtained, ordinary hand fire engines should be kept at the asylum, and the patent contrivance called 'L'Extincteur' may be also kept at hand."

Every asylum should be lighted throughout with gas, which is at once the safest, cheapest, and most effective mode of lighting. If gas cannot be conveniently obtained from a company's works, it may be made on the premises without difficulty, at a cost which will render it cheaper than any other kind of illumination such as it is necessary to have in an asylum.

Dr. Manning gives it as his opinion that open fireplaces, especially when built with air-chambers, as in use in English asylums, form the best, simplest, and cheapest mode of warming asylums in a moderately cold climate; but in America the elaborate system of heating by steam, which has been almost universally adopted, is perhaps the best which could be used.

Natural ventilation, with such accessories as may be deemed expedient—and the simpler these are the better—can alone be recommended for an asylum in a temperate climate.

The height of twelve feet, proposed by the American Association of Medical Superintendents, seems ample for all the purposes of an asylum room.

Every room should have its cubical contents painted on its door.

In all asylums separate day and diningroom accommodation should be provided. It will be well that one diningroom should be provided for each sex, and that they should be placed on each side of the kitchen. Day room accommodation should be provided for each section of the asylum, at the minimum rate of five hundred cubic feet for each person. A general dining hall, or two dining halls—one for each sex—should be built conveniently situate with reference to the kitchen, capable of containing three fourths of the entire number of inmates. Experience has shown in English asylums that this number may with safety and advantage be allowed to dine in common.

Two airing courts for each sex are all that are absolutely necessary for an asylum. If a third is added for the use of the sick, infirm, and for special cases, such as epilepsy, it will be found frequently useful. It may save the more feeble among the patients from the accidents which might happen to them in the large general court.

In every airing court there should be a sunshed and a verandah or covered walk, to afford shade and allow patients so inclined to take exercise in wet weather.

The floorings of all the day and diningrooms and dormitories should be of wood. The boards should be tongued; and the English and Scotch Commissioners suggest that there should be a disconnection of the floor and joists at all internal doorways, by means of a stone sill. In all cases where a fireproof construction is not adopted, similar separations, at not greater distances apart than fifty feet, should be made in the floor and ceilings. There is but little necessity for oiling or polishing the floor except in rooms devoted to dirty patients.

The walls should be plastered or cemented, and subsequently painted or colored so as to make the rooms as cheerful and bright as possible.

All rooms devoted to dirty patients should be whitewashed.

The keys for the male and female side of the house should be different, and each attendant provided with one key which will unlock all the doors on his or her side of the house. A simple railway key will serve for each attendant to turn on or off water, gas, or to chock the window sashes, close or open shutters, etc., so that each attendant will have two keys only.

Asylum stairs should be of stone or iron; the flights short and straight. Wooden or iron handrails should be provided for all stairs, and let into a groove in the wall.

One kitchen, in a central position, is all that is required for an asylum, and in it, if properly arranged, all the food·for patients, officers, and attendants can be cooked.

The laundry should be detached from the main buildings, and may be placed at some little distance, if water supply is thus made more easy.

The arguments for a special chapel in connection with every·asylum need not be repeated here. The best argument is the existence of such a chapel in the well ordered institutions of all countries.

For minor amusements, the day rooms of the institution are sufficient, but a room where the majority of the inmates can be collected for dances, concerts, theatrical performances, gymnastics, lectures, etc., is absolutely necessary in an asylum.

It is scarcely necessary to provide a special room for a library.

The building for the reception of the dead should consist of two rooms at least. One of these should be the reception room, fitted with shelves for the dead, in which they may be seen by their friends. The other, a room for post mortem examinations, in which every convenience for the purpose should be supplied—a central table, hot and cold water, etc.

It is desirable that the dead should be buried in the ordinary cemetery of the town or district.

The balance of the report is devoted to "Organization," "Dietaries," forms for asylum reports, and architectural plans.

ORGANIZATION.

A Board of Control should be appointed by the Government for each asylum, or for each district, and should consist of not less than five members, one or two of whom should be medical men, and the remainder men of high social standing, residing in the district in which the asylum is situated. The necessary expenses of the Board should be paid, and such remuneration made to the professional members as may be deemed fair, but the other members should not receive salaries, the position being entirely an honorary one.

The members of the Board may either retain their seats permanently, or one or two members may retire annually, and be eligible for reappointment.

The duties of the Board should be:

1st. The control of the finances of the institution, and the preparation of the necessary estimates for the consideration of the Government.

2d. The appointment and dismissal of all officers, viz: Superintendent, Assistant Medical Officers, Secretary, Chaplain, and Housekeeper, subject to the approval of the Government.

3d. The visitation of the asylum and inquiry into its management and the general conduct of officers and attendants.

4th. The inspection of the forms of admission sent with all patients, and the ordering of the discharge of all such as are recovered, or for whom their friends promise to make provision, one medical member of the Board being always present to examine the patient and affix his signature to the certificate of discharge.

The Board should also be charged with the presentation of an annual report to the Government, in which the general and financial condition of the institution under its care is set forth.

On the appointment of a Board of Control, asylum government will be thus divided:

Superintendence and Management.

The whole internal economy of the asylum will be under the control of the Superintendent, and with him should rest the patronage, so far as the appointment of attendants and servants is concerned.

Legislation.

The making of all general laws for the conduct of the asylum, and for the guidance of all officers and attendants, will be the duty of the Government. A general code of laws will serve for the government of all the asylums of the country; and all marked alteration in such laws should be made, or at least approved, by the General Government; whilst minor alterations, which are not contrary to their general spirit, may be made by the Superintendent or Board of Control.

Financial Administration

Will be under the Board of Control, exact accounts of the financial condition of the asylum being submitted to the Government, with the estimates for each year. The estimates should include a sum for incidental expenses, to be spent at the discretion of the Board, and not exceeded. (The sum placed under the control of the Board is fixed, in the case of the English county asylums and the State asylum, Broadmoor, at four hundred pounds for each year.)

Patronage.

The appointment of the Board of Control (and the Board of Inspection, to be hereafter considered) will rest with the Government. The Board of Control will appoint all the officers, who are immediately responsible to it, the Government approval being necessary to ratify the appointments. The Superintendent will appoint the attendants and servants who come immediately under his directions.

There remains to be considered the duties of

Inspection and Supervision.

Doctor Manning then speaks of the way in which this is managed in the United States, Great Britain and Ireland, France, Belgium, and Holland, and then gives his opinion of what it should be in New South Wales:

The duties of such a Board of Inspection should be:

1st. The inspection of all asylums, public and private, at fixed periods not less than twice a year. At such inspection inquiry should be made as to their management; as to the regularity of admissions and discharges; the number of attendants; the dietary, and the general conduct of the institution.

2d. The frequent inspection of the criminal asylum, which it is recommended in a subsequent part of this report should remain under the immediate control of the Government, without the intervention of a Board of Control.

3d. (Is of local application, referring to the" Reception House at Darlinghurst.")

4th. The examination of all criminal lunatics, either acquitted on the ground of insanity or found to be insane, in prison; and the direction as to their maintenance in the prison for observation, or their transfer to an ordinary or criminal asylum.

5th. The transference of patients from one asylum to another for any reasons that may be considered good.

6th. The registration, visitation, and official guardianship of all lunatics under certificate residing with friends or with persons paid for their maintenance, with power of inquiry in all cases of detention and ill treatment by relatives of any insane person, whether under lunacy certificate or not.

7th. The examination of all certificates in lunacy, to see that they are in proper form and that all necessary particulars concerning the history, circumstances, social and mental condition of the patient are given.

8th. Inquiry into all cases of complaints in asylums, and all cases in which the Lunacy Acts have been infringed.

Superintendent.

The Physician of every asylum should be Superintendent and chief executive officer of the establishment. He should have entire control of the medical, moral, and dietetic treatment of the patients; the power of appointment and discharge of all attendants and servants, and exercise a general supervision and direction of every department of the institution. He alone should be responsible to the governing body for the state and condition of every part of the institution, and he should be the recipient of all their orders.

Assistant Medical Officers.

The Assistant Medical Officers of asylums should be qualified medical practitioners, whose duty consists in assisting the Superintendent in the medical and general duties of his office, and representing him in his absence.

Doctor Manning is of opinion that "the medical staff of an asylum containing acute and chronic cases in the usual proportion, should never consist of less than one to every two hundred and fifty patients; that whenever the asylum population exceeds two hundred and fifty, an Assistant Physician should be appointed; and that when the number of five hundred is reached, an additional assistant is necessary."

COMMENTS UPON DOCTOR MANNING'S REPORT.

We are of the opinion that *no* asylum should be without an Assistant Physician, and that an asylum of five hundred patients should be provided with an additional assistant, as suggested by Doctor Manning. The Guislain Asylum, as well as many others in the Old World, are greatly at fault in this respect, and the bad effects of such policy are ever apparent.

We have thus given a brief sketch of this exhaustive and admirable report, and can only again express a regret at our inability to obtain a copy for the State Library, and still hope an order sent to New South Wales, through Messrs. Trübner & Co., No. 60 Paternoster Row, London, may succeed in procuring one.* In most of the conclusions arrived at by Dr. Manning, as well as suggestions made to his Government, we heartily concur. But, as we cannot do so in all, we deem it due to ourself and what appears to be the interest of the insane in our midst to point out a few of the most important points of difference:

1st. For reasons already stated elsewhere, we think that two hundred and fifty patients as large a number as can be treated in the *best possible manner in one asylum*, and that this number should never be extended beyond four hundred. We admit, however, that the practice of the present day is to build asylums for four hundred, five hundred, and six hundred patients, as he has suggested.

2d. We are satisfied that the number of single rooms for one third of the patients is too small to insure the best results. His conclusions coincide with the custom in Great Britain and the continental countries, where one third is the greatest number provided with single rooms, even in the best asylums; whereas we agree with the custom in our own country, where the best asylums are never provided with single rooms for less than two thirds of their patients, and many of them a larger proportion. Under no circumstances should this be reduced to a less number than one half. We are fully aware of the advantages to be derived from the association of patients, but think this can be done to best advantage during the day, in large and pleasant airing courts, sitting rooms, and pleasure grounds.

---

* NOTE.—Since the above was written the report of Doctor Manning has been received, and we recommend its perusal to the committees, Commissioners, and others especially interested in the subject.

3d. The recommendation for six divisions for each sex, in an asylum for five hundred patients, seems to be too small, and is two less than proposed by the Superintendents in the United States; eight divisions for either sex is a better number.

4th. Dining halls for three fourths of the patients of either sex, one on each side of the kitchen, does not commend itself to our mind as the best method. The system in the United States of having each division take their meals in their own wards is preferred, as classification is best preserved in this way. Here we must also admit that in all the asylums in Great Britain and on the continent where we witnessed the patients of hospitals taking their meals in common dining halls, and often where males and females ate in the same room, no inconvenience or excitement was observed; but it must not be overlooked, that in all or nearly all of the instances referred to the patients were paupers, and the asylums almost exclusively occupied by them. This custom does not prevail in the asylums intended for the independent classes. In our country, all are accommodated in the same asylum, with very rare exceptions. The rich, the poor, the educated, and the ignorant, the refined and the vulgar, are all in one and the same institution, hence greater attention to classification and separation is an absolute necessity.

Separate Asylum for Patients who Pay.

Some eminent men in all the countries we have visited have given as their decided opinion, that patients who pay and those who do not should never be kept in the same asylums nor placed under the same administration, as the privileges that will be allowed the one begets jealousies on the part of the other, while the necessities of a crowded asylum often enforces associations that would not be recognized at home, and with all the sensibilities sharpened by insanity, as sometimes happens, disgusts and dissatisfactions are engendered, and detrimental results the consequence.

What is *best* to be done and what *can* be done are two very different propositions, and in a majority of cases we have to accept the latter. If it were possible, however, there is no question it would be best for each State to furnish one asylum for the accommodation of all of its citizens who desired to pay for accommodations superior to those that can be given to the indigent. These should be charged a sufficient sum to defray all the expenses of such an establishment, including officers' fees, repairs, and other expenses, the State only furnishing the buildings. All other asylums should be *free* to every person belonging to the State who might elect to enter them, without the payment of *fee* of any kind. If this system could be adopted, many economical changes might be made in the construction of our asylums, without detriment to any class of patients. An asylum for one hundred pay patients would probably be sufficient for all of this class now in our asylum, or likely to be committed during the next ten years. It should be as much under the control and watchful supervision of State officers as the others, and all charges should be regulated by State authority, in order that no person should profit by its operations save and except the patients who paid for the privilege of having more quiet, more comfort, and more attention than the State could afford to give.

This idea, we fear, is in advance of American notions of propriety; yet believing it to be supported by sound policy, and with no injustice to any, we hope to see it carried out in our State at some no distant period in the future.*

5th. The common bath house on the ground floor, one for each sex, is another European custom adopted in nearly all asylums, many of which, admirable in all other respects, have not a single bath tub on the second or third floor. This is certainly a great defect, and must suggest many inconveniences to all who are acquainted with asylum management. We found in one asylum in Austria only one bath room for all the patients, the men using it one day and the women the next. One bath in fourteen days was all that could be obtained by each patient. This asylum was new, neat, comfortable, and well managed in all other respects, but the Medical Director could not prevail on his Board of Managers to supply even one other. We could but conclude that economy in this instance was a poor financier.

6th. We cannot see any special advantage to accrue from a law requiring one of the Board of Control to sign certificates of discharge, as suggested by Doctor Manning. Surely the Superintendent must first say that the patient may be discharged without detriment ere the Trustee affixed his name; hence it would only seem an additional complication without corresponding benefit. Let us give the patient every protection and throw around him every necessary guard, but at the same time incumber our rules with no useless requirements.

With these few differences with Doctor Manning, and some of them may be influenced by prejudice engendered by long habits of thought that observation has failed to remove, we most heartily indorse what he suggests, and commend his remarks to all readers. It has been our desire to present the ideas and opinions of others with quite as much freedom as our own, that our people may have the benefit derived from the experience of many observers.

---

* Note.—*Statement of the Number and Nativity of Pay Patients in the Insane Asylum of the State of California, January 1st, 1872.*

NATIVITY.	Males.	Females.	Total.
Germany	5	1	1
Ireland	4	2	6
England	1	3	4
Scotland		1	1
Mexico		1	1
France		1	1
Chili		1	1
Denmark	1		1
New Brunswick		1	1
	11	11	22
United States	8	3	11
Totals	19	14	33

The foregoing table shows how small a proportion of the patients in our asylum pay for their support and treatment. There are a few others, no doubt, who would gladly avail themselves of asylum care and the benefits to be derived from the skill and experience of its medical officers, if proper accommodations could be offered them, but who shrink from the disadvantages and discomforts of the overcrowded wards of our asylum, and are thus kept at home till all hope of recovery is passed or the means of support have been exhausted, when they are sent to the asylum, to become life burdens upon the public Treasury. Until the system suggested can be carried out, we think it would be far better to abolish all charges, so far as they relate to citizens of the State.

It is scarcely necessary again to call attention to ventilation, warming, lights, water closets, window guards, flooring, stairs, infirmaries, kitchens, laundries, chapels, dead houses, amusement halls, theatres, dances, employés, attendants, airing courts, keys, etc., as we have done so to a sufficient extent in the sketch from Doctor Manning's report, and especially as we must necessarily touch upon some of them in speaking of the character of asylums which we think best adapted to the nature of our climate and the characteristics of our people.

CHAPTER XI.

CRIMINAL INSANE.

Another question connected with the care of the insane should not be passed by without notice. In England, Scotland, Ireland, and some of the continental countries, and in New York, in this country, asylums have been erected for keeping the criminal insane separate from the others, and strong arguments have been advanced in favor of the universal adoption of this system. These have been divided into two classes:

1st. Those who have been convicted of crime, and become insane while serving out their sentence of punishment.

2d. Those who have committed criminal acts during their insanity.

We can see no good reason why those of the latter class should be deprived of treatment in an ordinary asylum. In the eyes of the law they have really been acquitted of any criminal intent, and cannot be punished; nor should they be disgraced by being confined in an asylum with those whose crimes have led them to insanity.

With the first, or convict class, the case is entirely different. Though they have become insane, and are thereby entitled to every consideration of sympathy, and every effort at restoration, they have not been cured of their immoral ideas, low cunning, gross vulgarity, and vicious habits. On the contrary, these are often whetted by insanity, and exhibited in an intensified degree. They have no power to conceal the real hideousness of their character, nor restrain the debased vulgarity of their nature. They are not only unfit associates for the unfortunate people who occupy the wards of an asylum, but have a detrimental influence upon their recovery.

But this whole subject has been so ably and forcibly argued in the report of the Worcester Hospital, we cannot better bring the matter to the favorable notice of the Legislature than by quoting from its pages :

FROM THE WORCESTER REPORT, 1862.

Criminal Insane.

The experience of nearly thirty years operation of this hospital, and the careful observation of the successive Boards of Trustees, of the Superintendents, and others engaged in the management of this institution, all go to establish and to strengthen their conviction that it is impolitic and wrong to place insane criminals in the same rooms, wards,

21

or even establishments with the honest and untainted patients, and require them to live together.

No one will assert that the prison is a proper place for a lunatic; and it is equally clear that the hospital, created for and occupied by patients from general society, is not a proper place for a criminal. Admitting that the insane convict should be removed from the one, it by no means follows that he should be carried to the other. Whether viewed in the light of humanity or of economy, it is better that he be detained in his prison than be admitted into the hospital, for, at the worst, if he be not removed, he may remain insane for life for want of the means of healing, while if he be placed in a ward filled with other and respectable patients, he may be an obstacle to their restoration, and prevent some, perhaps many, from ever regaining their health. The question is not simply whether the insane convict shall or shall not have an opportunity of being healed, but whether an attempt shall be made to save a criminal and worthless citizen, by the peril and perhaps the sacrifice of the restoration of some, possibly many, honest and valuable men who must live and associate with him in the hospital.

Insanity disturbs the mental health of its victims in various ways. Among the most common of these morbid conditions, is the exaltation of sensibility, which makes the patients timid, anxious, suspicious, irritable, and even sometimes quarrelsome. Some are depressed in spirits, and almost crushed with a sense of imaginary sinfulness, or an intense consciousness of unworthiness. To meet these morbid conditions of the patient, the hospital Managers endeavor to bring the most favorable influences to act upon him; they surround him with everything soothing, gentle, and acceptable. They provide everything to cheer, encourage, and elevate him, and inspire him with confidence that his new position in the hospital is all for his good. They arrange all the circumstances, select his associates, and control the conversation; they determine the scenes that may be visited and the ideas that may be presented, according to their influence on the over sensitive and disordered mind.

It is among the best established principles of the treatment of insanity, that a patient should be opposed or interfered with as little as possible, consistently with his good; that his notions and arguments should not be disputed, his wishes and inclinations indulged, so far as they can be safely, his opinions and tastes treated with respect, when they are proper, but always with tenderness, and that everything should be done to encourage his self respect.

Among the patients in the hospital are always the members of our own families—our parents, our brothers and sisters, our sons and daughters. From their childhood they have been taught to love virtue and abhor vice, to avoid even the appearance of wickedness, to associate with good and shun evil company. They have been accustomed to run from the base, the degraded, and the corrupt. Their sensibilities, their tastes, and their consciences have been cultivated and shaped in accordance with their education and their habits. They lose none of these in their disease. Insanity tends to exalt and intensify them. They become morbidly sensitive, and even irritable, in respect to them.

To put a convict among such patients as these, to compel them to associate with him in the same halls, to eat at the same table, to hear his coarse and offensive conversation, his vulgar slang, his profanity, his curses at religion and honesty and religious and honest men, his contemptuous jeers at what they have been taught to regard with reverence, his tales of cunning and crime, of successful and unsuccessful villainy—all this is in contravention of the best principles of managing mental disorders, and diminishes if it does not counteract the influence of the curative measures that may be used.

It is at least a singular view of governmental responsibility that, looking for the highest good of the community and the moral and spiritual welfare of all its members, educates children and youth to walk in the ways of holiness, and encourages all of every age to associate only with the pure and the upright, when they are well and able to choose for themselves, but gives them felons for familiar companions when they are broken down with mental disease and too weak to choose their company.

The hospital is provided for all the families of the commonweath. In the chances of life any one of us may be exposed to the accidents or influences that cause insanity, as well as to those that cause fever. Any of our children may be afflicted with disease of the brain, as well as with disease of the lungs.

A daughter, the idol of her parents, becomes insane. Her anxious and almost agonized friends take her to the hospital and leave her there, in confidence that her intensely sharpened sensibilities will be soothed by the gentlest associates, the tenderest language and most refined manners of those that surround her; but she is shocked to find in the same hall with her, perhaps sitting next to her at table, a convict from the House of Correction, a woman that had previously been the keeper of a brothel, and still retains her vulgar obscenity and her lascivious ways. Or a son, trained in the same way, may become deranged on the subject of religion. Self chastening and downcast, he enters the ward and finds among the inmates a burglar from the State Prison, who has been educated and practiced in all manner of wickedness, and takes a pleasure in the display of his own corruption and in offending the sensibilities of such as he considers to be over nice and fastidious.

Among the insane there are always some whose recovery is doubtful, whose chances of mental life or death hang like a balance so evenly adjusted that the slightest weight will turn the scale, the least disturbing cause will decide the issue against them. These are watched by the officers and attendants in the hospitals with the tenderest solicitude, and guarded with anxious vigilance to protect them from every unfavorable influence. To such as these, standing on the verge of mental death, the presence and companionship of a felon from the prison may be sufficient to overthrow them and determine the fatal course of their disease.

These are cogent reasons, strongly put, and must carry conviction to the mind of every man as to their propriety and justice. The convict insane in California are not sufficiently numerous, however, to justify the establishment of a separate asylum for their accommodation, but it would be an easy matter to erect a suitable building in conjunction with the hospital at San Quentin, to be devoted to this class of patients. The hospital physician could give them the needful medical attention, and they would cost no more to take care of them there than at Stockton, where there is no suitable place to keep or retain them, to say nothing of the cost of transportation.

CHAPTER XII.

CHRONIC INSANE.

Provisions for Curables and Incurables in Separate Institutions.

SEPARATION.

This is a question that has excited some attention in all countries. And though it has been practicably decided as unwise and improper by the Association of Medical Superintendents of American Institutions for the Insane, and most of the bodies of a similar character in other countries, still it finds individual advocates in some of them. In Italy it is by no means uncommon, while in Austria and some of the German States it is rather the rule than the exception. It was one of the subjects to which we directed especial attention in our inquiries, and the opinions of every Superintendent with whom we met during our investigations was solicited. About one fourth of those in Italy, one half in Austria, Moravia, Bohemia, Saxony, and a few other of the German States, perhaps a tenth in other continental countries, and one in twenty of those in Great Britain and the United States, were in favor of separation, while all the rest were opposed to the principle and the practice. Economy seemed to be the leading argument of those who favored its adoption, though a few placed it upon higher grounds, and contended that while the chronic and incurable cases were quite as well cared for, and could be better employed, and allowed more liberties than in a curative establishment, that their removal increased the chances of recovery in the more recent cases; while another class seemed to favor the erection of different buildings for the two classes in proximity to each other, and under the same administration, in order that transfers might be made from the one to the other, as might in the judgment of the Superintendent be deemed expedient.

On the other hand, it is contended that all such institutions are more liable to degenerate into negligence, inattention, and decay; that they are cruel to the patients who are thus told of their hopeless condition and must therefore spend the rest of their days within asylum walls; that instead of being a disadvantage to the more recent and curable cases, the reverse of this is actually the case; that by their habits of obedience and order, others submitted more readily and cheerfully to the rules and requirements of the institution; and that by their example and willingness to labor and to take part in other occupations and amusements, the acute cases more readily joined in these necessary and healthful pursuits; with many other arguments familiar to all who have paid any attention to the subject, and which might be introduced here if deemed of the least importance. Candor compels us to say that our observations of the results of the two systems forces us to the conclusion that separation is wrong in principle and detrimental to the best interest of the insane. While this is decidedly our opinion, however, we most cheerfully admit that some of the asylums for the chronic insane were admirably managed in every respect, and their Superintendents intelligent, zealous, and attentive men, devoting their whole time and all of their energies to the unfortunate patients under their charge; and that this is true of some of these institutions in all the countries we visited. That at Ovid, on Lake Seneca, in the State of New York, with its splendid location and beautiful and picturesque surroundings, especially impressed us most favorably, and was such a paradise in comparison to the miserable wards of the poorhouses from which they had been taken that we cannot but regard its establishment as a boon to the insane poor of the State. We failed to discover, however, even the shadow of a reason why a person becoming insane in the neighborhood of this beautiful asylum should be sent to Utica because he was considered curable, and that one in Utica should be sent to Ovid because the reverse of this was true. It would seem infinitely better that each asylum should admit all of either class occurring in their respective vicinities. They should be as successfully treated at the one asylum as the other; while it is too plain a proposition to require argument that economy of transportation and convenience to family and friends would be best subserved by keeping them at the asylum nearest their homes.

With regard to the results of treatment, the facts elicted are altogether in favor of non-separation; the percentage of cures being less and that of deaths greatest in those countries where the system of separation is most generally pursued.

CHAPTER XIII.

TREATMENT OF INSANITY.

Treatment in English Asylums—*Mania*—Epilepsy connected with Insanity—Paralysis connected with Insanity—Melancholia—Observations on present Treatment of Insanity.

TREATMENT IN ENGLISH ASYLUMS.

In the further report (1847) of the Commissioners in Lunacy for England and Wales will be found a circular letter, addressed to the proprietors or Superintendents of Asylums, containing several questions in reference to their methods of treating cases of insanity, and the disorders complicated with it.

These questions referred especially to the treatment adopted:
First—In mania.
Secondly—In epilepsy connected with insanity.
Thirdly—Paralysis connected with insanity.
Fourthly—In melancholia.
Replies were received from fifty-three physicians in charge of these establishments, from which we extract the following as a fair specimen of the whole, as elucidating the most approved methods of treatment adopted at that time by the most learned men of the day.

MANIA.

First—in regard to Mania:

The Practice pursued at the Devon County Asylum, as described by Doctor Bucknill.

With hot scalp, full pulse, etc., from six to twelve leeches to the temples or behind the ears; the head shaved, and evaporating lotions applied; a warm bath for half an hour at bedtime; the bowels open, by one dose of calomel and jalap, followed, if necessary, by salts and senna; then one fourth or one third of a grain of tartar emetic in solution, every three or four hours. The patient is not kept upon low diet; he is clothed warmly, and in the open air as much as possible, and the opportunity of muscular exertion and fatigue is allowed. If he does not sleep, two drachms of tincture of henbane, with camphor mixed, are given at bedtime; if this does not succeed, one drachm of laudanum, with one drachm of sulphuric æther, are given when the acute symptoms have yielded.

When the head is cool, the face pale, the pulse compressible, I give warm baths, with æther and ammonia, and sometimes æther and laudanum, or Hoffman's anodyne, with aloetic aperients. When these symptoms are accompanied by great unsomnolence or restlessness, with illusions, and when I can ascertain that the patient has been a drunkard, I give wine, æther, and large quantities of opium, the indications of treatment being the same as in delirium.

When the patient, with the ordinary symptoms of mania, presents those of typhus fever, with sordes on the teeth, picking the bedclothes, etc., I give warm negus, frequently ammonia, camphor, æther, with occasional doses of calomel. I have fortunately never lost a patient suffering under acute mania.

Remarks.

General bloodletting I never use, and cannot, therefore, give an opinion upon.

Local Bloodletting

I use frequently, by leeches, to the groin, temples, or neck; or by cupping the nape of the neck. In inflammatory diseases within the chest, I find that free cupping between the shoulders, followed by the use of antimony or mercurials, is sufficient, and that bleeding is not required.

Emetics

I have given, with benefit, where exacerbation of melancholy is accompanied by fœtid breath, or discharge of gluey mucous from the stomach; also in incipient dementia with lethargy and indigestion, and for chronic cough.

Purgatives.

Patients are often admitted with obstinate constipation, and for them the stronger purgatives are necessary; but afterwards, this condition is not allowed to prevail, and an occasional, or, if need be, a small daily dose of compound rhubard pill, or castor oil, or decoction of aloes, or house medicine, is all that is requisite. Five or six grains of calomel are given when the state of the liver requires it, but I have now discontinued the use of drastic purgatives. I have used them with decided benefit in maniacal cases, but have made up my mind that antimonials are more manageable and safe. The house medicine above mentioned is made of the sulphate of magnesia and soda, with senna, and extract of liquorice, decocted, and peppermint water added, when cool; the patients like it, and a dose, to produce two or three dejections, will often cut short beginning excitement.

Antimonials.

1 use tartar emetic frequently in acute and recurrent mania, dissolving three or four grains in mint water, with simple syrup, and giving one twelfth part every three, or four, or six hours. After a few doses the medicine does not usually produce sickness, the appetite is not diminished, and the patient often gains flesh during its use. Two or three gamboge colored evacuations are generally passed in the day. I believe that this medicine acts less by its depressing agency than by some influence upon the congested capillaries of the brain, enabling them to contract. I find that repeated doses of ipecacuana, though more nauseating, are not equally useful.

Opiates and Anodynes

I use sparingly. In the cases before referred to as resembling delirium tremens, opium is given in large quantities. It is not given if there is heat of the scalp and a strong pulse. In other cases of sleeplessness, where it is not thus contra-indicated, it is usually combined with sulphuric ether, or with camphor. Hyoscyamus, in combination with ammonia and camphor, is often given as a sleeping potion, but sleep is more frequently induced by warm baths, cooling lotions to the head, or some food in the middle of the night, than by means of narcotics. A plaster of extract of belladonna is sometimes used to the epigastrium or pericardium as an anodyne. Other narcotics have been tried without encouraging results.

Antispasmodics.

The compound galbanum pill and mixture, containing the fœtid spirits of ammonia or the tincture of assafœtida, are sometimes given to females with uterine derangement; but the only antispasmodic in frequent use is the spirits of turpentine, given to epileptics with a view of reducing the number and the severity of the fits.

Tonics.

Vegetable bitters, with ammonia and aromatic stimulants, or with mineral acids, or with liquor potassæ, or with small doses of iodide of potassium, are frequently used; also, chalybeates, in the form of steel wine or compound steel pills, or iodide of iron dissolved in simple syrup, which prevents its decomposition, are given in numerous cases with benefit. The only tonic not in general use which has been given is the sulphate of strychnia, in doses from the thirtieth of a grain upwards. It is never given to produce nervous twitchings. It requires occasional doses of aloetic medicines, and is useful in some cases of melancholia in old people.

Stimulants

Are frequently used medicinally. Those preferred are æther and ammonia, strong beer, porter, and wine. They are mostly given to patients who are admitted in a reduced condition, or to those whose strength is failing from general decay, paralysis, or other cause.

Bathing.

Tepid, warm, shower, and vapor baths are used. A tepid bath is given to all the patients once a week in Summer and once a fortnight in Winter, for the sake of cleanliness. Warm baths are constantly used to allay excitement and to induce sleep. Shower baths are used as a tonic to dyspeptic and hysterical young patients, but not to old ones. They are also sometimes given to the refractory as a penal remedy. Vapor baths have been tried upon some old persons suffering from melancholy, with dry and harsh skin, it is thought with benefit, but further experience is required.

Practice pursued at Middlesex (or Hanwell) County Asylum, as described by Doctor Conolly.

A kind and soothing reception, immediate removal of restraints, a warm bath, clean clothing, comfortable food, encouraging words, a medical treatment first directed to any manifest bodily disease which may occasion the cerebral disturbance, as of the uterus, stomach, etc., or the general loss of strength; and if such disease or debility is not manifest, attempts to allay the irritation of the brain more directly by leeches occasionally applied to the head, gentle aperients, moderate doses of tartarized antimony, sometimes combined with sedatives, cold applications to the head, blisters behind the neck, shaving the head, and friction of the scalp with the tartarized antimony, the warm bath, or in violent cases the cold shower bath efficiently applied; tranquility, occasional exercise in the open air, exercise and occupation in chronic cases, cleanliness, order, good diet, attention to relieve heat and thirst, particularly in the night, a careful avoidance of everything that can irritate the brain, including the avoidance of the strait waistcoat, etc. Antimony and all sedatives are of uncertain effect, and sometimes of none, *time* seeming alone to effect a cure, provided proper and constant care be taken of the patient.

General Remarks.

It will be observed that I consider the direct treatment of any form of insanity by mere medicinal application to be very limited; but the indirect treatment of mental maladies by innumerable means acting upon the body and mind of immeasurable importance. These means can, I believe, seldom be efficiently applied, except in well constructed and well conducted asylums, superintended by well educated men, aided by benevolent and active attendants. By such means I believe many insane persons to be capable of cure, and all, however incurable and hopeless, capable of improvement and relief.

I will merely add, that I am convinced that general bloodletting is rarely admissible, and generally dangerous in insanity, and that local bleeding by leeches is safe and serviceable in most cases. I have no faith in emetics. I think purgatives are often needlessly employed. Antimony is often of temporary service; sedatives, though occasionally most efficacious, are also most uncertain in their effects. The acetate of morphia, the hyoscyamus, and the cannabis indica, have appeared to me to be the most frequently useful. Tonics and stimulants are frequently of service, and every form of bathing in different instances. I have ceased to employ the douche bath, as it occasions more distress to the patient than the shower bath or than cold affusion, without corresponding benefit.

A liberal diet, moderate use of malt liquor, exercise out of doors, employment, recreation, mental occupation, friendly intercourse, and judicious religious attentions, are all important anxiliaries to amendment.

Practice in the Surrey County Asylum, as described by Sir Alexander Morison.

If the patient is brought under mechanical restraint, this is removed and the warm bath is generally employed. The hair, if considerable, is thinned, and in some cases removed; and recourse is had to laxative medicines, as jalap, rhubarb, senna, calomel, sulphate of magnesia, croton oil, castor oil. Nauseating medicines are sometimes given to allay excitement—in particular, small doses of tartrate of antimony; also sedatives, as hyoscyamus, morphia, camphor, nitre. Cooling lotions are applied to the head. Topical bloodletting by cupping or by leeches (general bloodletting has not been employed). Blisters to the nape of the neck. Animal food daily. Porter or wine have in some cases been given. . Few recent cases of mania have been received, owing to the vicinity of the public hospitals of Bethlem and St Luke's.

Practice pursued at Stafford County Lunatic Asylum, as described by Mr. James Wilkes.

In the medical treatment of the cases of mania sent to this Asylum the first indication is sought in the careful examination of the patients' general condition, in ascertaining how far the cerebral excitement depends upon increased vascular action, and in detecting the nature of any bodily disorder that may be present. Although the latter is often obscure, still some derangement of the thoracic or abdominal organs, either functional or organic, is a constant complication of mania, and remedies directed to their relief are often sufficient to cure the mental disorder.

In many instances the patient when brought to the asylum is in so prostrate a condition; either from exhaustion, produced by the disorder itself, from having refused food, or from the extent to which bleeding, purgatives, and low diet have been carried, that the course of treatment is at once clear, and good nourishing diet, stimulants, and tonics often restore the patient, unless, as is too frequently the case, the symptoms of sinking have already set in.

The injurious effect of active medical treatment in cases of mania, and the tendency there is to exhaustion and sinking is so fully established that the general practice in this asylum is chiefly directed to supporting the vital powers, subduing the cerebral irritation, and correcting the existing physical derangement, not by any peculiar or specific mode of treatment, but upon ordinary principles.

In pure cases of mania, however great the excitement may be, general bleeding is never employed. The cerebral irritation is often materially relieved and every advantage gained by local bleeding, without materially depressing the patient's strength. For this purpose, leeches to the temples or behind the ears, and cupping on the same parts or on the nape of the neck, are the means usually employed, due regard being had in using these to the amount of vascular action and condition of the patient.

Any obvious derangement in the patient's general health, or in the function of any particular organ, is attended to, and appropriate remedies prescribed; but the usually defective state of the digestive and assimilative organs renders attention to them of much importance. The bowels, when torpid, are freely acted upon, and if there is nothing to contra-indicate such a course, the morbid and accumulated secretions are removed by a dose or two of calomel, either alone or combined with colocynth; and if the patient refuses medicine, croton oil and enemata are employed. If there is much exhaustion, an enema alone is prescribed.

The various narcotics and sedatives are constantly used in this asylum in the treatment of cases of mania, both acute and chronic, and though they are uncertain, and no very precise rule can be laid down for their employment, they are, on the whole, found to be highly serviceable. They appear to be of the most benefit in cases attended with great nervous excitement, and are of little use and often positively injurious when there is much febrile disturbance, especially in typhoid symptoms or vascular determination to the head. The description of narcotics to be used, and also the dose, can only be determined by experience in individual cases. The free action of the bowels should be previously obtained, and then either solid opium, the tincture, Battley's sedative solution, or morphia, are prescribed, combined in some cases with antimony or ipecacuana, hyoscyamus, camphor, or æther. In cases of great excitement any of these, in small doses, rather increase it, and it is important to prescribe it in full doses and frequently to keep up the narcotic action by repeating it every four or six hours. The Indian hemp has latterly been used here, and, when genuine, is a valuable and powerful remedy. In several cases in which I have employed it the excitement has been subdued and sleep obtained, when large and repeated doses of opium and morphia only added to the restlessness of the patient. Its after effects also seem to be less injurious than those of opium; constipation is not produced, and the constitutional disturbance is often relieved.

When there is much febrile disturbance, with heat of skin and thirst, the saline mixture (composed of liq. ammoniæ, acet. vin. antimon., pot. tart., tinct. hyoscyami, potassæ nitras, and mixtura camphoræ) is frequently prescribed with good effect, the action of the skin being promoted by it and the restlessness relieved.

In certain cases of acute mania, and also in the chronic form, the employment of tonics is found to be of much use, especially in enfeebled constitutions with weak pulse and depressed vital powers. Quinine, iron, and the vegetable bitters, combined with stimulants and aromatics, are prescribed in these cases.

The exitement in mania is rather increased than relieved by low diet, and the usual difficulty is to get the patients to take sufficient food. The diet used here is ample and nutritious, and the principle of supporting the patient's strength and making up for the waste and exhaustion which are going on in the system, by an abundant supply of nutriment, is here fully acted upon.

Thus, patients who are laboring under much excitement are not restricted to the ordinary dietary, but are supplied with meat daily, soup, milk, eggs, sago, arrow root, etc., and often with wine, brandy, ale, and other stimulants; and daily experience proves that in many chronic cases life may be prolonged by a liberal diet, and that in recent cases it alone often cures the patient and even supersedes medical treatment.

The use of the warm and shower bath is found here to be of much importance in the treatment of mania. The warm bath seems to exert a sedative influence in many cases of excitement, and may generally be employed in safety. The tepid or cold shower bath, when cautiously employed, is also a powerful means of subduing the paroxysm, and many patients acknowledge that it alone has cured them. It seems to be of the greatest benefit in cases of mania attended with heat of scalp and increased vascular action, and when unattended with much general disturbance of the system or symptoms of thoracic or abdominal disorder. In the latter complications the use of the shower bath is at once contra indicated, and the warm bath may be substituted for it.

Cold lotions, ice, and cold affusion to the head are constantly employed whenever heat of scalp, suffused eyes, and increased arterial action indicate fullness of the cerebral vessels.

In acute cases of mania, blisters are not often used here, as they serve to add to the excitement by the irritation they produce. In cases of chronic mania they are employed, and especially when there is evidence of slow mischief going on in the brain.

Remarks.

Emetics.—These, as directed to the treatment of insanity, are never employed in this asylum, nor are the depressing doses of tartarized antimony which some practioners recommend. In cases of gastric or biliary derangement, in which emetics would be indicated under other circumstances, they are occasionally employed.

To the observations on general bleeding I may add that not only is there a want of proof of relief having been obtained by this popular remedy in any of the cases brought to this asylum in which it has been practiced, but its injurious effects have been so repeatedly and decidedly witnessed, either in producing fatal exhaustion or reducing the patients to a hopeless state of imbecility, that in cases of simple mania, uncombined with inflammation, its adoption cannot be too strongly deprecated.

In reference to the diet of the insane, daily observation increases my conviction that a liberal supply of good, nutritious food both adds to the recoveries and diminishes the mortality in institutions for the insane, being an important means of cure in recent cases and of prolonging life in the chronic and incurable.

Practice pursued at Brislington House, as described by Doctors F. and C. Fox.

In cases of mania, which, we must observe, seldom come under our notice in the incipient stage, we have rarely seen benefit derived from general bleeding. Small quantities of blood are often abstracted by the cupping glasses from the nape of the neck; the bowels are evacuated freely by aloetics combined with nauseating doses of tartar emetic taken each night, and succeeded by castor oil in the morning. The cold plunge or shower bath is usually taken each morning, and it is repeated with much advantage in the evening in cases of sleeplessness. In the more protracted cases of mania, the principal medical treatment has consisted of counterirritants to the scalp or to the pit of the stomach, with attention to the state of the skin and bowels, the maintenance of a warm atmosphere in the sleeping apartments, a plain and nutritious diet, and the use of much exercise, unattended with violent bodily exercise.

Remarks.

We have found it impossible to comprise under either of the foregoing heads a large proportion of the cases which have been in this asylum, or to describe any uniform mode of treatment as applicable to the cases in either of the divisions. In those cases of moral perversion which occur without the existence of any delusion, we have seen much benefit derived from the system adopted in an asylum. In this form of insanity we have generally discovered a propensity to excess in diet and to intoxication, or to the indulgence of lascivious habits; and we have found a spare diet, cold bathing, saline purgatives, early rising, and active exercise, with a prolonged separation from the scenes and habits of former excitement, most useful to such patients. We believe that such a system can be enforced only in an asylum, and that moral treatment and the services of a chaplain are of much importance in these cases.

General bloodletting is only resorted to by us in those cases of mania in which the physical condition of the patient induces the apprehension of apoplexy, and never for the purpose of quieting a paroxysm of excitement. Previously to admission, most of our patients have been under medical treatment, and we have often had reason to suspect that the general bloodletting to which they have been subjected has been detrimental, and that it has in some cases induced permanent fatuity. We have found general bleeding useful in some cases of melancholia. In most forms of insanity, we find benefit derived by the local abstraction of blood from the head or nape of the neck; in some cases, by the application of leeches to the pit of the stomach, and in females, to the groin.

We value antimonials in the treatment of insanity much less for their emetic action than the change which they effect in the circulation, and we find that this object is gained by nauseating doses, which tend to allay maniacal excitement and to procure sleep.

We consider that the use of purgatives is indicated in almost all forms of insanity in the incipient stages, and we find them especially useful in melancholia, until they can be dispensed with by attention to diet and exercise. Opiates and anodynes have frequently been resorted to by us, with a hope of success which has but rarely attended their use. In paralysis and epilepsy we have derived benefit from the use of antispasmodics, tonics, and stimulants, and in some cases of melancholia dependent upon uterine disturbance, but we have not found these remedies in the treatment of mania.

We attach much value to the use of hot and cold bathing. In mania, we chiefly use the cold plunging and cold shower bath, and we find the warm bath and the cold shower bath, with the feet of the patient immersed in hot water, more applicable in cases of melancholia.

We are of opinion that maniacal and melancholic patients almost invariably require a generous and nutritious diet; this we find to be equally necessary in cases of chronic insanity. In epilepsy and paralysis, connected with insanity, we often find it necessary to place the patients upon a very restricted system of diet.

EPILEPSY IN CONNECTION WITH INSANITY.

Secondly—in regard to epilepsy, we quote:

Remedies used in Cases of Epilepsy at Devon County Asylum, as described by Dr. Bucknill.

The patients are placed on a wholesome and nutritious diet and regimen. Indigestion is treated by tonics and other appropriate remedies; costiveness is removed by small daily doses of co. rhubarb pills, decoct. of aloes, castor oil, or house medicine; when the fits are severe, one drachm of spt. of turpentine, with mx. of liq. of potass. every four hours; sinapism to the legs and feet, and three or four ounces of blood from the neck by cupping.

Turpentine undoubtedly diminishes the strength and frequency of the fits, and I have only seen it once produce bloody urine. In young patients, the frequent application of croton oil to the scalp, and the long continued use of mercurial alteratives (hyd. chloria. is preferred) have apparently effected cures.

Remedies used in Cases of Epilepsy at the Middlesex (or Hanwell) Asylum, by Doctor Conolly.

Cases of epilepsy being generally associated with occasional mania, are treated on the principles before mentioned. In the fit, care is taken that the patient sustains no injury. Epileptics should sleep on low beds or cribs, or beds on the floor. In the excited or maniacal state nothing is done to irritate the patient. When restraints were resorted to the epileptics were often furious, and generally dangerous; since their disuse, the epileptic ward has become the quietest in the asylum. . I have never seen a case of epilepsy in an adult permanently cured by any medicine whatever. Attention to the general health, the occasional application of leeches to the head, blisters behind the neck, and, in some cases, an incision in the scalp, have served to lessen the cerebral congestion. Setons appear to me to be useless, as well as issues, and all other modes of severe counter-irritation.

Remedies used in Cases of Epilepsy at the Surrey County Lunatic Asylum, by Sir A. Morison, M. D.

Many cases of this description have been admitted. In them attention is given to the general health by remedies tending to improve the state of the digestive organs.

Leeches, in. some cases, have been of service; also, rubefacients, counter-irritants, and blisters, and tartrate of antimony, externally applied.

Preparations of silver and turpentine have been given internally, but with little good effect.·

Organic mischief, to a greater or less extent, has been found in the brain in all the cases of epilepsy, connected with insanity, which have been examined in this asylum.

Remedies used in Cases of Epilepsy at the Stafford County Asylum, by Mr. Wilkes.

The cases of epilepsy usually sent to this asylum are usually connected with congenital defect, or are of such long standing and so intense in degree that any hope of cure or material relief is out of the question; and the only indication seems to be, to attend to the patient's general health, and guard against and relieve cerebral congestion. In cases of obvious debility the employment of tonics is of use, especially those of the mineral class, as the preparations of iron, zinc and the nitrate of silver. The excessive state of congestion which frequently occurs is here treated by the free exhibition of purgatives, as large doses of calomel and croton oil; the application of leeches or cupping to the temples; ice, cold lotions, and cold affusions to the head, blisters to the nape of the neck, stimulating pediluvia and enemata, especially those containing turpentine and assafœtida. While the diet should be nourishing, it should not be stimulating; and the disposition to over-nutrition should be carefully guarded against. As a general rule, the free action of the bowels is kept up by the frequent exhibition of purgatives.

Remedies used in Cases of Epilepsy, at Brislington House, by Doctors F. and C. Fox.

If such cases are of recent date, we have sometimes seen good results from the use of nitrate of silver, with small doses of turpentine; an incision on the scalp, leeches on the perinæum, the tepid shower bath, much friction of the skin, as much pedestrian exercise as the patient can accomplish, and a restricted vegetable diet, have often been useful. By paying close attention to the periodical tendency which this disease so frequently displays, and by meeting the gradual increase of nervous irritability by a small local bleeding and a moderate anodyne, we have sometimes succeeded in prolonging the intervals between the attacks, and on some occasions in effecting a cure.

PARALYSIS CONNECTED WITH INSANITY.

Thirdly—In regard to paralysis, we quote:

Remedies used in Cases of Paralysis at Devon County Asylum, by Doctor Bucknill.

When the patients are not admitted in a bedridden and ulcerated condition, good diet and regimen generally improve the strength, and the progress of the disease appears to be very slow. A few leeches are sometimes applied to the temples, when the face is apt to flush and the scalp to become heated. Having observed that some patients who had sore legs appeared to be more comfortable when the suppuration was free, I have tried setons, but cannot as yet give an opinion about their utility. In sinking cases, wine and porter are freely given, and sloughing sores are dressed with equal parts of tinct. of kino and liq. of subacetate of lead, and a yeast cataplasm is applied for three or four hours every second day.

Remedies used in Cases of Paralysis at the Middlesex (or Hanwell) County Asylum, by Doctor Conolly.

The paralytic complication (*paralysie générale* of the French) makes great care necessary to prevent injury to the patient. Good food, porter, occasional tonics, and in all cases warmth and comfort, evidently prolong life for many years. The patients neither bear reduction nor excitement; even baths are scarcely to be recommended. Leeches and aperients are sometimes required to lessen congestion in the head. Small doses of calomel and squills have occasionally seemed useful, but I am satisfied that all specific modes of treating this form of paralysis are ineffectual as regards a cure. Many of the miseries of the malady, as uncleanliness, ulceration, and fits of violent anger, are prevented or long retarded by kind treatment and the absence of all bodily restraint.

Remedies used in Cases of Paralysis at the Surrey County Asylum, by Sir Alexander Morison, M. D.

The same may be said as to the existence of organic mischief in cases of this description, of which a large number have been examined. The remedies employed have been laxatives, leeches, blisters, generous diet, and tonics, especially quinine. In most cases recourse has been had to water beds on account of the extensive ulceration which frequently attends the termination of these unfortunate cases.

Remedies used in Cases of Paralysis at the Stafford County Asylum, by Mr Wilkes.

Cases of paralysis connected with insanity, like those of epilepsy, are rarely sent to this asylum before the disease is in an advanced stage, and as far as my experience goes, the patient in a hopeless and incurable state. Life, in many cases, is prolonged by care and attention, and it is especially needful to guard against congestion of the brain, and so to regulate the diet as not to encourage undue nutrition and plethora, which is often attended with serious aggravation of the symptoms. The occasional exhibition of purgatives, and even those of an active character, are necessary to relieve congestion, and the tendency, which usually exists, to constipation. Local bleeding, by means of leeches and cupping, to the temples, behind the ears, or nape of the neck, is also employed, together with blisters and other counter-irritation, especially when there are symptoms of coma. The iodide of iron and a mild mercurial course, combined in some cases with tonics, have been tried in this asylum, but without permanent benefit; the organic changes in the brain, upon which the disease depends, appearing to be beyond the influence of medical treatment.

Remedies used in Cases of Paralysis at Brislington House, by Doctors F. and ·C. Fox.

We have arrested this disease by the use of iodide of mercury, by the prolonged application of open blisters to the parietal junction of the scalp, and by the use of the electro-galvanic apparatus to the affected portions of the body. ·

As such cases have generally occurred in aged or wasted constitutions we have often had recourse to chalybeate medicines, but have experienced their injurious effects upon the mental disease. These cases are rarely presented to our notice in a curable state.

MELANCHOLIA.

Fourthly—in regard to melancholia, we quote:

Remedies used in Cases of Melancholia in the Devon County Asylum, by Doctor Bucknill.

I endeavor to appreciate and to treat the bodily condition wherever it is disordered. In young women with suppression of the menses, I order leeches to the vulva, hip baths, aloetic aperients, and often chalybeates. In elder women, at the critical period, an occasional blue pill, a small daily dose of decoction of aloes, vegetable tonics, sometimes galbanum, or assafœtida, or chalybeates. In various cases with dyspepsia, I have given bitter infusions with mineral acids or alkali, or gr. iij. doses of iodide of potassium with liq. potassæ or lime water.

In some cases emetics have been very beneficial, and shower baths are good tonics and safe in the Summer months. When pain, sense of burning, etc. is felt in the head, I have given blue pill to twitch the gums, and used counter-irritation to the scalp. When the skin is dry, warm bath with friction, or vapor baths are used. I have found the electro-galvanic apparatus beneficial in some cases, when used moderately so as not to produce fear or pain.

Remedies used in Cases of Melancholia at Middlesex (or Hanwell) Asylum, by Dr. Conolly.

The attention is first directed to any manifest bodily disorder, or to existing debility or plethora, often with the effect of curing the patient. Leeches behind the ears or to the forehead, blisters behind the neck, small and sometimes large doses of sedatives, give relief in some cases. The warm bath is soothing; and, in some instances, the shower bath has great effect. Occupation of mind and body, cheerful and encouraging conversation, and the absence of all restraints or apparatus calculated to alarm the patient, are of great importance; direct attempts to stimulate the faculties, by various impressions, by frequent change of scene, or by wine or spirituous liquors, are seldom successful, and sometimes very hurtful. Tonics are, in some cases, serviceable, as calumba, cascarilla, or preparations of iron. When plethora is manifestly present, daily saline aperients are generally useful.

Remedies used in Cases of Melancholia in the Surrey County Asylum, by Sir Alexander Morison, M. D.

Few recent cases of this description have been sent to this asylum, owing to the cause stated in regard to recent cases of mania.

Laxatives, sedatives, tonics, warm baths, shower baths, and blisters, have been chiefly employed.

The most numerous cases are those of dementia, in a more or less advanced stage. The object in them has been to improve the general health. Warm baths, shower baths, and blisters, have been occasionally employed.

In all cases where practicable, recourse is had to occupation, useful or agreeable. As little restraint is employed as is deemed to be consistent with the safety of the patient and of others, and this is continued for as short a time as possible.

Remedies used in Cases of Melancholia at Stafford County Asylum, by Mr. James Wilkes.

This state is generally found .to be connected with a low condition of health and a depressed state of the vital powers, independent of direct symptoms of cerebral disorder, and the medical treatment followed in this asylum is chiefly directed to restore the functions of any organ which may seem to be impaired, and to invigorate the patient's general health. The frequent association of melancholia with various forms of dyspepsia and disorders of the assimilative organs is not overlooked; neither are the defective quality and quantity of the urine, and the changes which so often take place in its chemical composition.

The employment of purgatives is rarely to be dispensed with, and these are often required in large and repeated doses to obviate the tendency to constipation which usually exists. The various combinations of tonics and stimulants with purgatives are here advantageously used, as the bitter infusions with sulphate of magnesia, and compound spirits of ammonia, aloes, quinine, and iron, in the form of pills, with sulphate of iron; alterative doses of calomel, or blue pill, are also given when the functions of the liver are disordered. When there is headache and symptoms of fullness in the head, the application of leeches is of service; and much benefit is often derived in cases of melancholia from the regular use of the shower bath whenever there is no obvious reason for not applying it.

Sedatives and narcotics in various forms are used in this asylum with great benefit, the restlessness of patients being subdued by them and the nervous system tranquilized. The preparation of opium (especially Battley's sedative solution), morphia, Indian hemp, hyoscyamus, conium, camphor, lactucarium, in different combinations, are given with the best effect. The diet in cases of melancholia requires regulating in reference to the state of the digestive organs, but should always be nutritious, and in many cases may be advantageously combined with stimulants.

Remedies used in cases of Melancholia at Brislington House, by Doctors F. and C. Fox.

In melancholia which has succeeded to an attack of mania we have so often found that the disorder has again reverted to the maniacal form, that we generally confine the medical treatment to moderate evacuations of the patient's bowels, with regulation of the diet, and we encourage that increased indication to quiet and to sleep which such cases usually exhibit. Melancholia, as an idiopathic disease, is the only form of insanity in which general bleeding has appeared to us to be useful. In such cases we often open the vena saphæna, prescribe warm and aloetic purgatives, counter-irritation to the region of the stomach, warm bathing, carriage and horse exercise, and animal diet.

TREATMENT AT THE PRESENT DAY.

The foregoing extracts show the most approved treatment of insanity

23

as practiced in the English asylums twenty-five years ago. In many respects it is essentially the same at the present time. A few of the remedies then employed have been laid aside, or are regarded with less favor now, while a few others have been discovered or brought more prominently to notice, and have been substituted for them or given in conjunction with them.

General Bleeding.

General bloodletting was not approved by any of the authorities we have quoted, though we see that the practice was spoken of as one too much in vogue, and as detrimental in the extreme. Such is the universal opinion of the physicians at this time, and in no instance nor in any form of insanity was it recommended by those with whom we met as a proper remedy to be employed.

Local Bleeding.

Local bleeding, by cups or leeches, is still practiced by some physicians, and regarded with as much favor as ever, while it is rarely resorted to by others, and therefore not so generally employed.

Counter-irritants.

Shaving the scalp, blisters, and counter-irritants, including setons, are also less employed than formerly, while tartar emetic and digitalis have become extremely unpopular with many, and are now cautiously and sparingly used by all.

Baths.

Baths in all forms seem to be less used in England than formerly, and in the asylums of the United States have a less prominent place than they deserve, while in Italy, the German States, and in some portions of France and Holland they are relied on as of paramount importance. Indeed, they seem to be the chief agents employed in some of these countries, and are administered in one way or other in nearly all forms and phases of the disorder. The shower bath, the douche, the plunge, and continued bath, are all supposed to have their peculiar virtues as stimulants, tonics, or sedatives, and are used *ad libitum et ad infinitum.* We have often seen half a dozen patients in one bathroom, each with the head only visible, the body being immersed in warm water, and the bathtub covered with a lid having a hole in one end to fit around the neck. Here they usually remain from one to three hours; in some cases six to eight hours, and in occasional instances for days at a time. Doctor Gudden of the Asylum at Zurich, in Switzerland, informed us that he had on one occasion kept a man thus confined in a bath five days. In this instance there was a high state of excitement connected with bed-sores; and the treatment was for the double purpose of allaying the one and relieving the other. The patient is represented as having slept well during a portion of the time spent in the bathtub, while the bed-sores were entirely healed. The most remarkable feature in this case was the entire freedom from exhaustion or any other evil consequence. We would have supposed that such relaxation of the physical powers would have ensued as to have rendered resuscitation impossible. We were also informed that in a case at Vienna, where a man had been scalded by steam, Doctor Hebra had him placed in a tepid bath and kept there for a period of three weeks, until a new cuticle had formed over the entire body. The patient recovered without inconvenience. This case was not one of insanity, and has been introduced to show how much endurance is possessed by some persons under peculiar circumstances, and to direct attention to this treatment. The water, of course, was kept of uniform temperature, and at such degree as was most agreeable to the patient. The agonizing pain usually attendant upon scalds is said to have been effectually overcome. In most of the asylums in these countries there is a general bathroom for either sex, and in many of them, especially Santa Maria della Pieta at Rome, and St. Ann at Paris, are fitted up in the most elaborate manner. In addition to the ordinary appliances for the warm and vapor bath, the douche, plunge, and shower bath, there are the Turkish and medicated baths, and a peculiar contrivance made with metallic pipes an inch in diameter, forming circles like the hoops of a barrel. These tubes are perforated with innumerable holes on the inner side, so as to send small streams of water under heavy pressure upon every inch of the body at the same time. This the poor fellow has to submit to till the doctor or master of the bath concludes that the object sought to be accomplished has been attained. It seemed to us a frightful ordeal through which to pass, and from the contortions and grimaces of the patients we infer it was regarded in the same unfavorable light by them.

At the Asylum San Yon, at Rouen, presided over by Doctor Morel, a writer well known to the scientific world, a man of ability, and a worthy successor of Esquirol and other celebrated men who had charge of this famous old asylum in bygone days, we also found them both much employed, and especially in the treatment of epilepsy. The shower bath is used twice a day in these cases, after which the patient is wrapped in a sheet. He reports one case of great violence entirely cured by this method, in which bro. pot. and other remedies usually resorted to had signally failed. He had also seen great benefit in other cases, and entertained the opinion that no remedy equalled it with which he was acquainted.

There can be no question about the efficacy of baths in the treatment of insanity, when judiciously prescribed and properly administered, but like all other powerful agents they are liable to abuses, by which they are brought into disfavor. Doctor Blanche, of Paris, and Doctor Skae, of Edinburgh, informed us that after many years of persistent and successful use of the warm bath in the treatment of acute mania, they had been induced to abandon it entirely, for notwithstanding the happy effects derived from it in most cases, they had become convinced that several patients for whom they had prescribed the warm bath had died in consequence of its depressing influence.

We conclude, therefore, that baths, like most other valuable agents, are too much used in some countries and too little in others. No remedy is so general in its effects as to be applicable to all cases, and its failure to accomplish *all* that may be expected of it is no reason why it should be totally abandoned. Chloroform and opium are sometimes fatal when administered in ordinary doses, yet they are too valuable to be abandoned on this account. Let us use all the remedies of value that science has given to our profession, but let us watch their effects and administer them with prudence.

Purgatives.

With regard to purgatives, no change seems to have taken place for many years. They are regarded as absolutely necessary in certain conditions in all phases of insanity, the particular kind to be employed being a mere matter of taste with the physician prescribing them. Those employed twenty-five years ago are as much in vogue to-day as they were then.

Emetics.

Emetics are even less popular now than formerly, and are not often administered. Indeed, what we have said of tartarized antimony in its sedative and other capacities may also be said of it as an emetic. None of the emetics are popular remedies at this time.

Anodynes, Narcotics, etc.

Anodynes and narcotics, which have occupied such a high place in the confidence of most medical men who have been engaged in the treatment of insanity during the last quarter of a century, are now being subjected to earnest criticism by some, and almost angry, if not unreasonable, opposition by others. They are remedies used in some form, though in various degree, by nearly all the Superintendents of asylums with whom we have met, regardless of country or differences of opinion on other subjects. Hence, we might naturally expect to find that they have been misused in some, and greatly abused in other instances. Dr. Maudsley, the President of the Psychological Association of Great Britain, in an able and interesting address, read before that association August third, eighteen hundred and seventy-one, made narcotics the subject of special notice, and deprecated their use, in most cases, in decided terms, denominating them the "chemical restraint," that had been substituted for the mechanical restraint of former times. It was, perhaps, natural that this class of remedies should have been used to excess in a country where public opinion had been so much excited by and had waged such vigorous war against the employment of mechanical restraint—even in its mildest forms—in any asylum in the realm. In almost every asylum of ordinary size, there are a few patients who at times become so much excited, and have such irresistible propensities to injure themselves or others—to tear their clothing, indecently to expose their persons, or commit other equally unreasonable acts—that it becomes absolutely necessary to restrain them by some means—mechanically, if you choose, by seclusion in padded rooms; by the muscular power of attendants, or by narcotics, anodynes, etc., the "chemical restraint" of which Dr. Maudsley now complains. Mechanical restraint being tabooed by public opinion, was not to be thought of ten or twenty years ago. It would have cost any Superintendent in England his official head to have undertaken it, and let the fact be known. Seclusion, when long continued, is attended with many evil results—loss of appetite, depression of spirits, the engendering of filthy habits, or other effects detrimental to physical health and mental integrity. Attendants, unfortunately, are not always blessed with that amount of sweetness of temper, of untiring patience, and unlimited self-control, that will enable them, either through a sense of duty or from Christian principles, when "struck upon one cheek to turn the other," even though the offender be a lunatic. Hence the necessity, in England, more than in other countries, of resorting to sedatives and other chemical restraints to produce the quietness and relief that could not otherwise be attained. The debate that followed the reading of Doctor Maudsley's address revealed the fact that all did not agree in the views he had expressed; but, on the contrary, many stoutly maintained that anodynes were among the most valuable agents employed in the treatment of insanity; while all admitted that cases did occur in which it was necessary to employ them in some form. In such a discussion, it was natural to inquire which of the many neurotic medicines was best calculated to accomplish the desired end with least injury to the patient. Opium, morphine, Battley's sedative, hyosciamus, cannabis indicus, bromide of potash, chloral hydrate, and, in some instances, a mixture of two or more of these drugs, was given preference. But the most remarkable and varied views were entertained with regard to the effects and efficacy of the hydro-chloral. It is thought, by Doctor Rhys Williams and a few others, to be of little consequence either one way or the other. Doctor Browne, of Wakefield, has reported three cases of death from it in the asylum under his care—two of these having occurred the same day, and within half an hour after taking thirty grains of chloral. While Doctor Clouston, of the Cumberland and Westmoreland Asylum, near Carlisle, and many others, have administered it in large doses with no dangerous symptoms, but the best results. It is used with more or less freedom in very nearly all the asylums of Italy, Austria, the German States, Switzerland, and Holland; but very rarely in France and Belgium. Doctor Lehman, of Pirna, in Saxony, gives it in doses of from thirty to one hundred and twenty grains; Doctor Köeppe, of Halle, in doses of forty-five to one hundred and thirty-five grains; Doctor Guentz, of Thonberg, near Leipzig, gives from forty-five to seventy-five grains; and Doctor Ludwig, of Heppenheim, administers from thirty to ninety grains, repeating the dose three times a day; while Doctor Leiderdorf, of Döblins, near Vienna, expresses the opinion that chloral hydrate will supersede all other remedies as a quieting agent.

Dr. Professor Neri, of Perugia, Dr. Serafino Biffi, of Milan, Dr. Roller, of Illenau, and others, have also used it, and express the highest opinion of it as a quieting, sleep-producing agent. Dr. Roller thinks, when long continued, it has a tendency to produce congestion of the skin; while Dr. Lehman thinks it has a tendency, under similar conditions, to produce stranguary; but as he also gives very large doses of cannabis indicus, it may possibly have been confounded with the effects of that drug. In the asylums of the United States it has been more or less employed for the last two years, and the testimony in its favor has been very general. But few, if any, of the Superintendents claim for it curative properties, while nearly all regard it as one of the best hypnotics known to the profession. We must conclude, therefore, from all the testimony we have been able to collect from various sources, that chloral hydrate is not only one of the most innocent but one of the best remedies that can be used in most cases where sleep alone is the object desired. We know that it, like most other remedies of its class, will fail to produce like effects upon all persons; and it may be so much adulterated as to be either worthless or dangerous; and in no other way can we account for the varied results observed by the English Superintendents. We have spoken more especially of this remedy because less is known of it by the general reader than almost any other of equal importance. We prefer to administer it in twenty grain doses, given at bedtime, and repeated every hour till sleep is produced; and never to give it, or any other remedy of its class, except when the end to be accomplished is esteemed an absolute necessity. Of this necessity the physician must be the judge in each case as it presents itself. If chemical restraint seemed to be the proper remedy, we would use it. If mechanical restraint should seem of more importance in any given case, we should not hesitate to employ that instead of the other; nor can we see any good reason why the physician should be left with unlimited power to use the more dangerous remedy, while the other is entirely prohibited. The camisole or muff is the only kind of mechanical restraint that should ever be employed under any circumstances, except for surgical reasons, and these only by the order and in the presence of the physician. In these views we are confident that two thirds of the Superintendents in Great Britain will heartily concur, and at least nine tenths of those in other countries, including our own. In truth, we are disposed to believe that mechanical restraint is too freely used in most of the asylums in our country as well as on the continent; and in this respect we go quite as far wrong in one direction as they do in England in the other.

Dr. Morel, of St. Yon, is one of the warmest advocates of the non-restraint system with whom we met in all France. He had paid a visit to Dr. Conolly, at Hanwell, where he had seen its practical operations under the eye of the master, of whom he was an ardent admirer. Having imbibed Dr. Conolly's views, he made to his Government one of the ablest reports on the subject that we have read, and so thoroughly was he convinced of the propriety and practicability of the system that he at once put it in practice in the asylum over which he presided, nor did he abandon it, even in surgical cases, until a deformity in a case of fracture of the leg demonstrated the absurdity of treating lunatics and those possessed of their reason alike in all cases. Had this patient been strapped to the bed during the process of union, this calamity would have been avoided, and so it may be said of others of like character. Hence, Dr. Morel now thinks the use of the camisole as necessary in rare instances as any other remedy intrusted to the judgment and discretion of the physician, nor does he hesitate to prescribe its use when he thinks the patient will be benefited, but under no circumstances does he permit an attendant to employ it without his direction. The chemical restraint, opium, morphine, chloral, etc., are prescribed by the physician only, and so should it ever be with mechanical restraint, the camisole.

Epilepsy.

We have seen that the remedies employed in this fearful disease were principally the metallic salts—nitrate of silver, oxide of zinc, citrate of iron, bichloride of mercury, etc., assisted by setons, blisters, cups, purgatives, and anti-spasmodics—and that all were equally unavailing. The disease is still considered incurable by almost all who have been called upon to treat it, though it is now claimed by a few that in rare cases among the young, and especially in those cases where insanity supervenes on a previously existing epilepsy, it is not necessarily incurable, and that, in a large majority of cases, the frequency and severity of the attacks may be lessened, thus modifying the disease and ameliorating the unhappy condition of the patient. We have already stated the treatment by shower bath pursued by Doctor Morel, at San Yon, and given the results. Similar claims have been made by different persons in favor of each of the remedies above enumerated. Thus, Doctor Leiderdorf, of Döbling, near Vienna, reports one case, cured with ox. zinc; another, when there was a syphilitic taint, with iod. pot. Doctor

Fischel, of the Royal Bohemian Asylum at Prague, attributes the cure in one case to Fowler's solution; and so on through the entire list. But the remedy most used in the present day, and that in which there is most confidence, is unquestionably the bromide of potassium. It is given by nine tenths of the profession who have charge of asylums; and while but few ascribe to it curative powers, most of them claim that it greatly ameliorates the attacks, and often wards them off entirely during its administration, thus giving its victims long intervals of relief and repose, while in a few instances complete restoration is effected. It is given in doses varying from five to one hundred and twenty grains, according to the urgency of the case and the peculiar views of the physician. Nor is its employment confined alone to the treatment of epilepsy. Some use it in the treatment of nymphomania and kindred affections, while it is the only neurotic medicine employed by Doctor Blanche in his asylum at Passy. He gives fifteen or twenty grains three times a day as a quieting agent. It is often administered in combination with other sedatives, anodynes, or narcotics—and is thought to increase their efficiency, and is one of the few remedies that have attained almost universal popularity.

Paralysis.

In the treatment of this disease as connected with insanity but little change has taken place within a quarter of a century, unless, we should say, it is not so much treated as formerly. Blisters, the galvanic battery, counter-irritation of all kinds, and the shower bath, seem to be less used than formerly; while the only new remedy employed, so far as we know, is the ergot of rye, as prescribed by Doctor Chrichton Browne, of the Wakefield Asylum in England. He thinks good effects have been accomplished by its use, but sufficient time has not yet elapsed to test its efficacy.

MORAL TREATMENT.

The moral treatment of insanity is considered of more importance by many persons having charge of the insane than the medical, and the tendency to this opinion seems to be gradually increasing. It comprehends all of those means which operate on the feelings and habits of the patient, and exerts a salutary influence by tending to restore them to a natural and healthy condition. The means to be employed under this head are as varied as the diseases leading to or the symptoms developed by insanity. It is in the judicious employment of the remedies of this class that the physician and the attendants are called upon to use the greatest skill and tact of which they are capable, whether as connected with individual cases or collective numbers. One important particular belonging to moral treatment has been already alluded to in our remarks on the non-restraint system. The English Commissioners in Lunacy say:

" There is nothing more important in the moral treatment of the insane than the proper use of means which contribute to their employment, both mental and bodily, and tend to withdraw their attention from thoughts and feelings connected with their disordered state."

The provision made for the attainment of these objects in our asylums cannot be too strongly recommended, nor insisted upon with too much pertinacity by those whose duty it is to watch over them.

Employment in agricultural labor, in the vegetable garden, among the vines and fruit trees, or in cultivating flowers for their amusement and entertainment, will be of the greatest advantage to all of the insane who can be induced, either by persuasion or slight compensation, to participate in them. The general health will be improved by this exercise in the open air, the appetite increased, the nervous system is less easily disturbed, the mind more composed, sleep is sweeter, sounder, and more refreshing, and the patient, with less opportunity to brood over his disease or imagined troubles and wrongs, gravitates naturally and by degrees into old habits of thought, health, and cheerfulness; the equilibrium is restored, and the patient is well.

Single Rooms.

Another matter coming under the head of moral treatment or management may be properly mentioned here. It is the general opinion, expressed in words and carried out in practice, that all excited patients should be kept by themselves in single rooms, or cells, as they are unfortunately called throughout Europe; and especially, that they should be so kept at night. Doctor Morel is decidedly of the opposite opinion, and while he admits their necessity in a few isolated cases, has demonstrated to his own satisfaction that the theory is wrong and the practice injudicious in most instances. He has, therefore, taken out the partition walls between most of these cells and converted them into dormitories, and assured us that where four noisy, restless, sleepless patients were formely kept in single rooms, sixteen were now passing quiet nights, sleeping well, and giving every evidence of being better satisfied. He argues that most of the excited, noisy patients are afraid to be left alone at night, and that this very fear disturbs their quiet and prevents them from sleeping.

Schools.

He has also recently organized a class of excited patients, which he examines each day when passing through the wards. Thirty were in attendance on the day of our visit, and we found them more quiet and orderly than at any other time. All would clamor for the privilege of showing how well they could read, or repeat some little piece of prose or verses of poetry that they had committed for the occasion, but as soon as the doctor would decide who was entitled to the floor, all became quiet and listened attentively till the piece was spoken, when they would rise to their feet and again put in their claims, and so on to the end of the recitation. They really seemed to take great interest in these exercises, and doubtless many moments of comparative happiness were passed in learning their lessons that would otherwise have been spent in miserable contemplation of their unhappy condition. These schools have long existed in some of the continental asylums, and a few in Great Britain and Ireland, though this was the first and only one we have seen especially devoted to the excited patients. Music, drawing, and singing are taught in most of the Italian asylums and in some of those in other countries. At Aversa, near Naples, there is a regular band, who play for their own amusement and that of the other patients. A theater has been fitted up, in which they play, give concerts, and other entertainments; and here, as at York, in England, and Morningside, in Scotland, a printing press has been provided, and the patients encouraged to write articles that are set up and printed by themselves. Here, too, as at Lyons, in France, Ghent, in Belgium, and Wakefield, England, we saw many looms, on which the patients wove the cloth used by the asylums. At San Servalo, in Venice, the band plays every day from eleven to twelve, and the patients are as much delighted as if at a regular concert, while those who belong to the band gave signs of evident satisfaction.

In some of the asylums in Milan, schools have also been established, but we will only make an extract from our notes of a visit to one of them, the last we visited in Italy:

April 3d—To-day we visited the private asylum of Doctor Serafino Biffi, one of nature's noblemen, who seems as generous as a prince and as kind as a woman, one of those real loveable men with whom we sometimes meet in our journey through life. The asylum is a quiet, homelike place, such as we might expect to grow up under the care and management of so good a man. No pains have been spared to make it in reality a home for the homeless, and a retreat for the heavy hearted and afflicted. Two teachers are employed, who, in addition to other branches, teach vocal and instrumental music. They play and sing with as much accuracy and expression as if no illusion or hallucination disturbed their minds. They played and sang several pieces and tunes for our benefit, and showed us some of their paintings and drawings that would have been a credit to artists of no ordinary pretentions. Twenty of the seventy-four patients in this asylum were engaged in these occupations at the time of our visit, and as good order prevailed as at any school to be found. Others were reading, playing billiards or draughts, while others still were promenading about the beautiful grounds.

This, as we have stated, is a private asylum, where patients are charged from sixty cents to two dollars per day, and is not given as a specimen of the public institutions, which are greatly inferior to it.

The most thoroughly organized school that we have anywhere seen, however, was in the Richmond Asylum, at Dublin. The system has been completely established, and the organization as perfect as any schools in the country. The able Superintendent, Doctor Lalor, has taken great interest in and paid particular attention to the subject, demonstrating not only the possibility of promoting good order and discipline by means of schools, but also of increasing the knowledge and improving the morals of persons while in a state of insanity. There were about nine hundred patients in the asylum at the date of our visit— August twenty-ninth, eighteen hundred and seventy-one—more than a fourth of whom attended school. In the school for males we saw one hundred and twenty engaged in their recitations and exercises, which were conducted with perfect order and propriety. Reading, writing, arithmetic, object lessons, music, drawing, and painting are taught, and Doctor Lalor informed us that considerable advancement had been made by some, while all had been benefited in a moral point of view; self-control, power of concentration, and regularity of habits had been attained in many instances where they had been totally absent before; and that he regarded the school as one of the chief agencies in promoting good order and in establishing a comparative degree of contentment and cheerfulness in his asylum. The school for females is conducted on similar principles, though needlework is added to the list of studies in this department. Six teachers, three of either sex, are regularly employed, at salaries about double the amount paid attendants, and in addition to their duties as teachers are required to assist in "keeping the house in order." Some of them always accompany the patients in their walks outside the asylum walls, in the public park, and other places to which they are permitted to go. These teachers, being better educated, more intelligent, and of a higher order than those whose services can be obtained for the ordinary wages paid attendants, exercise a salutary influence over the patients at all times. Their morals, habits, and manners, being thus cultivated and controlled, are necessarily improved, and we confess our surprise at having seen this kind of occupation introduced into so few of the asylums of our own country.

DIRECTORS AND SUPERINTENDENTS.

Unfortunately the custom still prevails in some of the asylums on the continent of placing a Director at the head of the institution. Its general management, the power to employ and discharge all the attachés and attendants, and to say how the patients shall be fed, clothed, and occupied, are invested in him, though generally a non-medical man. The Medical Superintendent occupies a subordinate position. He of course prescribes the medical treatment for all, and the diet for the sick, but no other powers are assigned to him. As may readily be supposed, this divided responsibility begets evil results. The physician is lessened in public estimation; the employé and attendant look to the Director for his position or his place, and naturally take sides with him in any conflict of opinion that may arise. They place themselves in antagonism to the wishes of the physician, and but half carry out his orders, and thus destroy the harmonious workings of the institution.

In Great Britain no man is chosen as Superintendent of an asylum who has not served as an assistant. He must be armed with recommendations as to his qualifications, standing, and moral character, and is subjected to a searching examination. Having passed this ordeal and obtained the position, he retains it for life, unless removed for cause. He has supreme control of the asylum over which he presides, nominates his assistants and other officers, and selects his attendants. He is paid a liberal salary, and given one mouth's leave of absence each year for recreation; and after serving fifteen years is allowed an annuity equal to three months of his salary, provided he desires to retire from service. Harmony is the result of this system, and the consequence is good order and thorough discipline in every asylum in Great Britain.

Under these circumstances, men of the highest order of intellectual capacity and thorough education prepare themselves for the position of Superintendent, and being under a local Board of Managers, and subjected to periodical visitations by the Commissioners in Lunacy, strive to merit their good opinion. These Commissioners are always men of first class ability, high character, independence, and influence, who make searching examinations, and comment upon matters as they find them, without fear or favor, and are a power in the land that cannot be ignored nor disregarded.

The vigilance exercised by the Boards of Commissioners in Great Britain, and the admirable organization above referred to, make their system superior to any that elsewhere exists, and should be adopted in all countries with centralized Governments and circumscribed boundaries. The form of our Government, composed of thirty-seven States, each managing its own local affairs and having its own method of providing for the insane (even if the vast extent of territorial limits did not forbid), would render it impossible for such a system to be adopted in the United States, while the small number of asylums in most of the

States would not justify the establishment of Boards of State Commissioners.

In Ireland and in some asylums on the continent, in addition to the resident officers, a Visiting Physician is appointed, who makes regular visits and consults with the Superintendent. The advantages claimed for this custom by the Directors are, that he forms a link between the asylum and the outer world; that the people have more frequent opportunities to converse with one who.is in constant communication with the patients within; that they can make more frequent inquiries about their afflicted friends; and that a physician engaged in general practice is better prepared to treat diseases of a purely physical character than one who has devoted his time to the study and his energies to the treatment of insanity alone.

An asylum should be open to the friends of patients at all times, except when such visits might be thought by the Superintendent to be injurious to the patient; and even in this case the desired information as to his condition might as properly be communicated by the Superintendent as by the Consulting Physician. We are well aware of the injurious effects upon the patients of too much indiscriminate visiting by families or friends, but the propriety of these visits must be left to the discretion of the ,Superintendent or other resident medical officer, and these should ever be accessible to all who desire to make legitimate inquiry as to the condition, prospects, and treatment of their friends. They should be the "connecting link" mentioned by our friends in Ireland. The last reason referred to is of still less weight. We cannot comprehend how any physician who does not thoroughly understand the pathology and treatment of physical diseases can successfully treat persons who are insane, since we hold that all cases of mental derangement are in some way connected with or dependent upon physical disease.

ATTENDANTS.

To accomplish the best results, however, in addition to a skillful medical staff and proper hospitals it is all-important that intelligent, patient, and self-sacrificing attendants should be procured; those who will not only be attentive to their duties, but are kind and cheerful in disposition, and who are possessed of tact and discriminating judgment.

For these reasons, liberal wages should be paid, and a system of rewards established for those who are faithful to their trust and continue in the service. Reasonable leave of absence should be given at regular intervals to admit of visits to family or friends, and comfortable quarters provided, that proper rest may be procured and contentment prevail. Seeing that their comforts, happiness, and interests are not overlooked, they will become interested in the duties assigned them and in the general welfare of the institution with which they are identified.

In some asylums in this country and in Europe the wages of attendants are regularly increased for a given number of years, and in some of those in England and on the continent an annuity is allowed after a continuous service of fifteen years. These are all good features that may well be considered in the organization of a hospital for the insane, as nothing is more detrimental to the harmonious management of an asylum than inefficient and constantly changing attendants. The best authorities agree that there should be at least one attendant for every ten patients; and we are thoroughly convinced that the number has not been placed too high, for though some classes of patients require less than this proportion, others need more, and cannot be properly treated or managed without them.

We also observed in a few of the English asylums a man and wife acting as attendants in the wards for infirm men, and learned from the Superintendents who had adopted the system that it gave great satisfaction to the patients, and always added to the neatness and cheerfulness of the wards. That the restraining influence of woman and the soothing effects of her tender care were as apparent among the insane as among sane men; and if this be true, all will admit the propriety of the system. For ourself, we would at any time rather be nursed by one woman than ten men, and in this respect we probably agree with all classes of our fellow men.

We have thus given a brief synopsis of the treatment of insanity and the management of insane persons, as practiced in some of the best asylums in most of the enlightened countries of the world; and it may fairly be presumed that the medical men who have charge of them are among the most able and learned of the profession to which they belong. From this we hope the non-professional reader may be able to form some idea of the methods of general treatment ordinarily adopted in the usual forms of insanity. No specific treatment can be laid down that would be applicable to the same class, as this must vary with the peculiarities of each case. But we desire to impress this important fact upon the public mind, that "insanity is a disease of the brain affecting the mind," and that an asylum is nothing more than a hospital adapted to the treatment of this peculiar malady; that patients committed to its care will be skillfully treated and kindly nursed, and that if sent in the early stage of the disorder a large majority will be restored to health and to reason.

CHAPTER XIV.

INSANITY IN GENERAL.

Increased attention to Insanity—Growth of Hospitals in United States—Increase of Hospitals in United States—Increased Accommodation—Hospitals exhibit Insanity—Non-residents—Should other States send their Insane to California—Insanity in other States—Results of Treatment—Curability of the Insane—Effects of Early Treatment—Good Hospitals necessary to Favorable Results—Results in our Asylum—Doubtful and Hopeless Cases—Economy of Early Treatment—Probable Duration of Life in Chronic Cases—Increase of Patients in our Asylum—Causes tending to this Result—Will the Children of Foreigners be as liable to Insanity as their Parents—Observations upon Physical and Moral Causes producing Insanity—Intemperance a Leading Cause of Insanity—Duty of State relative to Asylums—Physicians not generally Informed on the Subject of Insanity—Psychology recommended to be Taught in Medical Schools—Effect of the Liberal and of the Economical Plan of Care and Treatment.

INCREASED ATTENTION TO INSANITY.

From the foregoing considerations, derived from various sources and authorities, setting forth the history of insanity, the receptacles in which the lunatics were kept, and the methods of treatment pursued towards them, we learn that it is only within a century that it dawned upon the world that lunacy was curable in any considerable degree. The doctrine, however, made very slow progress and but few converts. Even in the beginning of this century, hospitals were built to give to the insane a more humane confinement than the prisons in which they had been kept could afford; and it was not till within the recollection of many now living that the faith in the curability of the disease became general, even among professional men. Hence, hospitals began to be built for the twofold purpose of custody and curability, for beside the difficulty of managing and taking care of lunatics at home, it was found that comparatively few recovered. From this period hospitals began to be regarded as not only the best, but to most persons the only place for the insane. Hence an increasing demand for their accommodation, and though their numbers have multiplied with astonishing rapidity, and have greatly increased in size, they are still inadequate for the reception and accommodation of all who knock at their doors, and with piteous appeals seek admission for the treatment they afford and the benefits they are known to confer. At the beginning of this century there were only four receptacles for the insane in the United States, and only one of these, that at Williamsburg, Virginia, devoted exclusively to the treatment of insanity. Previous to its establishment, however, in seventeen hundred and seventy-three, a ward had been set apart for their accommodation in the Pennsylvania Hospital, and contained eighteen patients as early as seventeen hundred and fifty-two. Similar institutions followed in seventeen hundred and ninety-seven—the Maryland Hospital, at Baltimore, and the Bloomingdale Asylum, at New York. But little attention, however, had yet been paid to this subject, and, as will be seen from the following table, no other asylum was established till eighteen hundred and seventeen, when the Friends opened one at Frankford, near Philadelphia, followed the year after by the McLean Asylum, at Somerville, Massachusetts.

GROWTH OF HOSPITALS IN UNITED STATES.

Showing date of establishment of the following Asylums, with a list of those in process of erection.

The following hospitals first received insane patients before the year eighteen hundred:

Philadelphia, Penn., Hospital..1752	Baltimore, Md......................1797
Williamsburg, Va., established	Bloomingdale, N. Y.:............1797
at that time......................1773	

Asylums Established between 1800 and 1820.

Frankford.........................1817	McLean.............................1818

From 1820 to 1830.

Bloomingdale.....................1821	Hartford, Conn.....................1824
Columbia, S. C....................1822	Staunton, Va.......................1828
Lexington, Ky.....................1824	

From 1830 to 1840.

Worcester, Mass...................1833	Columbus, Ohio, destroyed by
Baltimore, Md.....................1834	fire 1839
Brattleboro, Vt...................1837	Boston, Mass........................1839

From 1840 *to* 1850.

Nashville, Tenn....................1840	Insane Department of Phila-
Augusta, Me........................1840	delphia Almshouse............1845
Philadelphia, Penn., Hospital	Flushing 1846
for Insane......................1841	Providence, R. I.................1847
Concord, N. H.....................1842	Indianapolis, Ind................1848
Milledgeville, Ga.................1842	Jackson, La.......................1848
Utica, N. Y.......................1843	Trenton, N. J.....................1849

From 1850 *to* 1860.

Jacksonville, Ill.................1851	Dayton, O.........................1855
Fulton, Mo........................1851	Washington, D. C.................1855
Harrisburg, Pa....................1851	Dixmont, Pa.......................1856
Stockton, Cal.....................1852	Raleigh, N. C.....................1856
Longview, O.......................1853	Auburn, N. Y......................1858
Madison, Wis......................1854	St. Vincent, Mo..................1858
Taunton, Mass.....................1854	Northampton, Mass................1858
Hopkinsville, Ky..................1854	Kalamazoo, Mich..................1859
Jackson, Miss.....................1855	Troy, N. Y........................1859
Flatbush, L. I....................1855	Newburgh, O......................1859
Canandaigua, N. Y.................1855	

From 1860 *to* 1870.

Kellyville, Pa....................1860	Portland, Or......................1869
Tuscaloosa, Ala...................1861	Weston, W. Va.....................1866
Mt. Pleasant, Iowa................1861	Ossawatamie, Kansas..............1866
Blackwell's Island, N. Y..........1861	Mt. Hope Retreat, Md.............1867
Philadelphia City Asylum......	Alameda Park, Cal................1867
Immigrant, N. Y...................1861	Middletown, Conn.................1868
Austin, Texas.....................1861	St. Louis, Mo....................1869
St. Peter, Minn...................1866	Ovid, N. Y........................1869

From 1870.

Howard Grove, Richmond, Va..........................1870.

ASYLUMS IN PROCESS OF ERECTION.

Anna, Ill.	Poughkeepsie, N. Y.
Elgin, Ill.	Columbus, O.
Independence, Iowa.	Athens, O.
Catonsville, Md.	Danville, Pa.
Towsontown, Md.	Buffalo, N. Y.
Ward's Island, N. Y.	Middletown, N. Y.

ESTABLISHMENT OF ASYLUMS IN THE BRITISH PROVINCES.

Toronto............................1841	St. John, N. B...................1848
Quebec.............................1848	Halifax, N. S....................1859

During the next ten years, eighteen hundred and twenty to eighteen hundred and thirty, the Bloomingdale Asylum was rebuilt, and four others added to the list. During the next ten years a like number were built, but it was not till after eighteen hundred and forty, about the time the mind of the English public was directed to the abuses existing in· the asylums of that country, and the heroic efforts of Doctor Hill, Charlesworth, and Doctor Conolly to abolish the vile and cruel custom of confining nearly all patients sent to asylums with chains, handcuffs, and the straight jacket, had been crowned with success, that a general interest in the subject, and a corresponding impetus was given to the erection of asylums in this country. And as the result we see that during the next ten years eleven asylums were built. In the ten years that followed twenty-one were established; till to-day, as we see from the table, no less than sixty-six asylums in perfect operation, accommodating seventeen thousand seven hundred and thirty-five patients, exist in the United States, to say nothing of twelve others in process of erection. Some of these, in architectural elegance, completeness of design, convenience of arrangement, adaptation to the purposes for which they are intended, and beauty of location, are unsurpassed, if indeed they are equalled by any institutions in the world.

SHOWING INCREASE OF HOSPITALS IN THE UNITED STATES.

YEAR.	Population	Number of Insane	Number of Lunatic Hospitals	Number of Patients	Average capacity	Proportion of Insane supplied with Hospital accommodations
1844	17,069,453	*17,457	23	2,561	111	14.67
1850	23,191,876	15,610	28	4,730	168	30.30
1860	31,443,322	23,999	50	†8,500	170	35.42
1870	38,555,983	37,382	66	- 17,735	268	47.44

It is not in our country alone, however, that this increased attention has been paid to the requirements of these unfortunate people. We have already pointed out this fact with regard to Germany, and we might do so for every country we have visited—France, Italy, Belgium, Holland, Ireland, Scotland, and Canada—but will be satisfied with a table setting forth this progress in the United States and England, as specimens of the whole:

---

* Including idiots, as these two classes were not separated until the census of eighteen hundred and fifty.

† See Journal of Insanity, Vol. XVIII, p. 2.

TABLE,

Showing the per cent of the Insane provided with Hospital Accommodation in the United States and England at different periods.

	UNITED STATES.				ENGLAND.		
Year	Total number of Insane	Number of Insane in hospitals	Proportion of Insane supplied with hospital accommodation	Year	*Total number of Insane	Number of Insane in hospitals	Proportion of Insane supplied with hospital accommodation
1850	15,610	4,730	30.30	1847	26,516	13,832	52.00
1860	23,999	8,500	35.42	1857	33,791	21,344	63.00
1870	37,382	17,735	47.44	1867	49,082	31,914	67.00

INCREASED ACCOMMODATIONS.

From the above table it will be seen that of the whole number of lunatics in England in eighteen hundred and forty-seven, fifty-two of every hundred were provided with asylum accommodation; and in eighteen hundred and sixty-seven, sixty-seven per cent were provided for. In eighteen hundred and fifty, the asylums in the United States accommodated only thirty per cent, and in eighteen hundred and seventy, forty-seven per cent. As rapidly as insanity has appeared to increase in these countries within the twenty years specified, this shows that the provisions made for the care, comfort, treatment, and restoration of its victims have outstripped it by fifteen per cent in England, and in the United States by seventeen per cent.

---

*As given in the reports of the Commissioners in Lunacy, including idiots.

TABLE,

Showing Period under Treatment in Asylums of those Discharged Recovered.

Period under Treatment of Patients who Recovered.	Holland. 12 Asylums, (1841 to 1864.)			France. 111 Asylums, (1852.)			England. Asylum at Hanwell, (1855 to 1860.)			United States. Southern Ohio Asylum, (1855 to 1859.)			Total.			Per cent of Recoveries at each Period.		
	Male.	Female.	Total.	Male.	Female.	Total.	Male.	Female.	Total.	Male.	Female.	Total.	Male.	Female.	Total.	Male.	Female.	Total.
Under three months.	479	474	953	507	396	903	3	3	3	207	178	385	1,193	1,051	2,244	30.6	25.2	28.1
Three to six months.	533	603	1,136	312	272	614	11	21	39	135	137	269	1,012	1,087	2,049	25.1	26.8	25.9
Six to twelve months.	534	651	1,195	282	263	495	30	25	16	74	94	168	850	1,041	1,501	22.1	25.9	24.0
One to two years.	329	358	678	117	116	263	9	8	17	31	41	72	507	523	1,030	13.0	13.0	13.0
Over two years.	160	242	411	133	103	236	5	10	15	15	11	25	322	366	688	8.3	9.1	8.7
Unknown.				133	107	240			13				153	107	260			
Totals.	2,035	2,338	4,373	1,514	1,257	2,771	48	69	117	439	451	911	4,047	4,125	8,172	100.00	100.00	100.00

} 78.48 of recoveries took place within 1 year.

} 21.52 of recoveries after more than 1 year's treatment.

Although this table does not show that ninety, nor even eighty per cent have been restored in those cases treated within twelve months after the accession of the disease, it does show that of all the recoveries more than seventy-eight per cent were cured within that period, and that less than twenty-two per cent were cured where the treatment was commenced after the disease had existed more than one year. It is the experience of the Southern Lunatic Asylum, of Ohio, that only seventeen per cent get well where the treatment has been deferred for two years and over, and in some other asylums that only eight per cent recover under such circumstances. Let us add to the large percentage of recoveries of those treated in the early stages of this malady, the usual number of deaths occurring in asylums, and it is quite certain that a small proportion only would remain as chronic cases to be supported by the State during the remainder of their days, which, as will presently appear, is about seventeen years.

GOOD HOSPITALS NECESSARY TO FAVORABLE RESULTS.

These results, of course, can only be expected, under the most favorable circumstances, when all of the conveniences, comforts, and appliances of the most approved hospitals and the best medical treatment are brought to bear upon the disease. It is hopelessly impossible for any amount of care and attention, any degree of medical skill that the power of man can supply, to overcome the disadvantages and drawbacks of a poorly constructed hospital, with its ill ventilated and overcrowded wards, where proper classification and necessary sanitary regulations cannot be fully carried out, such, unfortunately, as are some of the wards in our own asylum. But notwithstanding all of these drawbacks and disadvantages, the percentage of cures to admissions is surpassed by a few only in any country.

RESULTS IN OUR ASYLUM.

In eighteen hundred and seventy there were but few asylums in the United States that showed so large a percentage of recoveries, while the average in all is far below ours. This may be accounted for in a measure from the fact that a large majority of the patients are sent to our asylum at an early period after the accession of the disease, while it is yet within reach of the physician's skill; and none can doubt that the same amount of care, watchfulness, and skillful treatment in a better, arranged and less crowded hospital would largely augment the percentage of cures and lessen the percentage of deaths. They are sent to the asylum at an early period because it is not only known that they will be received, but kindly and skillfully treated, and that the chances of recovery are greatly in their favor. The very character of the population, too, leads in some degree to this result. Many are without homes and families; but few are blessed with kind and steadfast friends to look after, watch, and nurse them when the evil day comes, and as there is no other place for them they are sent to the asylum, fortunately for them, in time to be treated while there is yet hope of recovery. Under these circumstances a large number get well and are restored to society and the State. But, as already stated, under more favorable conditions, with a hospital less crowded and better ventilated than many of the wards in our asylum are, with facilities for proper classification, and where there are not so many for the medical officers to watch and prescribe for, a much larger number would recover. Abundant evidence has been adduced in another place to show that large asylums are not considered the best in any point of view—neither for curative purposes nor on economical grounds; the latter being the only argument that has ever been brought forward to justify large establishments for the treatment of the insane.

DOUBTFUL AND HOPELESS CASES.

We are fully aware that many cases of insanity are incurable from the beginning. The very causes producing it places recovery beyond the bounds of probability, if not of possibility. Thus, when apoplexy, palsy, or consumption, epilepsy, or even masturbation is the cause producing mental alienation, there is but little hope, and all who have been deprived of treatment for more than two years have forfeited their best chances of recovery and gone within the limits of chronic insanity, from which but few return with mental integrity. Fortunately, there is not a large proportion of these committed to our asylum, and had the oft repeated recommendations of our Superintendent been heeded by our legislators the accumulated numbers would not have reached such appalling proportions.

SOME SELF-LIMITED, BUT MOST REQUIRE TREATMENT.

While the cases we have been considering are of such a hopeless character, others appear to be self-limited, and if left to themselves or removed from exciting causes and disturbing influences will recover. But far the greater number require treatment, medical and moral. In most instances this can only be accomplished in hospitals. Men of disordered mind, when they need a change of air or scene, cannot go to a hotel or private boarding house, or even to the house of a friend, when they are so fortunate as to have the one or possess the means to command the other. They require more caution, forbearance, and oversight than those who are mere invalids suffering from ordinary diseases. Many of them are suspicious, and annoying to those about them, and dangerous to themselves and others. They must therefore go to hospitals, places, or people devoted to their care, and prepared to give them the needful attention and watchfulness. But hospitals are too expensive to be provided even by the rich, while a large majority are poor or entirely destitute. It is therefore the duty of the State to provide these hospitals, that all may receive the early treatment so essentially necessary to their restoration, not only that they may cease to be a burden upon the State, but that they may return to it and to society the benefits of their labor and usefulness.

ECONOMY OF EARLY TREATMENT.

To show more clearly the economy of early treatment, the following table has been prepared and introduced. It shows that of all the cures effected in the Worcester Hospital during a period of fifteen years, those treated during the first year of the attack required an average of five months and ten days; while all who recovered whose treatment commenced after the expiration of one year, required to be treated ten months and ten days—showing conclusively that it cost the State only half as much to cure the earlier cases. And when it is considered that more than three times as many of those treated in the early stages got well than of those treated at a later period, it will be seen that the advantages of the former are immense.

Let us add to this the large proportion of those who never recover when treatment is postponed, and who consequently are added to the chronic list to be maintained through life, and some idea of the advantages of early treatment may be comprehended by the dullest mind. The table also shows that the average duration of treatment in those who died during this period was four years, three months, and twenty-two days.

TABLE,

Showing the duration of Insanity of those who recovered in the Worcester Hospital from 1833 to 1848.

Duration of Insanity previous to Admission.	Number of Cases.	Total Duration of Insanity.			Average Duration.			Total Time in Hospital.			Average Time in Hospital.		
		Years.	Months.	Days.	Years.	Months.	Days.	Years.	Months.	Days.	Years.	Months.	Days.
One year or less.	1,179	855	6	25	....	8	21	523	10	29	....	5	10
More than one year	201	1,181	2	6	5	10	12	173	1	7	....	10	10
Unknown	41	....	......	.....	....	......	......	33	6	2	....	9	24

Duration of Insanity of those who Died.

No. Cases.	Years.	Months.	Days.	Years.	Months.	Days.
272	1,171	5	29	4	3	22

Probable Duration of Life in the Incurable Insane.

Age.	Males.	Females.	Average Duration of Life.	
			Insane.	Sane.
20	21.31	28.66	24.99	36.32
30	20.64	26.33	23.46	34.54
40	17.65	21.53	19.59	23.46
50	13.53	17.67	15.60	19.59
60	11.91	12.51	12.21	15.60
Average...	....	....	16.74	29 years.

PROBABLE DURATION OF LIFE IN THE CHRONIC CASES.

This table shows the probable duration of life in the incurable insane to be about seventeen years, while that of the sane of similar ages is twenty-nine years. This is doubtless as applicable to California as to Massachusetts and other countries, and will enable us to estimate with tolerable certainty the length of time we will have to support a large majority of those in our asylum at the present time, as well as to appreciate the great difference between the cost of cure and the burden of maintenance.

INCREASE OF PATIENTS IN OUR ASYLUM IN TEN YEARS.

During the last ten years the average annual admissions in our asylum has been three hundred and fifty-eight, and the average annual increase sixty-seven. In eighteen hundred and sixty every fifteen hundred and thirty-two inhabitants of the State furnished one insane person from their numbers, and in eighteen hundred and seventy every nine hundred and sixty-four furnished a lunatic; or an average of one in twelve hundred and forty-eight for each year from eighteen hundred and sixty to eighteen hundred and seventy. This is an annual increase of twelve and six tenths per cent. Since the asylum was opened in eighteen hundred and fifty-one, there have been admitted five thousand six hundred and eighty-one patients, of whom forty-seven and sixty-eight one hundredths per cent were cured, nine and sixty-eight one hundredths per cent were discharged or removed uncured, twenty-three and forty-six one hundredths per cent died, and nineteen and eighteen one hundredths per cent remain, most of whom must be left as a charge upon the Treasury during the rest of their days. This is indeed a serious state of things, and behooves us seriously to look the facts in the face, endeavor to find the causes, and if possible devise means to arrest the progress of this fearful malady ere it gets beyond our power to control it. In eighteen hundred and forty-six, according to tables prepared by Doctor Campbell, of New South Wales, there was in that colony one insane person to eleven hundred and fifteen inhabitants, at the next census one to four hundred, and in eighteen hundred and sixty-seven the proportion had risen to one in three hundred and eighty-seven. This more nearly approximates the increase in California than that in any other country; and as there are many points of resemblance between the two, it will be well to note what observers there have said in regard to the subject. Doctor Norton Manning, who was appointed by that Government to make an investigation similar to the one in which we have been engaged in behalf of California, made to his Government one of the most able, complete, and interesting reports that we have seen. A synopsis of this valuable document will be found in this report. On the increase of insanity he uses the following language:

" This increase is to a great extent accounted for by the growth of a large mass of chronic insanity, which perhaps even yet has scarcely reached its limits. In the earlier emigrant days of the colony, notwithstanding, as has been said by an authority on this subject, that every emigrant ship brought one or two either insane or soon to become so, the vast mass of the population came in the prime of mental and bodily health. Their sick had been left behind in their fatherland. It would necessarily take some years for those becoming insane and remaining incurable to grow old within the asylum walls, and reach by accumulation to that number of old, chronic, and incurable cases with which all other countries are burdened. It may be fairly estimated that, if the full extent of increase from this cause has not already been reached, it must soon be so, and that the number of removals by death will reach the proportionate number of yearly entries on this greater chronic list, and so a balance will be effected. Upon the whole, then, though the contemplation of this mass of suffering humanity must occasion deep sorrow, the Colony of New South Wales has cause for a feeling of satisfaction on estimating the number of its lunatic population. With some causes in addition to those existing elsewhere, the ratio of its insane to population is not now markedly above that in most of those countries where the numbers have been ascertained with even tolerable exactness. These special causes will, it is to be expected, gradually disappear; the convict element will become fainter; the excitements of life will diminish; it may fairly be hoped that the use of poisonous alcoholic compounds, also, will decrease with the increase in quantity and diminution in price of wholesome colonial wine and beer, as well as under the better moral feelings of the future. With the diminution of these, the special causes of insanity in older countries may make their appearance; but it can scarcely be supposed that the ratio of insanity will rise higher than at present. A ratio equal to this, though the burden is great, is borne cheerfully by States not more wealthy than New South Wales, both in the Old World and the New."

In speaking of the causes, he says: "First, the earlier population came under exceptional circumstances—the relations of crime and insanity are very intimate; second, the ups and downs of early colonial life, the influence of the gold diggings; third, the lonely life of the shepherd, alternating with long periods of debauchery; fourth, the abuse of ardent spirits in a warm climate. On the other hand, the absence of grinding poverty and the salubrity of the climate tend to diminish mental disease."

With the exception of the convict element in the population of New South Wales, what is here said is as applicable to this State as to that colony.

CAUSES TENDING TO THIS RESULT.

These causes have acted as powerfully here as there, and Dr. Manning might have added, with equal propriety, other causes that act quite as potently in producing this malady as any of the foregoing:

First—The total change in the habits of life.

Second—The absence of those salutary restraints imposed by the presence of well organized society.

Third—The separation from family and friends; and, above all, the strange and mysterious influence of being away from HOME in a foreign land. In many cases with no mother nor sister near to watch over and care for them in sickness; no wife by to soothe their sorrows with cheerfulness and smiles, and by tender sympathy drive away the gloom of despondency, and with heroic fortitude encourage them after failure in some cherished project again to buckle on the armor of determination and fight for success.

All of these causes, and doubtless many others, must be operating, with various degrees of activity and power, on the foreign born citizens of our country and State—in what degree in the different States and Territories will be seen in the table next hereafter; while the succeeding table has been prepared to show the relation of California in this respect to the whole country; the next to show the rate of increase of the population, the insane, and the idiotic, from the birth of the State to eighteen hundred and seventy; the next to show the percentages of these elements; the next table shows that more than sixty-two per cent of the population of California in eighteen hundred and seventy were born in the United States, while less than thirty-six per cent of the insane were supplied from their number—being a proportion of one to eight hundred and fifty-eight. The proportion of citizens of foreign birth is thirty-seven and forty-five one hundredths per cent, and the proportion of the insane from their numbers sixty-four and thirty-nine one hundredths per cent, or one to two hundred and eighty-four; thus showing that persons of foreign birth are three times as susceptible to the invasions of insanity as those who were born in the United States. By reference to the table next hereafter, it will be seen that the proportion of the foreign element is much greater in California than in any other State, and therefore we need not be surprised at the greater increase of insanity in our midst. And as the same causes, operating under similar circumstances, will always produce the same results, we may reasonably expect the growth of lunacy to continue till these conditions are changed.

UNITED STATES.

TABLE *showing total Native and Foreign Population, with total Native and Foreign Insane, and proportion of each class of the Insane to its respective Population; also proportion of the Foreign to the Native Insane.*

STATES AND TERRITORIES.	Total Population	Native Population	Foreign Population	Total Insane	Native Insane	Foreign Insane	Proportion of total Insane to total Population	Proportion of Native Insane to Native Population	Proportion of Foreign Insane to Foreign Population	Proportion of Foreign Insane to Native Insane
Total of the United States	38,555,983	32,989,437	5,566,546	37,382	26,161	11,221	1 to 1,031	1 to 1,261	1 to 496	1 to 2.33
Total of the States	38,113,253	32,640,907	5,472,346	36,786	25,832	10,954	1 to 1,036	1 to 1,263	1 to 499	1 to 2.35
Alabama	996,992	987,030	9,962	555	536	19	1 to 1,796	1 to 1,841	1 to 524	1 to 28.21
Arkansas	484,471	479,445	5,026	161	159	2	1 to 3,009	1 to 3,015	1 to 2,513	1 to 79.50
California	560,247	350,416	209,831	1,146	408	738	1 to 489	1 to 858	1 to 284	1 to .55
Connecticut	537,454	423,815	113,639	772	606	166	1 to 696	1 to 699	1 to 684	1 to 3.65
Delaware	125,015	115,879	9,136	65	56	9	1 to 1,923	1 to 2,069	1 to 1,015	1 to 6.22
Florida	187,748	182,781	4,967	29	28	1	1 to 6,474	1 to 6,527	1 to 4,967	1 to 28.
Georgia	1,184,109	1,172,982	11,127	634	622	12	1 to 1,868	1 to 1,885	1 to 927	1 to 51.83
Illinois	2,539,891	2,024,098	515,198	1,625	930	695	1 to 1,563	1 to 2,177	1 to 741	1 to 1.33
Indiana	1,680,637	1,539,163	141,474	1,504	1,223	281	1 to 1,117	1 to 1,258	1 to 503	1 to 4.35
Iowa	1,191,792	987,735	204,057	742	504	238	1 to 1,606	1 to 1,959	1 to 857	1 to 2.11
Kansas	364,399	316,007	48,392	131	90	41	1 to 2,781	1 to 3,511	1 to 1,180	1 to 2.19
Kentucky	1,321,011	1,257,613	63,398	1,245	1,082	163	1 to 1,061	1 to 1,162	1 to 388	1 to 6.63
Louisiana	726,915	665,068	61,827	451	324	127	1 to 1,612	1 to 2,052	1 to 486	1 to 2.55
Maine	626,915	578,034	48,881	792	712	80	1 to 792	1 to 811	1 to 611	1 to 8.90
Maryland	780,894	697,482	83,412	733	593	140	1 to 1,065	1 to 1,176	1 to 595	1 to 4.23

This page contains a single wide statistical table (1870 census data, states M–W and the Territories). No column headers are printed on this page. The first four data columns are ratios expressed as "1 to X"; the last three large columns are components of total population (column C8 + column C9 = column C10).

State	1 to (C1)	1 to (C2)	1 to (C3)	1 to (C4)	C5	C6	C7	C8	C9	C10
Massachusetts	2.11	413	610	547	855	1,807	2,062	353,319	1,104,032	1,457,351
Michigan	1.84	987	1,734	1,455	286	528	814	268,010	916,049	1,184,059
Minnesota	.08	897	2,268	1,456	179	123	302	160,697	279,009	439,706
Mississippi	26.22	1,243	3,460	3,379	9	236	245	11,191	816,731	827,922
Missouri	1.92	514	1,743	1,362	432	831	1,263	222,267	1,499,028	1,721,295
Nebraska	.55	1,708	9,224	4,392	18	10	28	30,748	92,245	122,993
Nevada		9,400		21,246	2		2	18,801	23,690	42,491
New Hampshire	7.80	493	659	639	60	438	498	29,611	288,689	318,300
New Jersey	1.61	538	1,264	987	351	567	918	188,943	717,153	906,096
New York	1.01	361	1,011	690	3,146	3,207	6,353	1,138,353	3,244,406	4,382,759
North Carolina	193.75	757	1,378	1,375	4	775	779	3,029	1,068,332	1,071,361
Ohio	2.74	408	916	781	911	2,503	3,414	372,493	2,292,767	2,665,260
Oregon	2.58	341	901	745	34	88	122	11,600	79,323	90,923
Pennsylvania	2.55	497	1,063	904	1,006	2,799	3,895	545,261	2,976,530	3,521,791
Rhode Island	2.80	675	704	697	82	230	312	55,396	161,957	217,353
South Carolina	26.75	672	2,172	2,119	12	321	333	8,074	697,532	705,606
Tennessee	36.	772	1,376	1,361	25	900	925	19,316	1,239,204	1,258,520
Vermont	5.58	449	460	458	105	616	721	37,155	293,396	330,551
Virginia	5.86	764	1,094	1,089	18	1,107	1,125	13,754	1,211,400	1,225,163
West Virginia	26.75	449	1,204	1,181	38	336	374	17,091	424,923	442,014
Wisconsin	61.50	677	2,240	1,247	538	308	846	364,499	690,171	1,054,670
Total of the Territories	1.23	352	1,059	742	267	329	596	94,200	348,530	442,730
Arizona	11.	5,809		9,658	1	11	1	5,809	3,849	9,658
Colorado	.50	6,509	3,024	3,322		1	12	6,599	33,265	39,864
Dacota	1.	1,407	477	4,727	2		3	4,815	9,366	14,181
District of Columbia		68		274	257	242	479	16,254	115,446	131,700
Idaho		7,885	6,308	14,999	1		1	7,885	7,114	14,999
Montana	24.		1,796	10,297		2	2	8,489	12,016	20,505
New Mexico	.66	2,810	5,608	1,837	2	48	50	5,620	86,254	91,874
Utah		2,046	1,262	3,471	15	10	25	30,702	56,084	86,786
Washington	1.87	628		1,041	8	15	23	5,024	18,931	23,955

26

RESULTS OF TREATMENT.

Having considered the subject of the treatment of insanity and the
rapid growth of hospitals, and having shown how rapidly insanity itself
has apparently, if not actually, increased in all countries during the last
forty years, let us consider the far more important subject of the results
of treatment in the various countries under consideration. The first of
the accompanying tables shows the number resident at the beginning of
the year, the admissions, numbers treated, recoveries, and deaths, with
proportions of recoveries and deaths in the asylums of the several countries from which returns could be obtained and of the latest dates that
could be procured:

While the last table sets forth similar facts for one hundred and thirty-
six of the one hundred and forty-nine asylums visited, the results as
exhibited in this table are for the year eighteen hundred and sixty-nine
in the United States and Canada, and for eighteen hundred and seventy
in the other countries. Though these tables differ in results in some
respects, they agree in showing that the largest proportion of recoveries to numbers treated and the smallest percentage of deaths to numbers
admitted are in the United States. This, of course, may be the result of
accident, as it requires a series of years and a knowledge of all the facts
to enable us to draw positive conclusions in matters of this character.
The average per cent of cures to admissions in all the asylums visited
was thirty-four, while in the United States it was thirty-seven. The
average of deaths to admissions in all was twenty-seven, and in the
United States only seventeen. This we believe to be owing to the fact
that the patients in our asylums are allowed a more liberal diet than in
any other country, and that the debilitating effects of the continued bath
so commonly used on the continent are entirely ignored in this country.
There may be other causes operating to produce this remarkable difference (sixty-three per cent) in the mortuary lists of all other countries, as
compared with our own, though the two above cited seem fully adequate
to the result.
As already seen in the foregoing table, of all the patients admitted
during the year, in the one hundred and thirty-nine asylums under consideration, thirty-four per cent were cured, and twenty-seven per cent
died, leaving thirty-nine per cent, most of whom must be added to the
chronic list, and thus swell the number of the insane. This is doubtless
as favorable a showing as could have been made had all the institutions
in the world been comprised in the list, as many of these are considered
among the best asylums ever established, and are conducted by as able
and learned men as have lived in any age. Well may we inquire, then,
"if this is a necessary part of our natural condition or our civilization,
to make this annual sacrifice of regiments of men and women on the
altar of mental destruction, can the causes producing these effects in any
way be avoided, and some of this sacrifice be prevented?" We will permit
others of more experience and wiser heads to answer the question.

CURABILITY OF THE INSANE.

"In a perfect state of things, where the best appliances whi ch the
science and skill of the age have provided for healing are offered to the
lunatics, in as early a stage of their malady as they are to th ose who
are attacked with fever or dysentery, probably eighty, and possibly

ninety, per cent would be restored, and only twenty, or perhaps ten, per cent would be left among the constant insane population."—Dr. Jarvis.

Referring to this assertion, it is stated, in reference to the Utica Asylum, that "its influence has been such that every acute case happening in the county is at once placed under hospital treatment. The result is that only *five* per cent of those treated in the early stage of the disease remain as incurables; thus more than verifying the assertion of Doctor Jarvis.*

Doctor Tuke says: "It is of great practical importance to remember that the chances of cure are very much greater in recent than in chronic cases. This is clearly shown by the experience of the Retreat, in the following table:†

Proportion of Recoveries on per cent of Admissions..

DURATION OF DISORDER WHEN ADMITTED.	York Retreat—1796 to 1857.		
	Male.	Female.	Average.
First attack and within three months........	72.97	73.23	73.10
First attack, above three and within twelve months..	43.07	44.2	43.66
Not first attack, and within twelve months	59.44	67.01	63.77
First or not first attack, and more than twelve months...................................	13.29	22.59	18.20
Totals.......................................	49.54	49.50	49.44

EFFECTS OF EARLY TREATMENT.

The Superintendent of the Southern Ohio Lunatic Asylum, in his report for eighteen hundred and sixty-nine, shows how the expectation of recovery diminishes almost in exact proportion to the length of time the disease has existed, thus:

DURATION.	Admissions.	Recoveries.	Per Cent.
One month..............................	530	363	68.49
Two months	219	141	63.01
Three months...........................	164	88	53.65
Four months............................	98	53	54.08
Six months..............................	177	83	46.32
Twelve months..........................	239	103	43.09
Two years...............................	163	47	28.83
Over two years..........................	191	33	17.32

* See Journal of Insanity, Vol. XXVII, p. 382.
† See Bucknill and Tuke on Insanity, p. 261.

The above table is for the period of years from eighteen hundred and fifty-five to eighteen hundred and sixty-nine inclusive.

This is a universally admitted fact which has been proved by the experience of hospitals almost without exception, and is by far the most powerful agent that can be employed in preventing the increase of insanity in our midst—at least in preventing its accumulation in our asylums. But as the experience of individual asylums may not be considered a fair test of so important a matter, we add the following table showing the results in many asylums in several countries for a series of years:

TABLE 1.
Results of Treatment.

COUNTRIES.	DATE.	GENERAL RESULTS.					PROPORTION OF—			
		Numbers Resident..	Admissions	Numbers Resident..	Recoveries	Deaths	Recoveries on Admissions	Recoveries on Numbers Treated	Deaths on Admissions	Deaths on Numbers Treated
United States *	1870	15,792	10,229	26,021	3,357	1,851	33.	13.	18.	7.
England	1870	35,913	11,462	47,375	3,955	3,790	34.	6.	33.	8.
Scotland	1870	5,317	2,015	7,332	832	491	41.	11.	24.	7.
Ireland	1870	7,121	2,532	9,653	1,068	708	43.	†11.	27.	7.
France	1860	28,761	10,785	39,546	†4,337	4,970	†40.		46.	12.
Italy	1867	8,101	4,909	13,100		1,504			30.	11.
Belgium	1865	5,441	1,851	7,292	642	595	34.	8.	32.	8.
Holland	1868	3,179	994	4,173	380	358	38.	9.	36.	8.
Norway	1867	667	423	1,090	140	41	33.	12.	9.	3.
Sweden	1864	1,095	332	1,427	†163	91	†49.	†11.	27.	6.
Totals		111,477	45,532	157,009	14,894	14,309	37.	10.	32.	9.

* This report is for forty-nine asylums only, it being impossible to obtain returns from the remainder.

† In the Swedish and French reports the numbers *discharged improved* are included with the *recovered*, which makes the percentage appear higher than it really is.

TABLE 2.

Report of Asylums Visited in Different Countries.

COUNTRIES.	No. Asylums visited from which Reports were obtained	General Report of Asylums Visited.					Proportion Per Cent of—				Average weekly cost for Pauper Patients
		No. Resident	No. Admitted	No. Cured	No. Died	No. Treated	Cures on Admissions	Cures on Number Treated	Deaths on Admissions	Deaths on Number Treated	
United States	39	12,907	8,039	3,240	1,519	21,504	37.	15.	17.	7.	$3 50
Canada	1	518	77	35	26	295	45.	5.	33.	4.	
England	24	12,819	3,966	1,458	1,272	16,785	36.	8.	32.	7.	2 28
Scotland	6	1,995	1,030	365	206	3,025	35.	12.	20.	6.	2 28
Ireland	7	2,437	1,206	457	256	3,643	37.	12.	21.	7.	2 15
France	13	*7,998	3,324	‖873	‖1,292	‖11,262	26.	7.	38.	11.	1 62
German States	10	2,495	1,046	276	290	3,541	35.	7.	27.	8.	1 60
Prussia	2	1,065	297	105	110	1,362	21.	9.	37.	8.	1 95
Austria	6	2,302	1,741	377	543	4,043	38.	13.	31.	13.	1 39
Italy	15	*4,259	†1,907	†764	†621	25,316	38.	8.	31.	10.	1 77
Switzerland	2	462	¶83	¶32	¶19	¶378	30.	6.	22.	5.	1 16
Belgium	8	3,029	†769	†232	†311	†3,567	38.	7.	40.	8.	1 05
Holland	3	1,245	321	123	145	1,566	38.	7.	45.	9.	1 88

* One of the largest of these, La Salpêtrière, is for chronic cases only; omitting this, the per cent of cures on admissions would be twenty-seven.

‖ In eleven of these asylums. † In thirteen asylums.

§ In twelve asylums. * In fourteen asylums.

¶ In one asylum. † In five asylums.

TABLE,

Showing the Total, the Native, and the Foreign Population, with the Total Native and Foreign Insane, and the Proportion of the Total, the Native, and the Foreign Insane to their respective Population, and the Proportion of the Foreign to the Native Insane, for the year eighteen hundred and seventy.

UNITED STATES.

Total Population	Native Population	Foreign Population	Total Insane	Native Insane	Foreign Insane	Proportion of the Total Insane to the Total Population	Proportion of the Native Insane to the Native Population	Proportion of the Foreign Insane to the Foreign Population	Proportion of the Foreign Insane to the Native Insane
38,555,983	32,989,437	5,566,546	37,382	26,161	11,221	1 to 1,031	1 to 1,261	1 to 496	1 to 233

Proportion of Foreign Population to Native Population, 1 in 5.92.

CALIFORNIA.

TABLE,

Showing the Population and Numbers of Insane and Idiots in 1850, 1860, and 1870, with the proportion per one thousand of Insane and Idiots to Population, and the Annual Rate of Increase of Insane, Idiots, and total Population.

CALIFORNIA.

YEAR.	Population.	Number of Insane.	Number of Idiots.	Total Insane and Idiots.	Ratio per 1,000 of—			Annual Increase of—		
					Insane to Population.	Idiots to Population.	Insane and Idiots to Population.	Population.	Insane.	Idiots.
1850	92,597	2	7	9	.02	.07	.09	} 15.16	72.1	19.62
1860	379,994	456	42	498	1.20	.11	1.31			
1870	560,247	1,146	87	1,233	2.04	.15	2.20	3.95	9.6	7.55

TABLE,

Showing Total Population with Native and Foreign Population, and proportion of the Native and of the Foreign to the Total Population.

YEAR.	Total Population.	Native Population.	Foreign Population.	Proportion of Native to Total Population.	Proportion of Foreign to Total Population.
1850	* 92,597	70,340	21,802	75.96	23.54
1860	379,994	233,466	146,528	61.43	38.56
1870	560,247	350,416	209,831	62.54	37.45

* In eighteen hundred and fifty the nationality of four hundred and fifty-five persons was unknown.

TABLE,

Showing Total Number of Insane, with Native and Foreign Insane, and proportion of the Native and of the Foreign to the Total Insane, and of the Foreign to the Native Insane.

YEAR.	Total Insane.	Native Insane.	Foreign Insane.	Proportion of Native to Total Insane.	Proportion of Foreign to Total Insane.	Proportion of Native Insane to Native Population.	Proportion of Foreign Insane to Foreign Population.
1850	2	2	....	100	....	1 to 35,170	....
1860	456	....	....	....	....	....	....
1870	1,146	408	738	35.60	64.39	1 to 858	1 to 284

TABLE,

Showing the total number of Idiotic, with Native and Foreign Idiotic, and proportion of the Native and of the Foreign to the total Idiotic, and of the Foreign to the Native Idiotic.

YEARS.	Total Idiotic.	Native Idiotic.	Foreign Idiotic.	Proportion of Native to Total Idiotic.	Proportion of Foreign to Total Idiotic.	Proportion of Foreign to Native Idiotic.	Proportion of Native Idiotic to Native Population.	Proportion of Foreign Idiotic to Population.
1850.......	7	6	1	85.71	14.28	16.66	1 to 11,723	....
1860.......	42	....	....	....	....	....	....	....
1870.......	87	70	17	80.45	19.54	24.28	1 to 5,005	1 to 12,343

CALIFORNIA NO EXCEPTION.

This shows that California is not an exception to the general rule; for while the insane have increased within her borders more rapidly than in any other country during the same period of time, it must not be overlooked that her citizens have not only been exposed to a greater number of causes by which this malady is developed, but that she is perhaps the only State in the Union, if not the only Government in the world, that has never refused admission to a single person who has sought to enter her asylum, notwithstanding it is a well known fact that among those received there have been and still are many citizens of other countries, who have not claimed California as a home, but who have come here hoping to better their fortunes and enrich themselves at her expense, and then return to their own homes and country; but failing to realize their dreams of wealth, give way to despondency, break down in health, or enter upon a course of reckless dissipation that leads them to insanity and to our asylum, either to be cured by our treatment or maintained through life at the expense of the State.

How far this evil may be remedied or ameliorated by judicious legislation, is a problem that we are not prepared to solve; but surely it would seem that some preference should be given, some difference made, between this class and our own citizens; but if we must keep them, it does seem that the comity of nations should prompt them to reimburse us for the expenditure made. The doctrine has been proclaimed, and repeatedly confirmed by the superintendents of American institutions for the insane, and by those who have paid any attention to the subject the world over, "that it is the duty of every State to provide for its own insane." In this sentiment we heartily concur, and earnestly urge its adoption by our noble State, without equivocation or reservation. But the other is a very different question; nor do we now remember any instance of a declaration to the effect that it is the duty of one Govern-

27

ment to defray the charity expense of another. In other countries, and even in different divisions of the same country, persons of this class are often transferred to the communities to which they belong. The question is at least worthy of consideration.

SHOULD OTHER STATES SEND THEIR INSANE TO CALIFORNIA?

In this connection another question, though intrinsically different, is nevertheless analagous to some extent, and deserves notice, not so much on account of its present importance as its future results. It is to inquire how far a sister State may be justified in establishing her institutions within the borders of another? Is it just or proper for one State to send all of her insane in the limits of another, even though she may pay the expense of care and maintenance? It is fair to presume that when they are considered sufficiently recovered to require no further medical treatment that they will not be returned to the State from which they come, but turned loose upon the community where the asylum is located. Should a speedy relapse follow their discharge, they would of course be sent back to the asylum in which they had been treated; but when a few months have elapsed they would be committed under our laws, and sent to our asylum, and thus become an additional charge upon the State. We all know that a large majority of the insane are from that class who are not able to pay, and that persons who have been afflicted with this malady are more liable to be attacked than an equal number who have not been thus affected. The burden of all these will inevitably fall upon us. For these reasons it would seem proper for the State to express an opinion on this subject.

WILL THE CHILDREN OF FOREIGNERS BE AS LIABLE TO INSANITY AS THEIR PARENTS?

We do not know and have no means of ascertaining how far this liability extends to the children who are born of parents of foreign birth, but venture the opinion that it will be only in a small degree. If this hypothesis be correct, it must necessarily follow that the proportion of insane will diminish very nearly in proportion to the increase of the native over the foreign element in the mass of the people. This will of course become more and more rapid with each successive generation; for while the one is supplied with emigration from the other States and all the children born in the State, regardless of the nativity of their parents, the other must be increased by immigration alone.

PHYSICAL AND MORAL CAUSES PRODUCING INSANITY.

Having considered some, perhaps most, of the prominent causes of insanity, so far as it is affected in a social or political point of view, it may be expected that we will enter upon the consideration of the more prominent of the physical and moral causes leading to this malady; but we scarcely consider it necessary to do more than allude to some of them. We have already given a table showing a few of the more prominent assigned causes in all the countries visited during the prosecution of our mission, but without special comment. By referring to that table it will be seen that they very generally agree with those operating in our State, but differing in degree and intensity in some countries. Thus, hereditary predisposition and intemperance are assigned as prominent causes in all countries, and in Prussia and the German States they are the only causes of prominence, In Italy we find pellagra (disease of the skin peculiar to that country) added to the other two, while in most other countries we find added to the list ill health, pecuniary and domestic troubles, and spermatorrhœa, including self-abuse, etc. In our State, we see by the report of Dr. Shurtleff, just published, that masturbation still holds its place at the head of the list of assigned causes, though we agree with him that it is high time for " Committing Boards " to be more careful in their conclusions with regard to this particular cause. Many patients who have been received at the asylum with this charge of self-pollution resting upon them, have, after weeks or months of watchfulness, been proved to be entirely free from such evil practices. That it is a cause in some cases we have every reason to believe; and further than this, when it is the cause its victims rarely recover; they seem to be doomed from the very beginning. There are other cases in which it is merely a symptom of a diseased brain, or some of its appendages—an effect, not a cause. These cases are more hopeful when treated in time. Indeed, many men of prominence with whom we have met on the continent, in Great Britain, and in the United States, believe that it is almost universally the effect of insanity, and not its cause.

INTEMPERANCE A LEADING CAUSE OF INSANITY.

With regard to intemperance the case is altogether different. It seems to be the bane of all countries, and claims its victims in every civilized nation and under every form of government. It is the common enemy of mankind, the destroyer of domestic happiness, the copartner of every crime, from petit larceny to murder. It is the father of poverty, the creator of ·debauchery, and the principal working tool of the Devil. No man is bold enough to defend it, and yet it is tolerated by all classes of society. It finds its way alike to the house of the rich and the home of the poor. It is a boon companion at the festive board of the aristocrat, and the poorly provided table of the cottager. It has caused more heartaches, produced more tears, engendered more sorrows, starved more *babies*, and led to more insanity than any other agent in existence—if not more than all others combined. We are strongly inclined to the opinion that directly or remotely it is more potent in producing these results than ALL other causes. It is the sin of civilization that it has found out manifold ways of extracting alcohol from natural substances, so that it is offered in tempting forms and accessible abundance to the weak and incautious, who would not instinctively seek it, as well as those whose appetites demand it. If, then, civilization is responsible for the introduction of this destructive element among mankind, it is certainly its duty and it should be compelled to provide for its victims. How to arrest its progress, if, indeed, it be possible, we must leave to the wiser heads of the legislator and the statesman; and he who can solve the problem will be the wisest of men, and a greater benefactor to his fellow men than has ever yet appeared among them.

We have thus briefly considered this last, as it is the most prolific, among the causes that have given us so large a number of persons deprived of their reason; who crowd the wards of our asylum till there is scarce sleeping room or breathing space for the numbers they contain, to say nothing of the accumulations that must take place ere additional accommodations can be provided for their reception. The question must be determined as to what is best to be done in performing our duty and relieving their distress.

The State must elect whether it will build other hospitals, and thereby pay the cost of cure, or support all those for life who become incurable from our failure to provide sufficient and suitable accommodation for their early treatment—whether to make the effort to regain a productive citizen, or support a non-producer for seventeen years. We must either provide hospitals for the reception of every citizen who may become insane within our borders and under our jurisdiction, or surrender this noble charity to degeneracy and decay. As already stated, this has been done. No other State, so far as our knowledge extends, has done so much; a fact that is doubtless a source of gratification and pride to every man who claims California as a home. We regret, however, that candor compels us to say that some of the wards of the male department of our asylum are wretched in the extreme, and would be disgraceful if not taken in connection with the fact, that the number of applicants have been so far beyond expectation as to render it next to impossible to provide accommodations for them all. Received they have been, but during the last two years at the discomfort of many who were thus compelled to give up a portion of the space, already too small, that had been allotted to them. Doctor Shurtleff in his report just published, has truly said "the rooms are not only *full*, but *crowded.*" In addition to this, two hundred and twenty-seven patients are sleeping on beds nightly prepared for them in the halls. The number in excess of the accommodations has grown to proportions too vast to admit of being properly provided for by the erection of cheap detached wards. The institution, in point of numbers, is already *double* the size of the average of similar institutions in the other States. With the completion of the new building, therefore, all further expansion should be discontinued. This done, aside from the cost of support, every other effort and expenditure in behalf of the asylum at Stockton should be directed to repairs, the construction of inclosures, and the improvement of the grounds, etc.

"If this view be concurred in, the only alternative left is for the State to make further provision elsewhere. The character, extent, and location of such provisions are questions upon which every possible light should be shed. In character, nothing less than a first class hospital, with all the modern improvements and appliances for the curative treatment of such as may be benefited thereby, and for the proper care of all classes of the insane, will meet the general approval of the most experienced;" and, we may add, the expectations of the people of the State. Doctor Shurtleff continues: "If additional provision for the care of the insane be made at some other place than Stockton, the question of locality is one of no less importance than those of character and extent. Topographical and climatic fitness are matters of such primary importance that they will not be likely to be overlooked. Convenience to the greatest number who will be likely to need its benefits is a very important consideration, in many respects, in the location of a hospital for the insane. Officers' fees and travelling expenses, which depend on the distance, and are a public charge generally, the difficulty and even danger in conveying the insane, and the visits of friends, are all matters which should be considered and have their influence in arriving at conclusions. In this connection it should be borne in mind that of the five hundred and twenty-three patients admitted during the last year, about three hundred came from the counties bordering on the Bay of San Francisco, and that two hundred and twenty-two—more than two fifths of the whole—came from the City of San Francisco alone. This proportion is no exception to those of several years past."

These suggestions, emanating from Doctor Shurtleff, a close and accurate observer, with a correct judgment, and a larger experience than any man on this coast, should not be lightly passed over nor disregarded. They are the results of serious reflection on an important subject with which he has been intimately identified for years, and his conclusions can be maintained with manifold reasons of the strongest character. With a single exception, that of size of hospital, they entirely accord with the views expressed to your Excellency soon after the completion of our visit to nearly one hundred and fifty asylums, wherein we had noted with especial interest, among other things, and observed with more than ordinary scrutiny and careful consideration, the effects of overcrowded wards and courtyards, the location and sites of asylums, their nearness to and distance from some city or important town, the character of scenery, quantity and quality of land, the sources of water supply, the facilities of communication, the convenience and cheapness with which fuel, supplies of all kinds, and building material could be obtained, as well as all other matters in any way connected with the construction, ventilation, warming, organization, etc., of hospitals for the insane, and which are treated more or less at length under their proper heads; and above all, to the importance of locating these institutions in the midst of those most likely to require the benefits they confer.

In many of the States inadequate provisions are made for treating the insane, followed by the most disastrous results. Large numbers who desired to gain admittance have been turned away and told, "not in words, but in acts that are more powerful than words," to wait till somebody gets well or dies, and then after the disease has fastened itself upon your brain so firmly that it cannot be removed, when all hope of recovery has passed, you may come in, and in your turn keep some other equally unfortunate person out till he, too, becomes hopelessly incurable, lost to himself, lost to his family, and lost to the State—yet a burden to the public treasury so long as he shall live. No one who is at all familiar with the nature of this malady will deny these facts; every person who has written or spoken upon the subject during this generation has asserted them till they have ceased to be denied.

Last year, as we learned from personal information obtained from some of the superintendents of asylums, and from the published reports of others, the following facts existed:

At Staunton, Virginia, of two hundred and eight applicants, only fifty-nine were admitted; rejected......................................	149
In the Michigan Asylum, rejected	155
In the Asylum in North Carolina, rejected.............................	150

Dr. Everts, of the Indiana Asylum, informed us that not more than one third could be accommodated in that State, and as three hundred and fourteen were admitted, it follows that six hundred and twenty-eight must have been rejected. Yes, strange as it may appear, this young and vigorous State, the sixth in point of population in the American Union, and, as we are informed, the only one free from the burden of debt; with low taxation and abundant resources; with one million six hundred and eighty thousand six hundred and thirty-seven inhabitants, has turned away from her asylum two thirds of her own unfortunate children who have sought relief at her hands. Who could have believed it possible in this enlightened age that any community of American citizens could be guilty of such cruel practices and such parsimonious conduct as this? And yet the fact is as stated. Doctor Hills, of West Virginia, reports from sixty to seventy-five in the jails of that young State; and the State Board of Charities report thirteen hundred and twenty-six in the poorhouses of New York. The States of Maine, Iowa, Illinois, and others are no better off. Unlike Indiana, however, most of these States are making noble efforts to remedy this evil, because they recognize the obligation and the duty, and feel no disposition to shirk the responsibility nor to avoid the expense. Indeed, we would like to know what right a State has to make such unjust distinctions between its citizens; to say to one, "Come and be healed," and to another, "Go hence; you shall not partake of the benefits you have helped to create." To one, "You shall come in, be fed, clothed, housed, and nursed; our physician shall minister to your diseased frame and release your troubled mind from its agonizing thraldom." To the other, "We have no house to shelter your head from the pitiless storms; no food to appease your hunger; no raiment to cover your nakedness or add to your comforts; no nurses to watch over you in sickness and minister to your necessities. For you there is no sympathy; you must take care of yourself, pay your own expenses, and provide for your necessities as best you can. For you 'there is no balm in Gilead, there is no physician there.' "

What is the result of this policy? Nine tenths of these people have no means of consequence. While in the possession of health, and endowed with that greatest of earthly blessings, their reason, they were able to support themselves, and, it may be, lay up a little something for their families; and if this had not already been exhausted by ill health or other cause that has led them gradually to insanity, this calamity has deprived them of the chief part if not all of their capital—the ability to work. The family who have hitherto depended upon these resources must now look to other means and other persons for support. They cannot afford to send this afflicted member of the family to a private asylum—it may be in another and distant State—nor can they afford to keep him at home and have him properly treated. They are out of relation with social and domestic life, and should go away. It is often the case the very presence of family and home is a source of annoyance and vexation that they cannot endure.

THE INSANE CANNOT BE KEPT AND CURED AT HOME.

They are a great burden to the family, and disturb its quiet and its peace; and if retained, as is not unfrequently the case, drag all down to poverty and misery with themselves. Besides, they require to be managed with fitting wisdom, that few can give, however willingly and cheerfully disposed, and with that amount of patience and forbearance not often found outside of asylum walls. Indeed, many cannot be managed at home on account of a disposition to wander, to be violent, or

destructive. Some cannot be persuaded to submit to the needful remedies for their proper treatment, even when this could be obtained.

PHYSICIANS NOT GENERALLY INFORMED ON THIS SUBJECT.

Unfortunately, but few of the medical men in general practice in our
country or any other have made themselves familiar with this mysterious disease and its proper treatment. The reason of this is obvious—
it is a branch not taught in any of our medical schools as a part of the
course. It is not a part of the curriculum in the colleges of any country; hence, proficiency in this branch is not a "sine qua non" for a medical diploma. They are sometimes called upon to pronounce as to the
sanity of some unfortunate person and to decide whether or not he is a
proper subject to be sent to an insane asylum. In the majority of cases
they have never seen the patient before and never see him afterwards.
Again: when some criminal puts in the plea of insanity to save his neck
or his reputation, the physician is called upon to testify in the case, and,
as often happens, is mortified to find that the lawyer knows more about
the subject than himself. The one has "read himself up" for the occasion, and can ask more questions than an author of medical jurisprudence could answer satisfactorily to the Judge or jury; while the doctor,
perhaps, has given the subject but little thought or attention. We trust
this condition of things will soon be changed, as more attention is being
paid to the subject both in this country and Europe.

PSYCHOLOGY RECOMMENDED TO BE TAUGHT IN THE MEDICAL SCHOOLS.

The Superintendents of many of the asylums in Italy, Austria, Germany, France, and England are giving courses of lectures on the science
of psychology, and the Association of Medical Superintendents of American Institutions for the Insane has strongly recommended its adoption
as a branch in the medical schools of this country. When this suggestion has been carried out a wonderful advance will have been made in
the right direction and many persons saved from the calamity of chronic
insanity by having their diseases early detected and properly treated.
But let us return to our patient who has not been able to procure proper
treatment in an asylum in time to obtain even a chance of recovery while
relief was possible, and we find him at last admitted to a place made
vacant by the death of some patient who has paid his last debt to the
"grim tyrant," or the recovery of some other who, more fortunate than
himself, was received in proper time. But, alas! it is too late for him.
His case has become chronic, perhaps incurable, and he is doomed to eke
out a wretched existence—a burden to himself and to the State during
the remainder of his days.

EFFECTS OF LIBERAL AND ECONOMICAL PLAN OF CARE OR TREATMENT.

The following extracts from the report of the Worcester, Massachusetts, Hospital for eighteen hundred and sixty-two, will show the effect
of the two policies on the use of hospitals, and cure of patients:

" The natural effect of the liberal and the economical policies of offer-
ing the hospitals to the use of the people, is manifest in the different
ratios of the patients sent in the early and in the later stages of their
malady to the hospitals in Massachusetts and Ohio.

"In Ohio seventy-three and one seventh per cent, and in Massachusetts sixty-four and one eighth per cent of the patients in their State hospitals were sent in the first year after they were attacked.

"As a necessary consequence, those States which sent the largest proportion in the early and curable stage received back the largest proportion in health and power of usefulness, and had the smallest proportion left in confirmed immovable lunacy to be supported for life by their estates or the public treasuries.

"In the three public hospitals of Ohio, fifty-four and fifty-nine one hundredths per cent of all that were sent to them were restored, and forty-three and forty one hundredths per cent remained insane for life. In Massachusetts, forty-four and five one hundredths per cent were restored, and fifty-five and ninty-five one hundredths per cent remained a life burden on the people.

"It must be remembered in this connection that the reports of admission into the hospitals of Massachusetts include both the foreign or State paupers who are admitted free, and the American paying patients who are charged more than the cost for their support. If distinction were made in the reports, and it were shown how many of each of those two classes were sent in the several stages of their disorder, it would, without doubt, be found that a much larger proportion than thirty-five and two one hundredths per cent of the native patients were kept out of the hospital until their disease become more difficult and even impossible to be removed.

"It is not necessary to go abroad to find the connection between the terms of admission and support, and the readiness with which people avail themselves of hospital privilege for the cure or custody of their insane friends. We have proof of this in our own daily experience. Our Irish patients go free and stay without cost, and they are sent early and Have the best opportunities of restoration. The Americans go at their own cost, and pay all and more than all of the expense of their support, and consequently a large proportion are kept away, some for months and years, as long as their friends can endure or take care of them, and many for life, because their friends lack courage or money to take due advantage of the means of restoration so largely provided in the State. In eighteen hundred and fifty-nine, ninty-seven and five tenths per cent of all the foreign and only fifty-eight per cent of the native lunatics then living in the State had been sent to some hospital.

"The proportion of patients restored out of all admitted to the hospitals, is twenty-three per cent greater in Ohio than in Massachussetts. Now, no one will suppose that the hospitals of Ohio are managed with more skill than those of this State. But the difference in the result of their labors is due to the difference in the proportion of patients sent in the curable stages of their disorder.

"Looking upon this matter merely as a question of political economy, in its bearing upon the remote as well as present means and prosperity of the State, it is plain that there are important advantages on the side of the free and open system of managing these public charitable institutions. They send back to society a larger proportion of workers, producers, self-supporters, and contributors to the public treasury, and leave a smaller proportion of the useless and burdensome class. Inasmuch as they have a better or more available material to work upon, they produce a more successful result, and convert a larger proportion of costly men and women into profitable members of the body politic. The Worcester and Taunton Hospitals have received eight thousand four hundred and ninety, and restored three thousand seven hundred and forty to health. If these could have been sent at as early a stage of their disease, and as large a proportion restored as in Ohio, then twenty-three per cent, or eight hundred and sixty would have been added to the useful and self-sustaining citizens sent back to the world, and as many taken from the class that has been or must be supported and cared for through life.

" It must be further considered that it costs no more to administer these institutions on the free principles of Ohio than on the economical principles of Massachusetts. Both there and here provisions, groceries, clothing, labor, and salaries would be the same under either system. The only difference is in the way in which the cost is assessed upon the people. Here it is imposed upon those who receive the immediate personal advantage, many of whom are the least able to bear it, and always at a period when they are the weakest, and any burden is distressing. In the other case, this cost of rescuing the people from permanent insanity, like the cost of schools, roads, Government, justice, and police, is assessed upon the whole community, in the proportion that each one is able to pay; and in both cases it comes out of the aggregate property and income of the Commonwealth."

Any attempt to save money by failing to provide for the insane is indeed poor economy, and worse philanthropy. Let us, therefore, adhere firmly to the policy we have so wisely inaugurated, and which has placed us in the front ranks among the States of the Union and the nations of the world, and build asylums for all of our people who may be so unfortunate as to require their use and need their healing influence. In this connection, we deem it of some importance to introduce the following extract from a Message from Mr. Seward (when Governor of New York) to the Legislature:

" I cheerfully express my approbation of the undertaking. Nations are *seldom impoverished by their charities*. The number of the insane in this State is not exaggerated, and I am not prepared to say that any erection less extensive would afford the space, light, tranquility, and cheerfulness indispensable to this interesting department of the healing art. Among all His blessings, none call so loudly for gratitude to God as the preservation of our reason. Of all the inequalities in the social condition, there is none so affecting as its privation. He sees fit to cast upon our benevolent care those whom He visits with that fearful affliction; it would be alike *unfeeling and ungrateful to withhold it*. Let then this noble charity be carried forward, with what measure of munificence it remains with you to determine."

Like sentiments have been proclaimed by the intelligent executive officers of most of the States of the Union, our own included, but unfortunately in too many instances legislators are frightened, or driven from their duty by the " criticisms of that class of public benefactors who make capital from their sympathy with our overtaxed people," and no appropriation is made. Fortunately, at this time, however, no such objection can be urged. The Democratic party has seen the necessity of additional accommodations for the insane, and it only remains for the

Republican party, ever the friend of progress, to carry forward the suggestion and complete the work. It is a noble charity, and no excuses should be needed to justify any appropriation that may be required, under judicious expenditure, to meet the necessities of the case; nor should the subject of politics weigh a feather in the balance of any man's mind in his considerations or his actions upon the subject. It did not do so two years ago, when the investigation was ordered to be made of which this report is the result, and there is no reason why it should do so now. Our labors have been performed with the hope that suffering humanity would be the gainer by the results, and if this shall prove to be the case we will have reaped the most earnest desire of our heart, and a reward beyond price. Hence we have ventured the suggestion that the one party and the other will be equally responsible for any appropriations that may be made and equally entitled to the honors of so beneficent a deed.

"We can lose nothing by our charities in this direction." Let us not only provide ample accommodations for all of our insane, but let us so locate our asylums that they will be easily accessible to the greatest number of those who will probably require their use, and then with an enlightened public opinion all will be encouraged to seek the benefits of early treatment and speedy restoration. Comparatively a few only will be left as permanent charges to the State. A much greater number will be restored to usefulness and labor. The State will be the gainer by the operation, and humanity will smile at the triumph of wise legislation and judicious treatment over the most appalling disease with which the human race has ever been afflicted.

CHAPTER XV.

INSANE ASYLUMS—ECONOMY OF PROVIDING AMPLE CURATIVE ACCOMMODATIONS.

Before entering upon the discussion of the plan of building best adapted to the care and treatment of the insane, we desire to call the attention of the business man, the financier, and the taxpayer, as well as the legislator, to the ECONOMY of restoration and the amount saved the State by the cures already effected in our asylum.

A similar showing was made by Doctor Jarvis a few years since to the State of Massachusetts, and to him we are indebted for the idea and most of the facts set forth in this article. We have applied them to California, and in making the argument must necessarily touch upon some matters already considered. It is a proposition universally admitted that it is the first interest of every State to preserve itself, to develop its own strength, and to sustain it to the fullest degree. The strength and wealth of the State are the aggregate of the wealth and power of the individuals who compose it. If a member of the community is strong, his strength increases the power of the State. If he be a producer and create riches, this adds so much to the common wealth.

If, on the contrary, he become sick or weak and lose his power of production, his loss of personal power takes so much from the general power. His failure to add to his own estate is so much loss to the general prosperity. If, more than this, he loses power to provide for his own wants, his support becomes a charge upon property that he or others have created, or are at the time creating. If his own means or those of his family are insufficient for this purpose, then the public treasury must and does assume the burden.

Whether this support of a dependent citizen comes from his own or others' estate, or the general treasury, it inevitably comes from the property of the commonwealth, either that which has already been paid in form of taxes to the Government, or that which, in the hands of individuals, is the basis of taxation. In either case the body politic is the loser to the extent of the cost of supporting the disabled person.

In all cases this cost is first chargeable to the estate of the one supported. If that be wanting, then his natural friends should pay it; and if they fail, the expense falls on the town or State. This last resort is sure, for the town or State is .the responsible indorser of every sick, disabled, or insane person within its borders, to restore him to health or support him through life.

There is in every community, especially in such as have had a generation of existence, a large body of the insane who are a constant burden on its resources. In Massachusetts, in eighteen hundred and fifty-five, there was one insane person in every four hundred and twenty-seven living. In other States and counties there are estimated to be from one in four or five hundred to one in a thousand. A part of these are the recent cases, that have a hope of restoration; a larger part consists of old and incurable cases that have been submitted to the healing processes without avail, or have been neglected until the day of relief was past.

The burden of supporting these is constant, unavoidable, and very great. It is the first claim of humanity, as well as the duty and interest of the body politic, to keep the numbers of these as small as possible, by healing all that can be healed in the curable stage of their disorder, and allowing none but those whose disease is primarily incurable to fall into chronic and permanent lunacy.

Insanity, although it suspends the power of production, self care, and self support, is not in itself very dangerous to life. A man becoming insane at twenty, if not restored, has a prospect of living, on an average, twenty-one years in lunacy; but if restored his prospect is for thirty-nine years in health. The average of life for a permanent lunatic is twenty years, and for a sane man thirty-two years, from their thirty-first year; and these prospects are respectively seventeen and twenty-six years from their forty-first year. Persons taken with lunacy at these ages have, then, the doubtful prospect of living twenty-one, twenty, or seventeen years, more or less, according to the age when attacked, in dependence, a burden on their own or the public estate, if not restored; or of being cured and of living thirty-nine, thirty-two, or twenty-six years, more or less, in health, ability to take care of themselves, and add to the strength and wealth of the community.

Insanity is one of the most removable of grave diseases, if the proper measures are used in its early stages, as they are in cases of fever, dysentery, etc. The experience of hospitals shows that from seventy to ninety per cent may be thus restored to health. The average time required for restoration in hospitals varies from five and a half to seven, and even eight months. But the average of the whole, especially those taken early, does not exceed six months.

The average cost of supporting patients in the California asylum for the four last years was thirteen dollars and eighty-five cents ($13 85) a month. This is eighty-three dollars and ten cents ($83 10) for six months, and one hundred and sixty-six dollars and twenty cents ($166 20) for a year. The actual cost of restoration necessarily includes the whole expense of the experiment. It is impossible to determine in advance who may be restored—who must remain uninfluenced by remedial measures. These must then be used for the whole; some may be restored in a few weeks, others in all periods from this to two years and more—averaging six months to all; but none must be given up as incurable until they have had at least two years trial of the means of cure.

The cure of the seventy-five per cent thus necessarily involves the necessity of two years board and care of the other twenty-five per cent. This must also be included in the list of cases and assessed upon the seventy-five who are restored.

The cost of seventy-five cured, for six months is.....................	$623 25
The cost of twenty-five not cured, for two years each is........	831 00
Total...	$1,454 25

Assessing this equally upon them makes the average cost of curing the insane in California to be one hundred and ninety-three dollars and eighty-six cents.

It must be remembered that this cost of supporting seventy-five for six months and twenty-five for two years in a hospital—fourteen hundred and fifty-four dollars—for the restoration of the seventy-five is not so much additional expense thrown upon the people. These hundred persons were already insane, helpless, powerless, unable to support themselves. They were already thrown upon the community and its individual members, who were responsible for their maintenance whether they were sent to the hospital or not; whether any attempt was or was not made to restore them. The Commonwealth collectively, or its estates separately, must pay the cost of their board, care, and guardianship.

It is questionable whether out of a hospital, a private house, or other abodes, at home or with strangers, these patients could obtain food for less than it cost the asylum for them—three dollars and twenty cents ($3 20) a week. If not, then the curative measures in the asylum caused no additional expense to the State or its people, except the cost of the establishment itself. The interest on the capital; the wear and depreciation of the buildings; the cost of repairs; the insurance, and the taxes which would otherwise have been paid to the public treasury on this amount of property, are properly chargeable to the cost of curing the insane, and nothing more.

Here, on the contrary, must be weighed the gain to the community from the restoration of the insane to health. The annual earnings of a man over and above the expense of his living may be considered as an annuity, or so much annually contributed to the commonwealth. According to the best European calculations of these values—the earnings and expenditures—the present worth of the excess of the former over the latter, for an unskilled laborer at twenty-five, is twelve hundred and eight dollars ($1,208). That is, such a laborer at that age is worth so much to the body politic. This is the English, and very nearly the German valuation. In this country wages are higher and earnings more, and of course the annuity and its valuation are greater. This, too, is the estimated value of an unskilled laborer, who earns the lowest wages. The value of the skilled mechanic, the merchant, the professional man, whose earnings are larger, must be very much greater. It is at least safe, then, to assume the European calculation of twelve hundred and eight dollars as the average worth of men of all conditions and occupations in California who may become insane at the age of twenty-five.

This is lost by his lifelong insanity. Add to this the cost of his support, at least as great as that charged in the asylum—thirteen dollars and eighty-five cents a month, one hundred and sixty-six dollars and eighty-five cents a year, for an average of twenty-one years:

Making for each uncured patient a total expenditure for support	$3,490 83
Add the loss of the value as a producer	1,208 00
Showing a total loss of	$4,698 83

So much is gained by restoring an insane laborer twenty-five years old. It would have been less if he had been older, with a prospect of fewer years before him; it would have been more if he were a mechanic or man of business, with power to earn more if in health. The cost, only one hundred and ninety-three dollars, is neutralized by the consideration that it would have been as great for his support if no attempt had been made to restore him.

During the twenty years of the operation of the California Asylum, five thousand six hundred and eighty-one lunatics were admitted. Of these two thousand seven hundred and nine, or forty-seven and sixty-eight one hundredths per cent, were restored. This relieved the State and people of the burden of supporting these through life in their disease. Taking the numbers in their several ages, their average life, if not cured, would have been twelve years each; or the whole sum of their insane lives would have been thirty-two thousand five hundred and eight years, and their life support, at one hundred and sixty-six dollars a year, would have been four million four hundred and ninety-seven thousand and four dollars, which was saved for the State. Their average valuation, considered merely as laborers earning the lowest wages, when restored to health and productive power, was eleven hundred and two dollars each; making a total of two million seven hundred and sixty-three thousand and eighteen dollars which was regained. Both of these make a total of seven million two hundred and sixty thousand and twenty-two dollars which has been gained to the State and people by the restoration of these twenty-seven hundred and nine insane persons in the asylum at Stockton.

This calculation presupposes that all these were original cases, and then no readmission; but although the record does not state it, there must have been here, as elsewhere, periodical cases, some being more than once and some several times attacked, sent to the hospital, and there cured. These of course had shorter periods of health than this average, and their years should be deducted. This would reduce the sum, but would still leave a very great amount lost by uncured insanity.

CHAPTER XVI.

INSANE ASYLUMS—PLAN BEST ADAPTED TO CARE AND TREATMENT OF THE INSANE.

General Observations—Cottage System—Farm Asylums—Close Asylums—Pavilion Plan.

GENERAL OBSERVATIONS.

From the foregoing considerations, then, there will be no question that the State has a very great interest in the cure of the insane. Yet there may be a question as to the best manner of effecting it. We have already shown why they cannot be properly cared for, treated, and cured in private houses, at least in California; and also why we prefer moderately small to very large asylums. As it is not probable, however, that an appropriation could be obtained for two asylums with a capacity for two hundred or two hundred and fifty patients each, in accordance with our views, we trust that none for more than four hundred patients will ever be built. In saying this, we have not forgotten the suggestion made, that the north wing of the Female Asylum at Stockton should be finished. It must be remembered that the removal of two or three most uncomforable, unsightly, and objectionable wards was at the same time deemed a most desirable end to be accomplished, so soon as a new asylum could be erected; and furthermore, that having already constructed a centre building (always the most expensive part of any asylum), together with kitchen, chapel, engine house, boilers for heating, and other necessary comcomitants for an asylum to accommodate a given number, this improvement can be made at less cost than at any other place, to say nothing of the pressing demands for the room it would more speedily supply than in any other way. We have an asylum at Stockton which in some respects is not what it should be; and we desire to see these evils remedied. The improvements suggested would accomplish this object; nor do we consider this improvement at all inconsistent with the views expressed with regard to the size of asylums; this would only be the completion of a hospital already begun, and is simply a matter of necessity; whereas a different system may and should prevail in the construction of all asylums to be hereafter built.

THE COTTAGE SYSTEM.

We have already had occasion to speak of the different kinds of asylums in vogue in several countries, in our sketch of the report of Doctor Manning. What he had to say of the cottage system, as practiced at the Colony of Gheel, and the modification of that system, as adopted to some extent in Scotland, entirely agrees with the conclusions at which we ourselves had arrived: that however well adapted the system may be for old and thickly settled communities, it is "altogether inapplicable to a new or sparsely settled country." Much has been written upon this system by some of the foremost men of the Continent, of Great

Britain, and the United States; some advocating its adoption in their respective countries, while others condemn it in no mild terms as being unworthy even of respectful consideration. Esquirol, Guislain, Moreau, Parigot, Bulckens, DeMundy, Duval, Roller, Droste, Halliday, Stevens, Brown, Sibbald, Earle, Galt, Tyler, Bemis, and a host of others, have visited the famous old Colony at Gheel, and given the results of their experiences and observations to the world. Manning came next, and we followed in the wake of all, and had set forth our views at some length, not only with regard to Gheel, but also the Scotch system, of keeping a certain class of lunatics in private dwellings. But as we have no Gheel in America, and no such population as that among whom lunatics are kept in Scotland, it is unnecessary to print them. Nine tenths of the patients kept at Gheel in Belgium, and at Kennoway in Scotland, we believe, are better satisfied than they would be in hospitals; but it would be impossible to induce our people to take charge of such patients for the cost of keeping them in our asylums. Hence, it would be useless to discuss the cottage system with a view to its adoption in our country.

We refer the curious, and those who may desire to learn more of the history of Gheel and the cottage system, to the interesting essays of Dr. John Sibbald, of Scotland, who has written the most satisfactory account of them with which we have met, and which may be found in the *Journal of Mental Science* for April, 1861; to that of Dr. Henry Stevens, published in the same journal for April, 1858; and to that of Dr. Merrick Bemis, to be found in the Worcester Hospital Report for 1869—all of which, with numerous other articles upon this and kindred subjects, are among the books which now adorn the shelves of the medical department of our State Library. Indeed, with Winslow's *Psychological Journal*, the *Journal of Mental Science*, and the *American Journal of Insanity* in our library, to say nothing of the large number of other works that keep these company, it would be difficult, if not impossible, to touch upon any subject relating to insanity that cannot be found ably and thoroughly discussed in some of them. Had a tithe of the information which they contain been known by our people, or could they have been accessible to all, then, indeed, would this report have been a useless undertaking; but should it only serve to direct public attention to them, and to the subjects of which they treat, will much good have been accomplished.

For a thorough understanding of the Scotch system, we refer the reader to the interesting work of A. Mitchell, M. D., "On the Insane in Private Dwellings."

The plans that we have selected for publication in this report are chosen from a large list, and are believed to be specimens of the best in the world. There are many others equally good, and in giving preference to these we by no means intend or desire to disparage others. All cannot be published, and to insert an account of so many asylums, such as we find in our notes, would constitute a volume, and must therefore be omitted, however agreeable it would be to us to give our experience of each institution visited. We must therefore be content with descriptions of a few only, as samples of the best, and again refer the reader to the journals and other works on the subject already alluded to, for any additional information that may be desired.

FARM ASYLUMS.

The farm asylum—of which Clermont, with its colony of Fitzjames, about fifty miles from Paris, is perhaps the best specimen—possesses some advantages, in an economical point of view, but would scarcely be applicable in this country. It consists of an asylum proper, situated in the Town of Clermont, and is intended for all patients who cannot safely be trusted with the liberty given the patients at the colonies. One of these, called "Fitzjames," is near the town, and is approached by a wide avenue, finely shaded by trees. Here there are several buildings appropriated to the use of the different classes of patients, who pay from thirty francs a month to three hundred. Those paying the higher prices have rooms to themselves, a larger number of attendants, better diet, greater facilities for amusements and entertainments, and are not required to work. Of this class there are very few. Those who are charged thirty francs a month are paid for by the Department from which they came, and are expected to do such labor as may be required of them. The colonies contain one thousand acres of land, and the men work upon the farm, in the garden, and in the shops, while the women sew, do housework, wash, iron, etc. The buildings occupied by the men who work on the farm are two stories high, and consist of day rooms on the first and dormitories on the second floor. They eat in a common dining room, and no classification is attempted. The flouring mill, barns, stables, piggeries, sheep sheds, fowl yards, butcher shop, etc., are near these buildings, and are all kept in the most complete order. They are under the management of M. Jules Labitte, one of the three brothers to whom the establishment belongs, while Doctor Gustave Labitte is the Physician in Chief of the entire establishment, having an assistant in each department. The buildings for the laundry women are located a few hundred yards distant from the last mentioned, and are of similar character. The laundry itself is so constructed that a little river or stream, the Beronelle, traverses its entire length, and presents much the appearance of an ordinary mining flume, on either side of which the women stand and wash, after the custom of washerwomen throughout France. The other colony, "Villiers," is about four miles from Clermont, and is conducted on the same principle as that at Fitzjames. Of the fourteen hundred and seven patients at this establishment three hundred and fifty are at Fitzjames, one hundred at Villiers, and the rest at the establishment in Clermont. It is said to be a most profitable enterprise to its proprietors, and we were impressed with the idea that the patients were required to do more work than seemed compatible with their physical and mental condition; and the fact that nineteen and seven tenths per cent of recoveries and forty-five and two tenths per cent of deaths to numbers admitted were reported for eighteen hundred and seventy is an additional reason to confirm this conclusion. Ordinarily the labor of five lunatics is supposed to be equal to that of one person in perfect health, while many cannot labor for medical reasons; but here a much larger proportion are required to work, and more work required of them. Hence we conclude that this system could not be successfully carried out in our country and among our people.

CLOSE ASYLUMS.

This brings us to the consideration of the close asylums, including the corridor, house, and pavilion plans. All of these have their peculiar advantages and their strenuous advocates. Plans of each will be found in Appendix F of this report. All have notes of reference explanatory of the design, and some have been described.

The asylums in the United States have nearly all been constructed on the corridor plan, with centre building and wings. The plans of the proposed asylum at the City of Boston, the Pennsylvania Hospital for the Insane, and the Michigan State Asylum, though differing in some respects, are all of this character, and are considered among the best in this country, and we think are not surpassed by any in the world. None of them could be built for less than one thousand six hundred dollars per patient, and the Pennsylvania Hospital for the Insane—known as the New Kirkbride Asylum—with all of its appurtenances would probably cost two thousand dollars per patient. It is a corporate institution, intended for and patronized by the wealthy or independent classes, who pay from fifteen to thirty-five dollars per week, which enables it to furnish many advantages, comforts, and luxuries, and sources of amusement and diversion, that would be beyond the reach of institutions intended mostly for the accommodation of indigent or non-paying patients. Its capacity is for two hundred and fifty patients.

The Michigan Asylum is a State institution and was designed for three hundred, and cost four hundred thousand dollars; while the plan of the Boston Asylum was also intended for three hundred patients, and was estimated to cost four hundred and ninety-eight thousand five hundred and three dollars.

Descriptions of these asylums will be found elsewhere in this report, and it is only necessary to say here that all of them might be built in such manner as materially to lessen the cost and yet retain the general design of the structures and convenience of internal arrangement. We will mention a few of the most prominent. The expensive apparatus necessary to forced ventilation might in our climate be dispensed with. It is rarely cold enough in California at any season to render it necessary to close all the windows of a hospital, while in Summer the prevailing winds afford an abundance of fresh pure air. The Boston plan is fifty-six feet wide, but we believe that thirty-six feet would be sufficient for all necessary purposes. This would give twelve feet for the corridors and ten feet in the clear for rooms—eight by ten being large enough for single rooms. Large dormitories we do not and never did fancy; one in each ward for five patients would be sufficient for most classes of patients, and anything larger than this might easily be provided by having one wing on either side so constructed as to have the rooms only on one side the corridor, after the almost universal system of Great Britain and the continent, as may be seen in the plans of Apperdix F, figures six, ten, twelve, and thirteen—the connection of the wings to the centre building and to each other giving an abundance of light and air. The bay windows and open sitting rooms at the end of each corridor are beautiful and most desirable features of this plan, and worthy of imitation in any new structure for the treatment of the insane.

In the Michigan Asylum the ceilings are fourteen and sixteen feet, which we think unnecessarily high. Eleven or twelve feet would seem sufficiently high for the wards and fourteen feet for the centre building, thus saving another item of expense. In addition to these items that may be saved without sacrifice to comfort or design, it must be remembered that in our temperate climate not more than half the quantity of piping and other apparatus for heating the building will be required as are absolutely necessary in the colder regions in which they are located. A most desirable feature in the Michigan Asylum, too, is the infirmary for those who are suffering from physical diseases, whether connected or not with their mental condition. There is one for either sex, and it is often a great comfort—sometimes the last—for these sufferers to have a dear relation or friend with them in such times of trouble, sickness, and need.

With the features that we have pointed out in these two asylums, and with the wards for excited patients as they exist at the Pennsylvania Hospital for the Insane, combined to make one asylum for two hundred and fifty patients, supplemented with detached buildings, as elsewhere suggested, for one hundred and fifty more—such for instance as are being adopted in most of the first class asylums of Great Britain and the continent, we are confident that no better plan could be found in the world—whether for the purposes of cure or comfort; nor can we see any reason why such an establishment may not be as cheaply constructed as any other.

In making these suggestions and giving preference to the asylums of our own country for the main building, we do not wish our kind and enlightened friends " on the other side of the water " to conclude that we have failed to appreciate the admirable features of their institutions. It is true that we have expressed our disapprobation of their congregated system—the common dining halls and large associated dormitories—because we believe them to be incompatible with proper classification. It seems to work remarkably well in that country, where classes in society are distinctly divided, and where most of the poor are kept in asylums prepared especially for their reception and accommodation, while the independent patients are sent to hospitals suitable to their social condition, either in separate institutions or separate buildings under the same superintendence. There, too, the people are more accustomed to regard those vested with authority as superior beings, entitled to command, and an inherent right to be obeyed. These ideas are rather strengthened than otherwise by insanity, and are carried into the asylum with them, causing them to submit, without complaint, to the rules of the asylum and to the orders of those placed over them. The English and continental asylums, therefore, may be well adapted to the treatment of patients thus constituted, but in our country the case is very different. Every man considers himself as good as any other, and generally claims that he has as much right to command as those whom he may have assisted to place in authority. Our people have, in their condition of health, an exalted idea of liberty, which is only perverted, perhaps, by insanity. To be thwarted in their designs or restrained in their actions is conceived to be a trespass upon their inalienable rights, a curtailment of their freedom, which tends to excite and exasperate them. We cannot bring them together with impunity in such numbers as they are in other countries; besides, in this country, with few exceptions, the asylums receive alike the rich and poor, the cultivated and the ignorant, the refined and the vulgar, who can only be separated by our corridor system, where each ward constitutes its own little family, with their own sitting and dining room, parlor, bath room, etc., which would be impossible with the English system. We are well aware of the advantages of the day rooms of the European asylums, which enables the dormitories to be vacated during the day and thoroughly aired and ventilated. Hospital odors are less liable to accumulate, to become offensive and unhealthy, and it may be that the patients learn the better to control their feelings and their actions by being brought in daily contact with a larger number of their fellows. Indeed, we are disposed to think that a modification of our system in this respect might be made with advantage—that there might be one large dining hall, not for all, or for three fourths, but for one fourth of the patients in our asylums, where the men and women who were well enough and who desired to do so might meet and take their meals together. There is at present but one asylum in the United States (at Staunton, Virginia) where this is done, and we were assured by Doctor Stribbling that it was considered a great privilege by the patients, who used extraordinary efforts at self-control that they might not be deprived of it. Seventy-five out of three hundred and fifty patients were deemed proper subjects to be thus brought together, regardless of sex.

PAVILION PLAN.

The Virginia Asylum of which we have spoken, more nearly than any other in this country resembles the pavilion system now so generally adopted in all the new asylums that we saw in France, either as recently completed, or in process of construction, and of which the asylum at Auxerre (see plan App. F, fig. 14), may be considered a specimen. The plan recommended by the German Superintendents, and adopted by the authorities for the new asylum at Berlin, is also on the pavilion system. Many of the more recently constructed asylums in Great Britain have also adopted this plan to some extent, by supplementing the main hospital with detached blocks, such as we have suggested for a new asylum in California.

The asylums at Brookwood, Brentwood, Glamorgan, Warwick, Gloucester, Colney Hatch, Wakefield, The Friends' Retreat, Newcastle on Tyne, Cumberland and Westmoreland, Morningside, Cupar and Fife, Glasgow, the Richmond Asylum near Dublin, Cork, Quartre Mare, and the new Asylum San Yon at Rouen, Saint Ann at Paris, and many others, are either entirely on the pavilion plan, or are supplemented with detached blocks or cottages. The McLean Asylum at Somervillle near Boston, is another sample in our country; though we think the detached blocks in this asylum too small to be used profitably or with advantage in a State institution, as none should be built so small as to require less than two or three attendants, that at least one may be ever present in each ward where patients are kept.*

In addition to this feature as taken from the European system, we cannot too strongly urge the adoption of another, which to our mind is the most charming of them all—we allude to the extensive and beautiful pleasure grounds by which the asylums of the Old World, and especially those of Great Britain, are surrounded. The bright and beautiful lawns,

---

* For further information on the pavilion system, see *Journal of Mental Science*, for January, eighteen hundred and sixty-seven, an interesting paper by Doctor Lockhart Robertson, read at the annual meeting of the Medico-Psychological Association, held in Edinburgh, July thirty-first, eighteen hundred and sixty-six. Doctor Robertson is the able and well known editor of the *Journal of Mental Science*, ex-President of the Medico-Psychological Association, and for many years Superintendent of the Asylum at Hayward's Heath.

The opinions of the distinguished psychologists of Germany will be of peculiar interest to all who can read German. Indeed, the shelves of our library now contain the opinions and suggestions of the ablest and most experienced men who have written on this subject, not only with regard to asylums, and hospital construction, but upon all subjects in any way related to or connected with insanity.

The admirable Reports of the Commissioners in Lunacy for England and Wales, Scotland and Ireland, are full of information and interest. We again invite especial attention to these works.

handsomely laid out and planted with shade trees, shrubs, and flowers, impress the beholder with satisfaction and delight, and must produce on the mind of the patient and his friends a feeling of pleasurable relief, that the bare walls of a hospital, however beatiful in design and elegant in structure, can never afford.

It may be well in this connection to state that no asylum in Great Britain or upon the continent is built more than three stories, and in our opinion none should ever be in this or any other country. The centre building may be three, the first wings should be two, and the last but one. If covered with a French roof, the attic may be utilized either for dormitories for quiet chronic cases or for such other purposes as may be desired. No ward should be built without a wide stairway of iron or stone at either end, that free escape in case of fire may always be made. For the want of this necessary precaution many patients have lost their lives in the numerous fires that have occurred in the last few years in our own country. We ourselves have had two fires at Stockton within the last fifteen months, but fortunately not in the asylum wards. In the first instance the laundry was burned, and in the last an outhouse used as a hayshed, and had the wind been from a different direction the wooden cottages in which patients are kept might have been consumed with the rest.

We learn, too, that the private asylum of Doctor Chipley, near Lexington, Kentucky, has just been destroyed by fire. This admonishes us that we cannot guard with too much care against the danger and ravages of this fearful and devouring element.

Our views with regard to the kitchen, chapel, laundry, airing courts, etc., are in entire accord with those expressed by Doctor Manning, as previously noticed in this report. It is therefore unnecessary to speak of them here.

With an asylum of this kind, carefully watched during its construction that the endless details from a *closet* to a *doorlock* may neither be overlooked nor neglected, and so located as to possess all the advantages we have pointed out, the most favorable results may reasonably be expected. And if in addition to this we could only have a small asylum for the treatment of such of our citizens as may desire better accommodations than the State can afford to GIVE, our system would be as near perfect as any in the world. There would then be no jealousies on the part of the poor, and no complaints on the part of those who pay. The rich would have such accommodations as they desired and were disposed to pay for at non-speculative rates, and the poor would be as comfortably provided for as in any other country. As already stated, we can scarcely hope that provision will be made for the execution of this last suggestion at the present time. The others are absolute necessities, requiring immediate action or disastrous consequences, while this is only a desirable end devoutly to be wished for but not of absolute and pressing necessity.

CONCLUDING REMARKS.

In our introductory chapter we expressed our obligations to all who had contributed to our stock of information or facilitated our investigations. We feel that something more than this is due from us, not only for courtesies extended in consequence of our position as an officer of the State of California, but for individual acts of kindness.

The Commissioners in Lunacy for England and Wales, and especially Mr. Wilkes, in addition to valuable contributions for the State Library, gave us information that greatly aided us in our investigations. Doctor Mandsley, the President of the Medico-Psychological Association of Great Britain, kindly invited us to attend the annual meeting of that body, and thereby brought us in contact with a large number of the most able and learned men in the country, and enabled us to exchange views with and obtain the experience of such men as Doctor Bucknill, the accomplished author and Chancery Commissioner in Lunacy; Doctor Lockhart Robertson, also a Chancery Commissioner, and editor of the Journal of Mental Science; Doctor Tuke, the Secretary of the Association, and Doctors Arlidge, Blandford, Sankey, Hood, Monroe, Clouston, and others whose writings are familiar to the profession in this country, and a large number of Superintendents of asylums from all parts of the kingdom. Many of these we had seen, or afterwards visited at the asylums under their management. Doctor Brushfield, at Brookwood; Doctor Begley, at Hanwell; Doctor Marshall, at Colney Hatch; Doctor Rhys Williams, at Bethlem; Doctor S. W. D. Williams, at Hayward's Heath; and that noble trio of genial gentlemen, Doctors Yellowlees, Clouston, and Rogers, who reminded us so forcibly of three *young* Superintendents in our own country—Doctors Rodman of Hopkinsville, Kentucky, Callender of Tennessee, and Walker of Boston. Doctor Forbes Winslow did not attend the meeting of the Association, but we had the pleasure of seeing him at his own home. He is a man of such versatility of genius and such a fund of knowledge that to be in his presence is to imbibe information. We are under many obligations to him. A host of others were equally kind and hospitable, and to whom we gratefully tender our thanks.

In Scotland, our obligations are due to Sir James Coxe, one of the Commissioners in Lunacy, and President of the Medico-Psychological Association, for courteous attention and valuable reports. To Doctor Sibbald, Deputy Commissioner in Lunacy, for devoting an entire day in visiting with us the Colony of Kennoway, where insane persons are kept in private dwellings, after the fashion of Gheel in Belgium; and also for a copy of his essay on the cottage system, Doctor Mitchell's treatise on the insane in private dwellings, and other documents. To Doctor David Skae, the celebrated Superintendent of the Morningside Asylum, for giving us the results of his treatment in some cases of insanity, together with the effects of certain remedies elsewhere considered; and to the Superintendents of all the asylums visited, for similar favors.

Doctor Stewart, of the Belfast Asylum in Ireland; Doctor Lalor, of the Richmond Asylum at Dublin; Doctor Murphy, at Killarney; Doctor Nugent, one of the Inspectors of Asylums, and other gentlemen engaged in the specialty, also placed us under obligations.

In France, to Doctor Blanche of Passy; Doctor Lasègue, President of the Medico-Psychological Society of France; Doctor Motet, the Secretary of the Society; and to Doctors Falret, Dumesniel, Morel, Foville, Dagonet, Labitte, Arthaud, Carrier, Bruno, Hildebrand, and Ceilleux, we are indebted for many courtesies and all the information we were able to obtain of the condition and treatment of the insane in that country.

In Italy, Doctor Fidèle, of Rome, not only accompanied us to the asylum but to the numerous hospitals and other charitable institutions of the Imperial City, and gave us letters to several of the prominent physicians throughout the kingdom. Professor Neri of Perugia, whose asylum overlooks the broad Valley of the Tiber, gave us the only general statistics that we were able to obtain in Italy, and was not only well versed in psychological medicine, but was imparting his information to a class of twenty medical students who were studying the diseases of the brain that affect the mind. Doctor Cardini, of Florence; Doctor Fouscarti, of Bologna; Doctor Biffi, of Milan; Doctor Salerio, of Venice; Doctor Bramanti, of Padua, and, indeed, all the physicians and Superintendents whose asylums we visited cheerfully opened to us the doors of their institutions and aided us in every possible manner in the prosecution of our inquiries.

Nor can we say less than this of the Superintendents of the asylums in Bavaria, in Austria, in Prussia, and in other German States, in Switzerland, in Holland, and in Belgium.

Nor can we forget the services rendered us in our visits to the German and Swiss asylums by our young and accomplished countryman, Doctor B. B. Kent of Boston, who accompanied us to a dozen institutions, and from his knowledge of medicine and of the German language added greatly to the interest and pleasure of our investigations and our travels.

To the United States Ministers, Mr. Marsh, in Italy; Mr. Jay, in Austria; Mr. Bancroft, in Prussia; Mr. Washburne, in France; Mr. Jones, in Belgium; and the acting representative of our Government in England, Mr. Moran; and to the Consuls of the United States, wherever and whenever called upon, we are indebted for favors of various kinds. They were ever ready to assist us in our investigations in every possible way.

It is scarcely necessary for us to say more of the Superintendents in the United States than that they are all intelligent men, devoted to the cause of humanity, and equal in every respect to those of any other country. Among them are men of worldwide reputation, such as Doctors Ray, Jarvis, Earle, Gray, Butler, Kirkbride, Stribbling, Nichols, Bancroft, Read, Buttolph, Gundry, Curwen, and Workman and others are well known in our own country. To all of these gentlemen we owe and herewith tender our thanks; and to our friend, Doctor Edward Jarvis, who not only gave us free access to his splendid library, but who rendered us invaluable assistance in various ways. He is a faithful worker in the harness of humanity, and deserves the gratitude of the human race. There are many others to whom we are indebted for counsel, assistance, and good cheer, and to these, with the rest, we offer our thanks. If there is any one man in this State who more than any other is entitled to the gratitude of the unfortunate class of our citizens in whose behalf we have pleaded, that man is our friend Colonel E. J. Lewis of Tehama, who, sympathizing with their misfortunes and comprehending their sad condition, introduced the bill authorizing this inquiry in order that public attention might be directed to their necessities and relief.

APPENDICES.

Table 1.

Showing admissions, with principal causes of Insanity, and per cent of each to admissions, in twenty-six Asylums, in eighteen hundred and sixty-nine.

In five thousand three hundred and fourteen admissions, the principal causes of insanity were:	
Ill health and physical disease...	1486
Spermatorrhœa..	708
Domestic troubles..	544
Intemperance...	544
Religious excitement...	527
Epilepsy...	357
Per cent of each on number of admissions:	
Ill health..	27.96
Spermatorrhœa..	13.32
Domestic troubles..	10.23
Intemperance...	10.23
Religious excitement...	9.91
Epilepsy...	6.71

Showing, also, the Deaths, with principal causes, and per cent of each to total Deaths, in twenty-seven Asylums, in eighteen hundred and sixty-nine.

In one thousand and seven deaths, the principal causes of death were:	
Disease of the lungs...	162
Paralysis..	111
Exhaustion, from different causes..	107
Mania...	51
Marasmus...	40
Old age...	38
Per cent of each on number of deaths:	
Disease of lungs..	16.08
Paralysis..	11.02
Exhaustion	10.62
Mania...	5.06
Marasmus...	3.97
Old age...	3.77

UNITED STATES.] TABLE 2.

STATES	TOWNS	Character	Acres of Land	When Opened	Capacity	Material	Cost of Building	Number of Patients	Cost of Maintenance	CHARGES
Alabama	Tuscaloosa	State	300	1861	300	Brick		279		Three dollars fifty.
California	Stockton	State	120	1852	720	Brick		1,090	$3 22	
Connecticut	Hartford	Corporate	87	1824	150			157		
Connecticut	Middletown	State	230	1868	230	Brick		230		
Connecticut	Litchfield	Private	100			Brown stone		12		
Georgia	Milledgeville	State	1,250	1842	400	Brick	$350,000	220		
Illinois	Jacksonville	State	187	1851	400	Brick	350,000	460	4 00	Paid by the State.
Indiana	Indianapolis	State	160	1848	500	Brick		500	4 00	Paid by the State.
Iowa	Mount Pleasant	State	173	1861	300	Brick	415,000	438		Paid by counties.
Kansas	Ossawatamie	State		1866				41		
Kentucky	Lexington	State	240	1824	525	Brick		525	4 08	Four to ten dollars.
Kentucky	Hopkinsville	State	350	1854	325	Brick	289,000	325		Half paid by State.
Louisiana	Jackson	State	580	1848	166			163		
Maine	Augusta	State	300	1840	350	Granite	350,000	345	4 51	Four to seven dollars
Maryland	Baltimore	State	12	1834	120	Brick		125		Six dollars.
Maryland	Mt. Hope Retreat	Corporate		1867	200			193		
Massachusetts	Catonsville	State	136		350	Blue stone	600,000	425	4 01	Three fifty to ten dols
Massachusetts	Worcester	State	120	1833	300	Brick		403	3 83	Three fifty to five dols
Massachusetts	Taunton	State	137	1854	300	Brick	375,000	420	3 51	
Massachusetts	Northampton	State	200	1858	300	Brick		294	2 00	
Massachusetts	Tewksbury	State						230	4 98	
Massachusetts	Boston	City	2	1839	175	Brick		190		Fifteen to fifty dolls.
Massachusetts	Somerville	Corporate	130	1818	190	Brick		305	3 98	Five dolls. eight cts.
Michigan	Kalamazoo	State	200	1859	300	Brick	400,000	206		
Minnesota	St. Peter	State	210	1866				160		
Mississippi	Jackson	State		1855						

State	Place	By whom	No.	Year	Capacity	Material	Cost	No.	Rate	Remarks
Missouri	Fulton	State	500	1851	350	Brick	......	288	3 50	Three dollars fifty.
Missouri	St. Louis	County and city	......	1869	200	Brick	750,000	214	......	Paid by county.
Missouri	St. Vincent	Corporate	......	1858	250	Brick	......	250	......	Five to twenty-five ds
New Hampshire	Concord	State	128	1842	250	Brick	......	253	......	Five to ten dollars.
New Jersey	Trenton	State	......	1849	500	Stone	......	648	......	
New York	Utica	State	200	1843	600	Stone	428,980	658	......	Four to six dollars.
New York	Poughkeepsie	State	......	......	400	......	1,500,000	......	......	
New York	Auburn	State criminal	6	1858	64	Stone	......	62	......	Paid by State. ($3 50)
New York	Ovid	State	475	1869	500	......	350,000	243	2 00	
New York	Bloomingdale	Corporate	......	1821	......	Brick	......	165	1 96	
New York	Blackwell's Isl'nd	City	......	1861	600	Stone	......	1,300	......	
New York	Flushing	Private	......	1846	......	......	......	40	......	[dollars.
New York	Flatbush	County	......	1855	450	......	......	602	......	Eight to twenty-five
New York	Canandaigua	Private	100	1855	73	......	......	73	......	
New York	Troy	Corp'ate and county	......	1859	......	......	......	109	......	
New York	New York	Immigrant	......	1861	......	......	......	......	......	
North Carolina	Raleigh	State	125	1856	204	Brick	250,000	230	......	
Ohio	Columbus	State	380	1839	600	......	600,000	......	......	Paid by State.
Ohio	Newburg	State	......	1859	300	......	......	330	4 90	
Ohio	Dayton	State	75	1855	470	Brick	560,000	559	......	
Ohio	Longview	County	138	1853	500	Brick	......	571	......	[dollars.
Oregon	Portland	State	......	1841	......	......	500,000	122	......	
Pennsylvania	Philadelphia	Corporate	113	1841	500	Brick and stone.	500,000	360	8 81	Fifteen to thirty-five
Pennsylvania	Frankford	Corporate	80	1817	60	......	......	62	......	Eight fifty to thirty.
Pennsylvania	Harrisburg	State	135	1851	400	Brick	250,000	430	4 45	County patients, $3.
Pennsylvania	Dixmont	State	......	1856	......	......	......	401	......	
Pennsylvania	Danville	State	250	......	400	Brick	600,000	750	......	
Pennsylvania	Philadelphia	City	......	1847	400	......	......	160	1 98	Five to thirty-five
Rhode Island	Providence	Corporate	130	1822	150	Brick	81,300	250	7 00	Two to three fifty.
South Carolina	Columbia	State	40	1840	220	Brick	......	356	......	
Tennessee	Nashville	State	......	1861	300	......	......	48	......	
Texas	Austin	State	455	1857	75	......	......	518	......	Three to four dollars.
Vermont	Brattleboro	Corporate	500	1773	200	Brick	......	203	5 76	
Virginia	Williamsburg	State	......	1828	350	Brick	......	324	4 15	
Virginia	Staunton	State	......	1870	150	Wood	......	150	5 12	
Virginia	Howard Grove	State	......	1866	250	......	450,000	207	2 75	
West Virginia	Weston	State	104	1854	175	......	......	360	......	
Wisconsin	Madison	State	......	1855	350	......	......	541	......	
District Columbia	Washington	Government	......	......	......	......	......	......	......	

Table 2—(Continued.)

STATES.	TOWNS.	SUPERINTENDENTS.	Salary.	Number of Assistants.	Number of Attendants.	Number of Chaplains.	FUEL.
Alabama	Tuscaloosa	Peter Bryce		1			Wood.
California	Stockton	G. A. Shurtleff	$3,500	2	From one to nine.		Coal.
Connecticut	Hartford	John S. Butler		1			Coal.
Connecticut	Middletown	A. M. Shew			One to three		Coal.
Connecticut	Litchfield	H. W. Buel					
Georgia	Milledgeville	Thomas F. Green		2			Wood at $5 05 per cord; and coal.
Illinois	Jacksonville	Henry F. Carriel	2,500	2	One to thirteen		Coal.
Indiana	Indianapolis	Orpheus Everts	1,800	2	One to eleven	1	Coal at $6 a ton.
Iowa	Mount Pleasant	Mark Ranney	1,600				
Kansas	Ossawatamie	G. O. Gause		3			Coal.
Kentucky	Lexington	John W. Whitney	2,000	1	One to fifteen		
Kentucky	Hopkinsville	James Rodman	2,000		One to eighteen		
Louisiana	Jackson				One to nine		
Maine	Augusta	Henry M. Harlow	1,500	1	One to twelve	1	Coal at $7 a ton.
Maryland	Baltimore	R. F. Stewart	1,500	1			Coal.
Maryland	Mt. Hope Retreat	William H. Stokes					Coal.
Maryland	Catonsville			2			
Massachusetts	Worcester	Merrick Bemis	2,000	1		1	Coal.
Massachusetts	Taunton	William W. Godding	2,000	1	One to twenty		Coal at $7 21 per ton.
Massachusetts	Northampton	Pliny Earle	2,000	1	One to twenty		Coal at $8 65 per ton.
Massachusetts	Tewksbury					1	
Massachusetts	Boston	Clement A. Walker	1,800		One to four		Coal.
Michigan	Somerville	George F. Jolly	3,000	2	One to seven	1	Coal.
Michigan	Kalamazoo	E. H. Van Deusen	2,000		One to ten		Coal.
Minnesota	St. Peter						
Mississippi	Jackson	William M. Compton		2			
Missouri	Fulton	C. H. Hughes	2,000	1		1	
Missouri	St. Louis	Charles W. Stephens	2,500				

State	Location	Name		Quantity	No.	Employees	Fuel
Missouri	St. Vincent	James B. Bancroft		700	2	One to twelve	Coal.
New Hampshire	Concord	H. A. Buttolph					Coal at $8 80 per ton.
New Jersey	Trenton	John P. Gray		3,000	3	One to ten	Coal.
New York	Utica	J. M. Cleaveland					Coal at $6 40 per ton.
New York	Poughkeepsie	James W. Wilkie		1,500	1	One to sixteen	Coal.
New York	Auburn	J. B. Chapin		3,000	1	One to fifteen	Coal.
New York	Ovid	Tilden Brown					Coal.
New York	Bloomingdale	R. L. Parsons					
New York	Blackwell's Isl'nd	J. A. Barstow					
New York	Flushing	Edward R. Chapin					
New York	Flatbush	George Cook			1	One to five	
New York	Canandaigua	Joseph D. Lomax					
New York	Troy	George Ford					Wood at $3 25 per cord.
New York	New York	Eugene Grissom		2,500	1	One to ten	
North Carolina	Raleigh	William L. Peek		1,100			Coal.
Ohio	Columbus	J. M. Lewis		1,200	2	One to fifteen	Coal at $7 per ton.
Ohio	Newburg	R. Gundry		4,000	2	One to twenty-five	Coal.
Ohio	Dayton	O. M. Langdon					
Ohio	Longview	J. C. Hawthorne		4,000	3	One to five	Coal.
Oregon	Portland	Thomas G. Kirkbride		3,000	1		
Pennsylvania	Philadelphia	J. H. Worthington		2,500	2	One to ten	Coal.
Pennsylvania	Frankford	John Curwen					
Pennsylvania	Harrisburg	Joseph A. Reed		2,000			
Pennsylvania	Dixmont	S. S. Schultz					
Pennsylvania	Danville	D. D. Richardson					
Pennsylvania	Philadelphia	John W. Sawyer		1,600	1	One to ten	Coal at $7 per ton.
Rhode Island	Providence	J. F. Ensor		2,500	1	One to ten	
South Carolina	Columbia	J. H. Callender	1	3,000	2	One to eight	
Tennessee	Nashville				1		
Texas	Austin	William H. Rockwell					
Vermont	Brattleboro	D. R. Brower		2,500	1	Sixty employs	Wood.
Virginia	Williamsburg	F. T. Stribbling		3,500	2		
Virginia	Staunton	Daniel H. Conrad		3,000	1	One to twelve	Coal.
Virginia	Howard Grove	R. Hills					
West Virginia	Weston	Alexander MeDill					
Wisconsin	Madison	Charles C. Nichols			1		Coal.
District Columbia	Washington						Coal.

TABLE 2—(Concluded.)

STATES.	TOWNS.	LIGHTS.	HOW WARMED.	WATER SUPPLY.	Insane at Large*
Alabama	Tuscaloosa	Gas at $7 per M.	By steam and stoves	Pumped from a well by engine	276
California	Stockton	Gas	By steam		46
Connecticut	Hartford	Gas		Brought from a spring in pipes to the top of the building	373
Connecticut	Middletown	Gas			
Connecticut	Litchfield				
Georgia	Milledgeville	Gas at $4 per M.	By steam		414
Illinois	Jacksonville	Gas, $3.50 per M.	By steam	Water pumped by steam, first into reservoir, thence into building	1,165
Indiana	Indianapolis	Gasoline	By steam	Abundant. Pumped by steam	1,004
Iowa	Mount Pleasant		By steam	From reservoir. Scant	304
Kansas	Ossawatomie		By steam		90
Kentucky	Lexington	Gas	By steam	Pumped from reservoir. Not abundant	395
Kentucky	Hopkinsville	Candles	By steam	Pumped. Abundant	285
Louisiana	Jackson	Gas			447
Maine	Augusta	Gas at $4 per M.	By steam	From lake. Not sufficient	415
Maryland	Baltimore	Gas	By steam		
Maryland	Mt. Hope Retreat	Gas	By steam		
Maryland	Catonsville	Gas	By steam		
Massachusetts	Worcester	Gas	By steam	Pumped by engine	994
Massachusetts	Taunton	Gas, $3.25 per M.	By steam	Pumped from a spring	
Massachusetts	Northampton	Gas	By steam		
Massachusetts	Tewksbury	Gas	By steam		
Massachusetts	Boston	Gas	By steam		
Massachusetts	Somerville	Gas at $3 per M.	By steam	Pumped from a spring. Abundant	509
Michigan	Kalamazoo		By steam		96
Minnesota	St. Peter				85
Mississippi	Jackson	Gas at $4 per M.		Pumped from stream	501
Missouri	Fulton	Coal oil		Deficient	
Missouri	St. Louis	Gas		From the city. Abundant	
Missouri	St. Vincent	Gas		Pumped from spring. Abundant	245
New Hampshire	Concord	Gas	By steam		

State	City	Lighting	Heating	Water Supply	No.
New Jersey	Trenton	Gasoline	By steam	Pumped from spring. Inexhaustible	270
New York	Utica	Gas	By steam	Pumped from reservoirs furnished by springs	3,041
New York	Poughkeepsie			Pumped from river into a reservoir	
New York	Auburn	Gas			
New York	Ovid	Gas	By steam	From mountain stream; brought in pipes to the top of building	
New York	Bloomingdale	Gas			
New York	Blackwell Island	Gas	By steam		
New York	Flushing				
New York	Flatbush				
New York	Canandaigua				
New York	Troy				
New York	New York	Gas at $8 per M.	By steam		549
North Carolina	Raleigh				1,091
Ohio	Columbus				
Ohio	Newburg	Gas	By steam	Pumped by steam	
Ohio	Dayton	Gas, $1 25 per M.	By steam	Abundant, but pumped twice	
Oregon	Portland				1,872
Pennsylvania	Philadelphia	Gas	By steam	Pumped. Abundant	
Pennsylvania	Frankford		Furnace in basement		
Pennsylvania	Harrisburg	Gas	By steam	Pumped by steam. Abundant	
Pennsylvania	Dixmont				
Pennsylvania	Danville				
Pennsylvania	Philadelphia				152
Rhode Island	Providence	Gas	By steam		83
South Carolina	Columbia	Gas	Stoves and open fires	From the city. Abundant	571
Tennessee	Nashville	Gas	By hot air and steam		222
Texas	Austin				203
Vermont	Brattleboro	Gas (of rosin)	Wood fires	From springs	448
Virginia	Williamsburg	Gas, $3 50 per M.		Brought from a spring in pipes to top of building. Abundant	
Virginia	Staunton	Lamps	By stoves		
Virginia	Howard Grove				107
West Virginia	Weston				486
Wisconsin	Madison				
District Columbia	Washington	Gas	By steam	Pumped from spring	

* This includes all of the insane at large, or in jails, almshouses, and private residences.

UNITED STATES.

TABLE 3.

Asylums visited in the United States in 1869.

NAME.	Numbers resident	Numbers admitted	Treated. Males	Treated. Females	Treated. Total	Cured. Males	Cured. Females	Cured. Total	Died. Males	Died. Females	Died. Total	Proportion per cent of Recoveries to Admissions	Proportion per cent of Recoveries to Number Treated	Proportion per cent of Deaths to Admissions	Proportion per cent of Deaths to Number Treated
California	853	482	989	346	1,335	168	57	225	121	38	150	46.68	16.85	32.98	11.91
Fulton, Missouri	368	131	255	244	499	26	18	44	24	14	38	33.58	8.81	29.00	7.61
Virginia.															
Eastern Asylum	180	53	109	124	233	10	9	19	5	4	9	35.84	8.15	16.98	3.86
Western Asylum, ('68 and '69)	338	204	310	232	542	46	34	80	28	9	37	39.21	14.76	18.13	6.82
Maryland.															
Maryland Asylum	54	46	56	44	100	11	12	23	4	1	5	50.00	23.00	10.08	5.00
Mt. Hope Retreat	178	125	147	156	303	22	31	53	16	6	22	42.40	17.60	17.60	7.26
Kentucky.															
Eastern Asylum	320	230	287	263	550	31	30	61	18	12	30	26.52	11.09	13.04	5.45
Western Asylum	280	81			361	27	12	39	4	5	9	48.14	10.80	11.11	2.49
Tennessee	257	214	251	220	471	55	45	100	26	16	42	46.72	21.23	19.62	8.91
North Carolina	217	27	128	116	244	3	4	7	5	2	7	25.92	2.86	25.92	2.86
South Carolina	204	94	150	148	298	28	16	44	10	4	14	46.80	14.76	14.89	4.69
Government Asylum	369	180	145	404	549	33	8	41	15	3	18	22.77	7.46	10.00	3.50
Pennsylvania.															
State Lunatic Asylum	340	180	288	232	520	26	21	47	19	6	25	26.11	9.03	13.88	4.80
Penn. Hospital for Insane	336	220	288	268	556	62	53	115	18	13	31	52.27	20.68	14.09	5.57
Phila. Almshouse, Ins. Dp't	680	397	440	637	1,077	66	103	169	25	62	87	42.56	15.69	21.91	8.07
Friends' Asylum	52	33			85			14			5	42.42	16.47	15.15	5.88
New Jersey	520	248	361	407	768	29	42	71	31	25	56	28.62	9.24	22.58	7.29

Institution															
New York.															
Utica, State	570	463	535	498	1,083	81	75	156	38	26	64	33.69	15.10	13.82	6.19
Kings County, Flatbush	558	314	354	518	872	57	73	130	29	29	58	41.40	14.90	18.47	6.65
Bloomingdale	157	140			297			51			27				
Blackwell's Island	1,035	680			1,715			183			122				
Canandaigua		42						36				26.91	10.67	17.94	7.11
Connecticut.															
Middletown, State	209	134	185	158	343	27	16	43	18	3	21	32.08	12.53	15.67	6.12
Hartford Retreat	135	123	131	127	258	18	23	41	14	11	25	33.33	15.89	20.32	9.08
Vermont	515	124	340	299	639	32	36	49	23	19	44	39.51	7.66	35.48	6.88
Maine	339	150	234	255	489	32	36	68	23	19	42	45.33	13.30	28.00	8.58
New Hampshire	237	130	190	177	367	22	15	37	12	11	23	28.46	10.08	17.69	6.26
Rhode Island	150	73	119	104	223			33			8	45.20	14.79	10.95	3.58
Massachusetts.															
Worcester	382	337	359	360	719	69	80	149	28	19	47	44.21	20.72	13.61	6.53
Taunton	398	265	326	317	663	47	54	101	28	19	47	38.11	15.23	17.73	7.08
Northampton	421	169	254	336	590	31	18	49	13	12	25	28.99	8.30	14.79	4.23
McLean	176	108	145	139	284	23	28	51	9	9	18	47.22	17.95	16.66	6.33
City Asylum	202	75			277			14			37	18.66	5.05	49.33	13.35
Michigan (2 years)	229	314	278	265	543	45	49	94	29	17	46	29.93	17.31	14.64	8.47
Mt. Pleasant	344	400	382	362	744	88	99	187	53	34	87	46.75	25.13	21.75	11.69
Illinois, Jacksonville (2 yrs.)	406	708			1,114			211			78	29.80	18.94	11.01	7.00
Indiana, Indianapolis	291	314	316	289	605	61	63	124	16	16	32	30.49	20.49	10.19	5.28
Ohio.															
Longview	425	334	388	371	759	96	83	179	33	26	59	53.59	23.58	17.66	7.77
Southern Asylum	182	297	214	265	479	48	54	102	7	8	15	34.34	21.29	5.05	3.13
Total	12,907	8,639			21,504			3,240			1,519	37.50	15.06	17.66	7.06

UNITED STATES.

TABLE 4.

Movements in Asylums in 1870.

ASYLUMS.	Number Resident	Number Admitted	Number Treated. Male	Number Treated. Female	Number Treated. Total	Number Cured	Number Died	Number Remaining	Proportion per cent of Cures on number admitted	Proportion per cent of Cures on number treated	Proportion per cent of Deaths on number admitted	Proportion per cent of Deaths on number treated
Alabama	191	88	148	131	279	17	30		19.31	6.09	34.09	10.75
California	920	562	1,108	474	1,482	221	156	1,047	39.32	14.91	27.75	10.55
Alameda Park, Cal.	10											
Woodbridge, Cal.	25											
Middleton, Conn.	232	75	63	80	307	20	21	237	26.66	6.51	28.00	6.84
Hartford, Conn.	130	143			277	46	20	157				
Milledgeville, Ga., 1869–70.	220											
Jacksonville, Ill.	406	708			1,114	210	78	452	29.66	18.85	11.01	7.00
Indianapolis, Ind.	387	405	408	384	792	187	51	475	46.17	23.61	12.59	6.43
Mt. Pleasant, Iowa	398											
Kansas	31	62	51	42	93	38	2	41	61.29	40.86	3.22	2.15
Lexington, Ky.	430	248			678	70	60	525	25.80	10.32	24.19	8.84

Institution												
Hopkinsville, Ky	301	71	224	243	372	27	14	345	38.02	7.25	19.71	3.76
Jackson, La	163	130			467	48	37		36.92	12.78	28.46	7.93
Augusta, Me	337											
Baltimore, Md	114	120	166	144	310	62	24	409	51.66	20.00	20.00	7.74
Mt. Hope Retreat, Md	190	384	386	374	760	158	64	382	41.14	20.78	16.66	8.42
Worcester, Mass	376	375	368	390	758	112	38	405	29.86	14.77	10.13	5.01
Taunton, Mass	383	202	257	347	604	50	33		24.75	8.27	16.33	5.46
Northampton, Mass	402	263			530	27	46	233	25.71	8.51	17.49	8.97
Tewksbury, Mass	267	105	170	147	317	33	42	178	41.77	12.54	40.00	13.24
Boston, Mass	212	79	130	133	263	94	12	305	29.93	17.31	15.18	4.50
Somerville, Mass	184	314	278	265	543	51	46	206	35.56	16.77	14.64	8.47
Kalamazoo, Mich. 1869-71	229	143		31	304	18	25	160	58.06	9.72	17.48	8.22
St. Peter, Minn	161	31	95	90	185	91	3		30.53	13.66	9.67	1.62
Jackson, Miss	154	298			666	31	74	303	25.83	9.22	24.83	11.11
Fulton, Mo. 1869-70	363	120	138		336		18	253			15.00	5.35
St. Louis, Mo	216			198								
St. Vincent, Mo	250											
Concord, N. H	253	135	192	196	388	65	32	225	48.14	16.75	23.70	8.24

UNITED STATES.

TABLE 4—Continued.

Movements in Asylums in 1870.

ASYLUMS.	Number Resident	Number Admitted	Number Treated			Number Cured	Number Died	Number Remaining	Proportion per cent of Cures on number admitted	Proportion per cent of Cures on number treated	Proportion per cent of Deaths on number admitted	Proportion per cent of Deaths on number treated
			Male	Female	Total							
Trenton, N. J.	567	247	384	430	814	68	44	648	27.53	8.35	17.81	5.40
Utica, N. Y.	603	481	545	539	1,084	155	75	...	31.80	14.11	15.59	6.91
Flatbush, N. Y.	601	355	390	567	957	103	75	642	29.01	10.76	21.12	7.83
Bloomingdale, N. Y.	161	153	...	...	314	60	27	165	39.21	19.10	17.64	8.59
Monroe Co. Asylum, N. Y.	88	...	...	...	...	...	...	...	...	...	...	...
Blackwell's Island, N. Y.	1,110	780	...	...	1,890	212	132	...	27.17	11.21	16.92	6.98
Flushing, N. Y.	40	...	...	...	...	...	...	...	...	...	...	...
Troy, N. Y.	109	...	...	...	...	...	...	...	...	...	...	...
Ovid, N. Y.	142	167	...	...	309	8	14	282	4.79	2.58	8.38	4.53
Buffalo, N. Y.	30	...	...	...	...	...	...	...	...	...	...	...
Auburn, N. Y.	79	17	...	...	96	9	3	...	52.94	9.37	17.64	3.12
Canandaigua, N. Y.	63	72	...	...	135	21	6	...	29.16	15.58	8.33	4.44
Raleigh, N. C.	225	28	128	125	253	6	9	232	21.43	2.37	32.14	3.55
Newburgh, O.	316	193	247	262	509	103	23	330	53.36	20.23	11.91	4.51
Dayton, O.	346	407	363	390	753	160	34	559	39.31	21.24	8.35	4.51
Longview, O.	511	273	400	384	784	165	62	544	60.43	21.04	22.71	7.90

Institution												
Portland, Or.	91	92			183	32	17	122	34.78	17.48	18.47	9.28
Phil'a Hospital for Insane	313	261	299	275	574	94	35	344	36.01	16.37	13.40	6.09
Phil'a Alms House, Pa.	723	416	41	50	1,139	147	101		35.33	12.90	24.27	8.86
Frankford, Pa.	55	36			91	15	3	62	41.66	16.38	8.38	3.29
Harrisburg, Pa.	410	168	325	237	578	30	39	434	17.85	5.19	23.21	6.74
Dixmont, Pa.	334	228			562	60	38	401	26.32	10.67	16.66	6.76
Kellyville, Pa.	20		122	113								
Providence, R. I.	154	81	32		235	34	12	95	41.97	14.46	14.81	5.10
Columbia, S. C.	232	90			322	26	31	245	28.88	8.07	34.44	9.62
Nashville, Tenn.	294											
Austin, Texas	48	120	328	303	631	35	40	518	29.16	5.54	33.33	6.33
Brattleboro, Vt.	511	73	130	143	273	22	7	209	30.13	8.05	9.58	2.56
Williamsburg, Va.	200	59	212	171	383	26	13	335	44.06	6.78	22.03	3.39
Staunton, Va.	324	110	85	95	180	6	15	150	5.45	3.33	13.63	8.33
Howard Grove, Va.	70	42	116	128	244	16	14	207	38.09	6.55	33.33	5.73
Weston, West Va.	202	168	267	265	532	53	32	360	31.54	9.96	19.04	6.01
Madison, Wis.	364	194	491	157	648	63	44		32.47	9.72	22.68	6.78
Washington, D. C.	454											
Totals	17,735	10,229			27,964	3,357	1,851	12,506	32.81	12.90	18.08	7.11

CANADA.

TABLE 5.

ASYLUMS.	Number of patients resident.	Admitted.	Cured.	Died.	Number treated.	Proportion of cures to admissions.	Proportion of cures to number treated.	Proportion of deaths to admissions.	Proportion of deaths to number treated.
1869.									
Halifax....................................	216	79	33	13	295	41	11	16	4
Toronto...................................	518	77	85	26	595	45	5	33	4
Provincial Asylum, Frederickton......	238	130	62	30	368	47	16	23	8
Prince Edward's Island....................	31	25	17	2	66	68	30	8	3
1870.									
Halifax....................................	245	70	24	25	315	34	7	35	7
Toronto...................................	509	121	46	37	630	38	7	30	5
Provincial Asylum, Frederickton......	239	124	44	36	363	35	12	29	9

[APPENDIX B.]

ENGLAND.

TABLE 1.

	1847 No. of Asylums	1847 Private patients	1847 Pauper patients	1847 Total	1847 Avg. capacity	1857 No. of Asylums	1857 Private patients	1857 Pauper patients	1857 Total	1857 Avg. capacity	1867 No. of Asylums	1867 Private patients	1867 Pauper patients	1867 Total	1867 Avg. capacity
County and Borough Asylums	21	230	5,247	5,486	261	37	213	14,096	14,209	387	48	216	24,374	24,590	512
Registered Hospitals	11	727	384	1,111	101	15	1,556	175	1,731	115	15	1,842	374	2,216	148
Metropolitan Licensed Houses	45	1,108	1,664	2,767	61	37	1,279	1,299	2,577	70	41	1,579	914	2,493	61
Provincial Licensed Houses	96	1,530	2,332	3,862	40	79	1,511	1,087	2,598	33	63	1,649	336	1,985	31
Other Hospitals or Asylums	3	466	140	606	202	1	129		129	129	3	630		630	210
Total	176	4,065	9,767	13,832	79	169	4,687	16,657	21,344	126	170	5,916	25,998	31,914	188
Insane not in Asylums:															
In Workhouses			7,797	7,797				6,800	6,800				10,307	10,307	
With relatives or others		437	4,418	4,855			150	5,497	5,047			223	6,638	6,861	
In Jails				32											
Total Insane				26,516			4,837	28,954	33,791			6,189	42,943	49,082	

In 1847, fifty-two per cent of the insane population were provided with hospital accommodations; in 1857, sixty-three per cent; and in 1867, sixty-seven per cent.

TABLE 2.

Movements of English Asylums Visited in 1870 and 1871.

ASYLUMS.	NUMBERS RESIDENT. Males	NUMBERS RESIDENT. Females	NUMBERS RESIDENT. Total	Numbers Admitted.	Numbers Treated	Numbers Cured	Numbers Died	Per cent of Cures on Admissions	Per cent of Cures on Number Treated	Per cent of Deaths on Admissions	Per cent of Deaths on No. Treated
Liverpool	...	...	42	35	77	14	5	40.0	18.1	14.2	6.4
Rainhill (1869)	313	358	671	108	779	45	45	41.6	5.7	41.6	1.9
St. Luke's	53	88	141	120	261	45	5	37.5	17.2	4.1	1.9
Bethlem	113	140	253	233	486	116	30	49.7	23.8	12.8	6.1
Grove Hall, Bow	...	...	443	115	558	22	37	19.1	3.9	32.1	6.6
Hanwell	617	1,081	1,698	423	2,121	119	182	28.1	5.6	43.0	8.5
Colney Hatch	817	1,236	2,053	462	2,515	135	187	29.2	5.3	40.4	7.4
Brookwood	303	317	620	186	806	63	83	33.8	7.8	44.6	10.2
Hayward's Heath	318	382	650	166	816	61	57	36.7	7.4	34.3	6.9
Brentwood, Essex	261	338	599	197	796	68	55	34.5	8.5	27.9	6.9
Bristol, Borough	110	111	221	110	331	40	26	36.3	12.0	23.6	7.8
Glamorgan, County	198	163	361	114	475	25	33	21.9	5.2	28.9	6.9
Wotton	282	311	593	194	787	91	66	46.9	11.5	34.0	8.3
Barnwood House	...	...	77	26	103	8	5	30.7	7.7	19.2	4.8
Buckinghamshire, County	186	240	426	108	534	46	51	42.5	8.6	47.2	9.5

Birmingham	272	315	587	194	781	85	68	43.8	10.8	35.0	8.7
Warwick, County	221	243	464	83	547	43	33	51.8	7.8	39.7	6.0
Derbyshire, County	183	185	368	110	478	50	40	45.4	10.4	36.3	8.3
West Riding (1868)	593	607	1,202	446	1,668	211	125	45.2	12.6	26.8	7.4
Friends' Retreat	50	89	139	15	154	8	11	53.3	5.1	73.3	6.1
York	102	83	185	32	217	16	13	50.0	7.3	40.6	5.9
Newcastle-upon-Tyne	82	77	159	180	339	17	32	9.4	5.0	17.7	9.4
Cumberland and Westmoreland	199	174	373	130	503	60	23	46.1	11.9	17.6	4.5
Littlemore, Oxford	223	271	494	159	653	70	60	44.0	10.7	37.7	9.1
Total	......	......	12,819	3,966	16,785	1,458	4,272	36.7	8.6	32.0	7.5

ENGLAND.

TABLE 3.

	PRIVATE.			PAUPER.			TOTALS.		
	Males	Females	Total	Males	Females	Total	Males	Females	Total
*Number of patients Dec. 31, 1869..	3,298	2,623	5,921	13,730	16,262	29,922	17,028	18,885	35,913
Admitted for first time..........							5,124	4,966	10,090
Readmitted........................							641	731	1,372
Total........................							5,765	5,697	11,462
Total number under treatment......									47,375
Discharged cured..................							1,783	2,172	3,955
Discharged improved and not im-proved							1,461	1,298	2,759
Died..............................							2,107	1,683	3,790
Total discharged and died.........							5,351	5,153	10,504
Number remaining Dec. 31, 1870....									36,871
Proportion per cent of readmissions to admissions for first time.........							12.5	14.7	13.5

* On January 1st, 1870, there were three hundred and fifty-six private single patients not mentioned in the above table.

ENGLAND.

TABLE 3—*Continued.*

	Males.	Females.	Total.
Proportion per cent of recoveries to admissions	30.	38.	34.
Proportion per cent of recoveries to numbers treated	....	....	8.3
Proportion per cent of deaths to admissions.	36.5	29.5	33.
Proportion per cent of deaths to numbers treated	....	....	8.
1871.			
Proportion of pauper lunatics to total paupers	....	....	4.63
Proportion of pauper lunatics in asylums and workhouses	....	....	85.43
Proportion of lunatics maintained by relatives and others	....	....	14.57

Fifty-four English asylums made postmortem examinations in thirteen hundred and fifty-two cases, out of thirty-one hundred and thirty-five deaths, in the year eighteen hundred and seventy.

ENGLAND.

TABLE 4.

Showing the ratio of total number of Lunatics, Idiots, etc., to population in each year from eighteen hundred and sixty-two to eighteen hundred and seventy-one, both inclusive; also, number of patients in private houses, and number in asylums, workhouses, etc.

YEAR.	Population.	Total number of lunatics, idiots, etc., January 1st.	Ratio per 1,000 to population.	Number in private houses. Private.	Pauper.	Number in asylums, poorhouses, etc. Private.	Pauper.
1862	20,336,467	41,129	2.02	146	6,157	5,274	29,552
1863	20,554,137	43,118	2.09	153	6,405	5,354	31,206
1864	20,772,308	44,795	2.15	159	6,541	5,446	32,649
1865	20,990,946	45,950	2.18	212	6,557	5,662	33,519
1866	21,210,020	47,648	2.24	227	6,580	5,873	34,968
1867	21,429,508	49,086	2.29	223	6,638	5,920	36,305
1868	21,649,377	51,000	2.35	274	6,829	5,850	38,047
1869	21,869,607	53,177	2.43	324	6,987	5,900	39,966
1870	22,090,163	54,713	2.47	356	7,086	5,924	41,347
1871	22,704,108	56,755	2.49	392	7,331	6,062	42,970

ENGLAND.

TABLE 5.

Showing total number of Paupers and of Pauper Lunatics, Idiots, etc., with the proportion per cent of Pauper Lunatics to Paupers, the proportion per thousand of Pauper Lunatics to population, and proportion per one hundred thousand of non-Pauper Lunatics to population.

YEAR.	Total number of paupers of all classes on January 1st...	Total number of pauper lunatics, idiots, etc. January 1st...	Percentage of pauper lunatics, etc., to paupers...	Proportion per 1,000 of pauper lunatics, etc., to population...	Proportion per 100,000 of lunatics not paupers to entire population...
1862.......	946,166	35,709	3.77	1.75	26.6
1863.......	1,142,624	37,611	3.29	1.82	26.7
1864.......	1,011,753	39,190	3.87	1.88	26.9
1865.......	974,772	40,076	4.11	1.90	27.9
1866.......	924,813	41,548	4.49	1.95	28.7
1867.......	963,200	42,943	4.45	2.00	28.6
1868.......	1,040,103	44,876	4.31	2.07	28.3
1869.......	1,046,103	46,953	4.48	2.14	28.4
1870.......	1,083,532	48,433	4.46	2.19	28.4
1871.......	1,085,661	50,301	4.63	2.21	28.4

From the above we find there is one pauper lunatic to every twenty-two paupers; one pauper lunatic to every four hundred and fifty-one of the population, and one non-pauper lunatic to every three thousand five hundred and eighteen of the population.

ENGLAND.

TABLE 6.

Showing the proportion of stated Recoveries to the Admissions in each Year—1859 to 1870.

ASYLUMS.	Number of stated Recoveries to one hundred Admissions.												
	1859.	1860.	1861.	1862.	1863.	1864.	1865.	1866.	1867.	1868.	1869.	1870.	Av'ge.
County and Borough Asylums.	34.04	30.65	35.42	39.28	36.93	37.11	33.88	35.71	36.19	36.10	35.72	36.36	35.61
Registered Hospitals............	46.65	35.99	43.28	57.71	39.95	36.10	37.24	48.70	37.67	36.72	36.74	40.09	39.73
Metropolitan Licensed Houses.	32.04	30.79	28.29	29.85	32.01	30.93	23.04	23.75	21.24	24.05	24.24	21.83	26.83
Provincial Licensed Houses...	39.33	33.56	31.70	32.32	33.07	29.52	24.49	33.95	34.11	28.62	29.88	29.26	31.65
Naval and Military Hospitals..	25.22	23.13	18.16	21.12	17.94	19.56	16.94	5.26	22.33	15.28	31.82	17.98	19.56
Criminal Asylum...............					1.01	3.07	7.41	13.95	9.33	4.21	18.75	32.25	11.24
Private Single Patients.........	15.63	4.00	5.88	12.11	9.52	3.77	9.64	12.50	6.34	8.09	10.06	8.22	8.89
Proportion per cent of aggregate number of recoveries to aggregate number of admissions......	35.12	31.06	34.11	36.81	35.34	34.37	31.56	34.22	33.68	33.06	33.95	34.14	33.95

Table 7.

Showing the proportion of Deaths to daily average number resident each Year.

ASYLUMS.	Number of Deaths to one hundred of the daily average number Resident.												
	1859.	1860.	1861.	1862.	1863.	1864.	1865.	1866.	1867.	1868.	1869.	1870.	Av'ge.
County and Borough Asylums.	10.25	12.16	11.03	10.16	10.42	11.73	10.95	10.76	10.66	10.15	11.16	10.81	10.85
Registered Hospitals..........	6.53	6.45	7.38	7.61	7.93	6.89	7.99	7.97	8.57	7.52	9.12	7.33	7.60
Metropolitan Licensed Houses.	12.41	11.04	10.60	11.08	8.54	10.91	11.31	13.67	11.75	9.73	9.69	9.48	10.85
Provincial Licensed Houses....	7.60	8.56	6.78	7.11	7.41	7.17	7.95	9.72	8.08	9.97	10.64	10.19	8.43
Naval and Military Hospitals..	13.94	14.71	11.43	10.06	11.63	10.27	11.23	8.02	9.55	9.27	11.11	10.44	10.97
Criminal Asylum..........				......	......	3.35	3.29	4.23	2.31	1.59	3.03	2.87	2.95
Private Single Patients..........	5.88	6.66	6.72	6.71	3.85	5.95	3.65	6.22	5.24	5.69	4.70	4.02	5.44
Proportion per cent of aggregate number of deaths to aggregate daily number resident	9.90	11.28	10.33	9.77	9.81	10.88	10.42	10.59	10.29	9.78	10.72	10.29	10.33

ENGLAND.

TABLE 8.

Showing Length of Residence in Sixteen English Asylums of Patients who Died therein or were Discharged therefrom Recovered in 1870.

LENGTH OF RESIDENCE.	DIED.			Discharged Recovered.		
	Males.	Females.	Total.	Males.	Females.	Total.
Under 1 month.....................	52	32	84	15	10	25
Over 1 and under 3 months...	67	43	110	92	81	173
Over 3 and under 6 months...	56	31	87	105	182	287
Over 6 and under 12 months...	69	29	98	97	139	236
Over 1 and under 2 years......	76	52	128	52	53	105
Two years and over..............	212	235	447	38	54	92
Totals........................	532	422	954	399	519	918

TABLE 9.

Showing Proportion per cent of Numbers Died and Discharged Recovered in the following periods to the whole Number Died and Discharged Recovered.

Under 1 month	8.80	2.72	One year. } 78.55
Over 1 and under 3 months	11.53	18.84	
Over 3 and under 6 months	9.11	31.26	
Over 6 and under 12 months....................	10.27	25.70	
Over 1 and under 2 years	13.42	11.43	Two years } 21.45
Two years and over.........	46.86	10.02	
Total	....	....	100.00

ENGLAND.

TABLE 10.

Showing Numbers Resident, Admitted, Treated, Discharged, Died, and Remaining; also Proportion per cent of Recoveries and of Deaths to Admissions for Ten Years, 1861–1870.

PATIENTS.	Numbers.	Proportion per cent of Cures to Admissions	Proportion per cent of Cures Treated
Numbers resident January 1st, 1861	24,989		
Admitted	101,927		
Treated	126,916		
Discharged cured	34,716	34.05	27.3
Discharged not cured	22,826		
Died	32,087		
Total discharged and died	89,629		
Remaining	37,287		

SCOTLAND.

TABLE 11.

Showing number of Patients resident, number treated, admissions, recoveries, and deaths, with proportion of the recoveries and of the deaths to the admissions and to the number treated in the Lunatic Asylums visited in the year eighteen hundred and seventy-one.

ASYLUMS.	Number resident.	Number admitted.	Number treated.	Number cured.	Number Died.	Proport'n pr centum of recover's to Admissions.	Proport'n pr centum of recover's to Number treated.	Proport'n pr centum of deaths to Admissions.	Proport'n pr centum of deaths to Number treated.
Royal Edinburgh	754	265	1,019	118	67	44.52	25.28	11.57	6.57
Fife and Kinross	227	70	297	35	13	50.00	18.57	11.78	4.37
Dundee Royal	190	59	249	25	13	42.37	22.03	10.04	5.22
Inverness District	279	58	337	26	26	44.82	7.71	44.82	7.71
Stirling District		252	252	14	16	5.55	6.34	5.55	6.34
Glasgow Royal	545	326	871	147	71	45.09	21.77	16.87	8.15
Total	1,995	1,030	3025	365	206	35.05	12.06	20.03	6.80

SCOTLAND.

TABLE 12,

Showing Number of Patients in Lunatic Hospitals, with Admissions, Discharges, Recoveries, and Deaths for the Year 1870.

PATIENTS.	PRIVATE.			PAUPER.			GRAND TOTAL.		
	Males	Females	Total	Males	Females	Total	Males	Females	Total
Number resident December 31st, 1869	568	595	1,163	2,216	2,512	4,728	2,784	3,107	5,891
Admitted during the year	231	245	476	744	933	1,677	975	1,178	2,153
Treated during the year	799	840	1,639	2,960	3,445	6,405	3,759	4,285	8,044
Discharged cured	94	102	196	281	365	646	375	467	842
Discharged not recovered									371
Deaths	47	45	92	212	237	449	259	282	541
Remaining December 31st, 1870									6,290
Proportion of recoveries to number admitted									39.
Proportion of recoveries to number treated									10.
Proportion of deaths to number admitted									25.
Proportion of deaths to number treated									6.

Proportion of pauper lunatics to paupers, one in thirteen............ 7.

Percentage of pauper lunatics maintained in asylums and workhouses.............. 76.

Percentage of pauper lunatics maintained by relatives and others.............. 23.

Proportion of other classes to population............................ 1 to 2,564

SCOTLAND.

TABLE 13,

Showing Results of Treatment in Public, Private, and Parochial Asylums, and Lunatic Wards of Poorhouses in 1870.

	Seventeen Public Asylums.			Ten Private Asylums.			Five Parochial Asylums.			Fifteen Lunatic Ward Poorhouses.			Grand Total.		
	Males	Females	Total	Males	Females	Total	Males	Females	Total	Males	Females	Total	Males	Females	Total
Average number resident	2,237	2,249	4,486	120	212	332	212	336	548	246	356	602	2,815	3,153	5,968
Admissions	697	824	1,521	107	138	245	103	146	249	68	70	138	975	1,178	2,153
Recoveries	292	347	630	28	39	67	50	76	126	5	6	11	375	468	843
Discharged not recovered	205	246	451	37	66	103	35	47	82	7	12	19	294	371	655
Deaths	201	195	396	17	27	44	18	33	51	23	27	50	259	282	541
Proportion of admissions—per cent on number resident	31.1	36.6	33.8	88.6	64.9	76.7	48.4	43.4	45.9	27.6	19.6	23.6	48.9	41.1	45.0
Proportion of recoveries—per cent on admissions	41.9	42.1	42.0	26.2	28.4	27.3	48.5	52.0	50.2	7.3	8.6	7.9	30.9	32.7	31.8
Proportion of deaths—per cent on number resident	8.9	8.6	8.7	14.1	12.7	13.4	8.4	9.8	9.1	9.3	7.6	8.4	40.7	38.7	39.6

SCOTLAND.

TABLE 14.

The ratio per one thousand of the total number of Lunatics, Idiots, and persons of unsound mind, to the population in each year from eighteen hundred and sixty-two to eighteen hundred and seventy-one, both inclusive.

YEAR.	Population...	Total number of lunatics, idiots, etc., January 1st.	Ration per one thousand to population.—	Number in private dwellings...	Number in Asylums and Poorhouses.	
					Private..	Pauper...
1862	3,083,989	6,341	2.05	1,741	1,031	3,548
1863	3,101,345	6,327	2.04	1,679	1,023	3,604
1864	3,118,701	6,359	2.03	1,637	1,018	3,683
1865	3,136,957	6,468	2.06	1,609	1,055	3,783
1866	3,153,413	6,616	2.09	1,568	1,104	3,922
1867	3,170,769	6,762	2.13	1,548	1,143	4,046
1868	3,188,125	6,031	2.17	1,521	1,158	4,224
1869	3,205,481	7,157	2.23	1,500	1,128	4,494
1870	3,222,837	7,409	2.29	1,469	1,163	4,728
1871	3,358,613	7,808	2.32	1,430(?)	1,178	4,817
			1 to 438	1 to 2,548	1 to 2,936	1 to 697

SCOTLAND.

TABLE 15.

Showing Admissions, Numbers Treated, Recoveries, and Deaths, and Proportion per cent of Recoveries and of Deaths to Admissions and to the Numbers Treated in the Lunatic Asylums of Scotland for a Period of Ten Years—1861 to 1871.

| | Admitted | | | Treated | | | Recovered | | | Died | | | Proportion per cent of recoveries to | | | | | | Proportion per cent of Deaths to | | | | | |
| | | | | | | | | | | | | | Admissions | | | No. Treated | | | Admissions | | | No. Treated | | |
	Male	Female	Total	Male	Female	Total	Male	Female	Total	Male	Female	Total	Male	Female	Total	Male	Female	Total	Male	Female	Total	Male	Female	Total
Public Asylums	6,289	6,705	12,994				2,145	2,556	4,701	1,539	1,369	2,908	34.1	38.1	36.9				24.4	20.4	22.3			
Private Asylums	1,231	1,667	2,898				347	558	905	271	330	482	28.1	33.4	31.2				22.2	19.7	21.1			
Parochial Asyl'ms	1,038	1,267	2,305				509	624	1,138	232	250	482	49.0	49.2	49.1				22.3	19.7	20.9			
Lunatic Wards of Poorhouses	507	771	1,278				38	55	93	194	298	432	7.4	7.1	7.2				38.2	30.8	33.8			
Totals	9,065	10,410	19,475	11,139	12,798	23,937	3,039	3,793	6,832	2,239	2,187	4,426	33.5	36.4	35.0	27.2	29.6	28.4	24.6	21.0	22.7	20.2	17.0	18.4

I R E L A N D.

Table 16,

Showing Number of Patients, Admissions, Recoveries, and Deaths, with Proportion of the Recoveries and of the Deaths to the Admissions and to the Number Treated in Seven Lunatic Hospitals visited in 1870.

NAME OF ASYLUM.	Number of patients resident.			Admissions	Number treated	Recovered	Died	Proportion per cent of recoveries to admissions	Proportion per cent of recoveries to number treated	Proportion per cent of deaths to admissions	Proportion per cent of deaths to number treated
	Males	Females	Total								
Belfast District Asylum	135	99	234	186	420	72	25	38.7	17.1	13.4	5.9
Richmond District Asylum (Dublin)	396	503	899	425	1,324	191	124	44.9	14.4	29.1	9.3
Bloomfield Retreat (private)	16	32	48	11	59	3	1	27.2	5.0	9.0	1.7
Maryborough District Asylum	111	104	215	302	517	49	20	16.2	9.4	6.6	3.8
Cork District Asylum	304	296	600	216	816	102	49	47.2	12.5	22.6	6.0
Killarney District Asylum	177	94	271	49	320	30	31	61.2	9.3	63.2	9.6
Central Asylum for Criminal Lunatics	116	54	170	17	187	10	6	58.8	5.3	35.3	3.2
Total	1,255	1,182	2,437	1,206	3,643	457	256	37.8	12.5	21.2	7.0

IRELAND.

TABLE 17.

Showing the number and distribution of the Insane in Ireland in the Years 1848, 1851, 1855, 1856, 1861.

ASYLUMS.	1848.			1851.			1855.			1856.			1861.		
	Male	Female	Total	Male	Female	Total	Male	Female	Total	Male	Female	Total	Male	Female	Total
District and Local Asylums			2,968			2,913	1,720	1,802	3,522				2,165	2,124	4,289
Workhouses			1,940			2,393	734	1,266	2,000				965	1,569	2,534
Jails			338			280	101	55	156				184	109	293
Private Asylums			432			436	252	207	459				263	246	509
Central Asylums for Criminals						91	84	42	126				92	41	133
Lunatics at large			*6,000			8,985	4,035	3,195	7,230				4,959	4,032	8,991
Total			11,678			15,098	6,926	6,567	13,493			14,141	8,628	8,121	16,749

* Approximate number.

IRELAND.

TABLE 18.

Calculated Population of Ireland from 1841 to 1871.

Year.	Population.	Year.	Population.	Year.	Population.
*1841	8,175,124	*1851	6,552,385	*1861	5,798,967
1842	7,996,219	1852	6,472,830	1862	5,728,565
1843	7,821,253	1853	6,394,244	1863	5,659,012
1844	7,649,920	1854	6,316,628	1864	5,590,312
1845	7,482,687	1855	6,239,928	1865	5,522,437
1846	7,318,985	1856	6,164,171	1866	5,455,387
1847	7,158,800	1857	6,089,343	1867	5,389,161
1848	7,002,164	1858	6,015,400	1868	5,323,736
1849	6,848,931	1859	5,941,947	1869	5,259,100
1850	6,699,063	1860	5,870,226	1870	5,195,236

* From census returns—remaining years calculated.

TABLE 19.

Showing proportion of the Insane to the total of population of Ireland for the years 1848, 1851, 1855, 1856, and 1861.

YEAR.	Number of Insane...	Population	Proportion of Insane to population......	Number of Insane to ten thousand of population......
1848............	11,678*	7,002,164	1 to 600	17
1851............	15,098	6,552,385	1 to 414	23
1855............	13,493	6,239,928	1 to 462	22
1856............	14,141	6,164,171	1 to 435	23
1861............	16,749	5,798,967	1 to 346	29
1870............	17,194	5,195,336	1 to 302	33

*Approximately.

IRELAND.

TABLE 20.

Civil condition of Patients in Asylums of Ireland on the first of December, eighteen hundred and seventy.

CIVIL CONDITION.	Males.	Females.	Total.
Single..	3,006	2,251	5,257
Married.......................................	701	747	1448
Widowed......................................	113	310	423
Unknown......................................	170	162	332
Total........	3,990	3,470	7,460

TABLE 21.

Showing Duration of Disease on Admission of Patients Discharged Recovered from the District Asylums for the Year ending December 31st, 1870.

	Males.	Females.	Total.
Under three months..............................	339	313	625
From three to six months........................	35	46	81
From six to twelve months.......................	32	32	64
From one to two years...........................	21	25	46
From two to three years.........................	10	14	24
From three to four years........................	7	4	11
From four to five years..........................	4	1	5
From five to six years...........................	1	1	2
From six to eight years	1	1	2
Eight years and upwards.........................	11	5	16
Not specified....................................	57	48	105
Totals	518	490	1,008

IRELAND.

TABLE 22.

Showing the number of patients in the Lunatic Asylums of Ireland, with the admissions, discharges, deaths and escapes, and proportion of readmissions to admissions for the first time.

FOR THE YEAR ENDING DECEMBER 31, 1870.	Males	Females	Total	Males	Females	Total
Number of patients in Asylums Dec. 31, 1869.....	....	....	....	3,788	3,333	7,121
Number admitted for the first time.....................	1,141	971	2,112	....	....	....
Number of readmissions............................	224	196	420	....	....	....
Total admissions..	....	....	....	1,365	1,167	2,532
Total number under treatment........................	....	....	....	5,153	4,500	9,653
Number discharged recovered.........................	549	539	1,088	....	....	....
Number discharged relieved...........................	166	110	276	....	....	....
Number discharged not improved....................	61	50	111	....	....	....
Died......,........	378	330	708	....	....	....
Escaped..	9	1	10	....	....	....
Total discharged, died and escaped.................	....	....	....	1,163	1,030	2,193
Number remaining December 31, 1870...............	....	....	....	3 990	3,470	7,460
Proportion per cent of readmissions to admissions for the first time..................................	....	....	....	19.6	20.1	19.8

	Males.	Females.	Total.
Proportion per cent of recoveries to admissions................	40.	46₁	43.
Proportion per cent of recoveries to number treated........	10.6	11.9	11.2
Proportion per cent of deaths to admissions....................	27.7	28.2	27.9
Proportion per cent of deaths to number treated..............	7.3	7.3	7.3
Proportion per cent of pauper lunatics in asylums and workhouses..	....	....	55.2
Proportion of lunatics maintained by relatives and others	....	....	44.8

IRELAND.

TABLE 23.

The total number of insane (including idiots), December 31st, 1870, was..........	17,194
These were distributed as follows:	
In district asylums..........	6,655
In private asylums..........	638
In Workhouses..........	2,754
In Jails..........	1
In Lucan, supported by Government..........	43
In Central Asylum for Criminal Lunatics..........	167
At large..........	6,936
	17,194

Of this number about nine thousand four hundred and ninety-eight are paupers, supported in asylums or Workhouses; and the remaining seven thousand six hundred and ninety-six are supported by relatives or others in asylums or elsewhere.

The asylums are:

District asylums..........	23
Private licensed asylums..........	20
Asylum for criminal lunatics..........	1
Total..........	44

TABLE 24.

Numbers of Insane (exclusive of Idiots), December 31st, 1870.

	Males.	Females.	Total.
In police districts, exclusive of those in asylums, Jails or Workhouses..........	1,526	1,228	2,754
In Union Workhouses..........	448	697	1,145
In district asylums..........	3,440	3,007	6,447
In Jails..........		1	1
In private licensed asylums..........	281	327	608
In Central Asylum for Criminal Lunatics....	117	50	167
Totals..........	5,812	5,310	11,122

[Appendix C.]

BELGIUM.

Table 1,

Showing Number of Patients Resident, Admission, Recoveries, and Deaths, with the Proportion of Recoveries and of Deaths to Admissions, and Number Treated in five Lunatic Asylums visited in 1870.

NAME OF ASYLUM.	Number of patients resident.			Admissions	Number Treated	Recoveries	Deaths	Proportion per cent of recoveries to admissions	Proportion per cent of recoveries to number treated	Proportion per cent of deaths to admissions	Proportion per cent of deaths to number treated
	Male	Female	Total								
Hospice des Aliénés à Anvers	78	67	145	67	212	32	24	47.7	15.0	35.8	11.3
Hospice de St. Julien à Bruges	389	384	773	265	1,038	119	80	44.9	11.4	30.1	7.7
Hospice Guislain à Gand	485		485	122	607	15	66	12.3	2.4	54.1	10.8
Maison de Santé, du d'Assaut à Gand,		268	268	52	320	24	24	46.1	7.5	46.1	7.6
Maison de Santé, du Strop à Gand. (private)	65		65								
Hospice de Liége	81		81								
Maison de Santé d'Ans et Glain	55	30	85								
Etablissement de Gheel	537	590	1,127	263	1,390	42	117	15.9	3.0	44.4	8.4
Total	1,600	1,339	3,029	769	3,567	232	311	30.1	6.5	40.4	8.7

Note.—Per cent of recoveries to admissions for ten years, ending December 31st, 1862, twenty-eight; deaths thirty-two.

BELGIUM.

TABLE 2.

Charges in Belgium Asylums Visited.

ASYLUMS.	First Class.	Second Class.	Third Class.	Fourth Class
	Francs Per Week.	Francs Per Week.	Francs Per Week.	Francs Per Week.
Liege, St. Ans..............	38 to 76	23 to 28	2 to 15	....
Colony at Gheel............	7 to 11	6	5½	5.00 centi.
Asylum at Antwerp.......	....	....	....	6.86 centi.
Guislain Asylum, Ghent..	11	....	....	5.60 centi.
Female Asylum, Ghent...	19 to 57	....	7	5.88 centi.
Du Strop Asylum, Ghent.	19 to 57	....	....	....
St. Julian Asy., Bruges...	7	....	....	2.00 centi.

TABLE 3.

Showing the Number of Patients in Lunatic Hospitals, the Admissions, Discharges and Deaths, and the Per Cent of Recoveries and of Deaths to Admissions, and to Number Treated for the Year 1865.

	Males.	Females.	Totals.	Males.	Females.	Totals.
Number of patients January 1st, 1865.............	....	....	....	2,663	2,778	5,441
Admissions for the first time........................	....	....	....	865	690	1,555
Readmissions..	....	....	....	174	122	296
Total admissions....................................	....	....	....	1,039	812	1,851
Total number treated during the year.............	....	....	....	3,702	3,590	7,292
Discharged recovered...............................	325	317	642	....	....	....
Relieved	126	99	225	....	....	....
Not improved.......................................	239	160	399	....	....	....
Died...	341	254	595	....	....	....
Total discharges and deaths.......................	....	....	....	1,031	830	1,861
Remaining January 1st, 1866.......................	....	....	....	2,671	2,760	5,431

BELGIUM.

TABLE 3—*Continued*.

	Male....	Female...	Totals....
Proportion per cent of recoveries to admissions..................................	31.2	39.0	34.6
Proportion per cent of recoveries to number treated.........................	8.7	8.8	8.8
Proportion per cent of deaths to admissions.....................................	32.8	31.2	32.1
Proportion per cent of deaths to number treated.......................	9.2	7.0	8.1

TABLE 4.

Belgium, 1863, 1864, and 1865—Fifty-one Asylums.

YEAR.	Number Resident.			Total No. Admitted....	Whole No. Treated....	Total Number Cured ...	Total Improved or other-wise...........	Deaths...............	Total per cent of Cures on Admissions.............	Total per cent of Deaths on Admissions...........	Total per cent of Cures to Number Treated...	Total per cent of Deaths to Number Treated...
	Males...........	Females...........	Total............									
1863	2,587	2,583	5,170	1,694	6,864	•605	373	620	35.50	30.51	8.81	7.57
1864	2,673	2,693	5,366	1,669	7,035	577	427	590	34.57	35.35	8.20	8.38
1865	2,663	2,778	5,441	1,851	7,292	642	624	595	34.68	32.14	8.80	8.15
Total..	7,923	8,054	15,977	5,214	21,191	1,824	1,424	1,705	34.98	32.70	8.60	8.04

BELGIUM.

TABLE 5.

Increase of Insane Persons in Belgian Asylums for Ten Years (1856 to 1865), and Annual Increase.

YEARS.	Number of Insane.	Increase.
In 1856...	4,278	....
In 1857...	4,431	153
In 1858...	4,508	77
In 1859...	4,677	169
In 1860...	4,882	205
In 1861...	5,033	151
In 1862...	5,170	137
In 1863...	5,366	196
In 1864...	5,441	75
In 1865...	5,431	10 less
Total for ten years	49,217	....
Annual increase...	....	115

Number of asylums in Belgium...	51
For the reception of men...	17
For the reception of women..	17
For the reception of men and women.....................................	17
For pay and non-paying..	27
For pay patients only....................................	16
For paupers only...	8
Number of patients in all..	5,431

The superior medical officers of the asylums in Belgium are paid in proportion to the number of patients under their care, as follows:

NUMBER OF PATIENTS.		Francs.
In an asylum of 50 patients..		1,460
In an asylum of 100 patients..		2,500
In an asylum of 150 patients {	Head Physician.......................	2,500
	Assistant................................	700
In an asylum of 200 to 250 patients {	Head Physician................	2,800
	Assistant	850
In an asylum of 250 to 300 patients {	Head Physician...............	3,500
	Assistant	1,200

HOLLAND

TABLE 6.

Showing number of patients resident, the admissions, recoveries and deaths, and the proportion per cent of the recoveries and of the deaths to the admissions and to the number treated in the Asylums of Holland visited in eighteen hundred and seventy.

NAME OF ASYLUM.	Number of patients resident.			Admissions	Number treated	Recoveries	Deaths	Proportion per cent of recoveries to		Proportion per cent of deaths to admis'ns.	
	Males	Females	Total					Admissions	Number treated	Admissions	Number treated
Reinier van Arkel	198	191	389	134	523	54	47	40.3	10.3	35.0	8.9
Meerenberg	314	373	687	136	823	52	76	38.2	6.3	55.8	9.2
Rotterdam	69	100	169	51	220	17	22	33.3	7.7	43.1	10.0
Total	581	664	1,245	321	1,566	123	145	38.3	7.8	45.1	9.2

COST OF MAINTENANCE.

Reinier van Arkel.—First class, 700 florins, and 25 florins entrance fee; second class, 400 florins, and 12 florins entrance fee; third class, 225 florins, and are clad by the institute.

Meerenberg.—First class, 1000 florins; second class, 750 florins; third class, 500 florins; fourth class, 300 florins; fifth class, 270 florins.

Rotterdam.—For indigents alone, who pay 240 florins. There are twelve other patients, who pay one florin per day extra and have better accommodations.

HOLLAND.

TABLE 7.

Showing number of Patients in Lunatic Hospitals, with Admissions, Discharges, Recoveries, and Deaths for the Year.

	Male	Female	Total	Male	Female	Total
Number of patients January 1st, 1868	....	....	....	1,521	1,658	3,179
Admitted during the year	....	....	....	500	494	994
Treated during the year	....	....	....	2,021	2,152	4,173
Discharged during the year recovered	177	203	380	....	....	....
Relieved	36	33	69	....	....	....
Not improved	35	36	71	....	....	....
Died	193	165	358	....	....	....
Total discharged and died	....	....	....	441	437	878
Number remaining January 1st, 1869	....	....	....	1,580	1,715	3,295

	Male	Female	Total
Proportion per cent of recoveries to admissions	35.4	41.0	38.2
Proportion per cent of recoveries to number treated	8.7	9.4	9.1
Proportion per cent of deaths to admissions	38.6	33.8	36.0
Proportion per cent of deaths to number treated	9.5	7.6	8.5

Number of insane in asylums January 1st, 1868	3,179
Population of Holland in 1868	3,592,415
Proportion of insane to population	1 in 1,130

Principal causes of death: marasmus, consumption, apoplexy, and general paralysis.

HOLLAND.

Table 8.

AGE.	ADMITTED.								
	From 1844 to 1854.			From 1854 to 1864.			Totals.		
	Males...	Females...	Total...	Males...	Females...	Totals...	Males...	Females...	Totals...
Less than ten years	13	7	20	27	19	46	40	26	66
Ten to twenty years	142	94	236	255	162	417	397	256	653
Twenty to thirty years	551	490	1,041	788	852	1,640	1,339	1,342	2,681
Thirty to forty years	672	569	1,241	888	916	1,804	1,560	1,485	3,045
Forty to fifty years	564	462	1,026	692	652	1,344	1,256	1,114	2,370
Fifty to sixty years	303	382	685	490	497	987	793	879	1,672
Sixty to seventy years	135	198	333	242	292	584	377	490	867
Over seventy years	47	101	148	79	140	219	126	241	367
Totals	2,427	2,303	4,730	3,461	3,530	6,991	5,888	5,833	11,721
Married	1,040	927	1,967	1,334	1,274	2,608	2,374	2,201	4,575
Unmarried	1,387	1,376	2,763	2,127	2,256	4,383	3,514	3,632	7,146
Totals	2,427	2,303	4,730	3,461	3,530	6,991	5,888	5,833	11,721
Insane for the first time	1,985	1,790	3,775	2,762	2,736	5,498	4,747	4,526	9,273
Relapsed cases	442	513	955	699	794	1,493	1,141	1,307	2,448
Totals	2,427	2,303	4,730	3,461	3,530	6,991	5,888	5,833	11,721
Hereditary	366	457	823	879	1,039	1,918	1,345	1,496	2,741
Not hereditary	2,061	1,846	3,907	2,582	2,491	5,073	4,643	4,337	8,980
Totals	2,427	2,303	4,730	3,461	3,530	6,991	5,888	5,833	11,721
From intemperance	307	53	360	586	109	695	893	162	1,055
Not from intemperance	2,120	2,250	4,370	2,875	3,421	6,296	4,995	5,671	10,666
Totals	2,427	2,303	4,730	3,461	3,530	6,991	5,888	5,833	11,721
Mania	871	981	1,852	1,554	1,574	3,128	2,425	2,555	4,980
Monomania	436	331	767	212	221	433	648	552	1,200
Melancholia	322	434	756	635	883	1,518	957	1,317	2,274
Dementia	507	391	898	622	554	1,176	1,129	945	2,074
Idiotisme	98	70	168	162	99	261	260	169	429
Epilepsia	193	96	289	276	199	475	469	295	764
Totals	2,427	2,303	4,730	3,461	3,530	6,991	5,888	5,833	11,721

HOLLAND.

Table 8—(Continued.)

AGE.	CURED.								
	From 1844 to 1854.			From 1854 to 1864.			Totals.		
	Males...	Females	Totals...	Males...	Females	Totals...	Males...	Females	Totals...
Less than ten years	1	1	2	1	1	2	2	2	4
Ten to twenty years...	44	39	83	87	59	146	131	98	229
Twenty to thirty years	188	227	415	313	419	732	501	646	1,147
Thirty to forty years	222	244	466	312	437	749	534	681	1,215
Forty to fifty years............	182	176	358	246	267	513	428	443	871
Fifty to sixty years............	110	139	249	184	164	348	294	303	597
Sixty to seventy years........	45	49	94	80	76	156	125	125	250
Over seventy years............	6	22	28	14	18	32	20	40	60
Totals	798	897	1,605	1,237	1,441	2,678	2,035	2,338	4,373
Married	393	407	800	533	614	1,147	926	1,021	1,947
Unmarried	405	490	895	704	827	1,531	1,109	1,317	2,426
Totals	798	897	1,695	1,237	1,441	2,678	2,035	2,338	4,373
Insane for the first time	611	640	1,251	905	997	1,902	1,516	1,637	3,153
Relapsed cases	187	257	444	332	444	776	519	701	1,220
Totals	798	897	1,695	1,237	1,441	2,678	2,035	2,338	4,373
Hereditary........................	124	164	288	338	437	775	462	601	1,063
Not Hereditary	674	733	1,407	899	1,004	1,903	1,573	1,737	3,310
Totals	798	897	1,695	1,237	1,441	2,678	2,035	2,338	4,373
From Intemperance...........	135	21	156	231	50	281	366	71	437
Not from intemperance......	663	876	1,539	1,006	1,391	2,397	1,669	2,267	3,936
Totals	798	897	1,695	1,237	1,441	2,678	2,035	2,338	4,373
Mania	425	515	940	782	818	1,600	1,207	1,333	2,540
Monomania......................	154	135	289	84	79	163	238	214	452
Melancholia	132	198	330	260	442	702	392	640	1,032
Dementia	61	41	102	83	90	173	144	131	275
Idiotisme.........................	4	2	6	7	2	9	11	4	15
Epilepsia	22	6	28	21	10	31	43	16	59
Totals	798	897	1,695	1,237	1,441	2,678	2,035	2,338	4,373

HOLLAND.

TABLE 8—(Continued.)

AGE.	DIED.								
	From 1844 to 1854.			From 1854 to 1864.			Totals.		
	Males.	Females.	Totals.	Males.	Females.	Totals.	Males.	Females.	Totals.
Less than ten years	2	....	2	7	4	11	9	4	13
Ten to twenty years	28	7	35	35	34	69	63	41	104
Twenty to thirty years	107	70	177	183	107	290	290	177	467
Thirty to forty years	216	120	336	308	211	519	524	331	855
Forty to fifty years	258	133	391	317	204	521	575	337	912
Fifty to sixty years	170	150	320	261	204	465	431	354	785
Sixty to seventy years	88	111	199	146	213	359	234	324	558
Over seventy years	48	102	150	81	173	254	129	275	404
Totals	917	693	1,610	1,338	1,150	2,488	2,255	1,843	4,098
Married	437	265	702	557	378	935	994	643	1,637
Unmarried	480	428	908	781	772	1,553	1,261	1,200	2,461
Totals	917	693	1,610	1,338	1,150	2,488	2,255	1,843	4,098
Insane for the first time	815	618	1,433	1,186	1,006	2,192	2,001	1,624	3,625
Relapsed cases	102	75	177	152	144	296	254	219	473
Totals	917	693	1,610	1,338	1,150	2,488	2,255	1,843	4,098
Hereditary	100	87	187	230	252	482	330	339	669
Not hereditary	817	606	1,423	1,108	998	2,006	1,925	1,504	3,429
Totals	917	693	1,610	1,338	1,150	2,488	2,255	1,843	4,098
From intemperance	91	15	106	190	31	221	281	46	327
Not from intemperance	286	678	1,504	1,148	1,119	2,267	1,974	1,797	3,771
Totals	917	693	1,610	1,338	1,150	2,488	2,255	1,843	4,098
Mania	247	186	433	400	348	748	647	536	1,181
Monomania	124	88	212	77	77	154	201	165	366
Melancholia	70	89	159	182	200	382	252	289	541
Dementia	358	245	603	414	368	782	772	613	1,385
Idiotisme	40	29	69	63	42	105	103	71	174
Epilepsia	78	56	134	202	115	317	280	171	451
Totals	917	693	1,610	1,338	1,150	2,488	2,255	1,843	4,098

HOLLAND.

TABLE 8—(Concluded.)

PERIOD UNDER TREATMENT.	CURED.									DIED.								
	From 1844 to 1854.			From 1854 to 1864.			Totals.			From 1844 to 1854.			From 1854 to 1864.			Totals.		
	Males	Females	Totals	Males	Females	Totals	Males	Females	Totals	Males	Females	Totals	Males	Females	Totals	Males	Females	Totals
Less than three months	189	205	394	290	269	559	479	474	953	236	156	392	283	246	529	519	402	921
From three to six mos	212	215	427	321	388	709	533	603	1,136	118	75	193	171	114	285	289	189	478
From six to twelve mos	199	253	452	335	408	743	534	661	1,195	141	86	227	195	144	339	336	230	566
From one to two years	136	125	261	184	233	417	320	358	678	132	89	221	192	153	345	324	242	566
From two to three years	30	39	69	57	59	116	87	98	185	76	55	131	115	103	218	191	158	349
From three to four years	13	26	39	19	44	63	32	70	102	51	48	99	70	80	150	121	128	249
From four to six years	10	15	25	19	22	41	29	37	66	40	37	77	93	98	191	133	135	268
From six to eight years	4	9	13	3	12	15	7	21	28	33	40	72	60	61	121	93	101	193
From eight to ten years	2	3	5	4	3	7	6	6	12	21	26	47	58	50	108	79	76	155
More than ten years	3	7	10	5	3	8	8	10	18	70	81	151	101	101	202	171	182	353
Totals	798	897	1,095	1,237	1,441	2,678	2,035	2,338	4,373	917	693	1,610	1,338	1,150	2,488	2,255	1,843	4,098

HOLLAND.

TABLE 9.

	Admitted.			Cured.			Died.		
	1844 to 1854	1854 to 1864		1844 to 1854	1854 to 1864		1844 to 1854	1854 to 1864	
Married	41.6	37.3	39.4	47.2	42.8	45	42.9	37.3	40.1
Unmarried	58.4	62.7	60.6	52.8	57.2	55	57.1	62.7	59.9
	100	100	100	100	100	100	100	100	100
Insane for the first time.....	79.8	78.6	79.2	73.9	71.2	72.6	89	88.1	88.6
Relapsed cases...................	20.2	21.4	20.8	26.1	28.8	27.4	11	11.9	11.4
	100	100	100	100	100	100	100	100	100
Hereditary	17.4	27.4	22.4	17	28.9	22.9	11.6	19.4	15.6
Not hereditary..................	82.6	72.6	77.6	83	71.1	77.1	88.4	80.6	84.4
	100	100	100	100	100	100	100	100	100
From intemperance...........	7.6	9.9	8.8	9.2	10.5	10.3	6.6	8.9	7.3
Not from intemperance.....	92.4	90.1	91.2	90.8	89.5	89.7	93.4	91.1	92.7
	100	100	100	100	100	100	100	100	100
Mania	39.2	44.8	42	55.3	60	57.7	26.9	30.1	28.5
Monomania......................	16.2	6.2	11.2	17.2	6.1	11.7	13.1	6.2	9.7
Melancholia	16	21.7	18.8	19.3	25.8	22.5	10.2	15.5	12.9
Dementia.........................	19	16.8	18	6.1	6.5	6.3	37.2	31.5	34.3
Idiotisme	3.5	3.7	3.6	0.4	0.4	0.4	4.3	4.1	4.2
Epilepsia	6.1	6.8	6.4	1.7	1.2	1.4	8.3	12.6	10.4
	100	100	100	100	100	100	100	100	100

FRANCE.

TABLE 10.

Showing number of patients resident, admitted, treated, cured, and died, with proportion per cent of cures and of deaths to admissions and treated, in thirteen French Asylums visited in 1870.

ASYLUMS.	Number of patients resident.			Admitted.	Treated.	Cured.	Died.	Proportion per cent of cures to		Proportion per cent of deaths to	
	Males.	Females.	Total.					Admissions.	Treated.	Admissions.	Treated.
Stephansfeldt	331	450	781	204	985	53	92	25.9	5.3	45.0	9.3
Antiquaille	514	597	1,111	385	1,496	132	159	34.2	8.8	41.2	10.6
Saint Jean de Dieu	638		638	38	676	12	55	31.5	1.7	144.7	8.1
St. George's	400		400								
Asile de la Salpetriere	544		544	172	716		191			111.0	26.6
Dr. Blanche (private)	30	36	66								
Charenton	265	248	513	229	742	72	89	31.4	9.7	38.8	11.9
Clermont	792	615	1,407	440	1,847	87	199	19.7	4.7	45.2	10.7
Quatre-Mares, St. Yon	613		613	192	805	66	75	34.3	8.1	39.0	9.3
St. Yon, Rouen		908	908	198	1,006	89	73	44.9	8.8	36.8	7.2
Asile des Chartreuse	170	213	383	98	491	29	41	29.5	6.0	41.7	8.5
Auxerre	215	225	440	90	530	32	50	35.5	6.0	55.5	9.4
Sainte Anne	300	300	600	1,278	1,878	301	268	23.5	16.0	20.9	14.2
Total	4,383	3,556	7,938	3,324	11,262	873	1,292	26.2	7.7	38.8	11.4

The Asylum de la Salpetriere is for incurable and chronic cases, which accounts for the absence of cures.

ITALY.

TABLE 11.

Table showing the Number Admitted, Treated, Cured, Died, Improved, and the percentage of Cures and Deaths in Asylums visited in 1870.

NAMES OF ASYLUMS	Number Resident — Male	Female	Total	Number Admitted — Male	Female	Total	Number Treated — Male	Female	Total	Number Cured — Male	Female	Total	Improved or otherwise — Male	Female	Total	Number Died — Male	Female	Total	Per cent of cures on admission	Per cent of deaths on admission	Per cent of cures to number treated	Per cent of deaths to number treated
Genoa	285	245	530	30	13	43	72	35	107	20	9	29	9	7	16			3	67.	6.	27.	2.
Naples, Capo di Chino	42	22	64			125			772			30			16			88	24.	70.	3.	11.
Aversa	430	217	647	151	112	263	463	425	888	98	50	148			26	36	41	77	56.	29.	16.	8.
Rome	312	313	625			85			257			60						23	70.	27.	23.	8.
Perugia			172	150	137	345			855			136			70			132	39.	38.	15.	15.
Florence			510			296						73						45	25.	15.	12.	10.
Bologna	437		437	160		160	597		597	74		74	15		15	63		63	46.	39.	10.	12.
San Servalo		330	330		153	153		483	483		50	50		38	38		60	60	30.	39.	15.	12.
St. John and St. Paul, Venice	179	210	389	129	191	320	298	401	699	43	63	106	4	4	8	37	52	89	34.	28.	2.	12.
Milan, Senarva	150	150	300	30	31	61	180	181	361	4	5	9	8	3	11	11	12	23	14.	37.	14.	6.
Mombello	47	24	71	31	12	43	78	36	114	11	6	17	5	5	10	4	3	7	39.	16.	20.	6.
Dufour			33	18	17	35			68	9	5	14			10	3		3	40.	8.	15.	4.
Colombo			77			38			115			18						8	47.	21.		6.
Rossi	54	20	74																			
Stabilimento Sanitario																						
Totals						1,967			5,316			764			220			621	38.	31.	13.	10.

ITALY.

TABLE 12.

General Movement of Population of Lunatic Asylums—1867.

Number of patients in asylums January 1st, 1867	8,191
Number of patients admitted during the year...........................	4,909
Number of patients discharged during the year........................	3,210
Number of patients died during the year................................	1,504
Number of patients remaining December 31st, 1867	8,386
Proportion per cent of discharges on admissions*.....................	65
Proportion per cent of deaths on admissions...................	30
Proportion per cent of deaths on number treated.....................	11

* The discharges are all given together, hence it is impossible to say what proportion recovered.

TABLE 13,

Showing the Hereditary Tendency to Insanity among Patients Admitted and Cured during the Year 1868, and among those remaining January 1st, 1869, in the Lunatic Asylum at Florence.

CASES.	Admitted.			Cured.			Remaining.		
	Male...	Female...	Total...	Male...	Female...	Total...	Male...	Female...	Total...
Hereditary tendency admitted..........	67	41	108	28	17	45	80	102	182
Hereditary tendency not admitted....	44	55	99	18	24	42	104	110	214
Hereditary tendency uncertain..........	62	45	107	26	16	42	142	167	309
Not proved insane.............................	....	....	....	....	....	....	2	....	2
Total....................	173	141	314	72	57	129	328	379	707

THE GERMAN STATES AND SWITZERLAND.

TABLE 1,

Showing Number of Patients Resident, Number Treated, Admissions, Recoveries, and Deaths, with Proportion per cent of the Recoveries and of the Deaths to the Admissions and to the Number Treated, in the following Lunatic Asylums Visited in the Year 1870, in the German States and Switzerland.

ASYLUMS.	No. of patients resident. Male	No. of patients resident. Female	No. of patients resident. Total	Admitted	Treated	Cured	Died	Proportion per cent of recoveries to admissions	Proportion per cent of recoveries to number treated	Proportion per cent of deaths to admissions	Proportion per cent of deaths to number treated
GERMANY PROPER.											
Munich (Bavaria)	200	170	370	127	497	71	33	55.9	14.2	25.9	6.6
Irsee (Bavaria)	130	120	250	72	322	32	18	44.4	9.9	25	5.5
Deggendorf (Bavaria)	......	......	38	125	163	9	6	7.2	5.5	4.8	3.6
Sonnenstein (Saxony)	200	170	370	232	602	59	63	25.4	9.8	27.1	10.4
Pirna, private (Saxony)	12	12	24	28	52	11	3	39.2	21.1	10.7	5.7
Hubertusburg (Saxony)	810	......	810	120	930	14	60	11.6	1.5	50	6.4
PRUSSIAN GERMANY.											
Neustadt (Prussia)	269	240	509	139	648	55	45	39.5	8.4	32.3	6.9
Halle	293	263	556	158	714	50	65	31.6	7	41.2	9.1
GERMANY PROPER.											
Thonberg, private (near Leipsic)	27	25	52	29	81	16	8	55.1	19.7	27.5	9.8
Gottingen	121	155	276	84	360	10	23	19	4.4	27.3	6.3
Frankfort	68	82	150	102	252	35	33	34.3	13.8	32.3	13
Heppenheim	69	86	155	127	282	13	43	10.2	4.6	33.8	15.2

AUSTRIAN GERMANY.											
Tyrolese Provincial Asylum, at Hall	124	114	238	77	315	31	6	40.2		9.8	7.7	1.9
Institution for Care and Cure of the Insane, at Linz	86	90	176	110	286	27	33	24.5		9.4	30.9	11.5
Royal Institution for the Care and Cure of the Insane, at Vienna	242	244	486	550	1,036	140	170	25.4		13.5	30.9	16.4
Döbling, private institution			68	40	108	9	9	22.5		8.3	22.5	8.3
Brunn (Moravia)	202	193	395	389	784	56	127	14.3		7.1	32.6	16.1
Prague (Bohemia), four asylums	516	423	939	575	1,514	107	198	18.6		7	34.4	13
Total			5,862	3,084	8,946	751	943	24.3		8.3	30.5	10.5
Klosterneuburg. (Opened in 1870; hence no report for the year. It is for incurables, yet one patient was cured in ten months)	54	69	123									
Illenau. (For ten years)	203	223	426	4,086	4,512	1,570	597	38.4		34.7	14.6	13.2
SWITZERLAND.											
Waldau (Berne)	152	143	295	83	378	32	19	38.5		8.4	22.8	5
Zurich. (Opened less than a year)	66	101	167									

GERMANIC CONFEDERATION.

*Descriptive List of the Lunatic Asylums of Germany.

NAME OF INSTITUTION.	WHERE LOCATED.	CHARACTER, WHEN ESTABLISHED, ETC,	Number of Patients, Jan. 1st, 1864	Admitted during the Year	Recovered
Annunciaten Institution for Care of Insane	Aix-la-Chapelle		87	56	
Institution for the Insane in Alexianer Convent	Aix-la-Chapelle	Has received for 500 years the incurable insane	47	10	
Provincial Institute for Care and Care of the Insane	Allenberg	A public self-supporting institution for East Prussia	260	83	
Local Lunatic Hospital, St. Getreu	Bamberg	Opened in 1805	36	6	3
St. Georgen Hospital	Bayreuth		67	10	1
Private Institute for Jewish Insane	Bayreuth	Established in 1861	8	2	
Asylum for Treatment of Diseases of the Brain and Nerves	Bendorf	Private. Owned and conducted by Dr. Brosius	21	15	
Private Institution for the Insane	Coblenz	Private. Owned and conducted by Dr. Erlenmeyer	74	36	
Institution for the Insane for the City of Berlin	Berlin	This institution is a part of the Charity Hospital	56	182	
City Hospital for the Insane	Berlin		340	356	15
Private Institution for Insane Women	Berlin	Founded in 1846, by the mother of present owner	20	2	
Doctor Klinsmann's Institution for Male and Female Ins.	Berlin	Called "Dr. Klinsmann's Institution."	47	19	7
Private Institution for Insane Women	Bernau	Established in 1856	15	1	
Institution for Care and Custody of Insane in Blankenburg Convent	Blankenburg		90	13	
Karl Friedrich's Hospital for Insane and Invalids	Blankenhain		86	7	
Albers' Institution for Insane and Nervous Patients	Bonn		11	8	8
Private Institution for the Insane and Melancholy	Bonn		21	17	
Institution for Care and Cure of the Insane	Brake		98	34	
Provincial Institution for the Insane	Braunschweig	Public institution for Lippe Detmold	65	25	
Department for the Insane in Hospital at Bremen	Bremen	This institution is only for the curable insane	76	38	
Department for the Insane in City Hospital at Breslau	Breslau	Built in 1850	50	89	15

Institution	Location	Remarks			
Provincial Institution for Care of the Insane	Brieg		173	5	47
Moravian Institution for the Care of the Insane	Brünn		208	229	2
Provincial Institution for the Care of the Insane	Bunzlau		227	143	
Private Institution for Care and Cure of the Insane	Burgdorf	This institution was opened in November, 1863	12	4	
Doctor Rühle's Private Institution for Insane	Canstatt	Only quiet, melancholy, nervous patients received	15	25	
Asylum Carlsfeld (a private Institution)	Carlsfeld	Founded by Dr. Heinrich Niemeyer	21	10	
Institution for Care and Cure of Insane Women	Charlottenburg	Founded in 1841. A private institution	9	2	
Brothers of Charity Hospital for Sick and Insane	Coblenz	A private institution			
Provincial Hospital for the Sick	Coburg	This hospital rarely receives chronic insane cases	63	12	
Citizens' Hospital for the Sick	Cologne	Has a department for the harmless insane	615	83	
Royal Provincial Institution for Incurable Insane	Colditz	For male patients	49	19	
Ducal Institution for Care and Cure of Insane	Dessau	In 1860 the sexes were separated	126	10	
Institution for the Insane in Dömitz Fortress	Dömitz	Only for incurable and dangerous of lower classes	433	164	
Department Institution for the Insane	Düsseldorf	A public institution only for incurables	268	54	
Institution for Care and Cure of the Insane	Eichberg	This institution was enlarged in 1864	38	64	17
Private Institution for Care and Cure of Insane	Eitorf	Receives from twenty to thirty patients	33	27	
Department of City Institution for the Incurable Insane	Ellerfeld	Opened in 1863	205	78	
Private Institution for Nervous Patients	Endenich		21	10	
District Institution for the Insane	Erlangen		101	73	22
Private Institution for the Insane	Eupen		9	26	
Institution for Insane and Epileptics	Frankfurt			7	
Provincial Institution for Incurables	Gesecke		226	91	
Asylum St. Gilgenberg	Near Bayreuth	Founded in 1841			
Institution for the Insane in Alexianer Convent	Gladbach	A private institution opened in 1862	33	33	
St. Vincenz Private Institution for Insane	Ginünd				
Private Institution for Care and Cure of Nervous and Melancholy Patients	Göppingen	A private institution—owns 120 acres land, with a farm house in which is a colony of patients	165	78	39
Institution for Care and Cure of the Insane	Görlitz	Opened in 1864	33	49	
Institution for Care and Cure of the Insane	Göttingen		16	6	
Provincial Institution for the Insane for Steiermark	Gotha	A new institution, calculated to accommodate 200	399	42	
Public Institution for the Cure of the Insane	Gractz	In September, 1851, had eighteen patients	114	45	
Institution of Villa Bochlen	Greifswald	A private institution	488	113	
Institution for the Care of the Insane and Sick	Grimma				
Provincial Institution for the Insane	Haina	Formerly Convent of Monks—made hospital in '53			
Institution for Care and Cure of the Insane	Hall				
Friedrichsberg Institution at Barmbeck	Halle	An institution for the Province of Saxony			
Private Institution for Melancholy and Nervous Patients	Hamburg	Opened in November, 1864	3	14	
Transylvania Provincial Institute for the Insane	Helmstädt	Has been established two years			
Public Institution for Cure and Care of the Insane	Hermannstadt	Opened November 19th, 1863	810	179	
Provincial Hospital for the Insane	Hildesheim				
Private Institution for the Insane at Kiel	Hofheim	Horticultural Colony for 40 patients. Estab. in '64	428	88	5
Insane Hospital for Women and Children	Hornheim				
	Hubertusburg	Opened in 1845	722	112	13

GERMANIC CONFEDERATION—(Continued.)

NAME OF INSTITUTION.	WHERE LOCATED.	CHARACTER, WHEN ESTABLISHED, ETC.	Number of Patients, Jan. 1st, 1864	Admitted during the Year	Recovered
Institution for Care and Cure of the Insane	Jena		74	53	9
Illenau Institution for Care and Cure of the Insane	Illenau	Opened in 1842—was formerly at Heidelberg	439	345	
Private Institution for Melancholy and Nervous Patients	Illten	Opened in October, 1863		76	
Institution for Care and Cure of the Insane	Irsee			22	
Lutheran Institution for Female Patients	Kaiserwerth		29	19	
Institution for Cure of the Insane	Kennenburg		20	11	
Private Institution for Melancholy and Nervous Patients	Kessenich		2		
Institution for Cure and Care of Insane	Klagenfurt	A branch of the General Hospital	326	123	
Institution for Cure and Care of the Insane	Klingenmünster	Opened December 31st, 1857			
Institution for Cure and Care of the Insane	Königshütter			25	
Private Institution for Cure and Care of the Insane	Kowanówko		27		
Provincial Institution for the Insane	Laibach	A branch of the General Hospital	16	76	
Private Provincial Institution for the Insane	Laichingen	Established in 1834	189	250	
House of St. George	Leipzig	Serves also as a hospital and House of Correction			
Institution for the Insane	Lemberg	A department of the General Hospital			
Institution for Cure and Care of the Insane	Lengerich				
Provincial Institution for Cure of the Insane (public)	Lenbus	These institutions are connected and under the same supervision	110	256	53
Provincial Institution for Cure of the Insane (pensionat)	Lenbus		36	15	5
Private Institution for Care and Care of the Insane	Lindenburg		296	101	
Private Institution for Care and Care of the Insane	Lindenhof		15	37	
Institution for Care and Cure of the Insane	Linz	Is a part of the Prov. Charitable, Upper Austria		96	
Institution for Care of Insane Catholic Women	Linz, on Rhine	Under the care of the Sisters of Charity	53	15	
Public Institution for Cure and Care of the Insane	Lubeck				
Institution for the Insane in an Ursuline Convent	Luxemburg	The Sisters of the Convent care for the Insane		144	
Public Provincial Institution for Cure and Care of Ins.	Marsberg		469	11	
Institution for the Care of Chronic Insane and Infirm Women	Merkhausen		200		

Institution	Location	Remarks			
Royal District Institution for the Insane	Munich	In 1864, building enlarged at expense of 90,000fl.	265	104	
Insane Department of Clemens Hospital	Münster	Sisters of Charity take care of the insane patients.	11	5	
Provincial Institution for the Insane	Neu-Ruppin		157	87	36
Provincial Institution for the Insane in Alexianer Convent	Neuss	For male patients only; cared for by Convent Bros.			
Department for the Insane in St. Joseph's Hospital	Neuss	Calculated for only a few patients.			
Institution for Care and Cure of the Insane	Neu-Eberswalde	A new institution, now nearly complete.			
Institution for Care and Cure of the Insane	Neu-Eberswalde	A private institution			
Provincial Institution for the Insane	Osnabrück	New; calculated for 200 patients; compl. in 1866.			
Institution for Cure and Care of the Insane	Owinsk, Posen	Calculated for 100 patients. For Province of Posen.	490	98	
Institution for Cure and Care of the Insane	Pforzheim	For the Grand Duchy of Baden			
Private Institution for Cure of the Insane	Pfullingen	A private institution for ten to twenty patients	16	12	
Private Institution for Cure of the Insane	Pirna	Originally founded by Doctor Pienitz	32	25	
Institution for the Care of the Insane	Pöpelwitz	Opened in 1852	25	17	
Provincial Institution for the Insane	Posen	Department of City Hospital for incurable insane.	744	386	
Private Institution for the Insane at Blockdick	Rockwinkel	Founded in 1750—rebuilt in 1839			
Institution for Cure and Care of the Insane, Carthaus, Prüll	Near Regenburg.		201	84	
Curative Hospital at	Roda	Combined with this is a District Hospital	130	54	
Institution for Cure and Care of the Insane	Rostock	Enlarged in 1860. April 1st, '61, had 86 patients.	42	8	4
Institution for Cure and Care of the Insane	Rudolstadt.		116	5	
Provincial Institution for Cure and Care of the Insane	Rügenwalde.		233	91	
Institution for Cure and Care of the Insane	Sachsenberg		39	29	
Provincial Institution for the Insane	Salzburg				
Leprosenhaus—a department for harmless and epileptic patients	Salzburg	Receives harmless insane patients			
Department for Insane in a Convent	Scheibe	Receives about thirty patients	639	109	
Lunatic Hospital at	Schleswig		8	1	1
Private Institution for Cure and Care of the Insane	Schleswig	Founded in 1855, by Doctor Klink	20	5	
Private Institution for Cure and Care of the Insane	Schmidchorg		46	36	
Asylum Schweizerhof	Near Berlin	A private institution for female patients			
Provincial Hospital and Institution for the Insane	Schwetz	Both departments are under the same supervision	207	262	
Provincial Institution for the Insane	Sieburg	For curable patients	40	16	
Department for Insane in Prince Charles' Hospital	Sigmaringen	A public institution	369	212	123
Royal Lunatic Hospital	Sonnenstein		243	69	
Lower Lusatian Institution for Cure and Care of Insane	Sorau	Established in 1842			
Institution for the Insane and Infirm	Stralsund	Workhouse, House Correction, Lun. Hos., comb.	59	17	
Institution for the Insane and Infirm	Strelitz	Receives female insane, and sick of both sexes	31	35	
St. Rochus Hospital	Telgte		197	26	
Institution for Care of the Insane	St. Thomas		44		
Private Institution for Cure and Care of the Insane	Thornberg	Combines hospital, workhouse, and insane dept.			
Department for Insane in Almshouse at	Trier	A State charity institution for insane only	136		
Royal Provincial Institution for Cure and Care of Insane.	Trieste.				

GERMANIC CONFEDERATION—(Concluded.)

NAME OF INSTITUTION.	WHERE LOCATED.	CHARACTER, WHEN ESTABLISHED, ETC.	Number of Patients, Jan. 1st, 1864	Admitted during the Year	Recovered
Institution for the Care of the Insane	Trieste	A city institution. Department of the hospital	30		
Provincial Institution for Schlesien	Troppau		51		
Institution for Cure of the Insane	Wehnen	Opened April 1st, 1858	77	54	
Castle Werneck	Waigolshausen				
City Institution for Care of the Insane ("Hohehaus")	Wesel				
Provincial Institution for Care and Cure of the Insane	Wien		807	789	341
Private Institution for Care and Cure of the Insane	Wien	Opened in 1831	54	41	
Private Curative Institution for Nervous and Melancholy	Wien	Opened in June, 1860	43	34	26
Private Institution for Cure and Care of the Insane	Wien	Opened in 1830	30		
Private Institution for Cure and Care of the Insane	Wien	Opened in 1834	40		
Royal Curative Institution, Winnenthal, near	Waiblingen		134	97	
Department for Insane in Almshouse at	Wittstock	Idiots are cared for with the insane	143	49	
Department for the Insane in Julius Hospital	Würzburg		82	111	
Lower Austrian Provincial Institution for Insane	Ybbs		363	59	
Royal Curative Institution	Zwiefalten	For care of incurable ins., Kingdom Würtemburg	168	4	

* From a General Report of the Institutions of Germany, by Doctor H. Laehr, published in 1865.

[APPENDIX G.]

Fig. 1.

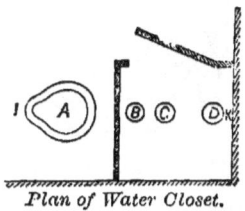

Plan of Baths at Evreux.

Reference:

D C—Douch Cocks.
B S—Barrel Shower.
H S—Head Shower.
L S—Lumbar Shower.
S S—Spinal Shower.
0 0—Foot Pans fixed.

Fig. 2.

Plan of Water Closet.

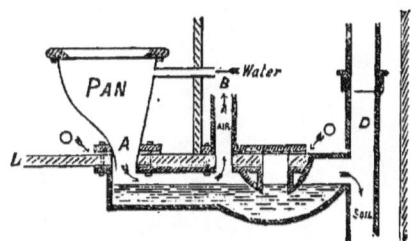

Section through I K.

Reference:

B—Ventilating Pipe.
L—Floor.
O—Rubber Gaskets.

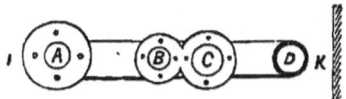

Plan of Water Closet, Washington.

Fig. 3.

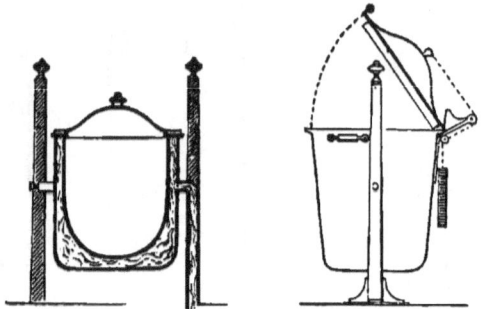

Kitchen Boiler on pivot, at Ville Evrard Asylum.

Fig. 4.

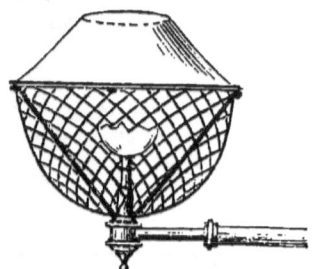

Gas Lamp at Evreux.

Fig. 5.

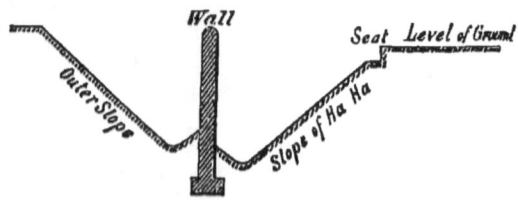

Ha-ha Fence and Seat at the Darby Asylum.

LIST OF ASYLUMS IN FRANCE.

WHERE SITUATED.		Name of Establishment.
Department.	Commune.	
Aisne...................	Laon (Prémontin).....	....
Ain......................	Bourg..................	St. Lazare.
Ain......................	Bourg..................	Ste. Madeleine.
Allier....................	Yzeure................	Ste. Catherine.
Ardèche.................	Privas	Ste. Márie Assompt'n.
Ariège..................	St. Lizier...............	St. Lizier.
Aude....................	Limoux................	St. Joseph de Cluny.
Aveyron	Rodez..................	Rodez.
Bous. du Rhône...........	Marseille...............	St. Pierre.
Bous. du Rhône...........	Aix	La Trinité.
Bous. du Rhône...........	St. Remy...............	St. Paul.
Calvados	Caen	Bon Sauveur.
Cantal...................	Aurillac................	Aurillac.
Charente................	Angoulême.............	Angoulême.
Charente Inf.............	La Rochelle............	Lafond.
Cher....................	Bourges...............	Bourges.
Corrèze	Mouestier-Merline.....	La Cellette.
Côte D'Or.....⁎..........	Dijon..................	La Chartreuse.
Côtes du Nord...........	St. Brieuc.............	St. Brieuc.
Côtes du Nord...........	Lehon	Sacrés Cœurs.
Doubs...................	Besançon..............	Mon. M. Guibard.
Eure....................	Evreux	Evreux.
Eure et Lôir.............	Chartres	Bonneval.
Finistère................	Quimper...............	St. Athanase.
Finistère................	Morlaix................	Morlaix.
Haute-Garonne	Toulouse	La Grave.
Haute-Garonne	Toulouse	Mon. Delage.
Gers....................	Auch	Auch.
Gironde.................	Bordeaux	Bordeaux.
Gironde.................	Cadillac	St. Léonard.
Gironde.................	Bouscat	Castel d'Andorte.
Hérault..................	Montpellier............	St. Charles.
Hérault..................	Montpellier............	Pont St. Côme.
Ille et Vilaine...........	Rennes................	St. Meen.
Iadre et Loire...........	Tours	Tours.
Isère	Ste. Egrève...........	St. Robert.
Jura	Dôle	Les Carmes.
Jura	Dôle	Les Capucins.
Loir-et-Cher.............	Blois..................	Blois.
Hte. Loire...............	Le Puy................	Montredon.
Loire Inférieure..........	Nantes	St. Jacques.
Loire Inférieure..........	Nantes	l'Grande Providence.

LIST OF ASYLUMS IN FRANCE—Continued.

WHERE SITUATED.		Name of Establishment.
Department.	Commune.	
Loire Inférieure............	Nantes	Mon. Gouin.
Loiret........................	Orléans....................	Orléans.
Lot	Leyme.....................	Leyme.
Lozère.....:................	St. Alban................	St. Alban.
Maine et Loire.............	Ste. Gemmes et Loire	Ste. Gemmes.
Manche	Pontorson	Pontorson.
Manche	St. Lô....................	Bon Sauveur.
Manche	Priauville...............	Bon Sauveur.
Manche	Le Mesnil Garnier.....	Ancien Convent.
Marne.......................	Châlons..................	Châlons.
Hte. Marne.................	St. Dizier...............	St. Dizier.
Mayenne....................	Mayenne.................	La Roche Gandon.
Meurthe....................	Laxon	Maréville.
Meurthe....................	St. Nicolas.............	St. François.
Meurthe....................	Jarville	La Malgrange.
Meuse.......................	Fains.....................	Fains.
Morbihan	Vannes...................	L'Humanité.
Moselle.....................	Gorze	Dépôt Mendicité.
Nièvre.......................	La Charité s. Loire...	La Charité s. Loire.
Nord........................	Lille......................	Lille.
Nord.........................	Armentières	Armentières.
Nord.........................	Marquelle................	Lommelet.
Oise.........................	Clermont	Mon. Labitte.
Orne	Alençon	Alençon.
Pas de Calais..............	St. Venant..............	St. Venant.
Puy de Dôme..............	Clermont-Ferrand	Ste. Marie Assompt'n.
Puy de Dôme..............	Riom.....................	Riom.
Bas-Pyrenées..............	Pau.......................	Pau.
Bas-Rhin	Brumath.................	Stephansfeld.
Rhône.......................	Lyon	L'Antiquaille.
Rhône	Lyon	St. Jean de Dieu.
Rhône	Lyon	St. Vincent Paul.
Rhône.......................	Lyon	Croix Rousse.
Rhône.......................	Lyon	Champ-Vert.
Rhône.......................	Calvère	St. Julien.
Rhône.......................	Vaugneray..............	Vaugneray.
Sarthe......................	Le Mans.................	Le Mans.
Savoie	Chambéry	Bassens.
Seine........................	St. Maurice.............	Charenton (Imperial)
Seine........................	Gentilly	Bicêtre.
Seine........................	Paris.....................	La Salpétrière.
Seine........................	Paris et environs......	Les 13 Asiles privés.
Seine Infre.................	Rouen	St. Yon.
Seine Infre.................	Sotteville les Rouen..	Quatre Mares.
Deux-Sèvres	Niort.....................	La Providence.

LIST OF ASYLUMS IN FRANCE—Continued.

WHERE SITUATED.		Name of Establishment.
Department.	Commune.	
Tarn	Alby........................	Bon Sauveur.
Tarn et Garonne..........	Montauban	St. Jacques.
Vaucluse.....................	Avignon..................	Mont de Vergues.
Vendée.......................	Napoléon Vendée......	Napoléon Vendée.
Vienne.......................	Poitiers...................	Poitiers.
Hte. Vienne...............	Limoges	Limoges.
Yonne........................	Auxerre...................	Auxerre.

THE TWELFTH ANNUAL COMMEMORATION

OF THE

OPENING OF THE SUSSEX LUNATIC ASYLUM

WILL BE HELD

On Tuesday, 25th July, 1871.

HOURS—12 noon—Morning Prayer, with Commemoration Sermon. Preacher, Rev. A. P. Perfect, M. A., Rector of St. John's, Lewes.

1–2 P. M.—Dinner in the Wards (Roast Beef and Plum Pudding).

1:30 P. M.—Luncheon for the Visitors in the Recreation Hall.

2–3:30 P. M.—Games on the Grounds. Athletic Sports. The Ockenden Band will play.

3:30 P. M.—Mr. Basil Young will give a Musical and Comic Entertainment.

6 P. M.—Tea.

7 P. M.—Patient's Ball. To conclude at 9 P. M.

THE BALL FOR THE HOUSEHOLD

WILL TAKE PLACE

On Thursday, July 27th. 9 P. M.–3 A. M.

Mr. Squire's Brighton Quadrille Band will play.

HAYWOOD'S HEATH, July, 1871.

———

THE ASYLUM, BOOTHAM, YORK.

PROGRAMME OF ENTERTAINMENTS. WINTER SESSION, 1870–1.

Thursday, October 13th, 1870—Ball.

Saturday, October 15th—Meeting of Singing Class.

Thursday, October 20th—Reading.

Saturday, October 22d—Discussion Club Conversazione and Meeting of Singing Class.

Thursday, October 27th—Vocal and Instrumental Concert.
Saturday, October 29th—Meeting of Singing Class.
Thursday, November 3d—Ball.
Saturday, November 5th—Meetings of Discussion Club and Singing Class.
Thursday, November 10th—Lecture, " Hull Worthies," by T. T. Lambert, Esq.
Saturday, November 12th—Meeting of Singing Class.
Thursday, November 17th—Reading and Musical Entertainment.
Saturday, November 19th—Meetings of Discussion Club and Singing Class.
Thursday, November 24th—Vocal and Instrumental Concert.
Saturday, November 26th—Meeting of Singing Class.
Thursday, December 1st—Ball.
Saturday, December 3d—Meetings of Discussion Club and Singing Class.
Thursday, December 8th—Magic Lantern Exhibition.
Saturday, December 10th—Meeting of Singing Class.
Thursday, December 15th—Lecture, "A Visit to a Coal Mine," by Dr. Procter, F.C.S.
Saturday, December 17th—Meetings of Discussion Club and Singing Class.
Thursday, December 22d—Reading and Musical Entertainment.
Friday, December 23d—Meeting of Singing Class.
Thursday, December 29th—Lecture, " The History of Music, with Illustrations," by the Rev. H. V. Palmer.
Friday, December 30th—Meeting of Singing Class.
Thursday, January 5th, 1871—New Year's Ball.
Friday, January 6th—Second ditto.
Saturday, January 7th—Meeting of Singing Class.
Thursday, January 12th—Lecture, " Thomas Gent, an Old York Printer," by the Reverend Canon Raine, M.A., Secretary to the Surtees Society.
Saturday, January 14th—Discussion Club Conversazione and Meeting of Singing Class.
Thursday, January 19th—Magic Lantern Exhibition.
Saturday, January 21st—Meeting of Singing Class.
Thursday, January 26th—Vocal and Instrumental Concert.
Saturday, January 28th—Meetings of Discussion Club and Singing Class.
Thursday, February 2d—Ball.
Saturday, February 4th—Meeting of Singing Class.
Thursday, February 9th—Lecture, " Some African Tribes," by Doctor Needham.
Saturday, February 11th—Meeting of Discussion Club and Singing Class.
Thursday, February 16th—Lecture, " Caverns and their Contents," by S. W. North, Esq., F.G.S.
Saturday, February 18th—Meeting of Singing Class.
Thursday, February 23d—Vocal and Instrumental Concert.
Saturday, February 25th—Meetings of Discussion Club and Singing Class.
Thursday, March 2d—Ball.
Saturday, March 4th—Meeting of Singing Class.
Thursday, March 9th—Magic Lantern Exhibition.

Saturday, March 11th—Meetings of Discussion Club and Singing Class.
Thursday, March 16th—Reading and Musical Entertainment.
Saturday, March 18th—Meeting of Singing Class.
Thursday, March 23d—Lecture, "The Northwest Highlands and Western Islands of Scotland," by the Rev. Canon Hey, M.A.
Saturday, March 25th—Meetings of Discussion Club and Singing Class.
Thursday, March 20th—Vocal and Instrumental Concert.
Saturday, April 1st—Meeting of Singing Class.
Thursday, April 6th—Ball.
Saturday, April 8th—Meetings of Discussion Club and Singing Class.
Thursday, April 13th—Reading.
Saturday, April 15th—Meeting of Singing Class.
Thursday, April 20th—Lecture, "An Analysis of the Franco-Prussian War," by W. Wallen, Esq.
Saturday, April 22d—Discussion Club Conversazione and Meeting of Singing Class.
Thursday, April 27th—Reading and Musical Entertainment.
Saturday, April 29th—Meeting of Singing Class.

The lectures and readings commence at six o'clock P. M.; the discussion meetings at half-past six; the balls at seven; the concerts at half-past seven; and the singing meetings at a quarter past eight.

NIGHT ATTENDANTS.

1. The duties of night attendants shall commence at eight P. M. on weekdays and nine on Sundays, and cease at six A. M., during which period they shall be responsible for the condition of the patients.

2. They are to obtain every night from the attendants on duty in each ward the names of such patients as require particular attention, either on account of their habits, fits, illness, or disposition to self-injury, and to see that sufficient changes are provided for those whose habits are dirty. Should they find any patients wet or dirty when they go on duty, they must require the day attendants in charge of such patients to attend to them and hand them over to the night attendants in a clean, dry, and proper state; and the night attendants must themselves deliver over to the day attendants all patients in a like proper condition.

3. They shall visit each ward at least seven times in the course of the night, and oftener if necessary, commencing their rounds at eight, nine, ten, and twelve P. M., and at two, four, and half-past five A. M.

4. They shall administer any medicines, extra diet, wine, etc., (which may have been ordered by the Superintendent), at the times appointed; but shall not disturb any patient whom they may find sleeping, for the purpose of administering either food or medicine. A dry cloth or bib shall always be used when any patient has to be fed.

5. They shall visit every epileptic patient on each round of the wards, and see that they are so lying as not to endanger life from suffocation during an accession of fits. Should any patient at any time be found out of bed or lying on his face, or with his head off the pillow, he must be put to bed, placed upon his back or side, with his head on the pillow, and shirt neck unbuttoned.

6. They shall devote particular attention to all supposed suicidal cases, and remove any articles by which they might possibly injure themselves.

7. They shall use every exertion to improve the dirty patients in their habits, by getting them up at the stated times, and by taking such measures as will tend to keep them clean. Whenever any bedding is found wet or dirty it shall be removed immediately, and fresh clean bedding substituted; or if necessary the patient shall be removed to another room, and the one previously occupied washed out. No patient shall be allowed to remain in a damp or dirty room.

8. The general quiet of the galleries must be strictly attended to, and any noisy patient visited and quieted, or if necessary removed to a room where he will not disturb the other patients. In going round the galleries, the night attendants must avoid disturbing the patients as much as possible; and for this purpose shall wear list shoes, and unbolt and shut the doors quietly. They must also lock and secure the various doors and windows of water closets, etc., on windy nights, to prevent rattling.

9. They shall see that the various galleries are properly ventilated, and shall personally attend to any fires which may require to be kept burning during the night.

10. In the event of any sudden illness, accident, escape, or death during the night, they shall report the same to the Superintendent with the least possible delay.

11. They shall call the day attendants at half past five A. M., stating to them any peculiarity which may have occurred to their respective patients during the night; and before going off duty shall fill up the report for the night, to be left in the Superintendent's room.

12. On Thursdays and Saturdays they shall be at liberty from two to eight P. M., and on Sundays from two to nine P. M.; but on other days they will be expected to perform certain light duties in the afternoon.

13. In all their intercourse with the patients, they must bear in mind that they are insane, and consequently not responsible for their actions. Should any of them make use of abusive language, or offer them violence, they must on no account take it as an insult, but, on the contrary, use every endeavor to gain an influence over them by firm yet kind and attentive treatment.

38

YORK ASYLUM.

Attendant's daily Reports for week ending .... 18...... Female Gallery...............

	Su.	M.	T.	W.	Th.	F.	S.	
Number patients..........................								
Number empty beds......................								
Number patients at work in kitchen......								
Number patients at work in laundry......								
Number patients at work in galleries.....								Names of patients unemployed—reasons why.
Number patients at work sewing..........								
Number patients at work knitting.........								
Number patients reading or otherwise employed...								
Number patients altogether unemployed..								Names of Patients refusing food.
Number patients wet or dirty.............								
Ill { Confined to bed.....................								
{ Not confined to bed................								
Number patients excited..................								Names of patients who are suicidal.
Number patients refusing food............								
Number patients requiring to be washed...								
Number patients who are suicidal.........								Names of patients who have had fits.
Number patients who have had fits........								
Number patients attending chapel.........								
Number patients attending amusements...								Names of patients never beyond boundaries, and reasons why.
Number patients out beyond boundaries....								
Number patients never out beyond boundaries...								

NOTE.—All accidents and injuries, however slight, illness, acts of violence, attempts to escape or commit suicide, and struggles with attendants, to be immediately reported to the Assistant Matron, and by her, in writing, to the Superintendent.

MISSING LIST.

_____ Ward, No._____   _____187

	Articles.	Patients.	Attendants.	

_____Attendant.   _____Laundress.

When signed to be given to the Head Attendant.

BROOKWOOD ASYLUM.

NEAR WORKING STATION, SURREY.

Application for Situation of...
(To be filled up in the candidate's own writing).

Name and age..

Married, single, or widowed...

Religious persuasion...

Post address...

Can you read and write? ....

Brought up to any particular trade, or class of work?...........................

Any knowledge of music, vocal or instrumental?...............................

Present occupation...

Name and address of various employers, in regular order, particularly of
all recent ones; length of time with each, and cause of leaving.

BROOKWOOD ASYLUM.

BATHS—REGULATIONS FOR THE GUIDANCE OF THE ATTENDANTS.

1. Every patient to be bathed immediately after admission, and once a week afterwards, unless exempted by medical order. Should there be the slightest doubt as to the advisability of bathing any patient, owing to sickness, feebleness, or excitement, immediate reference to be made to one of the medical officers.

2. The name of every patient not having the customary bath to be inserted in the daily report sheet.

3. In preparing a bath *the cold water is always to be turned on first.*

4. Before the patient enters the bath the temperature is to be ascertained by the thermometer, and is not to be less than eighty-eight degrees, nor above ninety-eight degrees. In case of the thermometer becoming inefficient from injury, etc., all bathing operations to be suspended until another be obtained.

5. Not more than —— patients to be bathed in the same water. Any infringement of this rule to be entered in the daily report sheet.

6. *Under no circumstances whatever* are two patients to occupy the bath at the same time.

7. During the employment of the bath, the room is never to be left without an attendant. At all other times the door is to remain locked, and the floor to be kept dry.

8. *Under no pretence whatever* is the patient's head to be put under water.

9. In the bath the body of each patient is to be well cleansed with soap. After coming out of the bath especial care must be taken to dry those patients who are feeble and helpless, and to clothe them as rapidly as possible.

10. The keys are never to remain on the bath taps, nor are they to be employed by patients. When not in use they are to be locked in the attendants' room.

11. Any marks, bruises, wounds, sores, local pain, evidences of disease of any kind, complained of by the patients, or noticed by the attendant during any of the bathing operations, to be immediately reported to one of the medical officers, and also to be entered in the daily report sheet.

12. Any deficiency in the supply of warm water, soap, towels, etc., to be entered in the daily report sheet.

13. The attendants are to bear in mind that, except under medical order, the baths are to be employed solely for the purposes of cleanliness.

14. Neither the cold nor the shower bath is ever to be employed, except under medical order, and then only in presence of one of the officers. When not in use the door of the latter is to remain locked, and the key to be kept in the dispensary.

15. It is the duty of the head attendant to be present at all baths employed under medical order, and to take care that the duration does not exceed the time specified in such order. He is also to supervise the whole of the ordinary bathing operations, to ascertain that the rules are rigidly carried out, and to report to the Medical Superintendent every infringement that may come to his knowledge.

T. N. BRUSHFIELD, M. D.,

June, 1867.   Medical Superintendent.

301

[Lunatics 1. (16 & 17 Vict.) Private Patient.]
"ORDER" FOR THE RECEPTION OF A PRIVATE PATIENT.

N. B.—Under all circumstances the "Order" and "Statement" below to be fillod up by the patient's relatives or friends.—Sched. (A) No. 1, Sects. 4, 8.

I, the undersigned, hereby request you to receive ——, whom I last saw at ——, on the (a) —— day of ——, 18—, a (b) —— as a patient into your hospital.

Subjoined is a statement respecting the said ——.

Signed: Name, ——; occupation (if any) ——; place of abode, ——; degree of relationship (if any), or other circumstances of connection with the patient.

Dated this —— day of ——, one thousand eight hundred and ——.

To the Superintendent of Bethlem Hospital, St. George's Road, Lambeth, S.

"STATEMENT."

If any particulars in this Statement be not known, the fact to be so stated.

Name of patient, with Christian name at length, ——; Sex and age, ——; Married, single, or widowed, ——; Condition of life and previous occupation (if any), ——; Religious persuasion, as far as known, ——; Previous place of abode, ——; Whether first attack, ——; Age (if known) on first attack, ——; When and where previously under care and treatment, ——; Duration of existing attack, ——; Supposed cause, ——; Whether subject to epilepsy, ——; Whether suicidal, ——; Whether dangerous to others, ——; Whether found lunatic by inquisition, and date of commission or order for inquisition, ——; Special circumstances (if any) preventing the patient being examined, before admission, separately by two medical practitioners, ——; Name and address of relative to whom notice of death is to be sent, ——.

How many previous attacks ? ——; Have any relatives of the family been similarly affected ? ——; State in what degree of relationship, ——; Has the patient been of sober habits ? ——; Number of children ? ——; Age of youngest ? ——; Degree of education ? ——.

Signed: Name, (e)——; occupation (if any), ——; place of abode, ——.

Degree of relationship (if any) or other circumstances of connection with the patient, ——.

(a) Within one month previous to the date of the order.
(b) Lunatic or an idiot, or a person of unsound mind.
(e) The "Statement" must be signed, but "where the person signing the statement is not the person who signs the order, the following particulars concerning the person signing the statement are to be added."

N. B.—Medical certificates of patients' examination, and the signatures, are required by the above statute to be dated within seven clear days of the patient's reception. In stating the residence, the number of the house must be specified when there is any.

The medical men signing the certificates must not be in partnership, nor one an assistant to the other.

By Order of the Commissioners in Lunacy.

1.—It is absolutely necessary that the medical men should write their certificates legibly, so as to afford the opportunity of an exact copy being made.

2.—"All alterations in the original certificates, unless by the certifying medical man, invalidate them; and the initials of the latter must be placed to every change or addition made."

3.—"If a registered medical man describes himself as 'a duly qualified registered practitioner,' it is not necessary that he should specify his medical qualifications in full in addition."

MEDICAL CERTIFICATE.—Sched. (A) No. 2, Sects. 4, 5, 8, 10, 11, 12, 13.

I, the undersigned, ——, being (a) ——, and being in actual practice as a (b) ——, hereby certify that I, on the —— day of ——, 18——, at (c) [here insert the street and number of house, if any,] ——, in the County of ——, separately from any other medical practitioner, personally examined ——, of (d), [state address and occupation, if any,] and that the said —— is a (e) ——, and a proper person to be taken charge of and detained under care and treatment, and that I have formed this opinion upon the following grounds, viz:

1. Facts indicating insanity observed by myself (f) [some definite fact or facts must be specified,] ——;

2. Other facts, if any, indicating insanity communicated to me by others (g), [state the name of the person giving the information,] ——.

Signed: Name, ——; place of abode, ——; dated this —— day of ——, one thousand eight hundred and ——.

[Here follows duplicate of above certificate.]

(a) Here set forth the qualification entitling the person certifying to practice as a physician, surgeon, or apothecary, ex gra.; Fellow of the Royal College of Physicians in London.

(b) Physician, surgeon, or apothecary, as the case may be.

(c) Here insert the street and number of the house, if any, or other like particulars.

(d) A. B., of ——, insert residence and profession or occupation, if any.

(e) Lunatic or an idiot, or a person of unsound mind.

(f) Here insert the facts. Some definite fact or facts must be specified. Please to write the facts legibly and on the lines.

(g) Here state the information and from whom received.

COMPLAINT AND COMMITMENT.

State of California, County of ———.

To Honorable ———, County Judge of said county. ——— respectfully represents that there is now in said county a person named ———, who is insane, and by reason of insanity dangerous to be at large, and is a proper subject for the Insane Asylum; and the said ——— being duly sworn, deposes and says that the foregoing statement is true; wherefore he prays that such action may be had as the law requires, and that the said ——— may be sent to the Asylum of California.

Subscribed and sworn to before me, this ——— day of ——— A. D. 186 .

The foregoing application having been made to me, ———, County Judge of said county, and ——— named in said application, being this day brought before me for examination on said charge of insanity, and having heard the testimony of ——— and ——— witnesses who have had frequent intercourse with the accused during the time of the alleged insanity; and doctors ——— and ——— graduates in medicine, after hearing the testimony of witnesses, and after a personal examination of the accused, having made the certificate by law required, and being myself satisfied that the said ——— is insane and dangerous to be at large, and is not a case of idiocity, or imbecility, or simple feebleness of intellect, or old case of harmless dementia, or of any class of old, incurable, and harmless insanity, nor a case of delirium tremens; and being further satisfied of the truth of all the matters set forth in the said physician's certificate; I do hereby order the said ——— to be taken to and placed in the Insane Asylum at Stockton, and ——— is charged with the execution of this order.

As to the ability of the said ——— or his kindred to bear the charges or expenses for the time ——— may remain in the Asylum, as well as all other matters pertaining to ——— interests or possessions, I find, after diligent inquiry the facts to be as follows:

1. The said ——— is ——— by possession of ——— able to pay ——— expenses in the Asylum.

2. I have ——— appointed ——— a guardian for the said ——— and directed a quarterly payment in advance, and a supply of necessary clothing, together with the bond, to be forwarded to the Asylum with the said ——— as by law required of paying patients.

3. The said ——— has ——— kindred in the degree, as by law defined, who are able to pay said expenses, and I have ——— made the assessment as by law directed in cases of kindred able to pay.

4. There is ——— due the said ——— for ——— and I have ——— taken steps as by law required to be taken in such cases.

5. There ——— money (in ——— own right) on the person of the said ——— and ———.

Witness my hand this ——— day of ——— A. D. 186 .

———————————, Judge.

PHYSICIAN'S CERTIFICATE.

State of California, County of ———

We, ——— and ——— being sworn, do depose and say that we are graduates in medicine; that at the request and in the presence of Hon. ———, County Judge of said County, we have heard the testimony, and carefully examined the said ———— in reference to the charge of insanity, and do find that ———— is insane and by reason of insanity dangerous to be at large. The facts in support of this opinion (elicited by said examination) are set forth in the answers to the following questions as nearly as can be ascertained:

QUESTIONS.

1. Name?
2. Age?
3. Nativity?
4. Married or single?
5. If children, how many, and the age of the youngest?
6. If female and married, maiden name and name of husband?
7. What State last from and how long in California?
8. What occupation?
9. What evidence have you of the presence of insanity?
10. Is there a homicidal, suicidal, or incendiary disposition?
11. Is the case a recent one, having occurred within twelve months last past.
12. When did this attack first appear?
13. Is this the first attack? If not, when did others occur and what their duration?
14. Is the disease increasing, decreasing, or stationary?
15. Are there rational intervals? If so, do they occur periodically?
16. Is there any permanent hallucination? If so, what is it?
17. In what way is the accused dangerous to be at large?
18. Is there a disposition to injure others? If so, is it directed especially to relatives, and is it from *sudden passion or premeditation?*
19. If suicidal, is the propensity *now* active, and in what way?
20. Is there a disposition to filthy habits, destruction of clothing, furniture, etc.?
21. Any relations, including grand parents and cousins, been insane?
22. Any peculiarities of temper, habits, disposition or pursuits, *before* the attack—any predominant passions or religious impressions?
23. Been intemperate in the use of ardent spirits, wine, opium or tobacco in any form?
24. Suffered from epilepsy, suppressed secretions, eruptions, discharges or sores, or injured on the head?
25. Any change in the physical health *since* the attack?
26. The supposed cause of insanity?
27. Of what class of insanity?
28. What treatment has been pursued, and with what effect?

———————— ———————, M. D.
———————— ———————, M. D.

Subscribed and sworn to before me, this ———— day of ———— A. D. 186 .

———————— ————————.

DIETARY

Breakfast.

One pint coffee, or more, to satisfy appetite; five ounces loaf bread; one half pound thick mush, made with corn meal or cracked wheat, flavored with syrup.

Dinner.

One quart soup, made from good fresh meat and beans, rice or fresh vegetables; four and one half ounces meat without bone; five ounces loaf bread; one half pound potatoes; beets, carrots, miscellaneous vegetables and fruits, grown on the Asylum grounds, are used when in season.

Supper.

One pint tea; five ounces loaf bread; three ounces gingerbread.

The attendants are instructed to furnish as much bread and soup as the patient may desire, except in cases of dementia with morbid appetite.

Patients employed on the farm and garden have a lunch of bread and butter at ten o'clock, A. M. and at four o'clock, P. M., in addition to the above.

The diet of the sick is prescribed by their medical attendant.

Different kinds of meats and fish are substituted for beef, and other variations made for a change occasionally, but not regularly, except Fridays, when fish is used as far as practicable.

RICHMOND, NEAR DUBLIN.

Ordinary Diet.—Breakfast: half pound of bread and a pint of tea, or eight ounces of stirabout with a pint of new milk. Dinner: ten ounces of bread to males, and eight ounces to females, with half pound of meat or a British pint of soup. Supper: half pound of bread and a pint of cocoa.

Extra Diet.—Breakfast, ordered by the medical officers, an egg. Dinner: a pint of beer or porter, half pound of chops, or half pint of beef tea and eight ounces of bread. Supper: a British pint of tea and eight ounces of bread.

Hospital Diet.—Beef tea, chops, eggs, wines, rice, arrowroot, etc.

SUSSEX COUNTY ASYLUM—DIET SCALE.

	SUPPER AT 6 P.M. Females			SUPPER AT 6 P.M. Males			DINNER AT 1 P.M. Females									DINNER AT 1 P.M. Males							BREAKFAST AT 8 A.M. Females		BREAKFAST AT 8 A.M. Males	
DAYS	Tea (Pt.)	Butter (Oz.)	Bread (Oz.)	Coffee (Pt.)	Butter (Oz.)	Bread (Oz.)	Vegetables (Oz.)	Meat stew (Pt.)	Mutton broth (Pt.)	Plum pudding (Oz.)	Baked pie (Oz.)	Suet pudding (Oz.)	Uncooked meat (Oz.)	Beer (Pt.)	Bread and dumpling (Oz.)	Vegetables (Oz.)	Irish stew	Mutton Broth (Pt.)	Suet pudding or pie (Oz.)	Uncooked meat (Oz.)	Beer (Pt.)	Bread or dumpling (Oz.)	Cocoa (Pt.)	Bread (Oz.)	Cocoa (Pt.)	Bread (Oz.)
Sunday	1	½	5	1	½	6	12						8	½	5	16		1	12	6	½	6	1	5	1	6
Monday	1	½	5	1	½	6	12					8	4	½	5	8				4	½	6	1	5	1	6
Tuesday	1	½	5	1	½	6	8				12		2	½		8			16	2	½	6	1	5	1	6
Wednesday	1	½	5	1	½	6	12	1					4	½	5	16	1			8	½	6	1	5	1	6
Thursday	1	½	5	1	½	6								½		8				4	½	6	1	5	1	6
Friday	1	½	5	1	½	6	12			12	12		4	½	5	16		1	16	2	½	6	1	5	1	6
Saturday	1	½	5	1	½	6	8		1				4	½	5	8				4	½	6	1	5	1	6
Weekly total	7	3½	35	7	3½	42	64	1	1	12	24	8	26	3½	25	80	1	2	44	30	3½	42	7	35	7	42

EDINBURGH ROYAL ASYLUM.

DIET TABLE.

Breakfast for Males.

Six ounces oatmeal or two pints of porridge, and three fourths pint of skimmed or buttermilk, or one fourth ounce of coffee; one half ounce of sugar; seven and a half ounces of bread, and one fourth ounce of butter.

Females.

Six ounces oatmeal or one and a half ounces of porridge, and three fourths pint of skimmed or buttermilk, or one fourth ounce of coffee; one half ounce of sugar; five ounces of bread, and one fourth ounce of butter.

Dinner.

Sunday—Four ounces of rice; one third ounce of sugar, and one half pint of sweet milk; seven and a half ounces of bread for males, and five ounces for females.

Monday—Seven ounces of uncooked meat boiled in broth, with two ounces of barley; seven and a half ounces of bread, or one and one eighth pounds of potatoes, for males, and five ounces of bread, or one and one eighth pounds of potatoes for females.

Tuesday—Seven ounces of uncooked meat, stewed or roasted, and eight ounces of vegetables, bread, or potatoes, as on Monday.

Wednesday—Broth made with two ounces of meat boiled down in the broth; eight ounces of dumpling of flour, suet, and currants; bread or potatoes as above.

Thursday—Seven ounces of uncooked meat made into Irish stew; bread or potatoes as above.

Friday—Pea soup made from two ounces of meat and four ounces of peas; bread or potatoes as above.

Saturday—Seven ounces of meat and broth, as on Monday; bread or potatoes as above.

Supper for Males.

Six ounces of oatmeal or two pints of porridge, and three fourths pint of skimmed or buttermilk, or one eighth ounce of tea; one half ounce of sugar; seven and one half ounces of bread, and one fourth ounce of butter.

Females.

One eighth ounce of tea; half ounce of sugar; five ounces of bread, and one fourth ounce of butter.

Luncheon for Workers.

Bread, two and one half ounces; cheese, one ounce; beer, one half pint.

QUATRES MARES, NEAR ROUEN.

Diet Table for Lunatics maintained at the cost of the Department.

DIVISION OF THE DAY.	DESCRIPTION OF PROVISIONS.	MEN. Quantities before preparation.	MEN. Quantities after preparation.	WOMEN. Quantities before preparation.	WOMEN. Quantities after preparation.
Daily — First	White bread for soup		3 ounces.		3 ounces.
Daily — Second	Medium bread		22 ounces		18 ounces.
Daily — Third	Cider and water, equal parts		2 pints.		1½ pints.
Breakfast	Thin broth		1 pint		1 pint.
Breakfast	Or milk		½ pint		½ pint.
Breakfast	Or cheese		1½ ounces.		1½ ounces.
Breakfast	Or butter		1 ounce		1 ounce.
Breakfast	Or fruits, in season		6 ounces		6 ounces.
Sunday, Tuesday, and Thursday — First	Meat soup		1 pint		1 pint.
Sunday, Tuesday, and Thursday — Second	Meat, for boiling	8 ounces	4 ounces	6 ounces	3 ounces.
Monday — First	Soup, à la graisse		1 pint		1 pint.
Monday — Second	Meat, for ragout	4 ounces		3 ounces	
Monday — Second	With fresh vegetables	6 ounces		6 ounces	
Monday — Second	Or potatoes	8 ounces		6 ounces	
Monday — Second	Or dried vegetables	1-10 of a pint		1-10 of a pint	
Dinner — Wednesday First	Soup, à la graisse		1 pint		1 pint.
Dinner — Wednesday First	Salt fish	6 ounces	4½ ounces	6 ounces	4½ ounces.
Dinner — Wednesday First	Or fricasseed eggs	2	2	2	2
Dinner — Wednesday Second	Potatoes	1 pound	10 ounces	1 pound	10 ounces.
Dinner — Wednesday Second	Or fresh vegetables	14 ounces	10 ounces	14 ounces	10 ounces.
Dinner — Wednesday Second	Or dried vegetables	¼ pint	½ pint	¼ pint	½ pint.
Dinner — Wednesday Second	Or rice	1½ ounces	7 ounces	1½ ounces	7 ounces.
Dinner — Fast days First	Thin broth, for soup		1 pint		1 pint.
Dinner — Fast days Second	As on Wednesday				
Supper — Sunday and Wednesday	Pork		2 ounces		2 ounces.
Supper — Sunday and Wednesday	Rice	1½ ounces	7 ounces	1½ ounces	7 ounces.
Supper — Other days	Or preserved pears or prunes		3 ounces		3 ounces.
Supper — Other days	Or thin soup		1 pint		1 pint.
Supper — Other days	Or cheese		1½ ounces.		1½ ounces.

GENERAL RULES

FOR THE

SURREY COUNTY LUNATIC ASYLUM,

AT BROOKWOOD,

Pursuant to the fifty-third section of the Act 16 *and* 17 *Vict. cap.* 97.

COMMITTEE OF VISITORS.

1. The Committee of Visitors for the time being, shall meet for the first time at the asylum within a fortnight after their appointment, and shall then (after electing a Chairman), appoint five members of the Committee of Visitors to be a House Committee for the purposes after mentioned, of whom three shall be a quorum. They shall continue their meetings at the asylum throughout the year, by adjournment to such times as they shall consider most convenient.

2. At their first meeting, and afterwards as occasion shall require, they shall make such appointments and perform such duties as may be necessary for carrying into full effect the various Acts of Parliament relating to lunatics (16 and 17 Vict. c. 97; 18 and 19 Vict. c. 105; 25 and 26 Vict. c. 111).

3. Minutes of the proceedings of the Committee of Visitors shall be kept and entered by the Clerk to the Visitors, and the same shall be read at the following meeting and signed by the Chairman.

4. The Committee of Visitors shall make, from time to time, such "regulations and orders" as they shall see fit, not inconsistent with the "general rules" for the time being, in force for the management and conduct of the asylum.

5. No general rule for the government of the asylum shall be rescinded or altered, except at a meeting of the Committee of Visitors specially convened for the purpose; and no alteration in the general rules shall take effect until it has received the approval of one of Her Majesty's principal Secretaries of State.

6. They shall cause all moneys received from every source to be paid to the account of the asylum at the bank of their Treasurer, and they shall make all payments by checks, to be signed by three of their body.

7. A special meeting of the Committee of Visitors may be at any time convened in the manner pointed out by the Act 16 and 17 Vict. cap 97, sect. 25, notice being given of the particular business to be transacted thereat.

8. They shall in addition to the report required by the Act 16 and 17 Vict. cap. 97, sect. 62, present at every General Quarter Sessions of the Peace for the county a summary of their transactions during the preceding quarter; and at every Easter session they shall present a report on the state and condition of the asylum, with an audited account of the whole of their receipts and expenditures for the year ending on the preceding thirty-first day of December.

HOUSE COMMITTEE.

1. The House Committee shall visit the asylum twice in the course of every calendar month, and their duties shall be as follows:

2. To inspect the food and see that all contracts are performed; also, to see all the patients and all the wards and premises appropriated to their use, and also to inquire and examine as to the convalescence and improvement of particular patients, and as to the treatment, health, and general condition of the whole establishment, and to perform the general duties imposed on them by the Act 16 and 17 Vict., cap. 97, sect. 61.

3. To audit all the accounts of the asylum, to superintend the farm and garden, to examine all bills due by the asylum, and recommend the same when correct, for payment; to examine all accounts for the maintenance of patients and for repairs previous to their being sent to the several parishes or to the County Treasurer, and to consider all applications for additional stores and for advances to the Steward for current expenses before they are submitted to the Committee of Visitors, and also to make orders for such advances, not exceeding one hundred pounds sterling.

4. To give orders, in all cases of emergency, for such works to be performed or such goods to be provided as shall be absolutely necessary for the service of the asylum, reporting such orders to the Committee of Visitors at their next meeting.

5. To keep a record of all their visits and proceedings, and to make such reports or recommendations as they may see fit; all of which are to be read and confirmed at the next meeting of the House Committee and of the Committee of Visitors, respectively.

CLERK TO THE VISITORS.

1. There shall be a Clerk to the visitors, who shall be considered the law officer and adviser of the Committee of Visitors, and shall prepare all contracts and legal documents. He shall convene and attend all general meetings of the Committee of Visitors, and also the meetings of the House Committee when required, and shall take minutes of all orders and resolutions, and take such steps as may be necessary for carrying them into effect.

2. He shall assist the visitors in their examinations of the asylum books of accounts, the quarterly abstract of expenditure or maintenance, and the accounts of the Treasurer, and in preparing the visitors' annual report for publication.

3. He shall furnish to the Superintendent a copy of all orders made by the committee relating to the institution or its inmates.

4. He shall transact all the ordinary duties of Clerk to the visitors as prescribed by the statute, and as may be directed by the committee.

RESIDENT MEDICAL SUPERINTENDENT.

1. There shall be a Medical Superintendent, who shall be a physician or surgeon and a registered medical practitioner. He shall be resident in the asylum, shall give up the whole of his time to the duties of his office, and shall not attend to or engage in any professional or other business or employment except that of the asylum.

2. He shall have paramount authority in the asylum, subject to that of the Visitors; shall have control over all the officers, attendants, and

servants, and shall superintend and direct their duties as prescribed by the regulations and orders of the Committee of Visitors. He shall be empowered to hire, suspend, or discharge all attendants and servants, subject to the approval and confirmation of the House Committee at their next meeting, when such hiring, suspension, or dismissal shall be reported.

3. He shall be responsible for the condition of the patients, and for the management of the establishment, and shall have the full direction of the medical, surgical, and moral treatment of the patients, and of all general arrangements within the asylum.

4. Should any case of difficulty or danger arise, he shall have authority to call to his aid in consultation any registered medical practitioner.

5. He shall visit the wards and offices daily, making occasional night visits also, and report to the House Committee any serious irregularities which may fall under his notice.

6. He shall examine every patient shortly after admission, and shall cause proper entries relative thereto to be made in the books kept for that purpose.

7. He shall regulate and determine the diet of the sick and infirm, and shall also from time to time examine and report on the quality of all provisions furnished for the use of the asylum.

8. He shall regulate and determine the bedding and clothing of the patients.

9. In all cases of fatal or dangerous accident, or other emergency, he shall immediately communicate the fact to the Chairman of the Committee of Visitors.

10. He shall not absent himself for more than one night from the asylum, without the previous written consent of one of the Committee of Visitors; nor for more than one week, without the sanction of the Committee of Visitors or the House Committee; and on no occasion shall he leave the asylum unless in charge of the Assistant Medical Officer, or of some other properly qualified medical substitute.

11. He shall have power to exclude from admission into the asylum persons affected with cholera, or any disease or malady which may be considered contagious or infectious, and persons coming from any district or place in which any such disease or malady may be prevalent.

12. He shall keep a journal, in which he shall record the name of every attendant and servant whom he shall hire, suspend, or dismiss, together with the date and cause of such hiring, suspension, or dismissal. Also the name of every patient fit to be discharged, or likely to be benefited by being allowed a period of absence on trial. Also the case of every escape, death, and inquest, with such particulars as may be necessary for the Committee of Visitors to be made acquainted. Also all such other facts, observations, and suggestions as he shall deem important, relative to the condition or management of the asylum or the patients therein. And all such entries shall be read as part of the proceedings at the next meeting of the House Committee, or Committee of Visitors, respectively.

13. He shall make a yearly report of the number of admissions, discharges, and deaths during the year, and shall, in the same report, describe the general condition of the patients, the state and management of the asylum, and such other matters as he shall deem necessary or the Committee of Visitors may direct.

ASSISTANT MEDICAL OFFICER.

1. There shall be an Assistant Medical Officer, who shall be a member of the Royal College of Surgeons of London, Edinburgh, or Dublin, and a Registered Medical Practitioner. He shall be nominated to the Committee of Visitors on his appointment by the Medical Superintendent, under whose control and direction he shall perform his duties. He shall be resident in the asylum and shall give up the whole of his time to the duties of his office.

2. He shall not leave the asylum when the Superintendent is absent, at which time he is to be held responsible for the management of the Institution. In his own occasional absence, he shall conform to the directions he may receive from the Medical Superintendent, as to its duration and the period of his return. Should, however, he desire to be away from the asylum for more than one night, the written consent of some member of the Committee of Visitors must also be obtained.

3. He shall exercise a general control over the conduct of the attendants and servants, and immediately report any misconduct, irregularity, or neglect of duty on their part to the Medical Superintendent.

4. He shall have charge of the dispensary, and shall be responsible for the safe and proper custody of the drugs, surgical instruments, and appliances.

CHAPLAIN.

1. There shall be a Chaplain, who shall be a clergyman of the Church of England, in priest's orders, and shall be licensed by the bishop of the diocese. He shall devote the whole of his time to the duties of his office, and not hold any other engagement.

2. He shall perform divine service, according to the rites of the Church of England, in the chapel of the asylum, every Sunday, Christmas day and Good Friday, preaching short sermons on each occasion.

3. He shall administer the holy sacrament to such of the officers and servants as may be desirous of receiving the same, at least four times in a year, and to such of the patients as he may think advisable, with the approbation of the Superintendent.

4. He shall consider all the household under his spiritual care.

5. He shall attend daily at the asylum, and administer religious consolation to the patients, subject however to the directions of the Committee of Visitors and of the Medical Superintendent.

6. He shall read morning prayers daily at such hours as the Committee of Visitors and the Medical Superintendent may direct.

7. He shall, under the general control and with the coöperation of the Medical Superintendent, organize and direct the schools for the patients of both sexes, and also classes for instruction in the Bible and in singing; and shall take charge of the library, and control the issue of books and periodicals.

8. He shall keep a daily journal in which he shall enter the hours of his attendance, and such other particulars as it may be desirable for the Committee of Visitors to know, which journal shall be laid before the Committee at every meeting.

9. He shall never absent himself from his duties on any Sunday, or for more than two days during the week, without leave in writing of one Visitor, and on providing some other clergyman, to be approved of by such Visitor, to supply his place.

10. He shall present an annual report to the Committee of Visitors, stating the result of his attendance on the patients.

TREASURER.

1. There shall be a Treasurer, to whom all monies shall be paid. He shall keep accounts of all monies received and paid by him and make them up to the thirty-first of December, annually, and state the balance (if any) then in his hands.

2. He shall give security for a sum to be named by the Committee of Visitors.

CLERK AND STEWARD.

1. There shall be a Clerk of the Asylum, who shall act as Steward. He shall perform all the duties of both those offices, under the control and direction of the Medical Superintendent, to whom he shall immediately report whatever he may know to be improper or contrary to the rules in the economy of the house or conduct of the servants. He shall be resident in the asylum and shall give up the whole of his time to the duties of his office.

2. He shall make all the necessary returns to the Commissioners in Lunacy and other authorities, as prescribed by the various Acts of Parliament relating to lunatics.

3. He shall take care of all the books and papers (except those relating to medical duties), and of all the stores, and shall be responsible for the quality, quantity, and safe keeping of all the articles received.

4. He shall examine and superintend the weighing and measuring of all the goods and provisions furnished to the establishment, and immediately report to the Superintendent any failure in the quality or quantity thereof, and take his instructions thereon. He shall order nothing except under the signature of the Superintendent, and receive nothing into the asylum without an invoice, which must be signed by himself in token of its correctness, and then filed.

5. He shall superintend the weighing and measuring out of the provisions so as to suit the diet tables; he shall take stock once a quarter and keep quarterly accounts of all moneys received of and paid to the Treasurer, and also of all goods ordered and payments made for the same, in such form as the Committee of Visitors shall direct.

6. He shall distinguish the building account from the maintenance account, and the accounts of the county from those of the unions and parishes; and shall lay an abstract of the accounts before the next meeting of the House Committee and of the Committee of Visitors, after the termination of each quarter, showing the moneys received and paid and the unions and parishes in arrear.

7. He shall keep all such books of accounts, and in such forms as may be ordered from time to time by the Committee of Visitors, so as to show the true state of the accounts. These books shall be kept in his office and be subject at all times to the inspection of any member of the committee and of the Medical Superintendent, to whom he shall supply such financial and other information as he may from time to time require.

8. He shall conduct such correspondence as the Medical Superintendent may direct, to whom he must submit all letters received by him

relating to the asylum and its inmates, all of which letters are to be considered the property of the institution. He shall keep copies of all correspondence, whether replies to letters or otherwise.

9. He shall keep inventories of all the household goods, furniture, farming and artisans' implements, official books, medical instruments, and other property of the institution.

10. In his occasional absence from the asylum he shall conform to the directions he may receive from the Medical Superintendent as to its duration and the period of his return. Should, however, he desire to be away from the asylum for more than one night, the consent of some member of the Committee of Visitors must be obtained.

11. He shall give satisfactory security by such sureties as the Committee of Visitors shall from time to time require.

HOUSEKEEPER.

1. There shall be a housekeeper, who shall perform her duties under the control and direction of the Medical Superintendent, to whom she shall immediately report whatever she may know to be improper or contrary to the rules in the economy of the house or conduct of the servants. She shall be resident in the asylum, and shall give up the whole of her time to the duties of her office.

2. She shall have charge of the entire kitchen and laundry departments, the officers' and servants' apartments, and central offices, and be responsible for their cleanliness and good order. She shall use her utmost endeavors to prevent waste, and to check any misapplication of stores.

3. She shall have authority over the female servants, directing them in their several duties; and be responsible for the safety and conduct of all patients employed in any of the departments over which she has control.

4. She shall superintend the preparation of the meals for the patients, officers, attendants, and servants, and shall see that the articles of food are properly cooked, and served with neatness and punctuality at the appointed hours.

5. She shall superintend and be responsible for the washing, airing, and regular distribution of all articles sent to the laundry department.

6. She shall receive from the steward once weekly all necessary materials to be converted into clothing, bedding, etc., for the establishment. She shall cut out and supply to the wards, through the head female attendant, all needlework necessary for the employment of the patients; and when made, return all the articles to the steward, stating their number, with a detailed account of the conversion of the raw material.

7. In her occasional absence from the asylum she shall conform to the directions she may receive from the Medical Superintendent as to its duration and the period of her return. Should, however, she desire to be away from the asylum for more than one night, the written consent of some member of the Committee of Visitors must also be obtained.

HEAD ATTENDANTS—MALE AND FEMALE.

1. There shall be a head male and a head female attendant, who shall perform their duties under the control and direction of and as prescribed by the Medical Superintendent, to whom they shall immediately report

whatever they may know to be improper or contrary to the rules in the economy of the house or conduct of the attendants. They shall give up their whole time and attention to the duties of their office.

2. They shall instruct the attendants in the performance of their duties, and shall at all times require the strictest obedience to any orders which they may give.

GENERAL MANAGEMENT.

1. The male and female patients shall be kept in separate wards, and no male attendant, servant, or patient shall be allowed to enter the female wards, nor any female to enter the male wards, except in discharge of their duty, or with adequate authority. In visiting the female patients, the medical officer shall be accompanied by the head attendant, or some other female officer, and no male shall enter the female wards, unless accompanied by a female attendant. Any male attendant or servant found in any portion of the women's wards, unless he can give a satisfactory explanation for his being there to the Superintendent, may be immediately dismissed.

2. There shall be such a number of attendants as shall be sufficient for the effective supervision of the patients, both by day and night; and no ward shall at any time be left without at least one attendant.

3. During the day the patients of both sexes shall be employed as much as practicable out of doors; the men in gardening and husbandry, the women in occupations suited to their ability; and as a principle in treatment, endeavors shall be continually used to occupy the minds of the patients, to induce them to take exercise in the open air, and to promote cheerfulness and happiness among them.

4. The male patients shall be encouraged to follow their particular callings, and to learn shoemaking, tailoring, and other common useful trades. Needlework, strawwork, and other suitable employments shall be provided for the female patients. And they shall be rewarded by such indulgences as the Superintendent may deem compatible with their welfare and encouragement.

5. An ample supply of books, and cheap publications of a cheerful nature, in addition to Bibles and prayer books, shall be provided, and replaced in case of destruction; and various methods of in and out door amusements shall be placed at the disposal of the patients of both sexes, and they shall be encouraged to have frequent recourse thereto.

6. Ample and special provision shall be made for the effective watching of the asylum and attention to the patients during the night.

7. No patient, on any account whatever, shall be struck, or threatened, or spoken harshly to; and no patient shall be placed in restraint or seclusion, or subjected to any bath (except for the purpose of cleanliness), except by the authority of one of the medical officers.

8. All the attendants shall be responsible for the safety, cleanliness, and general condition of the patients, and for the ventilation, proper warmth, and good order of their respective wards.

9. No officers, excepting the Treasurer and the Clerk to the Visitors, shall have any occupation unconnected with the asylum, nor shall they have any interest, directly or indirectly, in any other establishment for the reception and treatment of lunatic, imbecile, or idiotic patients.

10. No officer, attendant, or servant shall, directly or indirectly, take any fee, reward, or perquisite of any kind from any tradesman, patient, or other person, on pain of immediate dismissal.

11. Relatives and friends of patients shall be allowed to visit them once in every week, between the hours of ten and four o'clock, and on such other days and hours as the Superintendent shall in special cases permit; but no visitor shall be permitted to see any patient if the Superintendent shall state in writing that the visit will be injurious to the patient or otherwise inexpedient.

12. Patients shall be at liberty to hold private conversation with those who visit them, but no male visitor shall remain in a room with a female patient, nor a female visitor with a male patient, except in the presence of an attendant or other third person.

13. The person of every patient shall immediately after admission be carefully examined by the head attendant, who shall at once personally report in writing to one of the medical officers the bodily condition of the patient, and especially of any mark, bruise, or injury of any kind, bedsores, ruptures, or the slightest symptom of disease or disorder of any kind; and it shall be the duty of one of the medical officers, upon receiving notice of the existence of any injury or apparent bodily disorder, at once himself to make a personal examination of the patient; and no relieving officer or other person bringing a patient to the asylum shall be allowed to leave the premises until such report or examination shall have been made.

14. All parish officers shall be encouraged to visit the patients belonging to their union or parish once in every three months, or oftener, on a week day; and to make particular inquiries from time to time as to the treatment experienced by the patients, and their fitness for discharge.

15. Notice shall be given to the nearest relative in the case of serious illness to any patient, and especially where a fatal termination is anticipated. On the death of a patient, notice shall be immediately given to the coroner of the district, the parish officers, the registrar of the district, and the nearest relations of the deceased (if their address be known), and the body shall be delivered to the latter if requested. If the body be not removed early on the fourth day after death, it shall be buried under the direction of the Superintendent, who shall have power to order an earlier interment, if from any particular circumstance he shall consider such to be necessary.

16. Such patients as the Superintendent may direct shall in such number and at such times as he may think fit, be allowed, under proper care, to take walks or excursions beyond the grounds of the asylum; and he shall also be empowered, at his discretion, to permit patients to spend the day with their friends.

Approved.

(Signed)   GATHORNE HARDY.
WHITEHALL, 28th October, 1867.

PROPOSED CASE BOOK—(ENGLISH).

NAME.   ADMITTED.

AGE AND SEX.   STATE AS TO MARRIAGE.   EDUCATION.

WHERE FROM.   OCCUPATION.   RELIGION.

History:

CAUSATION. { Previous attacks. | Where treated.
Hereditary history. | Disposition and habits in
Predisposing. | health.
Exciting. }

DURATION OF DISEASE.

FIRST { Mental.
SYMPTOMS. { Bodily.

RECENT { Mental.
SYMPTOMS. { Bodily.
{ Suicidal.   Dangerous.

Other facts.

State on Admission.

MIND. { Exaltation.
Depression.
Excitement.
Enfeeblement.
Memory.
Coherence.
Can answer questions.
Delusions.
Other abnormalities. }

BODY. { Appearance.
Color of hair.   Color of eyes.
Muscularity.   Fatness.
Nervous system.
Reflex action.   Pupils.
Special senses.   Retina.
Lungs.
Heart.   Pulse.
Other organs.
Tongue.   Appetite.
Urine, specific gravity.   Urinary deposits.
Menstruation.   Temperature.
Hight.   Weight. }

NAME OF DISEASE.   GENERAL BODILY STATE.

Date.	Temperature.		Pulse.		Weight	Progress of Case.
	Morn'g	Even'g	Morn'g	Even'g		

[Memoranda to be put in beginning of Case Book.]

HISTORY.

PREVIOUS ATTACKS.   Number, character of each.

HEREDITARY HISTORY.   Age of parents, relationship of parents or grand parents, health of same, family diseases or peculiarities—consumption, epilepsy, drunkenness.

PREDISPOSING CAUSES.   Drunkenness, overwork, character of vocation or habits. Food, tobacco, tea, infantile diseases, adult diseases. Catamenial irregularities, marriage, children, difficult labors, miscarriages, lactation, etc.

EXCITING AND PROXIMATE CAUSES.   Disease of brain emotions—blows on the head, drinking bouts, fever, poisons, over-sexual excitement, childbirth.

STATE ON ADMISSION MORE FULLY AND SYSTEMATICALLY ARRANGED.

A.—BODILY CONDITION.   a, Hight.
b, Weight.
c, Temperature.
d, Color of hair (baldness).
e, Muscularity.
f, Fatness.
g, Expression of face and general appearance.
h, Any special injuries or wounds to be noted.

B.—VEGETATIVE FUNCTIONS.   a, Digestive—Tongue, stomach, appetite, condition of bowels.
b, Dermic—Conditions as to moistness, eruptions, and other abnormalities.
c, Circulatory—Pulse, cardiac murmurs, flushing of face, or inject of conjunctiva.

d, Respiratory—State of lungs, breath, rapidity of respiration.

e, Glandular—Exam. of urine, state of liver, spleen, thyroid, etc.

C.—REPRODUCTIVE FUNC-
TIONS.

a, Abnorm. of penis or testes in men—masturbation, syphilis, etc.

b, In women—Catamenia, discharges, syphili, pregnancy, nursing, etc.

D.—NERVOUS SYSTEM.

a, Paralysis, epilepsy, catalepsy, hysteria, and other abnormalities unconnected with the special senses or mental functions.

b, Special senses—

1.—Sight—*a,* Color of iris.
    b, Shape and size of pupils.
    c, Condition of retina.
    d, Vision.
    e, Knowledge of color.
    f, Hallucinations.
    g, Illusions.

2.—Hearing—*a,* External ear.
    b, Deafness.
    c, Hallucinations.
    d, Illusions.

3.—Smell—*a,* Any abnormality of nose.
    b, Sense of smell.
    c, Hallucinations.
    d, Illusions.

4.—Taste—*a,* Sense of.
    b, Hallucinations.
    c, Illusions.

5.—Touch and Nervous Sensibility—
    a, Sense of pain.
    b, Reflex action.
    c, Hyperæsthesia.
    d, Illusions and hallucinations, including those of internal organs.

E.—MENTAL SYMPTOMS,
unconnected with the
special senses.

a, Apparent consciousness.
b, Identity.
c, Attention.
d, Coherence of language.
e, Memory—*a* for recent events, *b* for past ditto.
f, Exaltation or depression of spirits.
g, Excitement of manner.

h, Habits and propensities (filthy, dangerous,
   suicidal, destructive, indecent, etc.)
i, As to sleep.
j, Delusions—not being hallucinations or illusions.
k, Other abnormalities.

———

NOVA SCOTIA CASE BOOK.

Registered No.   Previous Nos.
Name
  Admitted—
Where from
Brought by
Order of
Maintenance
Certificates
Age   last birthday
Sex   state as to marriage
Occupation
Natural disposition
Habits in health
Education
Religion
Address of nearest friend

HISTORY.

Age at first attack
 First ⎫ Bodily
Symptoms ⎭ Mental
No. and duration ⎰
of previous attacks ⎱
Where treated
    ⎰ Hereditary history
Causation ⎨ Predisposing
    ⎱ Exciting
Duration of present attack
 Recent ⎫ Bodily
Symptoms ⎭ Mental
Suicidal, and how
Dangerous, and how
Other facts

Name,

Date.	Temperature.		Pulse.		Weight	Progress of Case.
	Morn'g	Even'g	Morn'g	Even'g		

MICHIGAN ASYLUM FOR THE INSANE.

SITUATION.

The Michigan Asylum for the Insane is situated at Kalamazoo, upon the Michigan Central Railroad. The location is probaby as central and convenient as any that could have been chosen, having reference both to the present means of communication with the various parts of the State, and to any other routes of travel likely to be projected hereafter. The site selected for the building is upon an irregular eminence, about one mile from the village, and sufficiently elevated above the valley of the Kalamazoo River to secure an extensive prospect, and yet is well sheltered and easy of access from the plain below. The location is in every respect healthful and desirable, and well adapted to the purposes and objects of an institution for the treatment of mental diseases.

FARM.

The amount of land originally purchased for the use of the asylum was one hundred and sixty acres, but to secure a more desirable site for the buildings, an adjacent tract was subsequently added, making the whole amount of land in the possession of the institution one hundred and sixty-eight acres (167 76-100). Most of the land is finely timbered with the original growth of oak, hickory, and other trees, affording every facility which could be desired for beautifying the grounds. That in the rear of the building is broken, and falls, by a series of ravines covered with trees, about eighty feet to the valley below, through which flows a small but rapid stream of pure water. The buildings themselves will cover an area of one and one third acres. It is designed to preserve about fifty acres in groves and woodland, with walks and drives, and the remainder will be devoted to ordinary agricultural purposes.

41

GENERAL PLAN.

The ground plan was furnished by Doctor John P. Gray, the accomplished Superintendent of the New York State Lunatic Asylum at Utica, under whose directions the work was commenced. It might here be remarked that the principles laid down in a series of propositions relative to the construction and arrangement of hospitals for the insane, unanimously adopted by the "Association of Medical Superintendents of American Institutions for the Insane," have been fully carried out in the plans adopted by the Board. The form and internal arrangements of the institution will be readily understood by reference to the accompanying ground plan. The asylum building proper, the main front of which has an easterly aspect, consists of a centre and six wings. The centre portion of the main building is divided by the entrance hall into two nearly equal parts. That to the right contains, in front, the principal office of the institution, the apothecary shop, and an anteroom communicating by a private stairway with the Superintendent's apartments above, and in the rear the matron's room and ladies' reception room; while that to the left contains, in front, the public parlor and officers' dining room, and immediately behind these the steward's office and men's reception room. The second floor is appropriated exclusively to the use of the Medical Superintendent. Upon the third floor are the apartments of the Assistant Physicians, steward, and matron. The basement contains the laboratory connected with the apothecary shop, and the officers' kitchen and storerooms. Immediately behind the centre building is the chapel, and still further in the rear the engine and boiler house. Extending from the centre building toward the south for males, and toward the north for females, are the several wards of the institution, nine on each side, including the infirmaries.

MATERIALS.

The material used in construction is brick, covered with Roman cement and sand, and finished to represent freestone. The window caps, sills, and brackets, belt courses, and capitals in front, are of white limestone from the Athens quarries, near Chicago. The division walls throughout are of brick. The Asylum is built upon a system of fireproof construction, nearly all the floors being laid upon brick arches sprung from iron girders, which, beside providing against fire, give additional security to the building and insure its durability.

ARCHITECTURE.

The plans selected by the Board of Trustees were placed in the hands of A. H. Jordan, architect, of Detroit, for the necessary elevations, details, etc. The style adopted is the Italian, it being the lightest, most cheerful, and least expensive for the effect required in such an extensive range of buildings.

REFERENCES TO THE PLATE.

(A) public parlor; (B) general office; (C) Matron's room; (D) Steward's office; (E E) reception rooms; (F) officers' dining room; (G) apothecary shop; (H) anteroom, communicating by a private stairway with the Superintendent's apartments above; (I) Steward's storeroom;

(J J) matron's storerooms; (K) associated dormitories; (L) attendants' rooms; (M) day and recreation rooms; (N) parlors; (O) dining rooms; (U) chapel, having below it the kitchen and storerooms; (1) boiler house; (2) engine and fanrooms; (3) laundry; (4) drying room; (5) ironing room; (6) work shops; (7 7 7) covered corridors.

APPROPRIATION OF WARDS.

The various wards in the institution are appropriated as follows:

Nos.	Classification.	No. of wards.	Number of beds.		Total of each sex and class.
			Single rooms.	Associated dormit's.	
1 and 2	Convalescent and quiet..........	4	80	16	96
3 and 4	Less disturbed.....................	4	56	32	88
5 and 6	More disturbed....................	4	60	....	60
7	Demented	2	20	....	20
8	Demented and infirm.............	2	12	....	12
9	Acute cases, etc., (Infirmaries)..	2	12	....	12
	Total................	18	240	....	288

The divisions for the sexes are equal. Eight of these wards, inclusive of the infirmaries, are upon the first floor, six upon the second, and four upon the third floor of the transverse wings. It is considered that by means of these any desirable classification of patients may be carried out.

ARRANGEMENT OF WARDS.

Each ward has the usual arrangement of corridor, sleeping rooms, day rooms, and dining room, with two stairways, a clothes room, lavatory, bath room, water closet, soiled clothes shaft, drying shaft, and dust flue to each. The corridors in the first, second, and third wings are, respectively, one hundred and fifty-five, one hundred and sixty, and seventy feet long, and in the third stories of the first and second transverse wings, one hundred and nineteen and thirty-four feet long. They are uniformly twelve feet wide, and, in common with all other rooms, sixteen feet in height upon the first and third floors, and fifteen upon the second. The dimensions of the single sleeping rooms are eight and ten by eleven feet, with an average cubic capacity of fourteen hundred feet. The associated dormitories are fourteen by twenty-one feet, and the parlors or recreation rooms, eighteen by twenty. Lateral recesses, extending into the projecting towers in front, form additional day rooms in the first and second wings on either side. The dining rooms are sufficiently capacious to accommodate the number for which they are intended, and are supplied with detached sinks, cupboards, and dumb waiters. The closets, bath rooms, lavatories, and clothes rooms open upon an adjacent and not upon the main hall, giving a very desirable privacy. The bath and closet fixtures are of approved construction, and, to prevent all possible danger from leakage, the service pipes are conveyed in a separate pipe shaft—an arrangement which also facilitates and cheapens any repairs that may become necessary. Drying shafts, having lattice-work floors and communicating directly with the ventilating cupolas, furnish a ready means of drying mops, wet cloths, damp brooms, etc., and thus materially assist in promoting the cleanliness and healthfulness of the corridors. To prevent exposure, the bathrooms and lavatories have communicating doors, in order that the latter may serve, on " bathing days," as dressing rooms to the former.

INFIRMARIES.

In a detached building, in the rear of the first transverse wings, but connected with the wards by means of a covered corridor, an infirmary is provided for each sex. Fitted up with every convenience, they provide a very desirable place for the treatment of acute cases, of those who are seriously ill, or of any requiring special care and frequent medical attention. They can be reached at all hours of the night without disturbing any other portion of the house; they provide the means of isolation in case of the occurrence of any infectious or contagious diseases in the institution, and give to the friends of dying patients an opportunity of administering to them in their last moments.

WINDOWS.

The windows are fitted throughout with a castiron sash, the upper half of which alone is glazed. Posterior to the lower half, and immediately against it is a wooden sash of corresponding size and shape, moving free and suspended by a cord and weight; the former being attached to the bottom of the sash and passing over a pulley near its top, is always entirely concealed. The panes of glass are six by nine inches in size. The windows, where deemed desirable, are protected by a shutter of framed wicker work, sliding into the wall and retained there, as also in its position, by one and the same lock.

FLOORING.

The floors in all uncarpeted rooms are formed of one and one half inch oak plank, grooved and tongued, and none of them being more than three and one half inches in width. The sleepers and the iron girders supporting the arches rest upon an offset in the wall, which, when finished, also forms the cornice in the room below.

PROVISION AGAINST FIRE.

The horrible sacrifice of human life on the occasion of the burning of an institution for the insane in one of the eastern States, and the peculiar liability of these buildings to take fire, as shown by the frequent occurrence of such accidents, determined the Board of Trustees, although it would somewhat increase the price of construction, to make the asylum fireproof. The more recent partial destruction by fire of another institution has confirmed the wisdom of this decision. The use of iron girders and brick arches as a support for the floors was consequently determined upon, and to secure additional safety all connection between the wings and the center building is entirely cut off by the interposition of a verandah of iron and glass, with communication from one to the other only through fireproof doors. The location of the heating apparatus and the kitchen, in detached buildings, renders the institution quite exempt from danger of destruction by fire.

CHAPEL.

A separate building immediately in the rear of the centre building, seventy by forty feet in size, contains upon its first floor a room for chapel purposes capable of seating three hundred and eighty persons. It communicates with the different wards by means of covered corridors, is appropriately fitted up, properly warmed, and lighted with gas.

KITCHEN.

One central kitchen is intended to supply the whole institution. It is placed immediately beneath the chapel room, with storerooms near at hand, and communicates with the dumbwaiters of the different dining-rooms by means of a small car moving upon a covered railway. The building containing the chapel room and kitchen is surmounted by a bell and clock tower.

WARMING AND VENTILATION.

It is now admitted, as a principle, that the warming and ventilation of buildings corresponding in size and purpose with institutions for the insane should be effected by one and the same process; and also that means should be adopted for expelling the foul air to the same extent and simultaneously with the admission of fresh. The fact is also established, and in many asylums has been confirmed by a costly experience, that the ordinary system of making the ventilation depend upon the spontaneous action of warm-air currents failed to give satisfactory results. A perfect and equable distribution of fresh air, either warm or cold, and the necessary rapidity in the discharge of foul air, under all circumstances and in all seasons, can be secured only by a system of *forced* ventilation. This is found to be most efficiently and economically effected by means of a fan driven by a steam engine—effectual, because at all times under perfect control; and economical, because the warm air is more thoroughly and rapidly distributed. The primary cost is not great; it is not liable to get out of order, and the motive power is that required for other purposes. The system decided upon is a modification of that in use at the New York State Lunatic Asylum, the efficiency of which is shown by the fact that in five similar institutions in other States it has since been adopted in place of furnaces and other means of heating and ventilation already in operation. It consists of boilers, an engine, a fan, heating surface, and distributing ducts, and inlet flues, with exit flues, foul air ducts, and ventilating cupolas. The boilers are four in number; these, with the engine and fan (the latter peculiar from the circumstance of its delivering the air in the direction of its axis), and the heating surface, consisting of a series of wrought-iron pipes, are all in a separate and detached building. The air, after its delivery from the fan, passes directly forward beneath the chapel. The main duct conveying it gives off a small branch to the chapel, and another to the centre building; it then branches toward either wing, and another subdivision is made, one portion passing beneath the first longitudinal wing, and the other, entering the proximal end of the second wing, passes on to the end of the extreme wing. The air passage beneath the building occupies the middle portion of the basement, or rather the space immediately beneath the floors of the corridors, and the distributing flues pass up in the walls upon either side of them. Exit flues are carried up in the same walls, taking their departure from two points, one near the ceiling, and the other near the floor of the rooms on either side; these again conjoin in the attics to form the foul air ducts and empty out into the open air through the ventilating cupolas. Downward currents of air, for the ventilation of the water closets, will be secured through an arrangement of pipes terminating in the fire boxes of the boilers.

LAUNDRY AND WORKSHOPS.

The right wing of the engine and boilerhouse contains the washroom, drying and ironing rooms; and a similar wing upon the other side furnishes convenient rooms for the usual workshops. A close partition running from the rear of the chapel to the engine house, with a covered passageway on either side, provides ready and protected access to the shops and ironing rooms from the various wards in the house, and at the same time prevents all communication between the sexes.

WATER.

Water for drinking purposes is drawn from a well, while that for bathing and laundry purposes is forced up from a stream flowing in the valley, immediately in the rear of the institution.

DRAINAGE AND SEWERAGE.

Cast iron pipes will be used for connecting drainage in the rear of the wings, and will pass forward beneath the building at a single point only on either side. The drains and branch sewers will unite in front, and pour into the common sewer, which is of brick, egg-shaped, three feet high, and two feet wide. This runs down the ravine in front of the institution, and empties into a depot for the collection of solid material.

ILLUMINATION.

It is now universally conceded that gas is the only proper material to be used in lighting asylums for the insane. To obviate the only objection to its manufacture upon the premises, the gashouse will be placed just below the depot referred to. The gas main will be carried up to the institution in the sewer, attached to its upper arch.

The completeness of this description renders any further analysis of the internal arrangement of the institution quite unnecessary. To those familiar with the construction of asylums for the insane a reference to the engraving and lithograph will supply any omission that may have occurred. The plans of the building, as given in the preceding sketch, have been submitted to and received the unqualified approval of many of the more experienced physicians in charge of similar institutions; and from those most capable of judging, the Board have received the gratifying assurance that their efforts to combine in one the acknowledged excellences of several recently erected establishments, with such improvements as careful study and experienced assistance suggested, have not been unsuccessful.

In the accompanying plate, all portions of the institution represented in shaded lines 'are already built, with the exception of the " Infirmary for Males " and the chapel and kitchen. The portions represented in outline constitute, collectively, the north wing.

" Hall No. 1 " constitutes the portion known as the first longitudinal division. Adjoining it at the left is the first transverse division, which is connected with the second transverse division by the second longitudinal, designated as " Hall No. 3." " Hall No. 5 " and the wards beyond it are collectively known as the extreme wing. The transverse divisions are three and all other portions of the wing two stories high. The divisions of the north wing are the same.

REFERENCES.—A, Trustees' room; B, general office; C, Matron's room; D, Steward's office; E, E, reception rooms; F, dining room; G, medical office; H, safe on the left and water closet on the right; K, associated dormitories; M, recesses; N, day rooms; O, ward dining rooms; U, chapel and kitchen; 1, boiler room; 2, engine room; 3, laundry; 4, drying room; 5 and 6, ironing and distributing rooms; 8, fan room.

PENNSYLVANIA HOSPITAL FOR THE INSANE.

The Pennsylvania Hospital for the Insane, as now constituted, consists of two distinct buildings, each complete in itself, having separate pleasure grounds and inclosures, both situated, however, on the same tract of one hundred and thirteen acres of land originally purchased by the institution. The hospital just completed is styled " the Department for Males," and that which has been in use during the last nineteen years, " the Department for Females." Both departments remain as heretofore under the charge of a Physician in Chief, and who now has as associate officers one or more assistant physicians, a steward, and a Matron in each building.

This new hospital faces to the west, and consists of a centre building, with wings running north and south, making a front of five hundred and twelve feet; of other wings, connected with each of those just referred to, running east a distance of one hundred and sixty-seven feet, all three stories high, and these last having at their extreme ends communications with extensive one-storied buildings. All the exterior walls are of stone, stuccoed, and the interior are of brick.

This arrangement gives provision for the accommodation of sixteen distinct classes of male patients in the new building, as the same number of classes of females are now provided for in that previously in use. Each one of these sixteen wards has connected with it, besides the corridors for promenading and the chambers of the patients and attendants, a parlor, a dining room, a bath room, a water closet, a urinal, a sink room, a wash room, a drying closet, a storeroom for brushes and buckets, a clothes room, a dumb waiter, a dust flue, and a stairway passing out of doors, if desired, without communication with the other wards; and every room in the building, almost without exception, has a flue communicating with the fresh air duct for warm or cool air, according to the season (and hereafter to be referred to), and with the main ventilating trunks which terminate in the various ventilators on the roof of the building.

The centre building is one hundred and fifteen by seventy-three feet. It has a handsome Doric portico of granite in front, and is surmounted by a dome of good proportions, in which are placed the iron tanks from which the whole building is supplied with water. The lantern on the dome is one hundred and nineteen feet from the pavement, and from it is a beautiful panoramic view of the fertile and highly improved surrounding country, the Delaware and Schuylkill Rivers, and the City of Philadelphia, with its many prominent objects of interest. In the basement or first story of the centre building is the main kitchen, forty-two by twenty-four feet, in which are improved arrangements for cooking—a scullery, twenty-four by eleven; two storerooms, each about twenty by twenty-two feet; a trunk room, twenty-four by twelve feet; a general clothes room, a bread room, a dining room for the officers, another for the domestics, a lodging room for the seamstress, another for the supervisor of the basement, a stairway to the main story, and a dumb waiter leading from the kitchen to the cellar, and another to the upper rooms of the centre building. The cellars under the centre building, besides containing the hot air chambers for that division of the house, have three distinct rooms for storage, which are ventilated by means of flues leading out through the roof of the house. In front of the basement and under the steps and adjoining roadway are the vaults for coal for the kitchen and bake room, and the ice house, the latter being ventilated as mentioned for the cellars; and carts unload into both, through openings in the blue stone flagging, which forms the roadway upon the arches below. Adjoining the ice house is a small apartment with stone shelves, for keeping food cool in Summer; and alongside the coal vault is a space for the offal from the kitchen. There is also a small kitchen near the scullery, and intended for the Superintendent's family, whenever it is required for the purpose. In one of the storerooms is a dark apartment, and in another the tanks for the oxygen and hydrogen gases used in the dissolving apparatus.

On the second or principal story is the lecture room, forty-two by twenty-four feet, in the lecturer's table of which, water, steam, and gas, for experimental purposes have been introduced. It also contains commodious cases for apparatus, a blackboard running on a track behind the cases, and a smooth surface twenty-four by eighteen feet, at its eastern end, on which the dissolving views are shown. On the opposite side of the main corridor is a reception room for visitors, and a room for visits to patients by their friends, each being twenty-four by twenty-three feet. There are also on this floor two small rooms for more private visits, the medical office and library, which is also the Assistant Physician's office, twenty-four by fourteen feet, with a small storeroom, containing a sink, etc., adjoining; the lodging room for the Assistant Physician having charge of the medical office, with which it communicates; a general business office, which is also that of the steward, twenty-four by twenty feet; a manager's room, twenty-four by nineteen feet, which is also the Principal Physician's private office; a parlor twenty-four by nineteen feet, for the use of the officers of the house, and a fire-proof, eleven by nine feet, in connection with the general business office. In the third story front are four fine rooms, each twenty-four by twenty-one feet; a corridor, forty-two by sixteen feet, shut off from the adjoining portion by a ground glass partition; a bathing room, water closet, and clothes closets, intended at some future day for the use of the family of the superintending physician, whenever such an officer may be specially connected with that department. There are also on this floor, chambers for the Steward and Matron, for the Senior Assistant Physician, three others that may be used as deemed expedient, and a room twenty-four by eleven feet, lighted from the roof, and intended for a general storeroom for the bedding and other dry goods not actually in use. The corridors of the centre building, running east and west, are sixteen feet wide; those running north and south, in which are the stairways, lighted from the roof, are twelve feet wide. The height of the ceiling of the basement in the centre building, and of all parts of the wings, which is one foot more, is twelve feet. The ceilings in the second or principal and in the third story of the centre, are eighteen feet high.

The wings on each side of the centre building are almost exactly alike, except that on the south side in front, in the basement immediately adjoining the centre, is the ironing room, twenty-eight by eleven feet, with a drying closet, eleven by eleven feet, attached, and in the rear the small kitchen already referred to, and the lodging rooms of the female domestics; while on the north side in corresponding positions, are the bake room, the baker's store and lodging rooms, and the lodging room of the hired men not employed in the wards. On this floor on each side of the centre is also a museum and reading room, forty-two by fourteen feet, and accessible either from the grounds or from the inside of the building; two work rooms for the patients; two lodging rooms for persons employed in the work rooms; a bath room for the officers, and another for the domestics; two water closets, etc. The portion of the wing just described is shut off from the adjoining part (which constitutes the fifth ward) by a thick ground glass partition; this ward having in it a large room, twenty-nine by twenty-four feet, with a bath tub and water closets in a recess; another twenty-four by fourteen feet; a third twenty-three by eleven feet, and five rooms eleven by nine feet, a bath room, drying closet, and all the other conveniences already mentioned as forming a part of each ward. These apartments and arrangements are all intended for patients who are particularly ill, and who require special quiet and seclusion, where they may be visited, if deemed expedient, by their friends without annoyance to others, or interfering with the discipline of the house.

Besides the fifth ward, just described, and which is on the first floor, there are, on each side of the centre, two other stories, each of which constitutes a ward, and with all the conveniences already referred to. The rooms are arranged on both sides of the corridors, which are twelve feet wide, and have their extreme ends mostly filled with glass; while, wherever one wing joins another, there is entirely across it an open space for light and air eight feet wide, glazed with small sash from near the floor to the ceiling; and in the middle of each ward, on one side, is a similar open space, all of which may be used for keeping flowering plants, birds, etc., for having small jets of water, or any other object of interest, and which, in excited wards, may be guarded by ornamental wire work. Each story of the return wing makes a ward similar to those just described. Passing from the return wings into the Supervisor's office, the one-storied buildings are reached. Each of these has provision for twenty-six patients and six attendants, and every arrangement for their comfort. The rooms are here on one side of a corridor ten feet wide, and at the end of each of those running towards the east is a cross hall, in which are three rooms intended particularly for patients who from any cause may require special seclusion. One of the main halls is used for dining, and the other as a sitting room. Between the dining halls of these two wards (the seventh and eighth), and made private by sliding doors, are four rooms intended for excited patients who have special attendants. Opposite these last is a room one hundred and ten by fourteen feet, with an arched ceiling fifteen feet high, with skylights and windows out of reach, intended to be used as a kind of gymnasium, and accessible either from the adjacent garden and yards, or directly from the wards; and in the story below this is a room of the same size, in which are two fine bowling alleys, with reading tables, etc. Both these rooms may be well lighted with gas, and warmed by steam pipe, so that they can be comfortably used in the evening as well as by day, and in all kinds of weather.

The arrangement of these one-storied buildings makes for each two very pleasant yards, in size one hundred and ten by fifty-four feet, surrounded by broad brick pavements, and having grass in the centre, with an open iron palisade in front, giving a distinct though sufficiently distant view of two of the most traveled roads in the vicinity. There is also a yard, three hundred and forty-three by seventy-two feet, adjoining each sixth ward, fitted up as the others, and planted with shade trees. Brick pavements also surround the entire building, making, with those just referred to and those in front, a continuous walk of six thousand one hundred and fifty-two feet.

ENTRANCE.

The entrance to the department for males, as before mentioned, is from Forty-ninth street, between Market and Haverford streets. The gatekeeper's lodge has two comfortable rooms on the north, while on the opposite side of the gateway is a dead room and another for tools used about the grounds. Brick paths on either side of the main roadway lead to the centre building, and the space in front, planted with evergreen and ornamental trees, and having a fountain in the central grassplat, is three hundred and twenty-five by one hundred and seventy-five feet. From the front platform, eight steps lead up to the vestibule and seven steps inside of the building to the level of the principal floor. Visitors passing into the centre building may go out upon a pleasant balcony on its eastern side and overlook the improvements in that direction, but they cannot pass through the grounds.

Ten steps descend from the roadway to the pavement around the basement, which, except immediately at the front of the centre, where it is surrounded by a wide area with sodded banks, is everywhere above ground.

There is also a gate on Market street, near the engine house, used for bringing in coal or other heavy articles, and another on the eastern side of the grounds, for the use of the officers of the hospital only.

ENGINE HOUSE AND LAUNDRY.

The engine house, seventy-one feet from the nearest point of the hospital building, is a substantial stone structure, seventy by sixty-four feet, and two stories in height. The character of the ground is such that carts drive into the second story to discharge the coal directly into the vaults below, and the level of the railroad in the cellar of the hospital brings it upon the second floor of the engine house.

The first story, on the level of the ground on its southern and eastern side, contains vaults capable of containing near five hundred tons of coal. Adjoining these vaults is the boiler room, thirty by seventeen feet, and opening into the engineer's work room, in which will be placed lathes, grindstones, pipe cutting machines, etc., driven by the engines which are in the engine room, twenty three by nineteen feet in size, and separated from the last by a glass partition; while further west, also separated by glazed windows and doors, is the fan room, and the tower for supplying fresh air to the main duct, which leads from it through the entire building. The height of ceiling in this story is seventeen feet, and it is arched over the engine room and the engineer's work room, so as to give a proper support to the stone floor of the room above. In the second story of this building, into which the railroad passes, is the wash room, twenty-seven by twenty-four feet; the room for assorting and folding clothes, twenty-four by fourteen feet; the mangle room, forty-three by eight and a half feet; the drying closet, occupying a space twenty-six by thirteen feet; a water closet, and a large room over the coal vaults and boilers, surrounded by movable blinds, and intended for drying clothes without the use of artificial heat, for making soap, etc.

The carpenter shop, thirty-six by fifty feet, is of frame, two stories high, and forty-five feet from the engine house, from which steam may be taken for warming it in the winter. It has two rooms below, and a single large one above.

The carriage house and stables make a neat stone structure, fifty seven by thirty-six feet, and two stories high. It has accommodations for six horses and as many cows, and the carriages required for the different purposes of the institution. The lower floor is of cement, brick, or blue stone. The piggery is in the yard in the rear of the stables, and there is a carriage yard in front, both being surrounded by a stone wall.

SIZE OF ROOMS.

The height of the ceilings throughout the building, and the size of the parlors, and of all the rooms in the centre of the building, have been already given. The ordinary size of the patients' lodging rooms is nine by eleven feet, while there are some in each ward of a much larger size, many of which have communicating doors and are intended for patients who desire a parlor as well as a chamber, or for those having special attendants. The parlors in the first and third wards are thirty-three by twenty-four feet, and in the second, fourth, and sixth, they are twenty-three by thirty feet. The dining rooms are generally twenty-three by seventeen feet. The bath rooms are mostly nine by eleven feet. Sixteen rooms in each one-storied building have water closets in them, firmly secured, and with a strong downward draught. The sides of doors and windows in patients' rooms are generally rounded, by being built of brick made expressly for the purpose, and smoothly plastered.

WINDOWS AND WINDOW GUARDS.

The windows in patients' rooms are almost universally six feet by two feet nine inches, having twenty lights of glass, six by seventeen inches in each. In the front wings adjoining the centre, and in the third story of the return wings, both sashes are of cast iron, secured in wooden frames, so arranged as to balance each other, rising and falling only to the extent of five and a half inches, and doing away with the necessity for guards. In the other parts of the return wings, and in the one-storied buildings, the windows are of the same size, having the upper sash of cast iron and immovable, the lower being of wood, rising to its full extent and protected by an ornamental wrought iron guard, securely fastened on the outside. A few rooms in each one-story building have small windows out of reach of their occupants, and intended for the temporary seclusion of very violent or mischievous patients. In other parts, as well as in this, wire screens inside of the rooms are occasionally used to protect glass, and ornamental wire work is adopted in some of the parlors, at the ends of corridors and in other similar positions, as a guard outside of the windows.

DOORS.

The doors throughout are made of the best white pine lumber. In the wards they are one and three fourth inches thick, six feet eight inches high by two feet seven inches wide. Each door has eight panels in it, one of which makes a hinged wicket, and what is commonly known as bead and butt, very substantially put together, and wherever special strength is required it is obtained by transverse pieces of iron let into the wood, or by plates of boiler iron screwed on and painted so as to resemble an ordinary door. Each door has a good dead lock to it, and occasionally a mortise bolt is added. Over each door is an unglazed sash, thirty-one by seventeen inches, covered with fine wire on the inside, or a space thirty-one by five inches, which can be filled up at pleasure by a tight board or by wire. Lift hinges have been used for all these doors, which for patients' lodging rooms always open into the corridors.

FLOORS.

The floors throughout are of the best yellow pine, cut to order in Florida and piled up on the grounds two years before it was used. The boards are one inch and a quarter thick, varying in width from two and a quarter to four inches, and put down with secret nailing. Counter ceiling is everywhere used. The only exception to this kind of flooring is in the two kitchens, the scullery, a space in the basement hall in front, the bake room, all the sink, water closet, and wash rooms, the line between different wards, the entrance to the stairways, and the main wash room in the engine house, which are of brown German flagstones laid on brick arches; the engineer's work room, which is paved with brick; the front of the boiler room, which is of iron and blue stone flagging; and the engine room, one sink room, and all the ward stairways, which are of slate, admirably adapted to such a purpose, and which has also been used extensively for window sills, stairways, and other purposes.

STAIRWAYS.

All the stairways in those parts of the building occupied by patients are fire proof. The framework is of cast iron, built into the brick work on each side and covered with slate, which has many advantages. The rise of these steps is only seven inches, and there are platforms every five or six steps, with convenient handrails on both sides from top to bottom. They are all well lighted by windows by day and by gas at night. The well around which the stairs wind is used for hat or coat rooms for the different stories.

PLASTERING.

The inside plastering is what is called hard finish, composed of lime and sand, without plaster of Paris, except for ceilings, and well trowelled. This finish admits of being scrubbed for years without injury, and is at all times ready for painting. The outside of the building is rough cast, the material used being the pulverized stone of which the house is built and lime, to which an agreable shade of color is given by sand. Hydraulic cement is used near the ground in certain positions, in many of the sink and wash rooms, in the kitchen and scullery, in the main wash room, and as a substitute for the ordinary wash boards in many of the ward corridors and patients' chambers.

. ROOFING.

The roof is of Pennsylvania slate, fastened on lath, and plastered with hair mortar on the under and upper edges, and on the joints of the slate. The pitch is one fourth of the span. The water from the roof is carried off through four inch cast iron pipes, inside of the building, and easily accessible, into large drains leading into the main culvert.

. SEWERAGE.

The main culvert is two thousand and thirty-two feet in length. It is thirty-five inches from top to bottom in the clear, built of brick laid in hydraulic cement, egg-shaped, the smaller part being at the bottom. Beginning near the intersection of the north return wing and one-storied buildings, at which point it receives various pipes from the adjacent wards, it passes under the main chimney, by the engine house and barn, and extends to Mill Creek, into which it discharges just before it reaches Market street. Through this culvert all the drainage from the building and much of the grounds is carried off, being intersected by branch culverts at various points in its course.

BATH ROOMS, WATER CLOSETS, ETC.

There are twenty-one bath rooms and as many water closets in the building, in addition to those in the patients' rooms. Sixteen are in the wards. Each bath room has in it a cast iron bath tub, covered with zinc paint, and with improved arrangements for the admission and discharge of water through the bottom. In addition to the ordinary hot air flue, there is a coil of steam pipe for direct radiation in each, so that when hot baths are used the temperature of the room may be made so high as to prevent the sensation of chilliness when coming from the water. The water pipes in these rooms are generally of galvanized iron, left exposed, so as to be readily accessible, and passing from story to story through castings made for the purpose, so that in case of leakage the ceilings may not be injured.

The water closets are of cast iron, enameled, have no traps, but are open, so as to have a constant downward draught of air through them into the main chimney, as have all the sinks, bath tubs, etc., in the whole establishment. The water is let on by the opening of the door.

The wash basins in the wash rooms are of marble, with strong swing cocks. The sinks are of cast iron, and have hot and cold water at each. There is also an iron hopper to each, and into which the slops, etc., are emptied. There are permanent fixtures for securing the towels in each wash room. The drying closets are sufficiently large to contain a bed, and like the closets for buckets, etc., have flues leading into and from them, and thus secure a direct communication with the fan below and the ventilating ducts above. All these arrangements in each ward are clustered together, and have scarcely any wood in any part to absorb moisture or retain unpleasant odors.

SUPPLY OF WATER.

The new hospital is suplied with water from a well twenty-five feet in diameter, containing fifty thousand gallons, and into which, as measured at the dryest period of the last year, is a daily flow of thirty thousand gallons of excellent water. There is also a constant stream of spring water passing near the well, which can at any time be turned into it. By means of one of Worthington's combined direct acting steam pumps, capable of raising ten thousand gallons per hour, this water is forced through seven hundred and eight feet of six inch cast iron pipe into the four boiler iron tanks in the dome, and from which it is distributed through the entire building. These tanks are one hundred and three feet above the well, and contain twenty-one thousand gallons. They are so arranged that one or all may be used at pleasure; have overflows and pipes through which they may have the sediment washed out whenever deemed desirable. The elevation of these tanks is sufficient to secure the feeding of the steam boilers when carrying a pressure of forty pounds to the inch. These tanks were made at the works and put in place before the roof was on the building. It is intended that they shall always be about full of water, and a small pipe leading from them to the engine house tells the engineer on duty when that is the case. There is also in the engine room a single Worthington steam pump, capable of raising five thousand gallons per hour, and intended to prevent any possible deficiency of water should an accident happen to the larger engine. The rule is that both should be used some part of every day, so that in case of emergency there may never be a doubt of their being in working order.

The tank for supplying the centre building with hot water is twelve feet in length and twenty-three inches in diameter, and is placed above the cooking range, the heat being supplied through circulating pipe from a waterback behind one of the range fires, and is abundant for all purposes. The supply of hot water for the wards is derived from six iron tanks placed in the most convenient points in the cellar, in which situations they are easily accessible, and leakages can do little injury to the building. The heat is derived from steam coils coming from the summer pipe (as it is called) used for cooking and all other purposes except warming the building. The large steam boilers at the engine house are supplied with hot water by the condensed steam used in heating, which ordinarily returns to them by gravity, but when it does not is received into an iron tank and forced into them by a small steam pump. The laundry has hot water from a large tank placed in the oven, which covers the boilers, and through which the exhaust steam from the engines and pumps can be made to pass whenever desired, and which may be also used for feeding the large boilers. There are three wells of excellent water besides, at convenient points near the building, and which supplied all the water required in its erection. A fourth is now 'being sunk near the stable.

LIGHTING.

The hospital is lighted by gas from the city works. The fine meter is placed in the engine room, and a record is made every morning of the consumption during the preceding night. Stopcocks are placed at convenient points for checking the flow of gas through the main pipes, and the ordinary kinds of fixtures have been adopted throughout the building. The gas is also used for experimental purposes in the lecture room, and for boiling water, etc., in the medical office.

FURNITURE.

The furniture is intended to be neat and plain, but of a comfortable and substantial character; the amount in the various apartments being in a great measure dependent on the character of the patients occupying them. Carpets of some kind generally cover the parlors, and some portions of the corridors and chambers. Wardrobes, tables, mirrors, and other conveniences are frequently added to the bedsteads, which are of various kinds, mostly of wood, but many are of wrought or cast iron, painted of a light color, a few of which last are secured to the floor.

HEATING AND VENTILATION.

There is no fire used in any part of the hospital for heating, although provision for open fires has been made in all the parlors and in many of the other large rooms, should such an arrangement ever be deemed desirable. The only fires kept up in the building are those in the kitchens, bake and ironing rooms.

In the boiler room at the engine house there are three large tubular boilers. Each of these has a furnace five feet three inches wide by five feet three inches long and seven feet four inches high. The shell is seventeen feet eight inches long by four feet six inches in diameter. Combustion chamber four feet long, and ninety-eight tubes two and a half inches in diameter and eleven feet long. The total heating surface for each is seven hundred and forty-four square feet. The grate surface is twenty and a quarter square feet. The escaping gases enter a common flue, and the draft can be regulated by a damper at the back end of each boiler, or the supply of air graduated by a register in the ashpit door.

These boilers furnish steam for warming the entire hospital, and for driving all the machinery, pumping water, for ventilation, washing, cooking, etc. They are so arranged that one or all may be used at pleasure, either for heating or driving the machinery. The steam is carried from them in a five-inch welded iron pipe, and after reaching the hospital building, it is distributed in eighty-three air chambers, placed in its cellar, with direct flues leading from them to the apartments above. The gases from the boiler fires pass through an underground flue, four feet wide and six feet high, a distance of five hundred and fifty-seven feet, rising thirty-one feet in its course, till it comes to the foot of the main chimney, which is seventy-eight feet above the surface of the ground. The chimney is built double, the interior being round, formed of hard brick, without pargeting, six feet in diameter in the clear from bottom to top, the latter being formed of cast iron, while the foundation is of pointed stone work to a height of eleven feet, and the remainder of pressed brick. The underground flue alluded to contains the main steampipe until it reaches the nearest point of the building, and also that portion of it which is carried to the north section of the hospital, and is immediately over the main culvert. This chimney is made the ventilating power for securing a strong downward draft of air through all the water closets, urinals, sinks, and bath tubs in the entire establishment, and for this reason is placed in a central position on the eastern side of the building. The coils for heating are composed of welded iron pipes, three quarters or one inch in diameter, and are in two sections in all the air chambers, so that one or both may be used, according to the severity of the weather.

In the engine room are two horizontal high pressure steam engines of fine finish. They are exactly alike, each having a cylinder ten inches in diameter and a stroke of twenty-four inches. They are so arranged that either may be substituted for the other, and one may be made to do the work of both in case of emergency. Ordinarily, one drives the fan, and is therefore a part of the ventilating apparatus, while the second drives all the other machinery. The fan is of cast iron, its extreme diameter being sixteen feet and its greatest width four feet. It is driven directly from the shaft of the engine, and its revolutions vary from thirty to sixty per minute, according to the requirements of the house. The fresh air is received from a tower forty feet high, so that all surface exhalations are avoided, and is then driven through a duct, which at its commencement is eight and one half by ten and one half feet, into the extreme parts of the building. From the cold air duct openings lead into the different warm air chambers, which in the one storied buildings are covered with slate; but in all other parts of the hospital these chambers and air ducts are arched with brick laid with smooth joints. The warm air in nearly all cases is admitted near the floor and the ventilators open near the ceiling always in the interior walls. The only exception to this arrangement is in the one storied buildings, in which, in the patients' rooms, the warm air is admitted above and the ventilators are taken off near the floor. All the ventilating flues terminate in the attic in close ducts, either of brick or wood, smoothly plastered, increasing in size about thirty per cent more rapidly than the capacity of the flues entering them, and by which, through the different belvideres on the roof, they communicate with the external atmosphere. In the centre building the ventilation is through the main dome. There is no leaden pipe used in the building.

COOKING AND DISTRIBUTION OF FOOD.

All the cooking is done in the central kitchen, which has in it a large range with two fires and three ovens, a rotary roaster, a double iron steamer containing ninety gallons, a smaller one—iron outside and copper tinned on the inside—containing forty-five gallons, and six of tin for vegetables, besides the vessels for tea and coffee. The food prepared in this room is put into closed tin boxes, which are lowered by a dumb waiter to the car standing on the track of the railroad, where it passes under the kitchen, and is thus conveyed to the bottom of the various dumb waiters which lead directly to the different dining rooms above, of which, as before remarked, there is one for each ward. Each dining room has a steam table with carving dishes on it, and abundant provision for keeping meats and vegetables warm as long as may be desired. The dumb waiters are all controlled by the person having charge of the railroad; they are moved by a crank and wheel, and wire rope is substituted for that commonly adopted. The railroad is an indispensable part of the arrangements for distributing food. By its use a meal may be delivered in all the ward dining rooms (eight in number) on one side—the extreme ones being five hundred and eighty feet distant—in ten minutes after leaving the kitchen, or for the whole sixteen in twenty minutes. It also forms a very convenient mode of transporting articles from one section of the building to another, carrying clothing to and from the laundry, and gives a protected passageway in going from the centre building to the engine house, barn, and workshop, and for persons visiting their friends in the room set apart for the purpose between the sixth and seventh wards.

PROVISION AGAINST FIRE.

As already mentioned, no fires are required in the building for warming it, and gas is used for lighting. Wherever one wing comes in contact with another, or with the centre building, all the openings in the walls, which extend up through the slate roof, have iron doors in addition to the ordinary wooden ones, and which may be closed at pleasure. The floors of the kitchen and bakeroom, in which alone fire is used, are of German flagstone laid on brick arches, and all the stairways in the wings are fireproof. It is intended that there should always be about twenty thousand gallons of water in the tanks in the dome of the centre building, and fifteen thousand gallons per hour may be placed there by the pumping engines. A standpipe connected with this reservoir passes into every story and into every ward, in all of which it is intended to have a piece of hempen hose constantly attached, so that by simply turning a stopcock water may be put on a fire almost as soon as discovered. A steam pipe also passes up into the attic of each wing, and as one of the large boilers is constantly fired up, steam may at any moment be let into the building by simply turning a valve in the cellar. Hose is also kept near the steam pumps, so that it may be promptly attached and water thrown on the barn, carpenter shop, engine house, and contiguous parts of the hospital. A watchman is constantly passing through the house at night, and by means of two of Harris' watch-clocks, as made by H. B. Ames of New York, there is no difficulty in ascertaining not only how often each ward is visited, but almost the moment the visit was made, and of course the time taken in passing from one ward to another.

LAUNDRY ARRANGEMENTS.

The clothing, bedding, etc., collected in the different wards, after being sent to the cellar, are conveyed from that point by the railroad to the room for assorting clothes in the engine house, and thence into the large wash room, in which, besides the usual washing, rinsing, and blue tubs

43

and soap vat, is one of the valuable Shaker washing machines, in which six different kinds of clothes can be washed at the same time, and a centrifugal wringer, both of which are driven by one of the steam engines. From the wringer the washed articles are taken to the drying closet, in which by means of the heat derived from the exhaust steam from the engines passing through a large amount of cast iron pipe, and fresh air from the fan, they are in a very few minutes made ready for the mangle (also driven by steam power), or folded and taken by the railroad to the ironing room near the centre building, to which they are raised by the dumb waiter already referred to, or are sent directly to the principal clothes room, from which they are distributed by the same route as they may be required in the wards. All the divisions of the washing machine, of the rinsing and washing tubs, have hot and cold water and steam introduced directly into them, and the water from them all is carried off under the stone floor of the room to one of the iron columns below, through which it passes into the culvert on the outside of the building.

PLEASURE GROUNDS, GARDENS, AND YARDS.

This new hospital is situated in the midst of its pleasure grounds, embracing about fifty acres, and from most parts of which are fine views of the surrounding country; the boundary wall being so arranged, from the natural character of the ground, or made so by excavations, that little of it can be seen from any part of the building that is occupied by patients. There are two pleasant groves of natural forest trees within the inclosure, and several hundred others, evergreen and deciduous, that have already been planted or collected for the purpose, will give an ample amount of shaded drives and walks. A carriage road has already been made on the inside of the wall throughout its extent, and winding by the gardens and terraces around the buildings will ultimately be two miles long. The foot walks are not to be less extensive, and the brick pavements about the building have been already mentioned. There are also, as may be remembered, three pleasant yards on each side of the building, and connected directly with the adjacent wards. The vegetable garden will contain about eight acres, and is in full view from the north side of the building. Flower borders have been made near to and around the entire structure. The only fences inside of the inclosure are to give privacy to the patients in the yards, or to prevent those walking about the grounds from approaching certain parts of the building.

COST.

Without a statement of the cost, no account of such a building and such arrangements as have been described would be at all complete, and especially not of one like that under notice, which is entirely the offspring of the benevolence and liberality of a community, a result of practical christianity, and a generous recognition of the paramount claims which such afflictions of our fellow men have at all times upon our interests and our sympathies. The style of architecture is plain, and all useless ornament has been studiously dispensed with; but whenever the comfort and welfare of the patient were concerned, everything has been done in a thorough manner.

The amount of money paid on account of the new building and its varied fixtures and arrangements, up to the present time, is three hundred and twenty-two thousand five hundred and forty-two dollars and eighty-six cents, and a further sum of about thirty thousand dollars will be required to meet the other liabilities that have been incurred. Of this total sum, twenty thousand two hundred and seventy-six dollars and twenty-eight cents have been for the boundary wall and gate house; two thousand two hundred and forty-one dollars and forty-six cents for the carriage house and stabling; eight hundred dollars for the carpenter shop; four thousand four hundred and fifty-six dollars and three cents for machinery of different kinds; twenty-three thousand six hundred and twelve dollars and thirty-seven cents for heating and ventilating apparatus; fifteen thousand two hundred and one dollars and forty-seven cents for grading, for building, planting, and improving the grounds; and ten thousand four hundred and forty-one dollars and seventy-three cents for furniture.

PLANS, DESCRIPTIONS AND ESTIMATES OF THE BOSTON HOSPITAL FOR THE INSANE AT WINTHROP.

Boston Lunatic Hospital, }
Boston (Mass.), September 28, 1867. }

To the Board of Directors for Public Institutions:

Gentlemen: Three months ago the committee on the proposed new "Hospital for the Insane" referred the "plans" to the architect (N. J. Bradlee, Esq.) and myself, with the request that we would give them a thorough revision. That has been done and the result is before you.

While not doubting that experts of larger experience may discover defects and suggest improvements, we are at a loss to see how, without great expense, the plans can easily be materially improved.

Such a hospital structure, containing no provision that can well be dispensed with, and requiring not a dollar for mere ornamentation, will be no discredit to the humanity, intelligence, and good taste of Boston.

These plans have my hearty and unqualified approval.
Very respectfully,
CLEMENT A. WALKER,
Superintendent.

CONSTRUCTION OF THE BUILDING.

The exterior walls will be of brick, with granite trimmings, surmounted by a brick cornice and French roof.

The grouping of the several wings, falling back as they do from the centre and from each other, with their several projections and bays, will give a very pleasing effect to the whole.

BASEMENT.

This story, which will be from four to six feet above the level of the ground, will contain five hundred and four hot air chambers, each being two feet by five feet, for the pipes to heat the building. The basement of the rear centre building will contain store rooms and vegetable cellars.

PRINCIPAL STORY.

The general plan of the building consists of a centre building, three stories high, sixty feet by ninety-two feet, a building in the rear of the centre, two stories high, forty-nine feet by one hundred and fifty-six feet, and two wings of three sections each, two being three stories high. The first section on each side is fifty-six feet by one hundred and fifty-four feet; the second section, fifty-six by one hundred and forty-five feet nine inches; the third section, two stories high, fifty-seven feet by one hundred and twenty-one feet nine inches; one being at each side of and at an angle of forty-five degrees to the second section. This gives eight distinct wards for each sex, the *minimum* required (by unanimous vote of the Association of Medical Superintendents of American Institutions for the Insane) in a hospital for *two hundred* patients; this designed for *three hundred.*

The principal story of the centre building contains Superintendent's room, twenty feet square; private room, seventeen feet by twenty feet; Assistant Superintendent's room, seventeen feet by twenty feet; apothecary's room, twelve feet by seventeen feet; library, twelve feet by seventeen feet; dining room, twenty feet by forty feet; pantry, seventeen feet by twenty feet; and six large closets.

The rear centre building will contain: reception rooms, twelve feet by eighteen feet; attendants' dining room, eighteen feet by forty feet; store room, eighteen feet by twenty-six feet; kitchen, twenty feet by forty-two feet; laundry, twenty feet by forty feet; ironing room, twenty-two feet square; pantry, six feet by fifteen feet; bakery, fourteen feet square; bread closet, seven feet by twenty-three feet; tin closet, six feet by fifteen feet; oven, ten feet by twelve feet; drying room, ten feet by eighteen feet.

The first section on each side of the centre will contain fifteen single rooms, eight feet six inches by fourteen feet; sitting room, twenty-two feet by thirty feet; bay window, eighteen feet by twenty feet; reception room, thirteen feet by twenty-one feet; attendants' room, thirteen feet by twenty-one feet; bath room, nine feet by fourteen feet; storeroom, nine feet by fourteen feet; dormitory, seventeen feet by twenty-seven feet; dining room, sixteen feet by thirty-four feet.

The second section on each side will contain sixteen single rooms; general store room, twenty feet by twenty-three feet; the other rooms are the same as described for first section.

The third section will contain twelve single rooms, eight feet six inches by fourteen feet; open corridor, twenty-eight feet by sixty-two feet; dining room, seventeen feet by twenty feet; storeroom, ten feet by seventeen feet; attendants' room, fourteen feet by seventeen feet; bath room, ten feet by seventeen feet.

SECOND STORY.

The second and third stories of the first and second sections are divided the same as the first story of said buildings, and the second story of the third section is also like the first story of the same. The attics of the first and second sections will furnish pleasant and desirable infirmaries. The attics of the third section will afford ample and convenient room for the isolation of small pox and other contagious diseases.

The second and third stories of the centre building are arranged to accommodate the Superintendent and his family, with his assistants.

The second story of the rear centre building contains a chapel, forty-five feet by seventy-five feet; domestics' room, fourteen feet by twenty feet; billiard room, eighteen feet by forty-five feet; storeroom, twelve feet by twenty feet. The main centre building and the first section on each side, also rear centre buildings, are connected by corridors ten feet wide.

THE ENGINE HOUSE

Is located one hundred and three feet distant from the rear centre building, and is forty-seven feet by seventy-four feet, containing a boiler room thirteen feet by fifty-seven feet; engine room, fourteen feet by twenty-four feet; fan blower room, thirty-two feet by fourteen feet; fuel rooms, fourteen feet by twenty-three feet, and fourteen feet by thirty-four feet; connected with this house is the large chimney, fifteen feet square at the base by one hundred and eighty feet in height.

CONSTRUCTION.

The outside cellar walls are to be two feet thick of stone laid in cement mortar; the walls above are of brick twenty inches thick, laid hollow, the outer walls being twelve inches, an air space of four inches, and the inner wall four inches thick. The interior walls on the side corridors will be also twenty inches thick, so as to leave room for the ventilating and heating flues to pass through them. To render the building as nearly fireproof as possible without going to the expense of brick arches and iron beams or girders, all the plastering will be done directly upon the brick walls without furring; the floors will be plastered between the floor boards and the base or plinth around the rooms, and corridors will be of face brick, painted; all the inside partitions will be also of brick.

To give some idea of the size of the building, it may be stated that it will require one thousand seven hundred and seventy-five perches of stone for the foundation. Seven million seven hundred and fifty thousand two hundred and fifty bricks will be used in the walls; sixty-two thousand eight hundred and twenty-nine yards of plastering; three thousand two hundred and twenty-four feet of gutters, with two thousand twenty-two feet of conductors; eighteen thousand two hundred and fifty feet of gas pipe; one million two hundred and eighty-nine thousand four hundred and eighty-eight feet of lumber; one thousand two hundred and thirty-eight windows; fifty-nine thousand four hundred and twenty-four lights of glass, and nine hundred eighty-nine doors; five hundred and four being required for the pipe chambers in the basement.

HEATING AND VENTILATION.

The building will be arranged so as to hereafter decide upon the best method of heating, whether by hot water, high or low pressure steam, all of which systems have their strenuous advocates. The ventilation of all the waterclosets will be effected by the downward draft to the heated chimney; the ventilation of the wards will be likewise arranged for the downward draft; there will also be provided in the boiler house, a fan blower upon the Doctor Nichols plan, to be used as occasion may require.

The high chimney will be so constructed as to form a large ventilating flue entirely around the boiler flue, to assure a steady draft. The underground air flues will be eight feet in diameter, diminishing in size as they approach the third section, with small branches to each of the several hot air chambers in the basement story.

COUNTY OF SURREY ADDITIONAL LUNATIC ASYLUM.

At Brookwood, near Woking.

The additional asylum for the pauper lunatics of the County of Surrey is designed to accommodate six hundred and fifty patients, and stands on an estate of about one hundred and fifty acres in extent, at Brookwood, about three miles from the Woking station on the South Western Railway.

The site is bounded on the south by the Basingstoke Canal, and on the east and west by the high roads to Guildford and Chertsey. Few sites could be found in the country better adapted for such an institution. The soil, a primary consideration, is a dry sand, with occasional veins of gravel, loam, and clay. The ground rises gradually from the south and west about seventy feet above the level of the canal, and the buildings are erected on a plateau of some extent, with a fine range of views and southern aspect.

The plan of the building gives to every part uninterrupted views of the surrounding country, and free access to light and air.

The principal entrance with the visiting Justices', Superintendent's, Porter's, Steward's, and waiting rooms form the central portion of the north front of the main building.

To the west of the entrance block is the laundry wing, with the rooms for the female working patients and their attendants.

On the east side of the entrance block corresponding to the laundry wing just described, are the workshops and the apartments appropriated to the patients engaged in them.

In the centre are placed the kitchen, offices and stores, so arranged that the service on the male side is perfectly separated from the female side.

The apartments for the Assistant Surgeon and the matron, with dispensary and stores, are grouped together in the centre of the south building, near the wards for recent cases, which with the infirmaries form the rest of the south front of main building.

The height of the rooms occupied by the patients on the ground floor is twelve feet, and on the upper floors eleven feet.

Fifty superficial feet, or nearly six hundred cubic feet, are allowed to each patient in all dormitories, except those in the infirmaries, where the cubical contents exceed seven hundred feet per patient.

The smallest separate sleeping room is nine feet by seven feet, which gives seven hundred cubic feet; in the infirmaries they vary from eleven feet by eight feet seven inches to fourteen feet by ten feet.

The day rooms, except one on each side of the wards for recent and acute case, are all on the ground floor.

Lavatories, water closets, baths, slop rooms, store rooms, and closets are provided in all the wards. ·

To the east and west of the main building are placed detached blocks with associated day rooms and dormitories for the accommodation of ninety patients in each building. These blocks are connected with the main building by covered passages.

The buildings are constructed in stock brickwork, relieved with a few coloured brick dressings and sailing courses.

The stairs are of stone in all parts occupied by the patients, with the well holes built up.

The floors of all day and sleeping rooms and of the south corridors and corridors in infirmary wings are boarded.

The sashes generally are of wood, double hung with locks and keys, to prevent their being opened beyond a certain height.

The doors to all patients' rooms have solid panels, and all angles are rounded.

The day rooms and corridors have open fireplaces, in which are warm air grates, so constructed that warm air is admitted either into the room with the fireplace, or conducted to the chamber above. Provision has been made for the introduction of warm water pipes in case any auxiliary heating power should be required.

In both day rooms and dormitories ventilating flues for the extraction of foul air are formed, having sectional areas, in proportion to the sizes of the rooms, connected with the towers by large air shafts formed in the roofs.

The sewage is conveyed from water closets, sinks, etc., by means of pipe drains to filtering tanks, so placed and constructed as to permit of the distribution by gravity of the filtered water over a considerable portion of the land under cultivation.

The Superintendent's house is a detatched building placed to the southwest of the main building, near the boundary of the airing grounds for the female patients. Plans of the floors of this house are given, and show with sufficient clearness the arrangement and accommodation provided.

The house for the gardener, in which accommodation has been provided for twelve of the more quiet patients, is situated in the east of the main building, about two hundred yards from the entrance to male airing grounds, and near the kitchen garden.

The farm bailiff's house, in which accommodation has also been provided for twelve patients, adjoins the farm buildings. •

The gas works are placed to the northwest of the main building about sixty-five yards from the laundry block.

The chapel is a detached building, designed to accommodate three hundred and forty-three persons, very simply constructed, with plain gothic headed windows and doors. Ventilating dormers are provided in the roof, and the building is heated by Haden & Son's apparatus. There ⟋ is a chancel with vestry to the north. From the entrance of main building to the south porch of chapel the distance is about two hundred yards.

The detailed statement of the accommodation provided for the patients in the several parts of the building is as follows, namely:

RECENT CASES.

Female side—Ground floor: Single rooms, eight. First floor: Single rooms, eight; dormitories, twelve. Second floor: Dormitories, forty-five. Total, seventy-three.

Male side—Ground floor: Single rooms, eight. First floor: Single rooms, eight; dormitories, twelve. Second floor: Dormitories, forty-five. Total, seventy-three.

INFIRMARY.

Female side—Ground floor: Dormitory, six; single rooms, three. First floor: Dormitories, twenty-four; single rooms, four. Second floor: Dormitories, thirty-four. Total, seventy-one.

Male side—Ground floor: Dormitory, six; single rooms, three. First floor: Dormitories, twenty-four; single rooms, four. Second floor: Dormitories, thirty-four. Total, seventy-one.

SOUTH FRONT.

Female side—Second floor: Dormitories, thirty-two.
Male side—Second floor: Dormitories, twenty-two.

NORTH FRONT.

Female side—First floor: Dormitories, twenty-five. Second floor: Dormitories, twenty. Total, forty-five.

Male side—First floor: Dormitories, five. Second floor: Dormitories, eighteen. Total, twenty-three.

LAUNDRY BLOCK.

First floor: Dormitories, sixteen; single rooms, two. Total, eighteen.

WORKSHOP BLOCK.

First floor: Dormitories, sixteen; single rooms, two. Total, eighteen.

DETACHED BLOCKS.

FEMALE SIDE.		MALE SIDE.	
Ground Floor.		*Ground Floor.*	
Dormitories	20	Dormitories	20
Single rooms	2	Single rooms	2
First Floor.		*First Floor.*	
Dormitories	68	Dormitories	68
Total	90	Total	90

Recent cases	73	Recent cases	73
Infirmary	71	Infirmary	71
South front	32	South front	22
North front	45	North front	23
Laundry block	18	Workshop block	18
Detached block	90	Detached block	18
		Bailiff's house	12
		Gardener's house	12
Total	329	Total	321

The buildings, with all the necessary work and fittings having been completed, the institution was opened in the Summer of eighteen hundred and sixty-seven.

The cost of the buildings, exclusive of fittings, and engineer's and gas works, amounted to the sum of sixty-one thousand nine hundred pounds sterling.

C. H. HOWELL, Architect.

ERRATA.

Page thirteen, tenth line from bottom, for " eleven " read " seven."

Page forty-seven, nineteenth line from bottom, for "excess" read " sexes."

Page fifty, fifth line of second paragraph, for " courses " read "causes."

Page eighty-eight, ninth line from top, for " seventeenth " read " nineteenth."

The tables of " Results of Treatment," on pages two hundred and five, two hundred and six, and two hundred and seven, should come immediately after " Results of Treatment," on page two hundred and two.

Page sixty-four, first column figures, fifth line, for " 260,247 " read " 560,247."

Pl. 1.

30.

BOSTON HOSPITAL FOR THE INSANE.

BASEMENT

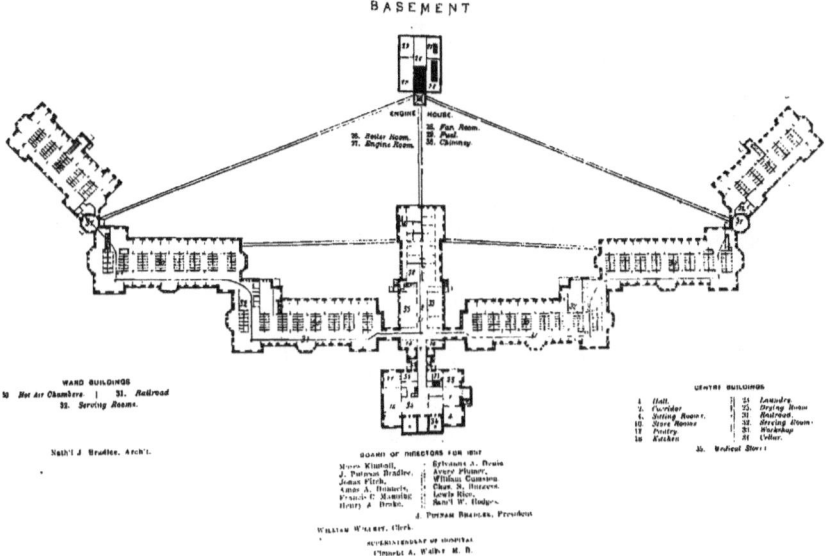

WARD BUILDINGS
30 *Hot Air Chambers* | 31. *Railroad*
32. *Serving Rooms.*

Nath'l J. Bradlee, Arch't.

CENTRAL BUILDINGS

1. *Hall.*   24. *Laundry.*
2. *Corridor.*   25. *Drying Room.*
4. *Dining Room.*   30. *Railroad.*
10. *Store Rooms.*   32. *Serving Room.*
17. *Pantry.*   34. *Workshop.*
18. *Kitchen.*   31. *Cellar.*
                          35. *Medical Stores.*

ENGINE HOUSE.
76. *Boiler Room.*   78. *Fan Room.*
77. *Engine Room.*   79. *Pool.*
                       34. *Chimney.*

P
P
P
T
ix,
on]
F

F.—Pl. 2.

1. *Hall.*
2. *Corrido*
3. *Bay Wi*
4. *Sitting-*
5. *Recepti*
6. *Attenda*

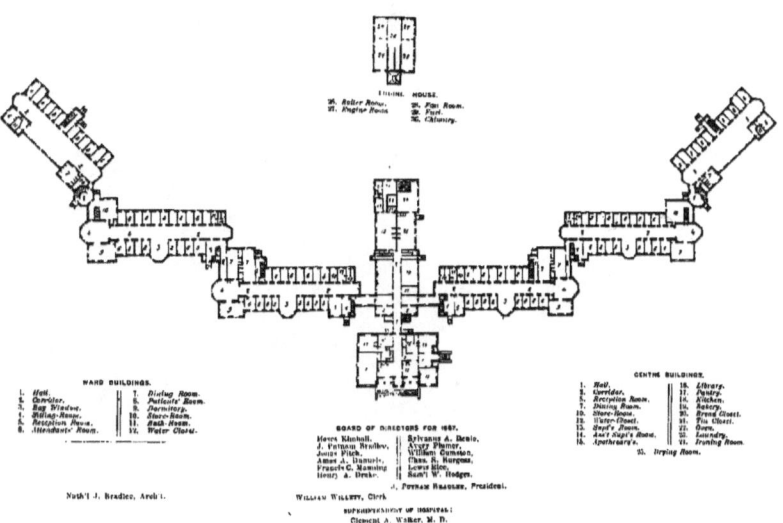

ENGINE HOUSE.

25. Boiler Room.
27. Engine Room.
28. Fan Room.
29. Fuel.
30. Chimney.

WARD BUILDINGS.

1. Hall.
2. Corridor.
3. Bay Window.
4. Sitting-Room.
5. Reception Room.
6. Attendants' Room.
7. Dining Room.
8. Patients' Room.
9. Dormitory.
10. Store-Room.
11. Bath Room.
12. Water Closet.

CENTRE BUILDINGS.

1. Hall.
2. Corridor.
5. Reception Room.
7. Dining Room.
10. Store-Room.
12. Water-Closet.
13. Supt's Room.
14. Ass't Supt's Room.
15. Apothecary's.
16. Library.
17. Pantry.
18. Kitchen.
19. Bakery.
20. Bread Closet.
21. Tin Closet.
22. Oven.
23. Laundry.
24. Ironing Room.
25. Drying Room.

BOARD OF DIRECTORS FOR 1867.

Moses Kimball.
J. Putnam Bradlee.
Jonas Fitch.
Amos A. Lawrence.
Francis C. Manning.
Henry A. Drake.

Sylvanus A. Denio.
Avery Plumer.
William Cumston.
Chas. R. Burgess.
Lewis Rice.
Sam'l W. Hodges.

J. Putnam Bradlee, President.

Nath'l J. Bradlee, Arch't.

William Willett, Clerk.

SUPERINTENDENT OF HOSPITAL:
Clement A. Walker, M. D.

]
]
]
]
ſ
six
on
]

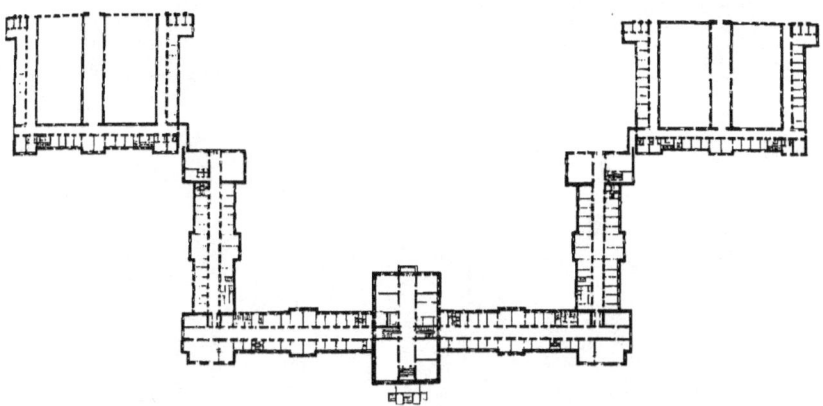

PLAN OF THE PENNSYLVANIA HOSPITAL FOR THE INSANE.

DEPARTMENT FOR MALES.

F. Pl. 4.

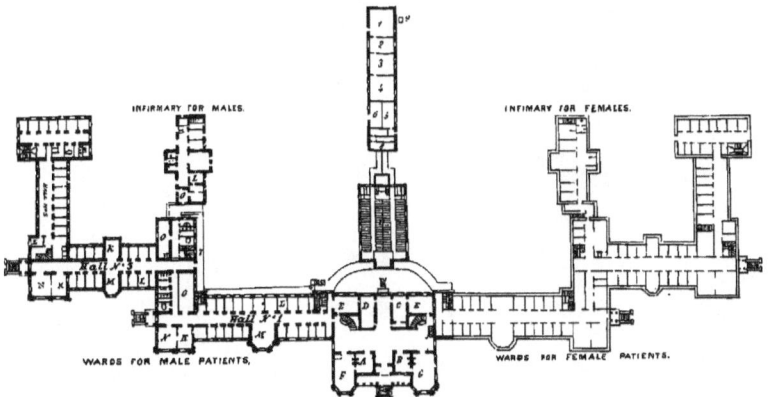

MICHIGAN ASYLUM FOR THE INSANE, KALAMAZOO.

six
on

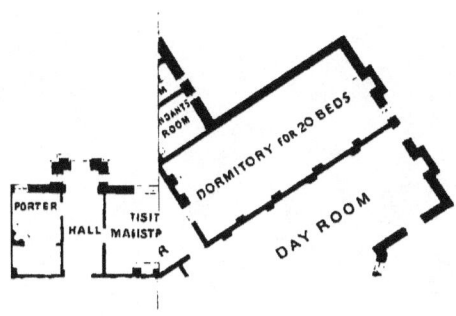

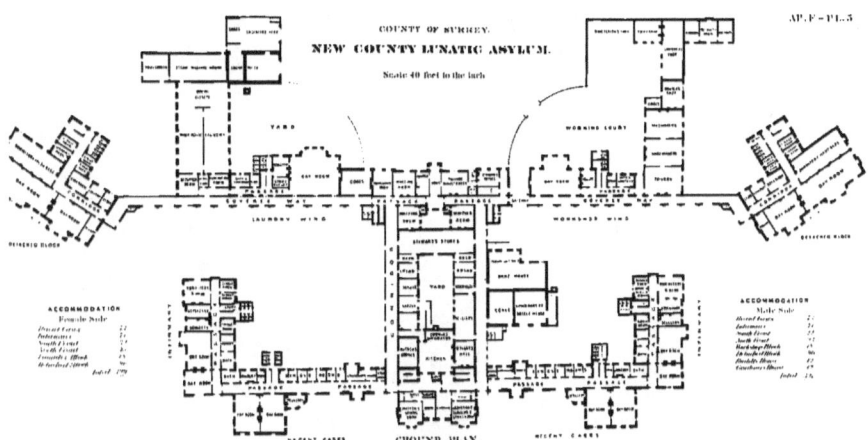

COUNTY OF SURREY.

NEW COUNTY LUNATIC ASYLUM.

Scale 40 feet to the inch

GROUND PLAN.

.F – PL.6.

OF SURR1

LUNATIC

ıt to the Inch

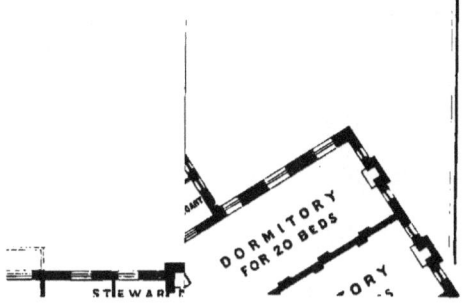

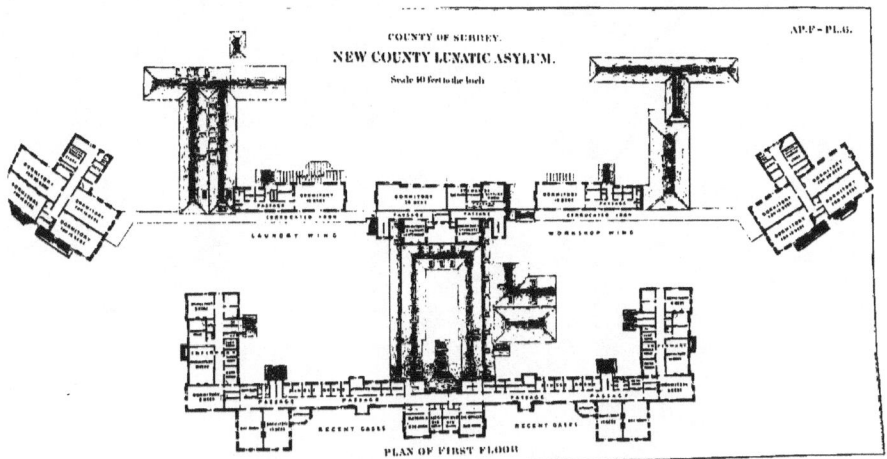

COUNTY OF SURREY.

NEW COUNTY LUNATIC ASYLUM.

Scale 40 feet to the Inch

AP.F - PL.6.

PLAN OF FIRST FLOOR

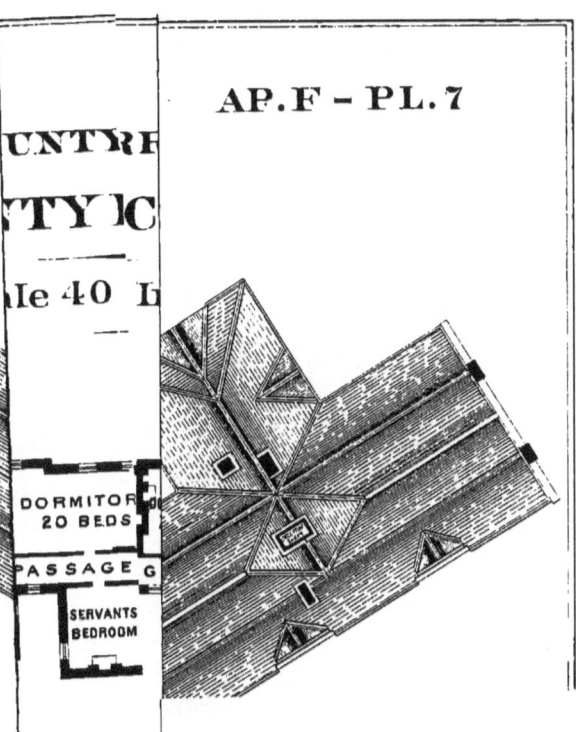

CNTRF

TY IC

le 40 1

DORMITOR
20 BEDS

PASSAGE G

SERVANTS
BEDROOM

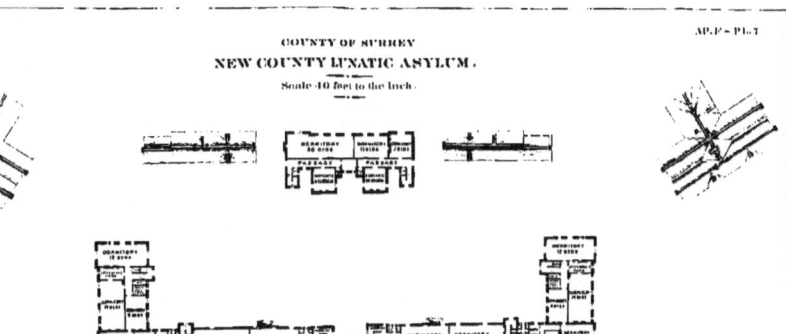

COUNTY OF SURREY

NEW COUNTY LUNATIC ASYLUM.

Scale 40 feet to the Inch.

PLAN OF SECOND FLOOR.

F . Pl.8.

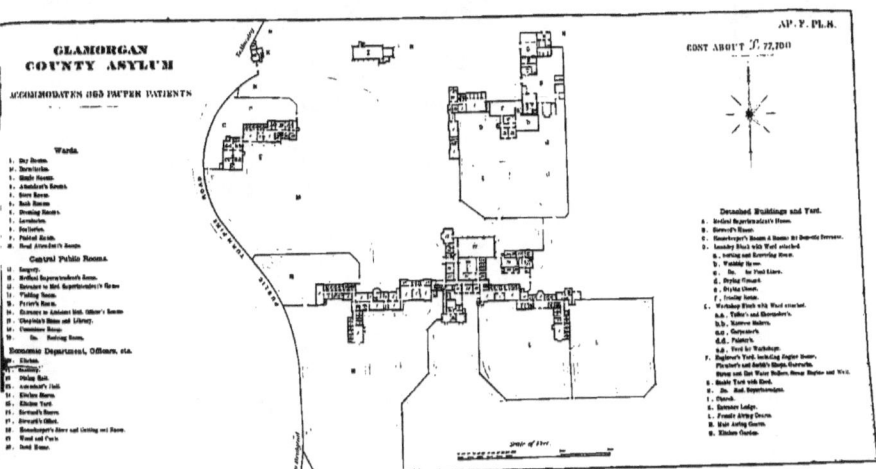

APP. F. PL. 8.

GLAMORGAN
COUNTY ASYLUM

ACCOMMODATES 665 PAUPER PATIENTS

COST ABOUT £.77,700

Wards.
1. Day Room.
2. Dormitories.
3. Single Rooms.
4. Attendant's Room.
5. Store Room.
6. Bath Room.
7. Dressing Room.
8. Lavatories.
9. Pantries.
10. Padded Room.
11. Head Attendant's Room.

General Public Rooms.
12. Surgery.
13. Medical Superintendent's Room.
14. Entrance to Med. Superintendent's Rooms.
15. Visiting Room.
16. Porter's Room.
17. Entrance to Assistant Med. Officer's Rooms.
18. Chaplain's Room and Library.
19. Committee Room.
20. Do. Retiring Room.

Economic Department, Offices, etc.
21. Kitchen.
22. Scullery.
23. Dining Hall.
24. Assistant's Hall.
25. Kitchen Stores.
26. Kitchen Yard.
27. Steward's Room.
28. Steward's Office.
29. Housekeeper's Stores and Sitting out Room.
30. Wood and Coals.
31. Dead House.

Detached Buildings and Yard.
A. Medical Superintendent's House.
B. Steward's House.
C. Housekeeper's Rooms & Rooms for Domestic Servants.
D. Laundry Block with Yard attached.
b. Sorting and Receiving Room.
b. Washing Room.
c. Do. for Foul Linen.
d. Drying Closet.
e. Drying Closet.
f. Ironing Room.
E. Workshop Block with Yard attached.
a.a. Tailor's and Shoemaker's.
b.b. Matron Makers.
c.c. Carpenter's.
d.d. Painter's.
e.e. Yard for Workshops.
F. Engineer's Yard, including Engine House, Plumber's and Smith's Shops, Gasworks, Ovens and Hot Water Boilers, Steam Engines and Well.
G. Stable Yard with Shed.
H. Do. Med. Superintendent.
I. Church.
K. Entrance Lodge.
L. Female Airing Courts.
M. Male Airing Courts.
N. Kitchen Garden.

Scale of Feet

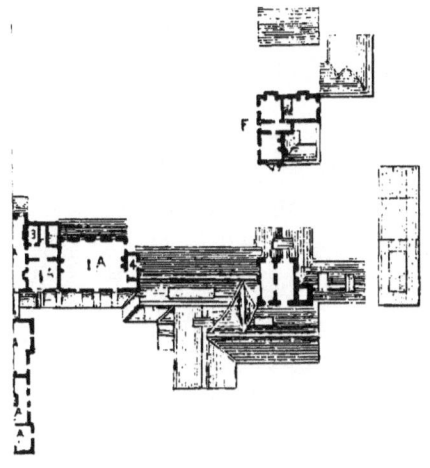

GLAMORGAN COUNTY ASYLUM.

PLAN OF FIRST FLOOR.

OCCUPIED ENTIRELY BY SLEEPING ACCOMMODATION AND THE NECESSARY CLOTHES STORES, LAVATORIES, ETC., ETC.

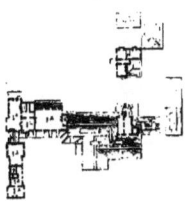

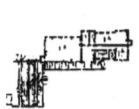

Reference

1. *Dormitories.*
2. *Single Rooms*
3. *Attendants.*
4. *Stores.*
5. *Bath.*
7. *Lavatories.*
10. *Head Attendant's Room.*
1B. *Assistant Medical Officer's Rooms.*
A. *Medical Superintendent's House.*
B. *Steward's House.*
C. *Housekeeper and Domestic Servants*
F. *Engineer's House*

Scale of Feet

sylum.

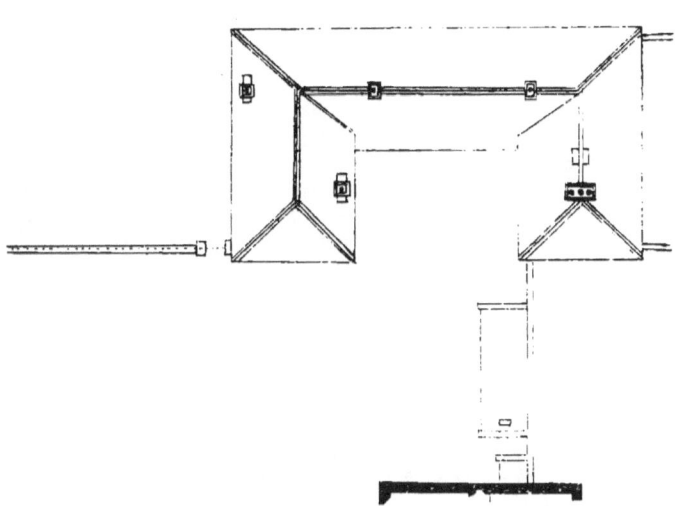

Perth District Lunatic Asylum.

PLAN OF UPPER FLOOR.

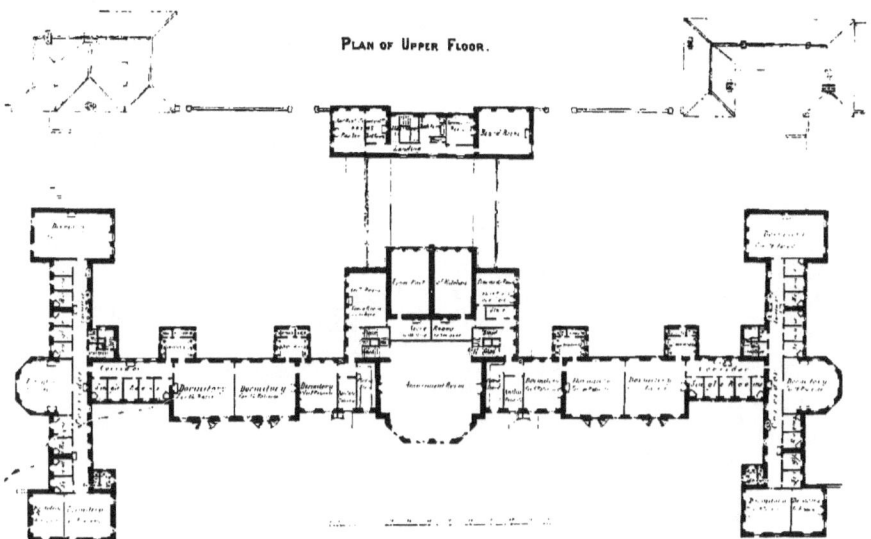

ד

LUNATIC ASYLUM.
MEERENBERG, NEAR HAARLEM.
Ground Plan and Elevation.

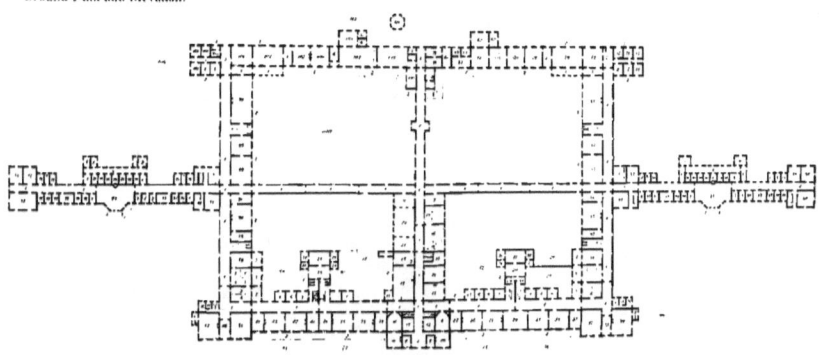

ASYLUM.

NEAR HAARLEM.

first Story.

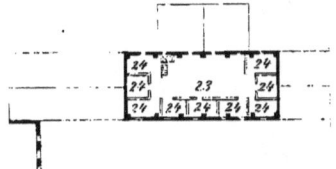

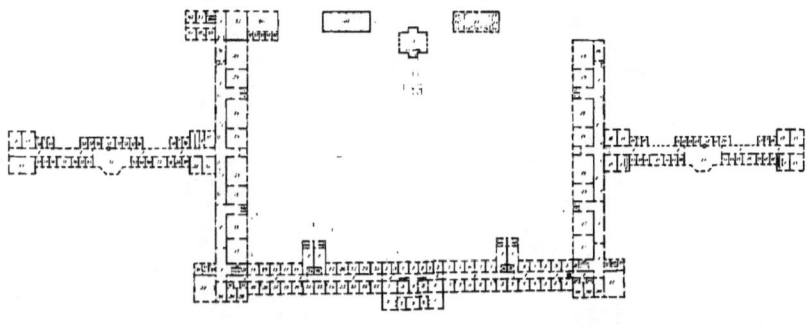

LUNATIC ASYLUM.
MEERENBERG, NEAR HAARLEM.
Plan of the first Story.

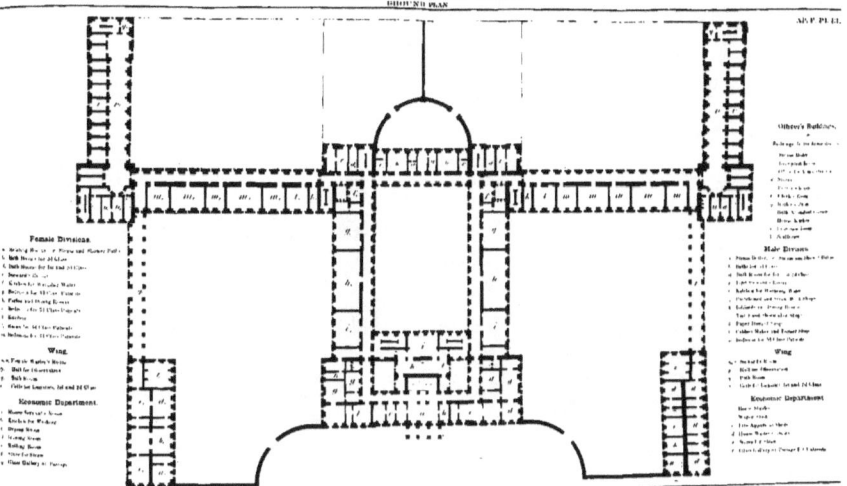

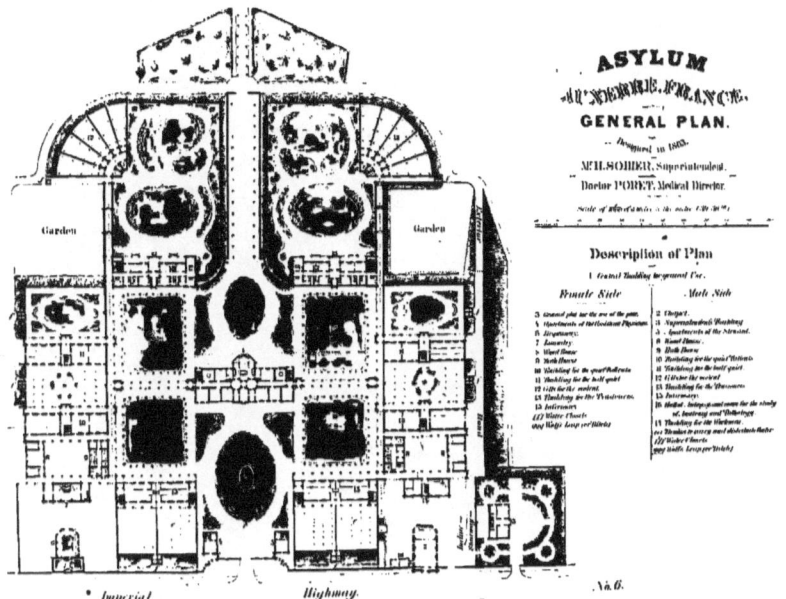

ASYLUM
d'AUXERRE, FRANCE.

GENERAL PLAN.

Designed in 1865.

Mr H. SOHIER, Superintendent.
Doctor PORET, Medical Director.

Scale of 660 of à metre = to the metre 1/10 in ty

Description of Plan

1 Central Building to ground Floor.

Female Side   Male Side

3 General plan for the use of the plan.   2 Chapel.
5 Apartments of the Resident Physician.   3 Superintendent's Building.
6 Dispensary.   4 Apartments of the Steward.
7 Laundry.   8 Bath House.
8 Wood House   9 Bath House.
9 Bath House   10 Building for the quiet Patients.
10 Building for the quiet Patients.   11 Building for the half quiet.
11 Building for the half quiet   12 Cloister for unrest.
12 Cells for the unrest   13 Building for the Uneasy ones.
13 Building for the Uneasy ones.   15 Infirmary.
15 Infirmary   16 Medical beings and rooms for the study
16 Water Closets   of Anatomy and Pathology
ggg Wings Icony per Wards   17 Building for the Workmen.
                                               ggg Theatre in every ward distributed Bathr
                                               18 Water Closets
                                               ggg Wells Icony per Wards

Garden   Garden

Imperial   Highway.   No. 6.

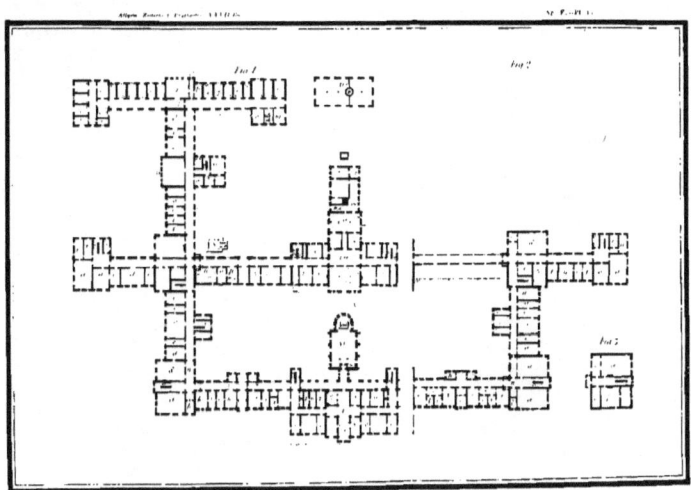

EXPLANATION OF TABLE NUMBER TWO.

FIGURE 1.

Plan of situation. Parterre and first story of Institution.

I. Building of administration. II. Section of quiet patients. III. Section of less quiet patients. IV. Section of idiotic (unclean) patients. V. Section of raving patients. VI. Church. VI. Household building. VIII. Coach room. IX. Ice cellar.

a. Day room;
b. Kitchen for dishwashing;
c. Room of attendants;
d. Sleeping apartment, third class;
e. Isolating room;
f. Room, first class;
g. Room, second class;
h. Garderobe room;

i. Depot room;
k. Room for somatic patients;
l. Cell;
m. Drying room;
n. Bath room, third class;
o. Dressing room;
p. Bath room, first and sec'nd class;
q. Single bath room.

1. Announcing room;
2. Visiting room;
3. Medical office;
4. Medical office;
5. Store room for material;
6. Room of the office porter;
7. Dispensary;
8. Room of the porter;
9. Sleeping room of the porter;
10. Office of the Administration;
11. Magazines;
12. Lodgings of Assistant Physic'n;
13. Room of accountant;

14. Sewing room (on the other side, lodgings of kitchen servants);
15. Kitchen for cooking;
16. Adjoining rooms thereof;
16' Formerly provisory kitchen;
17. Kitchen for washing;
18. Adjoining rooms thereof;
19. Room for washing machines;
20. Room for steam boiler;
21. Engine room;
22. Room of machinists;
23. Ventilation tower.

www.ingramcontent.com/pod-product-compliance
Lightning Source LLC
Chambersburg PA
CBHW021342110726
47900CB00005B/1573